# JACK HIGGINS

Jack Higgins lived in Belfast till the age of twelve. Leaving school at fifteen, he spent three years with the Royal Horse Guards, serving on the East German border during the Cold War. His subsequent employment included occupations as diverse as circus roustabout, truck driver, clerk and, after taking an honours degree in sociology and social psychology, teacher and university lecturer.

*The Eagle Has Landed* turned him into an international bestselling author, and his novels have since sold over 250 million copies and have been translated into fifty-five languages. Many of them have also been made into successful films. His recent bestselling novels include *Pay the Devil*, *Day of Reckoning*, *Edge of Danger*, *Midnight Runner* and *Bad Company*.

In 1995 Jack Higgins was awarded an honorary doctorate by Leeds Metropolitan University. He is a fellow of the Royal Society of Arts and an expert scuba diver and marksman. He lives on Jersey in the Channel Islands.

# JACK HIGGINS

# THE KEYS OF HELL

HarperCollins*Publishers*

This novel is entirely a work of fiction.
The names, characters and incidents portrayed in it are
the work of the author's imagination. Any resemblance to
actual persons, living or dead, events or localities is
entirely coincidental.

HarperCollins*Publishers*
77–85 Fulham Palace Road,
Hammersmith, London w6 8jb

www.harpercollins.co.uk

Special overseas edition 2001
This paperback edition 2002

9

Published simultaneously in hardback by
HarperCollins*Publishers*

First published in the USA by
Berkley Books 2001

ISBN 978-0-00-651467-1

Set in Sabon by Palimpsest Book Production Limited,
Polmont, Stirlingshire

Printed and bound in Great Britain by
Clays Ltd, St Ives plc

# PUBLISHER'S NOTE

THE KEYS OF HELL was first published in the UK by Abelard-Schuman, London, in 1965 under the authorship of Martin Fallon. The author was, in fact, the writer familiar to modern readers as Jack Higgins. Martin Fallon was one of the names he used during his early writing days. The book was later published in paperback by Coronet Books – under the authorship of Jack Higgins – but it has been out of print for several years.

In 2001, it seemed to the author and his publishers that it was a pity to leave such a good story languishing on his shelves. So Jack Higgins has created an entirely new framework to the original book, added some scenes and made some changes throughout. We are delighted to be able to bring back THE KEYS OF HELL for the pleasure of the vast majority of us all who never had a chance to read the original edition.

*There are no keys to hell –*
*the doors are open to all men.*
Albanian proverb

# Manhattan

## 1995

# 1

The dream was always the same. Plunging into the marsh, forcing his way through the reeds and mist, pushing the punt hard, Guilio Orsini standing at the front finding the way through and then the engine close by breaking into life and a burst of machine-gun fire.

Guilio went over head-first, always did, and Chavasse floundered through the reeds and the bitterly cold water and then, mysteriously, like a curtain, the reeds parted and there was the lagoon and the boat, the *Buona Esperanza*, and Orsini was at the rail leaning over, a hand outstretched.

'Now, Paul, now.'

And Chavasse reached and the mist seemed to increase and there was the roaring of the engine and the boat slapped away, vanished, and he was alone again.

\*   \*   \*

Chavasse was subject to dreams of the past, and had always suspected it was a legacy of his Breton father. An old race, the Bretons, an ancient people. But this dream he had not had for some years. Still . . . he got off the bed, went to the window of his suite and looked down at Manhattan. The lights sparkled in the evening dusk. He liked New York and always had. There as an excitement there, an infinite probability to things.

When the phone went he answered at once, 'Chavasse.'

'Ah, Sir Paul. Tino Rossi.'

'Good evening, Mr Rossi.'

'Listen, I know we're meeting later for dinner at the Saddle Room, but I wondered whether you'd mind coming round to my apartment at the Trump Tower first.'

'Is there a purpose to this?'

'Well, my lawyer, Mario Volpe, as you may know, is my nephew a couple of times removed. He seems to think there are a few things he could take care of before our meeting. You understand?'

'Perfectly,' Chavasse said.

'I'll send a limousine. Say half an hour?'

'No need. As it's only a couple of blocks, I'll walk.'

'Fine. I'll look forward to seeing you for dinner later.'

Chavasse put down the phone and thought about it, a slight frown on his face, then he went to the wardrobe, took out his rather old-fashioned carpet bag, pulled open a flap in the bottom and produced a short-barrelled Colt, only a .22, but deadly with hollow-point rounds. He checked it out, went into the bathroom and turned on the shower.

In the magnificent sitting room of his Trump Tower apartment Don Tino Rossi replaced the telephone. He was seventy-six years of age and still in good shape, his silver hair almost shoulder-length, his linen suit the best that Savile Row could provide.

The large man in the black suit with the shaven head came forward as the Don nodded, opened a silver box, offered a cigarette and a light. He was Aldo Vinelli, the firm's head of security. Don Tino's nephew, Mario Volpe, stood by the terrace window smoking a cigarette, thirty years of age, medium height, good-looking and like Rossi, impeccably dressed.

'So he's coming.'

'Why wouldn't he?' his uncle asked. 'He doesn't want a car. He's walking.'

'You trust this Chavasse?'

'As much as he trusts me. Our meeting in London made sense.'

'Good. I'll make arrangements.' Volpe nodded to Vinelli. 'I need you.' He went out.

The Don said quietly, 'Aldo, I assigned you to protect my nephew because I trust you and you've done a good job.'

'Thank you, Don Tino.'

'And where does your loyalty lie?'

'With you always.'

'Good.'

The Don held out his hand. Aldo kissed it and went out. Rossi sighed. Strange that facility he'd always had that told him when someone was lying to him. A gift from God really.

\* \* \*

Before it was fashionable, Tino Rossi alone amongst Mafia leaders had realized that life had to change, that the old days were long gone. He had turned the Rossi family to respectability. Real estate developments in New York, the same on the Thames in London. Investments in the electronics industry, shipping, banking. His early start meant that these days his only rivals were the Russian Mafia.

The young man he called nephew, Mario, was an important part of the organization. He'd never known his father, and his mother had also died at a young age. Her widowed sister, Signora Volpe, had brought the boy to New York, raised him in Little Italy. As Don Tino's niece her Mafia connection had assured the success of her café. Mario had gone to Columbia, had taken a law degree. Later, he'd done the same thing at London University and was now indispensable to the family on both sides of the Atlantic for his legal expertise.

He returned to the room. The Don said, 'Is everything in hand?'

'Sure. Look, I'll go with Aldo and monitor him. So he's crazy enough to want to walk

JACK HIGGINS

alone on a wet night in Manhattan, but that could be asking for it. I mean, this is an older guy. Sixty-five.'

'So I'm ten years older.'

'Heh, Uncle, I didn't mean . . .'

'Make this work, Mario, nothing is more important.'

'You trust this Chavasse?'

'As I told you, no more than he trusts me. Sir Paul Chavasse, knighted by the Queen of England, Mario.'

'So?'

'This man is what? Half English, half French. He speaks more languages than you've had hot dinners. University degrees coming out of his ears. In spite of all that, a killer by nature. For twenty years a field agent for the Bureau, the most secret of British intelligence units. You've seen his record. Shot three times, knifed twice.'

'So he was hot stuff.'

'More than that, Mario, for the past twenty years he's been Belfast Bureau Chief and that's no desk job, not with the IRA and all those other problems. Now he has Eastern Europe on his back. Bosnia, Serbia, Kosova, Albania, and we know who has the greatest input.'

'The Russian Mafia.'

'Exactly, and as they are not *our* friends we can help there. In return, Chavasse will help us.'

'When possible?'

'Of course. Look, I suspended all drug operations there years ago and not for moral reasons as you well know. If idiots want to kill themselves with heroin that's their affair. We make more out of cigarette smuggling from Europe into Britain than we ever would have with drugs.'

'Still illegal.'

'Yes, but as you being an expert in English law know, a drug runner pulls ten or twelve years. Get done, as the English say, for cigarette smuggling and what would your client get?'

'Twelve months and out in six.' Mario Volpe smiled. 'Still illegal, running cigarettes by the millions up the Thames, so where does that leave Sir Paul Chavasse?'

'Exactly as he is. A realist. We're not destroying the lives of stupid teenagers. We aren't harming the widows and orphans. He can live with that as long as we provide the expertise on Eastern Europe that he needs. You'll see that we do.'

'Of course, Uncle.'

'Good boy.' The Don nodded. 'You take care of things. Tell Sir Paul I'll see him later for dinner at the Saddle Room. You'd better go now, you and Aldo, to make sure he gets here in one piece.'

'Uncle.'

Mario Volpe went out. Rain battering the window, Don Tino reached for his unfinished glass of champagne. Such a clever boy. All the virtues really and yet capable of such stupidity. He swallowed the champagne, got up and walked out leaning on his Malacca cane.

When Chavasse emerged from the Plaza Hotel it was raining slightly. He wore a Burberry trench coat in dark blue and an old-fashioned rain hat slanted across his head. Inside, the Colt .22 rested in a special clip. Uncomfortable, but also comforting in its own way. Just a feeling, but that's why he was still here after all these years. He declined the offer of a cab from the doorman, went down the steps and started along Fifth Avenue.

Waiting in a black Mercedes town car, Mario Volpe and Vinelli watched him.

'Let's go, Aldo,' Volpe said, 'and don't lose him.' Not that there was much chance of that as they pulled away from the sidewalk. Not too many people as the rain increased.

Chavasse liked the rain. Somehow you could inhabit your own private world. It was what he called the cinema of the mind time. You considered the facts, tried to make sense, antici-pate the other side's next move, and there was certainly more to all this than met the eye. All his senses, the product of forty years of living on the edge, told him that.

Not that he distrusted Don Tino particularly. It was more that he didn't trust anyone. His special kind of life had taught him that. The way Eastern Europe was, the Don could be useful, which was what his meeting with Rossi and Vinelli at the Dorchester Hotel in London had indicated. If a few favours in return was the price, it was worth it, always supposing the price wasn't too high. So Rossi was a gangster. In essence, that was what Chavasse had been for years. You had to be a kind of gangster to be an intelligence agent. All that kept you alive really.

He paused, produced a silver case from an inside pocket, took out a cigarette and lit it in cupped hands. He was standing at the entrance of a darkened mall at the time and for the moment, the sidewalk was clear. As he started forward, a young man darted out of the mall and blocked his way.

'Heh, buddy, you got some change?'

At that moment, another one emerged, his twin, hard-faced in bomber jacket and jeans, only he was holding a Browning pistol.

'This one's got more than change. Let's get him in here.'

He rammed the barrel of the Browning against Chavasse's spine and drove him into the darkness.

All this was seen from the Mercedes.

Volpe said, 'Those bastards. Why the gun?'

There was the sound of a shot. Vinelli braked to a halt and got the door open.

*　　*　　*

In the mall the one with the Browning rammed it even harder into Chavasse.

'A nice fat wallet here I'd day, so let's stay friendly. You can call me Tommy.'

Chavasse raised his right elbow, struck backwards into the face, turned sideways, pushing the Browning away, grabbed for the barrel, twisted it free and had the gun in his hand.

'You should never get that close to anyone.'

He pivoted, rammed the barrel of the Browning into the back of Tommy's right knee and pulled the trigger. Tommy staggered into the wall and fell down with a cry.

The other one backed away, hands raised.

'Heh, man, don't do it.'

Vinelli arrived, a gun in his hand, Volpe behind him.

They looked at Tommy lying on the ground and Chavasse tendered the Browning to Vinelli.

'Not mine, his.' He looked down at the boy. 'Terrible class of muggers these days. Not too competent.'

Volpe held out his hand. 'Mario Volpe, Sir

Paul. We were worried about you so I figured we'd check the hotel. Aldo recognized you from London, so we were following. I mean, scum like this, what can I say?'

'Not much, I expect. Can we go now?'

'Sure.' Volpe turned to Vinelli. 'Take care of this, Aldo. I'll drive Sir Paul to the Trump, you follow on foot.'

He took Chavasse by the arm and led him away. Aldo turned, reached for the youth who was standing and pulled him close.

'You were supposed to jump him and wait for us to come to the rescue and what do we get? A gun, for Christ's sake.'

'It was Tommy. He's on crack.'

'Really?' Vinelli headbutted him, breaking his nose, sending him staggering.

The youth started to weep, blood everywhere. 'I'm sorry, Mr Vinelli, but what do I do with Tommy?'

'You get an ambulance. Three very large black guys beat up on you, and no fairy stories for the cops or the Rossi family will see to you on a more permanent basis.' He opened his wallet and took out ten hundred-dollar bills. 'I said a grand and

14

I'm a man of my word.' He dropped the money on Tommy.

'I'll do what you say, Mr Vinelli.'

'You better had, kid.'

Vinelli patted his face, turned his collar up against the rain and walked away.

In the sitting room of the Trump Tower apartment, Volpe helped Chavasse off with his Burberry and placed it on a chair. Chavasse removed the rain hat and put it on the coat carefully.

'Drink, Sir Paul? Martini? Champagne?'

'Irish whiskey,' Chavasse told him, 'Bushmills for preference.'

'Anything. We've got it all.'

'Good.' Chavasse took a cigarette from his silver case. 'And then you can tell me exactly what it is you want.'

Vinelli came in and stood by the door, face impassive. Volpe got the whiskey from the bar by the window and brought it over.

'I don't really want anything, Sir Paul. My uncle and you laid it out pretty clear at your meeting in London at the Dorchester. I mean, even Aldo here met you but I didn't, so I figured it was time. I handle all the family's legal business on both sides of the Atlantic. This whole deal is very important. I wanted to familiarize myself with you.'

'And why would you want to do that?'

'Well, on occasions, we'll be working together, but hell, no problem there. Your record in the intelligence business is amazing.'

'And how would you know that?'

'Bureau records are on file at the Public Records Office in London. Sure, maybe they're on a fifty-year hold, but there are always ways round that. The clerks aren't very well paid. Give them "a few bob" as you Brits say, and it's amazing what you get a copy of.'

Chavasse finished his whiskey. He said calmly, 'What you appear to be saying is that you've been checking up on my past record quite illegally.'

'Yes, but we've got to be careful with the London operation.'

'Does the Don know about this?'

'Of course.'

Chavasse nodded. 'So – where are we at?'

'One case of yours really got to me.' Volpe went to a side table and returned with a file. 'This was so amazing I had it copied. Read it. It's good stuff. I suppose you wrote it originally. I've got phone calls to make to all four quarters of the globe. I'll be about an hour then I'll take you to Don Tino at the Saddle Room. Anything you want, Aldo will get for you.'

He went out and Vinelli stood there, face impassive. 'Another whiskey, Sir Paul?'

'I think champagne might be more appropriate,' Chavasse said in excellent Italian.

'Of course.'

'Is he for real, the boy?'

'He is young.'

Aldo produced a bottle of Bollinger from the bar and Chavasse lit another cigarette, picked up the file and opened it. It was a fifty-page résumé of certain events in Albania in 1965. It was headed 'Bureau Case Study 203, Field Agent Doctor Paul Chavasse'.

Aldo stood at the door, still impassive.

It was very quiet, only rain drumming against the window.

*A long time ago*, Chavasse told himself, *a hell of a long time ago*.

He started to read.

# ROME

## MATANO

### 1965

# 2

When Chavasse entered the Grand Ballroom of the British Embassy, he was surprised to find the Chinese delegation clustered around the fireplace, looking completely out of place in their blue uniforms, and surrounded by the cream of Roman society.

Chou En-lai surveyed the scene from a large gilt chair, the Ambassador and his wife beside him, and his smooth impassive face gave nothing away. Occasionally, guests of sufficient eminence were brought forward by the First Secretary to be introduced.

The orchestra was playing a waltz. Chavasse lit a cigarette and leaned against a pillar. It was a splendid scene. The crystal chandeliers took light to every corner of the cream-and-gold ballroom, reflected again and again in the mirrored walls.

Beautiful women, handsome men, dress uniforms, the scarlet and purple of church dignitaries – it was all strangely archaic, as if somehow the mirrors were reflecting a dim memory of long ago, dancers turning endlessly to faint music.

He looked across to the Chinese and, for a brief instant, the white face of Chou En-lai seemed to jump out of the crowd, the eyes fastening on his. He nodded slightly, as if they knew each other, and the eyes seemed to say: *All these are doomed – this is my hour and you and I know it.*

Chavasse shivered and, for no accountable reason, a wave of greyness ran through him. It was as if some sixth sense, that mystical element common to all ancient races, inherited from his Breton father, were trying to warn him of danger.

The moment passed, the dancers swirled on. He was tired, that was the trouble. Four days on the run with no more than a couple of hours of uneasy sleep snatched when it was safe. He lit another cigarette and examined himself in the mirror on the wall.

The dark evening clothes were tailored well,

outlining good shoulders and a muscular frame, but the skin was drawn too tightly over the high cheekbones that were a heritage from his French father, and there were dark circles under the eyes.

*What you need is a drink*, he told himself. Behind him, reflected in the mirror, a young girl came in from the terrace through the french windows.

Chavasse turned slowly. Her eyes were set too far apart, the mouth too generous. Her dark hair hung loosely to her shoulders, the white silk dress was simplicity itself. She wore no accessories. None were needed. Like all great beauties, she wasn't beautiful, but it didn't matter a damn. She made every other woman in the room seem insignificant.

She moved towards the bar, heads turning as she passed, and was immediately accosted by an Italian Air Force colonel who was obviously slightly the worse for drink. Chavasse gave the man enough time to make a thorough nuisance of himself, then moved through the crowd to her side.

'Ah, there you are, darling,' he said in Italian. 'I've been looking everywhere for you.'

Her reflexes were excellent. She turned smoothly, assessing him against the situation in a split second and making her decision.

She reached up and kissed him lightly on the cheek. 'You said you'd only be ten minutes. It's really too bad of you.'

The Air Force colonel had already faded discreetly into the crowd and Chavasse grinned. 'How about a glass of Bollinger? I really think we should celebrate.'

'I think that would be rather nice, Mr Chavasse,' she said in excellent English. 'On the terrace, perhaps. It's cooler there.'

Chavasse took two glasses of champagne from the table and followed her through the crowd, a slight frown on his face. It *was* cool on the terrace, the traffic sounds muted and far away, and the scent of jasmine heavy on the night air.

She sat on the balustrade and took a deep breath. 'Isn't it a wonderful night?' She turned and looked at him and laughter bubbled out of her. 'Francesca – Francesca Minetti.'

She held out her hand and Chavasse gave her one of the glasses of champagne and grinned.

'You seem to know who I am already.'

She leaned back and looked up at the stars. When she spoke, it was as if she were reciting a lesson hard-learned.

'Paul Chavasse, born Paris 1928, father French, mother English. Educated at Sorbonne, Cambridge and Harvard universities. PhD Modern Languages, multilingual. University lecturer until 1954. Since then . . .'

Her voice trailed away and she looked at him thoughtfully. Chavasse lit a cigarette, no longer tired. 'Since then . . . ?'

'Well, you're on the books as a Third Secretary, but you certainly don't look like one.'

'What would you say I *did* look like?' he said calmly.

'Oh, I don't know. Someone who got about a lot.' She swallowed some more champagne and said casually, 'How was Albania? I was surprised you made it out in one piece. When the Tirana connection went dead, we wrote you off.'

She started to laugh again, her head back, and behind Chavasse a voice said, 'Is she giving you a hard time, Paul?'

Murchison, the First Secretary, limped across the terrace. He was a handsome, urbane man, his face bronzed and healthy, the bar of medals a splash of bright colour on the left breast of his jacket.

'Let's say she knows rather too much about me for my personal peace of mind.'

'She should,' Murchison said. 'Francesca works for the Bureau. She was your radio contact last week. One of our best operatives.'

Chavasse turned. 'You were the one who relayed the message from Scutari warning me to get out fast?'

She bowed. 'Happy to be of service.'

Before Chavasse could continue, Murchison took him firmly by the arm. 'Now don't start getting emotional, Paul. Your boss has just got in and he wants to see you. You and Francesca can talk over old times later.'

Chavasse squeezed her hand. 'That's a promise. Don't go away.'

'I'll wait right here,' she assured him, and he turned and followed Murchison inside.

They moved through the crowded ballroom into the entrance hall, passed the two uniformed footmen at the bottom of the grand staircase and mounted to the first floor.

The long, thickly carpeted corridor was quiet, and the music echoing from the ballroom might have been from another world. They went up half a dozen steps, turned into a shorter side passage and paused outside a white-painted door.

'In here, old man,' Murchison said. 'Try not to be too long. We've a cabaret starting in half an hour. Really quite something, I promise you.'

He moved back along the passage, his footsteps silent on the thick carpet, and Chavasse knocked on the door, opened it and went in.

The room was a small, plainly furnished office, its walls painted a neutral shade of green. The young woman who sat at the desk writing busily was attractive in spite of her dark, heavy-rimmed library spectacles.

She glanced up sharply and Chavasse smiled. 'Surprise, surprise.'

Jean Frazer removed her spectacles. 'You look like hell. How was Albania?'

'Tiresome,' Chavasse said. 'Cold, wet and with the benefits of universal brotherhood rather thinly spread on the ground.' He sat on the edge of the desk and helped himself to a cigarette from a teak box. 'What brings you and the old man out here? The Albanian affair wasn't all that important.'

'We had a NATO intelligence meeting in Bonn. When we got word that you were safely out, the Chief decided to come to Rome to take your report on the spot.'

'Nice try,' Chavasse said. 'The old bastard wouldn't have another job lined up for me, would he? Because if he has, he can damn well think again.'

'Why not ask him?' she said. 'He's waiting for you now.'

She nodded towards a green baize door. Chavasse looked at it for a moment, sighed heavily and crushed his cigarette into the ashtray.

The inner room was half in shadow, the only light a shaded lamp on the desk. The man who stood at the window gazing out at the lights of Rome was of medium height, the face somehow ageless, a strange, brooding expression in the dark eyes.

'Here we are again,' Chavasse said softly.

The Chief turned, took in Chavasse's appearance and nodded. 'Glad to see you back in one piece, Paul. I hear things were pretty rough over there.'

'You could say that.'

The older man moved to his chair and sat down. 'Tell me about it.'

'Albania?' Chavasse shrugged. 'We're not going to do much there. No one can pretend the people have gained anything since the Communists took over at the end of the war, but there's no question of a counter-revolution even getting started. The *Sigurmi*, the secret police, are everywhere. I'd say they must be the most extensive in Europe.'

'You went in using that Italian Communist Party Friendship cover, didn't you?'

'It didn't do me much good. The Italians in the party accepted me all right, but the trouble started when we reached Tirana. The *Sigurmi* assigned an agent to each one of us and they were real pros. Shaking them was difficult enough, and the moment I did, they smelt a rat and put out a general call for me.'

'What about the Freedom Party? How extensive are they?'

'You can start using the past tense as of last week. When I arrived, they were down to two cells. One in Tirana, the other in Scutari. Both were still in contact with our Bureau operation here in Rome.'

'Did you manage to contact the leader, this man Luci?'

'Only just. The night we were to meet to discuss things, he was mopped up by the *Sigurmi*. Apparently, they were all over his place, waiting for me to show my hand.'

'And how did you manage to get out of that one?'

'The Scutari cell got a radio signal from Luci as the police were breaking in. They relayed it to Bureau Headquarters here in Rome. Luckily for me, they had a quick thinker on duty – a girl named Francesca Minetti.'

'One of our best people at this end,' the Chief said. 'I'll tell you about her one of these days.'

'My back way out of Albania was a motor launch called the *Buona Esperanza*, run by a man named Guilio Orsini. He's quite a boy. Was one of the original torpedo merchants with the Italian Navy during the war. His best touch was when he sank a couple of our destroyers in Alexandria harbour back in '41. Got out again in one piece, too. He's a smuggler now. Runs across to Albania a lot. His grandmother came from there.'

'As I recall the original plan, he was to wait three nights running in a cove near Durres. That's about thirty miles by road from Tirana, isn't it?'

Chavasse nodded. 'When Francesca Minetti got the message from Scutari, she took a chance and put it through to Orsini on his boat. The madman left his crewman in charge, landed, stole a car in Durres and drove straight to Tirana. He caught me at my hotel as I was leaving for the meeting with Luci.'

'Getting back to the coast must have been quite a trick.'

'We did run into a little trouble. Had to do the last ten miles on foot through coastal salt marshes. Not good with the hounds on your heels, but Orsini knew what he was doing.

Once we were on board the *Buona Esperanza*,
it was easy. The Albanians don't have much of
a navy. Half a dozen minesweepers and a couple
of sub-chasers. The *Buona Esperanza* has ten
knots on any one of them.'

'It would seem that Orsini is due for a bonus
on this one.'

'That's putting it mildly.'

The Chief nodded, opened the file that contained Chavasse's report and leafed through it.
'So we're wasting our time in Albania?'

Chavasse nodded. 'I'm afraid so. You know
the way things have been since the 20th Party
Congress in 1956, and now the Chinese are in
there with both feet.'

'Anything to worry about?'

Chavasse shook his head. 'Albania's the most
backward European country I've visited and the
Chinese are too far from home to be able to do
much about it.'

'What about this naval base the Russians
were using at Valona before they pulled out?
The word was that they'd built it into a sort of
Red Gibraltar on the Adriatic.'

'Alb-Tourist took us on an official trip on our

second day. "Port" is hardly the word for the place. Good natural shelter, but only used by fishing boats. Certainly no sign of submarine pens.'

'And Enver Hoxha – you think he's still firmly in control?'

'And then some. We saw him at a military parade on the third day. He cuts an impressive figure, especially in uniform. He's certainly the people's hero at the moment. Heaven knows for how long.'

The Chief closed the file with a quick gesture that somehow dismissed the whole affair, placing it firmly in the past.

'Good work, Paul. At least we know where we stand. You're due for some leave now, aren't you?'

'That's right,' Chavasse said, and waited.

The Chief got to his feet, walked to the window and looked out over the glittering city, down towards the Tiber. 'What would you like to do?'

'Spend a week or two at Matano,' Chavasse said without hesitation. 'That's a small fishing port near Bari. There's a good beach, and Guilio

Orsini owns a place on the front called the Tabu. He's promised me some diving. I'm looking forward to it.'

'I'm sure you are,' the Chief said. 'Sounds marvellous.'

'Do I get it?'

The old man looked out over the city, an abstracted frown on his face. 'Oh, yes, Paul, you can have your leave – after you've done a little chore for me.'

Chavasse groaned and the older man turned and came back to the desk. 'Don't worry, it won't take long, but you'll have to leave tonight.'

'Is that necessary?'

The old man nodded. 'I've got transport laid on and you'll need help. This man Orsini sounds right. We'll offer a good price.'

Chavasse sighed, thinking of Francesca Minetti waiting on the terrace, of the good food and wine in the buffet room below. He sighed again and stubbed out his cigarette carefully.

'What do I do?'

The Chief pushed a file across. 'Enrico Noci,

a double agent who's been working for us and the Albanians. I didn't mind at first, but now the Chinese have got to him.'

'Which isn't healthy.'

'It never is. There's a boat waiting at Bari to take Noci over to Albania tomorrow night. All the details are in there.'

Chavasse studied the picture, the heavy fleshy face, the weak mouth – the picture of a man who was probably a failure at everything he put his hand to, except perhaps women. He had the sort of tanned beach-boy good looks that some of them went for.

'Do I bring him in?'

'What on earth for?' The Chief shook his head. 'Get rid of him; a swimming accident, anything you like. Nothing messy.'

'Of course,' Chavasse said calmly.

He glanced through the file again, memorizing the facts it contained, then pushed it across and stood up. 'I'll see you in London.'

The Chief nodded. 'In three weeks, Paul. Enjoy your holiday.'

'Don't I always?'

The Chief pulled a file across, opened it and

started to study the contents, and Chavasse
crossed to the door and left quietly.

# 3

Enrico Noci lay staring through the darkness
at the ceiling, smoking a cigarette. Beside him
the woman slept, her thigh warm against his.
Once, she stirred, turning into him in her sleep,
but didn't awaken.

He reached for another cigarette and heard
a distinctive rattle as something was pushed
through the letter box in the outer hall. He
slid from beneath the blankets, careful not to
wake the woman, and padded across the tiled
floor in his bare feet.

A large buff envelope lay on the mat at the
front door. He took it into the kitchen, lit the gas
under the coffee pot and opened the envelope
quickly. Inside was a smaller sealed envelope,
the one he was to take with him, and a single
typed sheet containing his movement orders.

He memorized them, then burned it quickly at the stove.

He glanced at his watch. Just before midnight. Time for a hot bath and something to eat. He stretched lazily, a conscious pleasure seeping through him. The woman had really been quite something. Certainly a diverting way to spend his last evening.

He was wallowing up to his chin in hot water, the small bathroom half-full of steam, when the door opened and she came in, yawning as she tied the belt of his silk dressing gown.

'Come back to bed, *caro*,' she said plaintively.

For the life of him, he couldn't remember her name and he grinned. 'Another time, angel. I must get moving. Make me some scrambled eggs and coffee, like a good girl. I've got to be out of here in twenty minutes.'

When he left the bathroom ten minutes later, he was freshly shaved, his dark hair slicked back, and he wore an expensive hand-knitted sweater and slacks. She had laid a small table in the window and placed a plate of scrambled eggs in front of him as he sat down.

As he ate, he pulled back the curtain with one hand and looked down across the lights of Bari to the waterfront. The town was quiet, and a slight rain drifted through the yellow street lamps in a silver spray.

'Will you be coming back?' she said.

'Who knows, angel?' he shrugged. 'Who knows?'

He finished his coffee, went into the bedroom, picked up a dark blue nylon raincoat and a small canvas grip and returned to the living room. She sat with her elbows on the table, a cup of coffee in her hands. He took out his wallet, extracted a couple of banknotes and dropped them on the table.

'It's been fun, angel,' he said, and moved to the door.

'You know the address.'

When he closed the outside door and turned along the street, it was half past twelve exactly. The rain was falling heavily now and fog crouched at the ends of the streets, reducing visibility to thirty or forty yards.

He walked briskly along the wet pavement, turned confidently out of one street into another and, ten minutes later, halted beside a small black Fiat sedan. He opened the door, lifted the corner of the carpet and found the ignition key. A few moments later, he was driving away.

On the outskirts of Bari, he stopped and consulted the map from the glove compartment. Matano was about twelve miles away on the coast road running south to Brindisi. An easy enough run, although the fog was bound to hold him up a little.

He lit a cigarette and started off again, concentrating on his driving as the fog grew thicker. He was finally reduced to a cautious crawl, his head out of the side window. It was almost an hour later when he halted at a signpost that indicated Matano to the left.

As he drove along the narrow road, he could smell the sea through the fog and gradually it seemed to clear a little. He reached Matano fifteen minutes later and drove through silent streets towards the waterfront.

He parked the car in an alley near the Club Tabu as instructed and went the rest of the way on foot.

It was dark and lonely on the waterfront and the only sound was the lapping of water against the pilings as he went down a flight of stone steps to the jetty.

It was quiet and deserted in the yellow light of a solitary lamp and he paused halfway along to examine the motor cruiser moored at the end. She was a thirty-footer with a steel hull, probably built by Akerboon, he decided. She was in excellent trim, her sea-green paintwork gleaming. It wasn't at all what he had expected. He examined the name *Buona Esperanza* on her hull with a slight frown.

When he stepped over the rail, the stern quarter was festooned with nets, still damp from the day's labour and stinking of fish, the deck slippery with their scales.

Somewhere in the distance the door of an all-night café opened and music drifted out, faint and far away, and for no accountable reason Noci shivered. It was at that moment that he realized he was being watched.

The man was young, slim and wiry with a sun-blackened face that badly needed a shave. He wore denims and an old oilskin coat, and a seaman's cap shaded calm, expressionless eyes. He stood at the corner of the deckhouse, a coiled rope in one hand, and said nothing. As Noci took a step towards him, the door of the wheelhouse opened and another man appeared.

He was at least six feet three, his great shoulders straining the seams of a blue pilot coat, and he wore an old Italian Navy officer's cap, the gold braid tarnished by exposure to salt air and water. He had perhaps the ugliest face Noci had ever looked upon, the nose smashed and flattened, the white line of an old scar running from the right eye to the point of the chin. A thin cigar of the type favoured by Dutch seamen was firmly clenched between his teeth and he spoke without removing it.

'Guilio Orsini, master of the *Buona Esperanza*.'

Noci felt a sudden surge of relief flow through him as tension ebbed away. 'Enrico Noci.'

He held out his hand. Orsini took it briefly and nodded to the young deckhand. 'Let's go, Carlo.' He jerked his thumb towards the companionway. 'You'll find a drink in the saloon. Don't come up until I tell you.'

As Noci moved towards the companionway, Carlo cast off and moved quickly to the stern. The engine burst into life, shattering the quiet, and the *Buona Esperanza* turned from the jetty and moved into the fog.

The saloon was warm and pleasantly furnished. Noci looked around approvingly, placed his canvas grip on the table and helped himself to a large whisky from a cabinet in one corner. He drank it quickly and lay on one of the bunks smoking a cigarette, a warm, pleasurable glow seeping through him.

This was certainly an improvement on the old tub in which he had done the run to Albania before. Orsini was a new face, but then there was nothing surprising in that. The faces changed constantly. In this business, it didn't pay to take chances.

The boat lifted forward with a great surge of power, and a slight smile of satisfaction touched Noci's mouth. At this rate they would be landing him on the coast near Durres before dawn. By noon he would be in Tirana. More dollars to his account in the Bank of Geneva, and this was his sixth trip in as many months. Not bad going, but you could take the pitcher to the well too often. After this, a rest was indicated – a long rest.

He decided he would go to the Bahamas. White beaches, blue skies and a lovely tanned girl wading thigh-deep from the sea to meet him. American, if possible. They were so ingenuous, had so much to learn.

The engines coughed once and died away and the *Buona Esperanza* slowed violently as her prow sank into the waves. Noci sat up, head to one side as he listened. The only sound was the lapping of the water against her hull.

It was some sixth sense, the product of his years of treachery and double-dealing, of living on his wits, that warned him that something was wrong. He swung his legs to the floor, reached for the canvas grip, unzipped it and took out a pistol. He released the safety catch and padded across to the foot of the companionway. Above him, the door opened and shut, creaking slightly as the boat pitched in the swell.

He went up quickly, one hand against the wall, paused and raised his head cautiously. The deck seemed deserted, the drizzle falling in silver cobwebs through the navigation lights.

He stepped out and, on his right, a match

flared and a man moved out of the shadows, bending his head to light a cigarette. The flame revealed a handsome devil's face, eyes like black holes above high cheekbones. He flicked the match away and stood there, hands in the pockets of his slacks. He wore a heavy fisherman's sweater and his dark hair glistened with moisture.

'Signor Noci?' he said calmly.

'Who the hell are you?' Noci demanded.

'My name is Paul Chavasse.'

It was a name with which Noci was completely familiar. An involuntary gasp rose in his throat and he raised the pistol. A hand like iron clamped on his wrist, wrenching the weapon from his grasp, and Guilio Orsini said, 'I think not.'

Carlo moved out of the shadows to the left and stood waiting. Noci looked about him helplessly and Chavasse held out his hand.

'I'll have the envelope now.'

Noci produced it reluctantly and handed it across, trying to stay calm as Chavasse examined the contents. They could be no more than half a mile from the shore, no distance to a man who had been swimming since childhood, and Noci was under no illusions as to what would happen if he stayed.

Chavasse turned over the first sheet of paper and Noci ducked under Orsini's arm and ran for the stern rail. He was aware of a sudden cry, an unfamiliar voice, obviously Carlo's, and then he slipped on some fish scales and stumbled headlong into the draped nets.

He tried to scramble to his feet, but a foot tripped him and then the soft, clinging, stinking meshes seemed to wrap themselves around him. He was pulled forward on to his hands and knees and looked up through the mesh to see Chavasse peering down at him, the devil's face calm and cold.

Orsini and Carlo had a rope in their hands and, in that terrible moment, Noci realized what they intended to do and a scream rose in his throat.

Orsini pulled hard on the rope and Noci lurched across the deck and cannoned into the low rail. A foot caught him hard against the small of the back and he went over into the cold water.

As he surfaced, the net impeding every movement he tried to make, he was aware of Orsini running the end of the line around the rail, of Carlo leaning out of the wheelhouse window waiting. A hand went up, and the *Buona Esperanza* surged forward.

Noci went under with a cry, then surfaced on a wave, choking for breath. He was aware only of Chavasse at the rail, watching, face calm in the fog-shrouded light, and then, as the boat increased speed, he went under for the last time.

As he struggled violently, water forcing the air from his lungs, and then suddenly he was aware of no pain, no pain at all. He seemed to be floating on soft white sand beneath a blue sky and a beautiful sun-tanned girl waded from the sea to join him, and she was smiling.

# 4

Chavasse was tired and his throat was raw from too many cigarettes. Smoke hung in layers from the low ceiling, spiralling in the heat from the single bulb above the green baize table, drifting into the shadows.

There were half a dozen men sitting in on the game. Chavasse, Orsini, Carlo Arezzi, his deckhand, a couple of fishing-boat captains and the sergeant of police. Orsini lit another of his foul-smelling Dutch cheroots and pushed a further two chips into the centre.

Chavasse shook his head and tossed in his hand. 'Too rich for my blood, Guilio.'

There was a general murmur and Guilio Orsini grinned and raked in his winnings. 'The bluff, Paul, the big bluff. That's all that counts in this game.'

Chavasse wondered if that explained why he was so bad at cards. For him, action had to be part of a logical progression based on a carefully reasoned calculation of the risk involved. In the great game of life and death he had played for so long, a man could seldom bluff more than once and get away with it.

He pushed back his chair and stood up. 'That's me for tonight, Guilio. I'll see you on the jetty in the morning.'

Orsini nodded. 'Seven sharp, Paul. Maybe we'll get you that big one.'

The cards were already on their way round again as Chavasse crossed to the door, opened it and stepped into a whitewashed passage. In spite of the lateness of the hour, he could hear music from the front of the club, and careless laughter. He took down an old reefer jacket from a peg, pulled it on and opened the side door.

The cold night air cut into his lungs as he breathed deeply to clear his head, and moved along the alley. A thin sea fog rolled in from the water and, except for the faint strains of music from the Tabu, silence reigned.

He found a crumpled packet of cigarettes in

his pocket, extracted one and struck a match on the wall, momentarily illuminating his face. As he did so, a woman emerged from a narrow alley opposite, hesitated, then walked down the jetty, the clicking of her high heels echoing through the night. A moment later, two sailors moved out of the entrance of the Tabu, crossed in front of Chavasse and followed her.

Chavasse leaned against the wall, feeling curiously depressed. There were times when he really wondered what it was all about, not just this dangerous game he played, but life itself. He smiled in the darkness. Three o'clock in the morning on the waterfront was one hell of a time to start thinking like that.

The woman screamed and he flicked his cigarette into the fog and stood listening. Again the screaming sounded, curiously muffled, and he started to run towards the jetty. He turned a corner and found the two sailors holding her on the ground under a street lamp.

As the nearest one turned in alarm, Chavasse lifted a boot into his face and sent him back over the jetty. The other leapt towards him with a curse, steel glinting in his right hand.

Chavasse was aware of the black beard, blazing eyes and strange hooked scar on the right cheek, and then he flicked his cap into the man's face and raised a knee into the exposed groin. The man writhed on the ground, gasping for breath, and Chavasse measured the distance and kicked him in the head.

In the water below the jetty came the sound of a violent splashing, and he moved to the edge and saw the first man swimming vigorously into the darkness. Chavasse watched him disappear, then turned to look for the woman.

She was standing in the shadow of a doorway and he went towards her. 'Are you all right?'

'I think so,' she replied, in a strangely familiar voice, and stepped out of the shadows.

His eyes widened in amazement. 'Francesca! What in the world are you doing here?'

Her dress had been ripped from neck to waist and she held it in place, a slight smile on her face. 'We were supposed to have a date on the terrace at the Embassy a week ago. What happened?'

'Something came up,' he said. 'The story of my life. But what are you doing on the Matano waterfront at this time of the morning?'

She swayed forward and he caught her just in time, holding her close to his chest for a brief moment. She smiled up at him wanly.

'Sorry about that, but all of a sudden I felt a little light-headed.'

'Have you far to go?'

She brushed a tendril of hair back from her forehead. 'I left my car somewhere near here, but all the streets look the same in the fog.'

'Better come back with me to my hotel,' he said. 'It's just around the corner.' He slipped off his jacket and draped it round her shoulders. 'I could fix you up with a bed.'

Laughter bubbled out of her, and for a moment she was once again the exciting girl he had met so briefly at the Embassy ball.

'I'm sure you could.'

He put an arm round her. 'Don't worry, I think you've had quite enough excitement for one night.'

There was the scrape of a shoe on the cobbles behind them, and he swung round and saw the other man lurching into the fog, hands to his smashed face.

Chavasse took a quick step after him and

Francesca caught his sleeve. 'Let him go. I don't want the police in on this.'

He looked down into her strained and anxious face. 'If that's the way you want it.'

There was something strange here, something he didn't understand. They walked along the jetty and turned on to the waterfront. As port towns went, Matano was reasonably tame, but not so tame that pretty young girls could walk around the dock area at three a.m. and expect to get away with it. One thing was certain. Francesca Minetti must have had a pretty powerful reason for being there.

The hotel was a small stuccoed building on a corner, an ancient electric sign over the entrance, but it was clean and cheap and the food was good. The owner was a friend of Orsini.

He slept at the desk, head in hands, and Chavasse reached over to the board without waking him and unhooked the key. They crossed the hall, mounted narrow wooden stairs and passed along a whitewashed corridor.

The room was plainly furnished with a brass bed, a washstand and an old wardrobe. As elsewhere in the house, the walls were white-washed and the floor highly polished.

Francesca stood just inside the door, one hand to the neck of her dress, holding it in place, and looked around approvingly.

'This is nice. Have you been here long?'

'Almost a week now. It's my first holiday in a year or more.'

He opened the wardrobe, rummaged among his clothes and finally produced a black polo-neck sweater in merino wool. 'Try that for size while I get you a drink. You look as if you could do with one.'

She turned her back and pulled the sweater over her head as he went to a cupboard in the corner. He took out a bottle of whisky and rinsed a couple of glasses in the bowl on the washstand. When he turned, she was standing by the bed watching him, looking strangely young and defenceless, the dark sweater hanging loosely about her.

'Sit down, for God's sake, before you fall down,' he said.

There was a cane chair by the french window leading to the balcony and she slumped into it and leaned her head against the glass window, staring into the darkness. Out at sea, a foghorn boomed eerily and she shivered.

'I think that must be the loneliest sound in the world.'

'Thomas Wolfe preferred a train whistle,' Chavasse said, pouring whisky into one of the glasses and handing it to her.

She looked puzzled. 'Thomas Wolfe? Who was he?'

He shrugged. 'Just a writer – a man who knew what loneliness was all about.' He swallowed a little of his whisky. 'Girls shouldn't be on the waterfront at this time of the morning; I suppose you know that? If I hadn't arrived when I did, you'd have probably ended up in the water after they'd finished with you.'

She shook her head. 'It wasn't that kind of assault.'

'I see.' He drank some more of his whisky and considered the point. 'If it would help, I'm a good listener.'

She held her glass in both hands and stared down at it, a troubled look on her face, and he added gently, 'Is this something official? A

Bureau operation, perhaps?'

She looked up, real alarm on her face, and shook her head vigorously. 'No, they know nothing about it and they mustn't be told, you must promise me that. It's a family matter, quite private.'

She put down her glass, stood up and walked restlessly across the room. When she turned, there was an expression of real anguish on her face. She pushed her hair back with a quick nervous gesture and laughed.

'The trouble is, I've always worked inside. Never in the field. I just don't know what to do in a situation like this.'

Chavasse produced his cigarettes, put one in his mouth and tossed the packet across to her. 'Why not tell me about it? I'm a great one for pretty girls in distress.'

She caught the packet automatically and stood there looking at him, a slight frown on her face. She nodded slowly. 'All right, Paul, but anything I tell you is confidential. I don't want any of this getting back to my superiors. It could get me into real trouble.'

'Agreed,' he said.

She came back to her chair, took a cigarette from the packet and reached up for a light. 'How much do you know about me, Paul?'

He shrugged. 'You work for us in Rome. My boss told me you were one of the best people we had out here and that's good enough for me.'

'I've worked for the Bureau for two years now,' she said. 'My mother was Albanian, so I speak the language fluently. I suppose that's what first interested them in me. She was the daughter of a *gegh* chieftain. My father was a colonel of mountain troops in the Italian occupation army in 1939. He was killed in the Western Desert early in the war.'

'Is your mother still alive?'

'She died about five years ago. She was never able to return to Albania once Enver Hoxha and the Communists took over. Two of her brothers were members of the *Legaliteri* in North Albania, which had royalist aims. They fought with Abas Kupi during the war. In 1945, Hoxha called them in from the hills to a peace conference at which they were immediately executed.'

There was no pain on her face, no emotion at all, except a calm acceptance of what for a long time must have been quite simply a fact of life.

'At least that explains why you were willing to work for us,' Chavasse said softly.

'It was not a hard decision to make. There was only an old uncle, my father's brother, who raised us, and until last year my brother was still in Paris studying political economy at the Sorbonne.'

'Where is he now?'

'When I last saw him, he was face-down in a mud bank of the Buene Marshes in Northern Albania with a machine-gun burst in his back.'

Out of the silence, Chavasse said carefully, 'When was this?'

'Three months ago. I was on leave at the time.' She held out her glass. 'Could I have some more?'

He poured until she raised her hand. She sipped a little, apparently still in control of her emotions, and continued.

'You were in Albania not so long ago yourself. You know how things are.'

He nodded. 'As bad as I've ever seen them.'

'Did you notice any churches on your travels?'

'One or two still seemed to be functioning,

but I know the official party line is to clamp down on religious observances of any sort.'

'They've almost completely crushed Islam,' she said in a dry matter-of-fact voice. 'The Albanian Orthodox Church has come out of it a little better, because they deposed their Archbishop and put in a priest loyal to Communism. It's the Roman Catholic Church that has been most harshly persecuted.'

'A familiar pattern,' Chavasse said. 'The organization Communism fears most.'

'Out of two archbishops and four bishops arrested, two have been shot and another's on the books as having died in prison. The Church has almost ceased to exist in Albania, or so the authorities hoped.'

'I must admit that was the impression I got.'

'During the past year there's been an amazing revival in the north,' she said. 'Headed by the Franciscan fathers at Scutari. Even non-Catholics have been swarming into the church there. It's had the central government in Tirana quite worried. They decided to do something about it. Something spectacular.'

'Such as?'

'There's a famous shrine outside the city dedicated to Our Lady of Scutari. A grotto and medicinal spring. The usual sort of thing. A place of pilgrimage since the Crusades. The statue is ebony and leafed with gold. Very ancient. They call her the Black Madonna. It's traditionally said that it was only because of her miraculous powers that the old Turkish overlords of ancient times allowed Christianity to survive in the country at all.'

'What did the central government intend to do?'

'Destroy the shrine, seize the statue and burn it publicly in the main square at Scutari. The Franciscan fathers were warned and managed to spirit the Madonna away on the very day the authorities were going to act.'

'Where is it now?'

'Somewhere in the Buene Marshes at the bottom of a lagoon in my brother's launch.'

'What happened?'

'It's easily told.' She shrugged. 'My brother, Marco, was interested in a society of Albanian refugees living in Taranto. One of them, a man called Ramiz, got word about the Madonna

61

through a cousin living in Albania at Tama. That's a small town on the river ten miles inland.'

'And this society decided to go in and bring her out?'

'The Black Madonna is no ordinary statue, Paul,' she said seriously. 'She symbolizes all the hope that's left for Albania in a hard world. They realized what a tremendous psychological effect it would have upon the morale of Albanians everywhere if it were made public in the Italian press that the statue had reached Italy in safety.'

'And you went in with them? With Marco?'

'It's an easy passage and the Albanian Navy is extremely weak, so getting into the marshes is no problem. We picked up the statue at a pre-arranged spot on the first night. Unfortunately, we ran into a patrol boat next morning on the way out. There was some shooting and the launch was badly damaged. She sank in a small lagoon and we took to the rubber dinghy. They hunted us for most of the day. Marco was shot towards evening. I didn't want to leave his body, but we didn't have much choice. Later that night, we reached the coast and Ramiz stole a small sailing boat. That's how we got back.'

'And where is this man Ramiz now?' Chavasse asked.

'Somewhere in Matano. He telephoned me in Rome yesterday and told me to meet him at a hotel on the waterfront. You see, he's managed to get hold of a launch.'

Chavasse stared at her, an incredulous frown on his face. 'Are you trying to tell me you intend to go back into those damned marshes?'

'That was the general idea.'

'Just the two of you, you and Ramiz?' He shook his head. 'You wouldn't last five minutes.'

'Perhaps not, but it's worth a try.' He started to protest but she raised a hand. 'I'm not going to spend the rest of my life living with the thought that my brother died for nothing when I could at least have tried to do something about it. The Minettis are a proud family, Paul. We take care of our dead. I know what Marco would have done and I am the only one left to do it.'

She sat there, her face very pale in the lamplight. Chavasse took her hands, reached across and kissed her gently on the mouth.

'This lagoon where the launch sank, you know where it is?'

She nodded, frowning slightly. 'Why?'

He grinned. 'You surely didn't think I'd let you go in on your own?'

There was a look of complete bewilderment on her face. 'But why, Paul? Give me one good reason why you should risk your life for me?'

'Let's just say I'm bored after a week of lazing around on the beach, and leave it at that. This man Ramiz, you've got his address?'

She took a scrap of paper from her handbag and handed it to him. 'I don't think it's far from here.'

He slipped it into his pocket. 'Right, let's get going.'

'To see Ramiz?'

He shook his head. 'That comes later. First we'll call on a good friend of mine, the kind of man you need for a job like this. Someone with no scruples, who knows the Albanian coast like the back of his hand and runs the fastest boat in the Adriatic.'

At the door, she turned and looked up at him searchingly. Something glowed in her eyes and colour flooded her cheeks. Quite suddenly, she seemed confident, sure of herself again.

'It's going to be all right, angel. I promise you.'

He raised her hand briefly to his lips, opened the door and gently pushed her into the corridor.

# 5

The air in the room was still heavily tainted by cigarette smoke, but the card players had gone. In the light of the shaded lamp, a British Admiralty chart of the Drin Gulf area of the Albanian coast was unfolded across the table. Chavasse and Orsini leaned over it and Francesca sat beside them.

'The Buene River runs down to the coast from Lake Scutari, or Shkoder as they call it these days,' Orsini said.

'What about these coastal marshes? Are they as bad as Francesca says?'

Orsini nodded. 'One hell of a place. A maze of narrow channels, salt-water lagoons and malaria-infested swamps. Unless you knew where to look, you could search for a year for that launch and never find it.'

'Anyone living there?'

'A few fishermen and wildfowlers, mainly *geghs*. The Reds haven't done too well in those parts. The whole area's always been a sort of refuge for people on the run.'

'You know it well?'

Orsini grinned. 'I'd say I've made the run into those marshes at least half a dozen times this year. Penicillin, sulphonamide, guns, nylons. There's a lot of money to be made and the Albanian Navy can't do much to stop it.'

'Still a risky business, though.'

'For amateurs, anything is risky.' Orsini turned to Francesca. 'This man Ramiz, what did he do for a living?'

'He was an artist. I believe he did most of his sailing at weekends.'

Orsini looked at the ceiling and raised his hands helplessly. 'My God, what a set-up. That he got you back safely to Italy is a miracle, *signorina*.'

The door opened and Carlo came in carrying cups on a tray. He handed them round and Chavasse sipped hot coffee. He frowned down at the map, following the main channel, then turned to Francesca.

'You say you know where the launch went down? How can you be sure? These lagoons all look the same.'

'Marco took a cross-bearing just before we sank,' she said. 'I memorized it.'

Orsini pushed a piece of paper and a pencil across and she quickly wrote the figures down. He examined them with a slight frown and then calculated the position. He drew a circle round the central point.

'X marks the spot.'

Chavasse examined it quickly. 'About five miles in. Another three or four to this place Tama. What's it like there?'

'Used to be quite a thriving little river port years ago, but it's gone down the slot in a big way since the trouble started between Albania and the satellite countries.' Orsini traced a finger along the line of the river. 'The Buene forms part of the boundary between Albania and Yugoslavia. Most of the main stream's been allowed to silt up. That means you have to know the estuary and delta region well to get as far inland as Tama.'

'But could you get us there?'

Orsini turned to Carlo. 'What do you think?'

'We've never had any trouble before. Why should we now?'

'The pitcher can go to the well too often,' Francesca observed softly.

Orsini shrugged. 'For all men, death makes the last appointment. He chooses his own time.'

'That only leaves the question of the price to be settled,' Chavasse said.

'No problem there,' Francesca put in quickly.

'*Signorina*, please.' Orsini took her hand and touched it to his lips. 'I will do this thing because I want to, and for no other reason.'

She seemed close to tears and Chavasse interrupted quickly. 'One thing I'm not happy about is Ramiz. Are you sure it was his voice on the telephone?'

She nodded. 'He came from the province of Vlore. They have a distinctive accent. I'm sure it was him.'

Chavasse decided that it didn't look too good for Ramiz. The *Sigurmi* had obviously traced them with no difficulty. Maybe they'd recovered Marco Minetti's body or, what was more probable, had got their hands on the people who had passed on the Madonna in Albania itself. Each man had his limits, his specific tolerance to pain. Once past that point, most would babble all they knew before dying.

And it was natural that the Albanians should go to so much trouble to trace the Madonna. Its disappearance must have meant a big loss of prestige politically, and the knowledge that it must still be in their own territory would be an added spur to recover it.

'If Ramiz did make that phone call, it was probably because he was made to. Either that or he was known to have made it.' He produced the slip of paper Francesca had given him at the hotel. 'Do you know this place?'

Orsini nodded. 'It's not far from here. The sort of fleabag where whores rent rooms by the hour and no questions asked.' He turned to Francesca. 'No place for a lady.'

She started to protest, but Chavasse cut in quickly. 'Guilio's right. In any case, you're out on your feet. What you need is about eight hours' solid sleep. You can use my room at the hotel.' He turned to Carlo. 'See she gets there safely.'

He pulled on his reefer jacket and she stood up. 'You'll be careful?'

'Aren't I always?' He gave her a little push. 'Lock yourself in the room and get some sleep. I'll be along later.'

She went reluctantly and Carlo followed her out. When Chavasse turned, Orsini was grinning hugely. 'Ah, to be young and handsome.'

'Something you never were,' Chavasse said. 'Let's get moving.'

It was still raining, a thin drizzle that beaded the iron railings of the harbour wall like silver as they walked along the pavement. The old stuccoed houses floated out of the fog, unreal and insubstantial, and each street lamp was a yellow oasis of light in a dark world.

The hotel was no more than five minutes from the Tabu, a seedy tenement, plaster peeling from the brickwork beside the open door. They entered a dark and gloomy hall. There was no one behind the wooden desk and no response to Orsini's impatient push on the bell.

'Did she give you the room number?'

Chavasse nodded. 'Twenty-six.'

The Italian moved behind the desk and examined the board. He came back, shaking his head. 'The key isn't there. He must still be in his room.'

They went up a flight of rickety wooden stairs to the first floor. There was an unpleasant musty smell compounded of cooking odours and stale urine and a strange brooding quiet. They moved along the passage, checking the numbers on the doors, and Chavasse became aware of music and high brittle laughter. He paused outside the room from which it came and Orsini turned from the door opposite.

'This is it.'

The door swung open to his touch and he stepped inside and reached for the light switch. Nothing happened. He struck a match and Chavasse moved in beside him.

The room was almost bare. There was a rush mat on the floor, an iron bed and a washstand. A wooden chair lay on its side beside the mat.

As Chavasse reached down to pick it up, the match Orsini was holding burned his fingers and he dropped it with a curse. Chavasse rested on one knee, waiting for him to strike another and was aware of a sudden dampness soaking through the knee of his slacks. As the match flared, he raised his hand, the fingers sticky and glutinous with half-dried blood.

'So much for Ramiz.'

They examined the room quickly, but there was nothing to be found, not even a suitcase, and they went back into the passage. High-pitched laughter sounded from opposite and Orsini raised his eyebrows inquiringly.

'Nothing to lose,' Chavasse said.

The big Italian knocked on the door. There was a sudden silence and then a woman's voice called, 'Come back later. I'm busy.'

Orsini knocked even harder. There was a quick angry movement inside and the door was jerked open. The woman who faced them was small, with flaming red hair. The black nylon robe she wore did little to conceal her ample charms. She recognized Orsini immediately and the look of anger on her face was replaced by a ready smile.

'Eh, Guilio, it's been a long time.'

'Too long, *cara*,' he said, patting her face.

'You still look as good as ever. My friend and I wanted a word with the man opposite, but he doesn't appear to be at home.'

'Oh, that one,' she said in disgust. 'Sitting around his room like that. Wouldn't even give a girl the time of day.'

'He must have been blind,' Orsini said gallantly.

'A couple of men came looking for him earlier,' she said. 'I think there was some trouble. When I looked out, they were taking him away between them. He didn't look good.'

'You didn't think of calling the police?' Chavasse asked.

'I wouldn't cut that bastard of a sergeant down if he were hanging.' There was an angry call from inside the room and she grinned. 'Some of them get really impatient.'

'I bet they do,' Chavasse said.

She smiled. 'You, I definitely like. Bring him round some time, Guilio. We'll have ourselves a party.'

'Maybe I'll do that,' Orsini told her.

There was another impatient cry from inside and she raised her eyebrows despairingly and closed the door.

Orsini and Chavasse went back downstairs and out into the street. The Italian paused to light a cheroot and flicked the match into the darkness.

'What now?'

Chavasse shrugged. 'There isn't really much we can do. I know one thing. I could do with some sleep.'

Orsini nodded. 'Go back to your hotel. Stay with the girl and behave yourself. We'll sort something out in the morning.' He punched Chavasse lightly on the shoulder. 'Don't worry, Paul. You're in the hands of experts.'

He turned away into the fog, and as Chavasse watched him go, tiredness seemed to wash over him in a great wave. He walked along the pavement, his footsteps echoing between narrow stone walls, and paused on a corner, fumbling for a cigarette.

As the match flared in his hands, something needle-sharp sliced through his jacket to touch his spine. A voice said quietly, 'Please to stand very still, Mr Chavasse.'

He waited while expert hands passed over his body, checking for the weapon that wasn't there.

'Now walk straight ahead and don't look round. And do exactly as you are told. It would desolate me to have to kill you.'

It was only as he started walking that Chavasse realized the voice had spoken in Albanian.

# 6

There were two of them, he could tell that much from their footfalls echoing between the walls of the narrow alleys as they moved through the old quarter of the town. The harsh voice of the man who had first spoken occasionally broke the silence to tell him to turn right or left, but otherwise there was no conversation and they stayed well behind him.

Fifteen minutes later, they emerged from an alley on to the sea wall on the far side of the harbour from the jetty. A house several floors high reared into the night, and beside it a flight of stone steps led down to a landing stage.

An old naval patrol boat was moored there, shabby and neglected, paint peeling from her hull. Across her stern ran the faded inscription *Stromboli – Taranto*.

The landing stage was deserted in the light of a solitary lamp and there was no one to help him. He turned slowly and faced the two men. One of them was small and rather nondescript. He wore a heavy jersey, and a knitted cap was pulled over his eyes.

The other was a different proposition, a big, dangerous-looking man badly in need of a shave. He had a scarred, brutal face, cropped hair and wore a reefer coat and seaboots.

He slipped a cigarette into his mouth and struck a match on the seawall. 'Down we go, Mr Chavasse. Down we go.'

Chavasse descended the steps slowly. As he reached the landing stage, the little man moved past him and led the way to the far end, where he opened a door set in the thickness of the wall. A flight of stone stairs lifted into the gloom and Chavasse followed him, the big man a couple of paces behind.

They arrived on a stone landing and the little man opened another door and jerked his head. Chavasse moved past him and stood just inside the entrance. The room was plainly furnished with a wooden table and several chairs. A narrow iron bed stood against one wall.

The man who sat at the table writing a letter was small and dark and dressed in a suit of blue tropical worsted. His skin was the colour of fine leather, the narrow fringe of beard combining to give him the look of a *conquistador*.

Chavasse paused a couple of feet away, hands in his pockets. Small, black, shining eyes had swivelled to a position from which they could observe him. The man half-turned and smiled.

'Mr Chavasse – a distinct pleasure, sir.'

His English was clipped and precise, hardly any accent at all. Chavasse decided that he didn't like him. The eyes were cold and merciless in spite of the polite, birdlike expression, the eyes of a killer.

'I'm beginning to find all this rather a bore.'

The little man smiled. 'Then we must try to make things more interesting. How would you like to earn ten thousand pounds?'

At the other end of the table was a tray containing a couple of bottles and several glasses. Chavasse walked to it calmly, aware of a slight movement from the big man over by the door.

One of the bottles contained Smirnoff, his

favourite vodka. He half-filled a glass and walked casually to the window, gazing forty feet down into the harbour as he drank, assessing the position of the *Stromboli* to the left, her outline showing dimly through the fog.

'Well?' the little man asked.

Chavasse turned. 'How are things in Tirana these days?'

The little man smiled. 'Very astute, but I haven't seen Tirana in five years. A slight difference of opinion with the present regime.' He produced a white card and flicked it across. 'My card, sir. I am Adem Kapo, agent for Alb-Tourist in Taranto.'

'Among other things, I'm sure.'

Kapo took out a case and extracted a cigarette which he fitted into a holder. 'You could describe me as a sort of middleman. People come to me with their requirements and I try to satisfy them.'

'For a fee?'

'But of course.' He extended the case. 'Cigarette?'

Chavasse took one. 'Ten thousand pounds. That's a lot of money. What makes you think I'd be interested?'

'Knowing who people are is part of my business and I know a great deal about you, my friend. More than you could dream of. Men like you are a gun for sale to the highest bidder. In any case, the money would be easily earned. My principals will pay such a sum in advance if you will agree to lead them to the position of a certain launch which recently sank in the marshes of the Buene River in Northern Albania. You are interested?'

'I could be if I knew what you were talking about.'

'I'm sure Signorina Minetti has already filled you in on the details. Come now, Mr Chavasse, all is discovered, as they say in the English melodramas. According to the information supplied to me by my clients, the body of an Italian citizen named Marco Minetti was discovered on a mud bank at the mouth of the Buene recently after an attempt had been made to smuggle a priceless religious relic from the country.'

'You don't say,' Chavasse said.

Kapo ignored the interruption. 'A few hours earlier, his launch had disappeared into the wastes of the Buene Marshes. Later, a priest and two men were taken into custody by the *Sigurmi* at the town of Tama. Apparently, the priest was stubborn to the end, a bad habit they have, but the two men talked. They named Minetti, his sister and an Albanian refugee, an artist called Ramiz. I was offered what I must admit was a very handsome fee to trace them.'

'And did you?'

'We've been watching Ramiz for weeks, waiting for him to make his move. Incredible though it may seem, he apparently intended to go in again. You see, he was an intellectual – one of those irritating people who feel they have a mission in life.'

'You speak of him in the past tense.'

'Yes, it's really quite sad.' Kapo sounded genuinely moved. 'I decided to have a little chat with him earlier this evening. When Haji and Tashko were bringing him here, there was some sort of struggle. He fell from the seawall and broke his neck.'

'An unfortunate accident, I suppose?'

'But of course, and quite unnecessary. It's surprising how easily one's motives can be misunderstood. I'm afraid an earlier attempt to get in touch with Signorina Minetti also met with a conspicuous lack of success.'

'Which leaves you with me.'

'One can hardly be blamed for thinking it rather more than coincidental that Mr Paul Chavasse of the British Secret Service just happened to be on the spot when the Signorina Minetti needed some assistance.'

Chavasse reached for the bottle of vodka and poured some more into his glass. 'And what would you say if I told you I still don't know what you're talking about?'

'If you persisted, you would leave me no choice. I would have to apply to the *signorina* again, which would distress me greatly.' Kapo sighed. 'On the other hand, women are so much easier to deal with. Don't you agree, Tashko?'

The big man moved to the end of the table, a mirthless grin on his face, and Chavasse nodded thoughtfully. 'Somehow I thought you'd say that.'

He reversed his grip on the bottle of vodka and struck sideways against Tashko's skull. The Albanian cried out sharply as the bottle smashed into pieces, drawing blood, and Chavasse heaved the table over, sending Kapo backwards in his chair, pinning him to the floor.

Haji was already moving fast across the room, a knife in his right hand. As it started to come up, Chavasse warded off the blow with one arm, caught the small man by his left wrist and, with a sudden pull, sent him crashing into the wall.

Tashko was already on his feet, blood streaming down the side of his face. He threw a tremendous punch, and Chavasse ducked under his arm and moved towards the door. Kapo pushed out a foot and tripped him so that he fell heavily to the floor.

Tashko moved in quickly, kicking at his ribs and face, and Chavasse rolled away, avoiding most of the blows, and scrambled up. He vaulted over the upturned table, picked up one of the chairs in both hands and hurled it through the window with all his force. The dried and rotting wood of the frame smashed easily and the window dissolved in a snowstorm of flying glass.

He was aware of Kapo's warning cry, of Tashko lurching forward. He lashed out sideways, the edge of his hand catching the big man across the face, scrambled on to the sill and jumped into darkness.

The air rushed past his ears with a roar, the fog seemed to curl around him; then he hit the water with a solid forceful smack and went down.

When he surfaced, he gazed up at the dark bulk of the house, at the light filtering through the fog from the smashed window. There was a sudden call, Kapo's voice drifting down, and another answered from the *Stromboli*, dimly seen in the fog to the right.

There was only one sensible way out of the situation, and Chavasse took it. He turned and swam away from the landing stage, out into the harbour towards the jetty on the other side. It was perhaps a quarter of a mile, he knew that. No great distance and the water was warm.

He took his time, swimming steadily, and the voices faded into the fog behind him and he was alone in an enclosed world. Everything seemed to fade away and he felt curiously calm and at peace with himself. Time seemed to have no meaning and the riding lights of the fishing boats moored close to the jetty appeared through the fog in what seemed a remarkably short time.

He swam between them and landed at a flight of steps which led to the jetty. For a moment or two he sat there getting his breath and then went up quickly and moved along the jetty to the waterfront.

His first real need was for a change of clothes and he hurried through the fog towards his hotel. After that, a visit to Orsini at the Tabu and perhaps a return match with Adem Kapo and his thugs, although it was more than probable that the *Stromboli* was already being prepared for a hasty exit.

The electric sign over the entrance to the hotel loomed out of the night and he opened the door and moved inside. The desk was vacant, no one apparently on duty, and he went up the stairs two at a time and turned along the corridor.

The door to his room stood open, panels smashed and splintered, and a light was still burning. A chair lay on its side in the middle of the floor and the blankets were scattered over the end of the bed as if there had been a struggle. He stood there for a moment, his stomach suddenly hollow, then turned and hurried back downstairs.

He noticed the foot protruding from behind the desk as he moved to the door and there was a slight groan of pain. When he looked over the top, he saw the old proprietor lying on his face, blood matting the white hair at the back of his head.

# 7

The landing stage was deserted when Chavasse, Orsini and Carlo drove up in the old Ford pick-up. The big Italian cut the engine, jumped to the ground and went to the head of the steps.

He turned, shaking his head. 'We're wasting our time, Paul, but we'll check the house just in case.'

They went down the steps quickly and crossed the landing stage to the door. It opened without difficulty and Chavasse went up first, an old Colt automatic Orsini had given him held against his right knee.

The door to the room in which Kapo had interviewed him stood ajar, light streaming out across the dark landing. Chavasse kicked it open and waited, but there was no reply. He went in quickly at ground level, the automatic ready.

Vodka from the smashed bottle had soaked into the floor, mixed with blood, and the table still lay on its side. Fog billowed in through the broken window and Orsini walked across, feet crunching on glass, and peered outside.

He turned, respect on his face. 'A long way down.'

'I didn't have a great deal of choice. What do we do now?'

The Italian shrugged. 'Go back to the Tabu. Maybe old Gilberto's remembered something by now.'

'I wouldn't count on it,' Chavasse said. 'That was a hard knock he took.'

'Then we'll have to think of something else.'

They returned to the pick-up and Carlo drove back to the Tabu through the deserted streets. As the truck braked to a halt, Chavasse checked his watch and saw that it was almost half past two. He jumped to the ground and followed the two Italians along the alley to the side door.

There were still a few customers in the bar at the front and, as they walked along the passage, the barman looked round the corner.

'Rome on the phone. They're hanging on.'

'That'll be my call to the Bureau,' Chavasse said to Orsini. 'I'll see what they've got to tell me about Kapo.'

'I'll have another word with old Gilberto,' Orsini said. 'He may be thinking a little straighter by now.'

Chavasse took his call in the small office at the back of the bar. The man on the other end was the night duty officer based at the Embassy. No one of any particular importance, just a good reliable civil servant who knew what files were for and how to use them efficiently.

He had nothing on Kapo that Chavasse didn't already know. Incredibly, everything the man had said about himself was true. At one time a high official in the Albanian Ministry of the Interior, he had been marked down for elimination in 1958 during one of Hoxha's earlier purges. He had been allowed to enter Italy as a political refugee and had since lived in Taranto earning a living as an import-export agent. Presumably on the basis that an Albanian of any description was preferable to a foreigner, Alb-Tourist had appointed him their Taranto agent in 1963. An official investigation by Italian

Military Intelligence in that year had indicated nothing sinister in the appointment.

Chavasse thanked the duty officer. No, it was nothing of any importance. He'd simply run across Kapo in Matano and had thought him worth checking on.

At the other end of the wire in his small office in Rome, the duty officer replaced the receiver with a thoughtful frown. Almost immediately, he picked it up again and put a call through to Bureau headquarters in London on the special line.

It could be nothing, but Chavasse was a topliner – everyone in the organization knew that. If by any remote chance he was up to anything and the Chief didn't know about it, heads might start to roll, and the duty officer hadn't the slightest intention of allowing his own to be numbered among them.

The telephone on his desk buzzed sharply five minutes later and he lifted it at once. 'Hello, sir . . . yes, that's right . . . well, there may be nothing in it, but I thought you'd like to know

that I've just had a call from Paul Chavasse in
Matano . . .'

Old Gilberto coughed as the brandy caught at
the back of his throat and grinned wryly at
Orsini. 'I must be getting old, Guilio. Never
heard a damned thing. It couldn't have been
more than twenty minutes after Carlo had delivered the young woman. One moment I was reading a magazine, the next, the lights were going
out.' He raised a gnarled and scarred fist. 'Old
I may be, but I'd still like five minutes on my
own with that fancy bastard, whoever he is.'

Orsini grinned and patted him on the shoulder.
'You'd murder him, Gilberto. Nothing like a bit
of science to have these young toughies running
around in circles.'

They went out into the passage, leaving the
old man sitting at the fire, a blanket around his
shoulders. 'A good heavyweight in his day,'
Orsini said. 'One with the sense to get out
before they scrambled his brains. Anything
from Rome?'

Chavasse shook his head. 'Everything Kapo

said about himself was true. He *is* the Alb-Tourist agent in Taranto, an old Party man from Tirana who said the wrong thing once too often and only got out by the skin of his teeth. According to Italian intelligence, he's harmless and they usually know what they're talking about.'

'That's what MI5 said about Fuchs and look where it got them,' Orsini pointed out. 'Nobody's perfect, and the good agent is the man who manages to pull the wool over the eyes of the opposition most effectively.'

'Which doesn't get us anywhere,' Chavasse said. 'They've gone, which is all that counts, taking Francesca Minetti with them.'

They went into the office at the rear of the bar and Orsini produced a bottle of whisky and three glasses. He filled them, a slight thoughtful frown on his face.

'Whoever took the girl, it couldn't have been Kapo and his men – the time factor wouldn't have allowed it. The men who attacked her on the jetty earlier – what can you tell me about them?'

'Judging by the language the second one used when he tried to stick his knife into me, I'd say he was Italian,' Chavasse said. 'Straight out of the Taranto gutter.'

'Anything else interesting about him?'

'He had a dark beard, anything but the trimmed variety, and his face was badly scarred. A sort of hook shape curving into his right eye.'

Orsini let out a great bellow of laughter and clapped him on the shoulder. 'But my dear Paul, this is wonderful.'

'You mean you know him?'

'Do I know him?' Orsini turned to Carlo. 'Tell him about our good friend Toto.'

'He works for a man called Vacelli,' Carlo said. 'A real bad one. Runs a couple of fishing boats out of here, engaged in the Albanian trade, the town brothel and a café in the old quarter.' He spat vigorously. 'A pig.'

'It looks as if Kapo must have employed Vacelli to get hold of the girl for him,' Orsini said. 'It's the sort of task for which Nature has fitted him admirably. Unfortunately, you arrived on the scene and messed things up.'

'Which doesn't explain why Kapo went to the trouble of having me pulled in for a personal interview.'

'He probably thought he could do some kind of a deal, you made a break for it and he had to leave in a hurry in case you decided to whistle the law down on him. No other choice.'

'And in the meantime, Vacelli and his boys picked up the girl?'

Orsini nodded. 'And Kapo had to leave before they could get in touch with him.'

'So you think Vacelli may still have the girl?'

Orsini opened the drawer of his desk, took out a Luger and slipped it into his hip pocket. He smiled and the great, ugly face was quite transformed.

'Let's go and find out.'

Vacelli's place fronted the harbour on the corner of an alley which led into the heart of the old town. The sign simply said *Café*. Inside, someone was playing a guitar. They parked the pick-up at the entrance and when they went in Orsini led the way downstairs.

There was a bead curtain and the murmur of voices from the bar beyond. The guitar player sat just inside the entrance, chair balanced against the wall. He was young with dark curling hair, the sleeves of his check shirt rolled back to expose muscular arms.

Orsini pulled back the curtain and looked down at the legs sprawled across the entrance. The guitar player made no effort to move and Orsini hooked the chair from under him, the sudden clatter stunning the room to silence.

There was a narrow, marble-topped bar, the wall behind it lined with bottles, and a few small tables and chairs ranged about them. The floor was of stone, the walls whitewashed and there were no more than a dozen customers, most of them men.

The guitar player came up fast, a spring knife in one hand, but Carlo was faster. His hand tightened over the wrist, twisting cruelly, and the youth screamed, dropping the knife. He staggered back against the wall, tears of pain in his eyes, and Orsini shook his head.

'God knows what's happened to the youth of this country. No manners at all.' He turned, looking the other patrons over casually. The bearded man with the scarred face, the one they called Toto, sat at the table by the wall, one arm in a sling.

Orsini grinned. 'Hey, Toto, you don't look too good. Where's Vacelli?'

There was a scrape of a boot on stone and a surly voice growled. 'What the hell do you want?'

Vacelli stood at the top of the flight of stone steps in the corner leading up to the first floor. He was built like Primo Carnera, a great ox of a man with a bullet-shaped head that was too small for the rest of his body.

'Hello there, you animal,' Orsini cried gaily. 'We've come for the Minetti girl.'

Vacelli's brutal face reddened in anger and he obviously restrained his temper with difficulty. 'I don't know what you're talking about.'

'What a pity.' Orsini picked up the nearest chair and threw it at the shelves behind the bar, smashing the mirror and bringing down a dozen bottles. 'Does that help?'

Vacelli gave a roar of rage and came down the steps on the run. Orsini picked up a full bottle of Chianti from a nearby table, jumped to one side and smashed it across Vacelli's skull as he staggered past.

Vacelli fell to one knee. Orsini picked up a

chair and brought it down across the great shoulders. Vacelli grunted and started to keel over. Orsini brought the chair down again and again until it splintered into matchwood. He tossed it to one side and waited.

Slowly, painfully, Vacelli reached for the edge of the bar and hauled himself up. He swayed there for a moment, then charged head-down, blood washing across his face in a red curtain. Orsini swerved and slashed him across the kidneys with the edge of his hand as Vacelli plunged past him.

Vacelli screamed and fell on his face. He tried to push himself up, but it was no good. He collapsed with a great sigh and lay still.

'Anyone else?' Orsini demanded.

No one moved and he turned to Carlo. 'Watch things down here. We won't be long.'

Chavasse followed him up the stairs and the big Italian pulled back a curtain and led the way along a narrow passage. A young woman in a cheap nylon housecoat leaned in a doorway smoking a cigarette.

'Eh, Guilio, have you killed the bastard?'

'Just about.' He grinned. 'He'll be inactive for

quite a while. Time enough for you to pack your bags and move on. There was a girl brought here tonight. Any idea where she is?'

'The end room. He was just going in when you arrived. I don't think he meant her any good.'

'My thanks, *carissima*.' Orsini kissed her lightly on one cheek. 'Go home to your mother.'

Chavasse was already ahead of him, but the door was locked. 'Francesca, it's Paul,' he called.

There was a quick movement inside and she called back, 'The door's locked on the outside.'

Orsini stood back, raised one booted foot and stamped twice against the lock. There was a sudden splintering sound, and the door sagged on its hinges, rotten wood crumbling. He stamped again and it fell back against the wall.

Francesca Minetti stood waiting, her face white. She was still wearing Chavasse's old sweater and looked about fifteen years old. Chavasse was aware of the breath hissing sharply between Orsini's teeth and then the Italian was moving forward quickly.

His voice was strangely gentle and comforting, like a father reassuring a frightened child. 'It's all right now, *cara*. There is nothing to worry about any more.'

She held his hand, gazing up into the ugly, battered face and tried to smile and then she started to tremble. She turned, stumbled across the wreckage of the door and ran into Chavasse's arms.

# 8

It was just after eight o'clock on the following evening when the *Buona Esperanza* moved away from the jetty and turned out to sea. It was a warm, soft night with a luminosity shining from the water. There was no moon, for heavy cloud banked over the horizon, as though a storm might be in the offing.

Orsini was at the wheel and Chavasse stood beside him, leaning forward to peer through the curved deckhouse window into the darkness ahead.

'What about the weather?' he said.

'Force-four wind with rain imminent. Nothing to worry about.'

'Is it the same for the Drin Gulf?'

'A few fog patches, but they'll be more of a help than anything else.'

Chavasse lit two cigarettes and handed one to the Italian. 'Funny what a day-to-day business life is. I never expected to set foot on Albanian soil again.'

'The things we do for the ladies.' Orsini grinned. 'But this one is something special, Paul. This I assure you as an expert. She reminds me very much of my wife, God rest her.'

Chavasse looked at him curiously. 'I never knew you'd been married.'

'A long time ago.' Orsini's face was calm, untroubled, but the sadness was there in his voice. 'She was only nineteen when we married. That was in 1941, during my naval service. We spent one leave together, that's all. The following year she was killed in an air raid while staying with her mother in Milan.'

There was nothing to be said and Chavasse stood there in silence. After a while, Orsini increased speed. 'Take over, Paul. I'll plot our course.'

Chavasse slipped behind him, and the Italian moved to the chart table. For some time he busied himself with the charts and finally nodded in satisfaction.

'We should move into the marshes just before dawn.' He placed a cheroot between his teeth and grinned. 'What happens after that is in the lap of God.'

'Do you want me to spell you for a while?' Chavasse asked.

Orsini took over the wheel again and shook his head. 'Later, Paul, after Carlo has done his trick. That way I'll be fresh for the run-in at dawn.'

Chavasse left him there and went down to the galley, where he discovered Francesca making coffee. He leaned in the doorway and grinned. 'That's what I like about Italian girls. So good in the kitchen.'

She turned and smiled mischievously. 'Is that all we're good for – cooking?'

She wore a pair of old denim trousers and a heavy sweater and her long hair was plaited into a single pigtail which hung across one shoulder. She looked incredibly fresh and alive and Chavasse shook his head.

'I could think of one or two things, but the timing's wrong.'

'What about the terrace of the British Embassy?'

'Too public.'

She poured coffee into a mug and handed it to him. 'There's a place I know in the hills outside Rome. It's only a village inn, but the food is out of this world. You eat it by candlelight on a terrace overlooking a hillside covered with vines. The fireflies dance in the wind and you can smell the flowers for a week afterwards. It's an experience one shouldn't miss.'

'I'm all tied up for the next couple of days,' Chavasse said, 'but after that, I'm free most evenings.'

'By a strange coincidence, so am I. And I'd like to point out that you still owe me a date.'

'Now how could I forget a thing like that?'

He ducked as she threw a crust of dry bread at his head, turned and went through the aft cabin into the saloon. Carlo had two aqualungs and their ancillary equipment laid out on the table.

'There's fresh coffee in the galley,' Chavasse told him.

'I'll get some later. I want to finish checking this lot.'

He never had much to say for himself, a strange, silent youth, but a good man to have at your back in trouble and devoted to Orsini. He sat on the edge of the table, a cigarette smouldering between his lips, and worked his way methodically through the various items of equipment. Chavasse watched him for a while, then went through into the other cabin.

He lay staring at the bulkhead, thinking about the task ahead. If Francesca's memory hadn't failed her and the cross-bearing she had given them was accurate, then the whole thing was simple. There couldn't be more than five or six fathoms of water in those lagoons and the recovery of the statue shouldn't take long. With any kind of luck, they could be back in Matano within twenty-four hours.

He could hear a rumble of voices from the galley, Francesca quite distinctly, and then Carlo laughed, which was unusual. Chavasse was conscious of a slight, unreasoning pang of jealousy. He lay there thinking about her and the voices merged with the throbbing of the engine and the rattle of water against the hull.

He was not conscious of having slept, only of being awake and checking his watch and realizing with a shock that it was two a.m.

Orsini was sleeping on the far bunk, his face calm, one arm behind his head, and Chavasse pulled on his reefer coat and went on deck.

Mist swirled from the water and the *Buona Esperanza* kicked along at a tremendous pace. There was no moon, but stars were scattered across the sky like diamonds in a black velvet cushion and there was still that strange luminosity in the water.

Carlo was standing at the wheel, his head disembodied in the light from the binnacle. Chavasse moved in and lit a cigarette. 'How are we doing?'

'Fine,' Carlo said. 'Keep her on one-four-oh till three a.m. then alter course to one-four-five. Guilio said he'd be up around four. We should be near the coast by then.'

The door banged behind him and a small trapped wind lifted the charts, raced round the deckhouse looking for a way out and died in a corner. Chavasse pulled a seat down from the wall and sat back, his hands steady on the wheel.

This was what he liked more than anything else. To be alone with the sea and the night and a boat. Something deep in his subconscious, some race image handed on from his Breton ancestors, responded to the challenge. Men who had loved the sea more than any woman, who sailed to the Grand Banks of the North American coast to fish for cod, long before Columbus or the Cabots had dreamed of crossing the Atlantic.

The door opened suddenly as rain dashed against the window and he was aware of the heavy aroma of coffee, together with another, more subtle fragrance.

'What's wrong with bed at this time in the morning?' he demanded.

She chuckled softly. 'Oh, this is much more fun. How are we doing?'

'Dead on course. Another hour and Orsini takes over for the final run-in.'

She pulled a seat down beside him, balanced her tray on the chart table and poured coffee into two mugs. 'What about a sandwich?'

He was surprised at the keenness of his appetite and they ate in companionable and intimate silence, thighs touching. Afterwards, he gave her a cigarette and she poured more coffee.

'What do you think our chances are, Paul?' she said. 'The truth now.'

'It all depends on how accurately your brother plotted the final position of the launch when she sank. If we can find her without too much trouble, the rest should be plain sailing. Diving for the Madonna will be no great trick in water of that depth. Depending on weather conditions, we could be on our way back by this evening.'

'And you don't anticipate any trouble in the Drin Gulf?'

'From the Albanian Navy?' He shook his head. 'From an efficiency point of view, it's almost non-existent. The Russians had a lot of stuff based here before the big bust-up, but they withdrew when Hoxha refused to toe the line. Something he hadn't reckoned on, and China's too far away to give him that kind of assistance.'

'What a country.' She shook her head. 'I can well believe that old story that when it came to Albania's turn God had nothing but trouble left to give.'

Chavasse nodded. 'Not exactly a happy history.'

'A succession of conquerors, more than any other country in Europe. Greeks, Romans, Goths, Byzantines, Serbs, Bulgars, Sicilians, Venetians, Normans and Turks. They've all held the country for varying periods.'

'And always, the people have struggled to be free.' Chavasse shook his head. 'How ironic life can be. After centuries of desperately fighting for independence, Albania receives it, only to find herself in the grip of a tyranny worse than any that has gone before.'

'Is it really as bad as they say?'

He nodded. 'The *Sigurmi* are everywhere. Even the Italian Workers' Holiday Association complain that they get one *Sigurmi* agent allocated to each member of their holiday parties. Even at a rough estimate, Hoxha and his boys have purged better than one hundred thousand people since he took over, and you know yourself how the various religious groups have been treated. Stalin would have been proud of him. An apt pupil.'

He took out his cigarettes and offered her one. She smoked silently for a while and then said slowly, 'Last year, two people who were

113

operating temporarily through the Bureau in Rome ended up missing. One in Albania, the other in Turkey.'

Chavasse nodded. 'Matt Sorley and Jules Dumont. Good men both.'

'How can you go on living the life you do? That sort of thing must happen a lot. Look how close you came to not getting out of Tirana.'

'Maybe I just never grew up,' he said lightly.

'How did it all begin?'

'Quite by chance. I was lecturing in languages at a British university, a friend wanted to pull a relative out of Czechoslovakia, and I gave him a hand. That's when the Chief pulled me in. At that time he was interested in people who spoke Eastern European languages.'

'An unusual accomplishment.'

'Some people can work out cube roots in their heads in seconds, others can never forget anything they ever read. I have the same sort of kink for languages. I soak them up like a sponge – no effort.'

She lapsed into Albanian. 'Isn't it a little unnerving? Don't you ever get your wires crossed?'

'Not that I can recall,' he replied faultlessly

in the same language. 'I can't afford that kind of mistake. If it's any consolation, I still can't read a Chinese newspaper. On the other hand, I've only ever met two Europeans who could.'

'With that kind of flair, plus your academic training, you could pick up a chair in modern languages at almost any university in Britain or the States,' she said. 'Doesn't the thought appeal to you?'

'Not in the slightest. I got into this sort of work by chance, and by chance I possessed all the virtues needed to make me good at it.'

'You mean you actually enjoy it?'

'Something like that. If I'd been born in Germany twenty years earlier, I'd probably have ended up in the Gestapo. If I'd been born an Albanian, I might well have been a most efficient member of the *Sigurmi*. Who knows?'

She seemed shocked. 'I don't believe you.'

'Why not? It takes a certain type of man or woman to do our kind of work – a professional. I can recognize the quality, and appreciate it, in my opposite numbers. I don't see anything wrong in that.'

There was a strained silence, as if in some

way he had disappointed her. She reached for the tray. 'I'd better take these below. We must be getting close.'

The door closed behind her and Chavasse opened the window and breathed in the sharp morning air, feeling rather sad. So often people like her, the fringe crowd who did the paper-work, manned the radios, decoded the messages, could never really know what it was like in the field. What it took to survive. Well, he had survived, and not by waving any flags, either.

*Then what in the hell are you doing here?* he asked himself, and a rueful smile crossed his face. What was it Orsini had said? *The things we do for the ladies*. And he was right, this one *was* something special – something very special.

The door swung open and Orsini entered, immense in his old reefer coat, a peaked cap on the side of his head. 'Everything all right, Paul?'

Chavasse nodded and handed over the wheel. 'Couldn't be better.'

Orsini lit another of his inevitable cheroots. 'Good. Shouldn't be long now.'

Dawn seeped into the sky, a grey half-light with a heavy mist rolling across the water.

Orsini asked Chavasse to take over again and consulted the charts. He checked the cross-bearing Francesca had given him and traced a possible course in from the sea through the maze of channels marked on the chart.

'Everything okay?' Chavasse asked.

Orsini came back to the wheel and shrugged. 'I know these charts. Four or five fathoms and a strong tidal current. That means that one day there's a sandbank, the next, ten fathoms of clear water. Estuary marshes are always the same. We'll go in through the main outlet of the Buene and turn into the marshes about half a mile inland. It's not only safer, but a damned sight quicker.'

The mist enfolded them until they were running through an enclosed world. Orsini reduced speed to ten knots and, a few moments later, Carlo and Francesca came up from below.

Chavasse went and stood in the prow, hands in his pockets, and the marshes drifted out of the mist and their stench filled his nostrils. Wildfowl called overhead on their way in from the sea and Carlo moved beside him and crossed himself.

'A bad place, this. Always, I am glad to leave.'

It was a landscape from a nightmare. Long, narrow sandbanks lifted from the water, and inland, mile upon mile of marsh grass and great reeds marched into the mist, interlaced by a thousand creeks and lagoons.

Orsini reduced speed to three knots and leaned from the side window, watching the reeds drift by on either side. Chavasse moved along the deck and looked up at him.

'How far are we from the position Francesca gave?'

'Perhaps three miles, but the going would be too difficult. In a little while, we must carry on in the dinghy. Much safer.'

'And who minds the launch?'

'Carlo – it's all arranged. He isn't pleased, but then he seldom is about anything.'

He grinned down at Carlo, who glared up at him and went below. Chavasse moved back along the deck and joined Francesca in the prow. A few moments later, the launch entered a small lagoon, perhaps a hundred feet in diameter, and Orsini cut the engines.

They glided forward and grounded gently against a sandbank as Orsini came out on deck and joined them. He slipped an arm around Francesca's shoulders and smiled down at her.

'Not long now, *cara*. A few more hours and we'll be on our way home again. I, Guilio Orsini, promise you.'

She looked up at him gravely, then turned to Chavasse, a strange, shadowed expression in her eyes, and for some unaccountable reason, he shivered.

# 9

Francesca cooked a hot meal, perhaps the last they would have for some time, and afterwards Carlo and Chavasse broke out the large rubber dinghy, inflated it and attached the outboard motor.

When they went below for the aqualung, Orsini was sitting on the edge of the table loading a machine pistol. The top of one of the saloon seats had been removed and inside the recess was an assortment of weapons: the submachine gun, a couple of automatic rifles and an old Bren of the type used by the British infantry during the war.

'Help yourself,' he said. 'We have a selection to suit all tastes.'

Chavasse picked up one of the automatic rifles, a Garrand, and nodded. 'This will do me. What about ammo?'

'There should be plenty in there somewhere.'

There were three boxes stacked together. The first contained grenades, the second, several pouched bandoliers. Chavasse picked one up and Orsini shook his head.

'That's an explosive we used during the war for underwater sabotage. I've had it for years.'

'A hell of a thing to have people sitting on,' Chavasse said.

Orsini grinned. 'Just the thing for fishing. You stick a chemical detonator in a piece as big as your fist, heave it over the side and wait. They come floating up by the thousand. I'll take some along, just in case we need to do any blasting.'

Chavasse found the ammunition in another box, loaded his Garrand and strapped a bandolier containing a hundred rounds about his waist. He helped Carlo up top with one of the aqualungs and they stowed it in the prow of the dinghy, along with several other items of equipment. As they finished, Orsini and Francesca came up on deck.

She was wearing an old reefer coat of Carlo's against the cold, the sleeves rolled back, and a scarf was tied around her head, peasant-fashion.

She seemed calm, but was extremely pale and there were blue shadows under her eyes.

Chavasse squeezed her hand as he helped her into the dinghy and whispered, 'Soon be over. We'll be on our way out again before you know it.'

She smiled wanly, but made no reply, and he clambered into the dinghy beside her and sat on one side, the Garrand across his knees. Orsini followed, seating himself in the stern. He glanced up at Carlo and grinned.

'If all goes well, we could be back by this evening. Certainly no later than dawn tomorrow.'

'And if it doesn't?'

'You always look on the dark side.'

Orsini pressed the automatic starter and the powerful motor roared into life. Wildfowl rose from the reeds in alarm, the sound of them filling the air. As Carlo released the line, the dinghy moved forward quickly. Chavasse had one final glimpse of his dark, saturnine face scowling at them over the rail and then the marsh moved in to enfold them.

\*     \*     \*

The reeds lifted out of the mist like pale ghosts on either side, the only sound the steady rattle of the outboard motor. Orsini consulted his compass, turning from one narrow waterway to another, always moving towards the position on the chart that Francesca had given them.

She sat in silence, her hands buried in the pockets of the reefer coat, and Chavasse watched, wondering what she was thinking. About her brother, probably. Of his death and her own struggle for survival in this waking nightmare. The stench of the marshes, heavy and penetrating, filled his nostrils and he hurriedly lit a cigarette.

It was perhaps an hour later that they emerged into a broad waterway and Orsini cut the motor. 'This is as near as I can make it from the position you gave me,' he told Francesca. 'Recognize anything?'

She stood up and gazed around her. When she sat down, there was a troubled look on her face. 'They all look the same, these waterways, but I'm sure this wasn't the place. It was much smaller. I can remember my brother running the boat into the reeds to hide her and then we suddenly emerged into this small lagoon.'

Orsini stood up and looked around, but the reeds stretched into the mist, an apparently impenetrable barrier. He turned to Chavasse and shrugged. 'This is definitely the position he charted, so this lagoon she speaks of can't be far away. We'll have to go looking for it, that's all.'

Chavasse started to undress. 'I hope to God you're right.'

He kept on his shirt, trousers and shoes against the cold, went over the side and struck across the channel. Orsini followed a moment or so later and swam into the mist in the opposite direction.

It was bitterly cold and Chavasse coughed, retching as the strong earthy stench caught at the back of his throat. He swam into the reeds, following a narrow waterway that turned in a circle, bringing him back into the main channel.

He tried another, emerging a few moments later into a shallow lagoon no more than four or five feet deep, and he swam across into the reeds, forcing his way through. Just then, Orsini called through the mist from the other side of the barrier and Chavasse pushed towards him. He came out on the perimeter of a lagoon no more than a hundred feet across, as Orsini surfaced in the centre.

The Italian floated there, coughing a little, hair plastered across his forehead. Chavasse looked down at the launch mirrored in five fathoms of clear water, then did a steep surface dive.

He swallowed to ease the pressure in his ears, then grabbed for the deck rail and hung there. The launch had tilted over on the shelving bottom and he worked his way round to the stern were he found the name *Teresa – Bari* inscribed in gold paint. He had a quick look at the general condition of the wreck, then released his hold and shot to the surface.

He trod water, gasping for air, and grinned at Orsini. 'Good navigating.'

'My mother, God rest her, always told me I was a genius.'

Orsini turned and swam across the lagoon, plunging into the reeds, and Chavasse followed. They emerged into the main channel within sight of the dinghy and swam towards it.

'Any luck?' Francesca asked.

Orsini nodded. 'Just as you described. Without that cross-bearing it would have been hopeless. We could have searched these marshes for a year without finding anything.'

They climbed back into the dinghy and he started the motor and steered for the wall of reeds. For a moment, they seemed an impossible barrier and Chavasse and Francesca pulled desperately with all their strength. Quite suddenly, the reeds parted and the dinghy passed into the lagoon.

Orsini cut the motor and they drifted towards the centre. Francesca gazed over the side, down through the clear water, her face very pale. She shivered abruptly and looked up.

'Will it take long?'

Orsini shook his head. 'We'll fix a line to hold us in position and one of us will go down. With luck we'll be out of here in a couple of hours.' He turned to Chavasse. 'Feel like another swim?'

Chavasse nodded. 'Why not? It couldn't be any colder than it is up here.'

The wind sliced through his wet shirt as he

lifted the aqualung on to his back and Orsini strapped it into place. Francesca watched, eyes very large in the white face, and Chavasse grinned.

'A piece of cake. We'll be out of here before you know it.'

She forced a smile and he pulled on his diving mask, sat on the rail and allowed himself to fall back into the water. As he surfaced, Orsini tossed him a line. Chavasse went under, paused to adjust his air supply, and swam down towards the launch in a sweeping curve.

The *Teresa* was almost bottom-up and he hovered over the stern rail to attach the end of his line and then swam towards the deckhouse, which was jammed against the sandy bottom of the lagoon at a steep angle.

There were jagged bullet holes in the hull and superstructure, mute evidence of the fight between the *Teresa* and the Albanian patrol boat. Some sort of a direct hit had been scored on the roof of the saloon and the companionway was badly damaged, the only entrance being a narrow aperture.

He managed it, pulling himself through by

force, the aqualung scraping protestingly against the jagged edges of the metal. The saloon table had broken free of its floor fastenings and floated against the bulkhead, together with several bottles and the leather cushions from the saloon.

There was no sign of the Madonna or anything remotely resembling it, and he swam towards the door leading to the forward cabin. The roof at this point had been smashed in by what looked like a cannon shell, and a twisted mass of metal blocked the door. He turned and swam out through the saloon, squeezed through the entrance and struck up towards the light.

He surfaced a few feet astern of the dinghy and swam towards it. Orsini gave him a hand over the side and Chavasse crouched in the bottom and pushed up his mask.

'The interior's in one hell of a mess. Stuff all over the place.'

'And the Madonna?'

'No sign at all. I couldn't get into the inner cabin. There's a lot of wreckage at that end of the saloon and the door's jammed.'

'But that is where it is!' Francesca said. 'I

129

remember now. Marco put it under one of the bunks for greater safety when the shooting started. It was wrapped in a blanket and bound in oilskin against the damp. The whole bundle was about five feet long.'

Orsini pulled a package from under the stern seat. 'A good thing I brought along some of that explosive. You'll have to blast your way in.'

He unfolded a bandolier and took out a piece of plastic explosive shaped like a sausage. 'That should be enough. We don't want to blow the whole boat apart.'

From another bundle he took a small wooden box containing several chemical pencil detonators, each one carefully packed in a plastic sheath.

'How long do these things give me?' Chavasse demanded.

'A full minute. I've got some that take longer, but I left them on the boat.'

'Well, thanks very much, friend,' Chavasse said. 'What are you hoping to do – collect on my insurance?'

'A minute should be plenty. All you have to

do is insert the fuse, break the end and get out of there. I'll go myself if you like.'

'Stop trying to show off,' Chavasse told him. 'In any case, you'll never get that frame of yours in through the saloon companionway.'

He was conscious of Francesca's face, white and troubled, as he gripped the rubber mouthpiece of his breathing tube between his teeth, pulled down his mask and went backwards over the side.

He went down through the clear water quickly, negotiated the companionway with no trouble and moved inside. He jammed the plastic explosive into the corner at the bottom of the door and inserted the detonator carefully. For a moment, he floated there looking at it, then he snapped the end.

The fuse started to burn at once, fizzing like a firecracker, and he turned and swam for the companionway. As he squeezed through the narrow opening, his aqualung snagged on the jagged metal. He paused, fighting back the panic, and eased himself through. A moment later, he was shooting towards the surface.

He broke through at the side of the dinghy

and Orsini pulled him over. There was a muffled roar and the dinghy rocked in the turbulence. The surface of the water boiled and wreckage bobbed up, sand and mud spreading in a great stain towards the reeds.

They waited for fifteen minutes, and gradually the water cleared again and the hull of the launch became visible. Orsini nodded and Chavasse went over the side.

There was still a lot of sand and mud hanging in suspension like a great curtain, obscuring his vision, but not seriously, and he went down towards the *Teresa*.

The explosion had even disturbed the entrance to the companionway, the turbulence blowing the wreckage back out on to the deck, and he passed through the saloon himself with no trouble.

Where the door to the cabin had been, there was now only a gaping hole, and he swam forward, paused for a moment and then moved inside.

The tiered bunks were still intact, but bedding floated against the bulkhead, moving languorously in the water like some living thing. He pushed his way through their pale fronds and looked for the Madonna. It became immediately obvious that he was wasting his time. There was no five-foot bundle wrapped in oilskins as Francesca had described.

The Madonna was carved out of ebony, a heavy wood, but one that would float, and he drifted up through the waving blankets, pulling them to one side, searching desperately, but he was wasting his time.

Back outside, he grabbed for the stern rail and floated there like some strange sea creature, his webbed feet hanging down. Perhaps Francesca had been wrong. Maybe her brother had moved it to some other place in the launch. And there was always the chance that it had been blown clear in the explosion.

He decided to start again, working his way from one end of the launch to the other. But first he had to let Orsini know what had happened.

He surfaced a few feet away from the dinghy and went under again in the same moment. Orsini was standing with his back to him, hands above his head. On the far side of the dinghy was a flat-bottomed marsh punt, an outboard motor at its stern. Its occupants were three Albanians in drab and dirty uniforms, on their peaked caps the red star of the Army of the Republic. Two of them menaced Orsini and Francesca with submachine guns while the third was in the act of stepping across.

Chavasse went under the dinghy in a shallow dive as submachine gun fire churned the water where he had surfaced. His aqualung scraped the bottom of the punt and he reached up, grabbed the thwart and pulled the frail craft completely over.

One of the soldiers sprawled against him, legs thrashing in a panic, and Chavasse slipped an arm around his neck and took him into deep water. His legs scraped painfully against the stern rail of the *Teresa* and he hung on with one hand, tightening his grip.

The soldier's face twisted to one side, hands clawing back, wrenching the breathing tube from his assailant's mouth. Chavasse tightened his lips and hung on. The man's limbs moved in slow motion, weakening perceptibly, until suddenly he stopped struggling altogether.

Chavasse released his grip and the body spun away from him.

The sand at the bottom of the lagoon had churned into a great cloud and he clamped the mouthpiece of his breathing tube between his teeth and struck out for the surface. Above him, there was a tremendous disturbance, limbs thrashing together in a violent struggle.

He came up into the centre of it, pulling his knife from his sheath, and struck out at a dim, khaki-clad shape. The soldier bucked agonizingly, shoving Chavasse away so that he broke through to the surface.

A couple of yards away from him, a fifteen-foot motorboat bumped against the dinghy. He was aware of Francesca struggling in the grip of two soldiers, of Orsini floating against the hull, blood on his face.

A soldier rushed to the rail, machine-gun levelled, and a man in a dark leather coat with a high fur collar ran forward and knocked the barrel to one side, the bullets discharging themselves harmlessly in the sky.

'Alive! I want him alive!'

For one brief moment, Chavasse looked up

into Adem Kapo's excited face, then he jack-knifed and went down through the water, his webbed feet driving him towards the edge of the lagoon. He swam into the reeds, forcing his way through desperately. A few moments later, he surfaced. Behind him, he could hear voices calling excitedly and then the engine of the motorboat coughed into life.

He broke through into the main channel, moved straight across it into a narrow tributary and started to swim for his life.

# 10

The motorboat turned out of a side channel into the main stream of the Buene River, the dinghy trailing behind on a line. In the stern, four soldiers huddled together, smoking cigarettes and talking in low tones. The bodies of their two comrades, killed in the lagoon by Chavasse, lay under a tarpaulin beside them.

Orsini was handcuffed to the rail and seemed half unconscious, his head roughly bandaged where a rifle butt had struck him a glancing blow. There was no sign of Francesca Minetti, but Adem Kapo paced the foredeck, impatiently smoking a cigarette, the fur collar of his hunting jacket turned up.

Orsini watched him, eyes half-closed, and after a while another man appeared from the companionway. He was as big as Orsini, with a scarred, brutal face, and wore the uniform of a colonel in the Army of the Albanian Republic with the green insignia of the Intelligence Corps on his collar.

Kapo turned on him, eyes like black holes in the white face. 'Well?'

The colonel shrugged. 'She isn't being very helpful.'

The anger blazed out of the little man like a searing flame. 'You said it would work, damn you. That all we had to do was wait and they'd walk right into the net. What in the hell am I supposed to tell them in Tirana?'

'What do you think he's going to do, swim out of here?' The big man laughed coldly. 'We'll run him down, never fear. A night out on his own in a place like this will shrink him down to size.'

'Let's hope you're right.'

Kapo walked across to Orsini, looked down at him for a moment, then kicked him in the side. Orsini continued to feign unconsciousness. Kapo turned away and resumed his pacing.

\*     \*     \*

As the motorboat rounded a point of land jutting from the mist into the river, Chavasse parted the reeds carefully. He stood up to his chest in water no more than fifteen yards away as it passed, and his trained eyes took in everything – Orsini and the soldiers, Kapo standing in the prow, the cigarette holder jutting from a corner of his mouth.

The most interesting thing was the presence of Tashko. When Chavasse had last encountered him, he had been dressed like any seaman off the Taranto waterfront; now he wore the uniform of a colonel in the Albanian Intelligence Corps, which explained a lot. Beyond him, through the deckhouse window, Chavasse could just see the head and shoulders of Haji, the knife man, standing at the wheel.

The motorboat passed into the mist and he waded on to a piece of comparatively dry land to take stock of the situation. The stench of the marsh filled his nostrils and the bitter cold ate into his bones.

There was a hell of a lot about the whole affair that didn't make sense, but the basic situation was obvious enough. Adem Kapo was no ordinary agent, but someone a lot more important than that. Probably a high-ranking *Sigurmi* officer. He'd have to be to have a Colonel of Intelligence taking orders from him.

In any event, he was a man who knew what he was doing. He'd obviously sailed straight for the Buene from Matano and his twenty-four-hour start had given him the time he'd needed to reach Tama and organize a suitable reception.

The *Buona Esperanza* must have been under observation from the moment it hit the coast, and tracking the dinghy would have been no great trick to men who knew the marshes.

He wondered what had happened to Carlo. He too was probably on his way to Tama by now. It was the only sizeable town in the area and certain to be Kapo's base.

The engine of the motorboat faded into the distance and he slid into the water and started to swim after it. Within an hour at the outside, they'd be out in force looking for him, probably concentrating their search towards the coast.

Under the circumstances, Tama would probably be a whole lot safer. At least there would be houses scattered along the river bank, and where there were houses there were dry clothes and food. There might even be a chance of doing something about the others, although he didn't hold out much hope of that.

About fifteen minutes later, the air in his aqualung ran out. He surfaced quickly and waded from the river into the reeds. He pulled off his rubber flippers, unbuckled the heavy aqualung and let it sink into the ooze.

He went forward through the reeds and the wildfowl called as they lifted from the water, disturbed by his passing. After a while he came out on higher ground and moved on through the mist, keeping the river on his left.

It was hard going through mud flats and marsh, and he constantly had to wade across narrow creeks, often sinking up to his waist in thick, glutinous mud. The salt water stung his eyes painfully and the intense cold steadily drove every trace of warmth from his body until his limbs had lost all feeling.

He moved into the grey curtain and the ground became firmer and he found himself stumbling across firm sand and springy marsh grass. He paused on a small hillock, head turned slightly to one side. He could smell woodsmoke, heavy and pungent on the air, drifting before the wind.

A narrow arm of the river encircled a small island and a low house looked from the mist. There was no sign of life and no boat was moored at the narrow wooden jetty. Probably the home of a fisherman or wildfowler out at his traps. Chavasse moved upstream, disturbing a wild duck, and walked into the river, allowing the current to sweep him in towards the island.

He landed in the reeds and moved through them carefully, drawing his knife. The house was no more than twenty yards away, a poor-enough-looking place of rough-hewn logs with a shingle roof and stone chimney.

Two or three scrawny hens picked apathetically at the soil and scattered as he moved across the patch of open ground. The back door was simply several heavy wooden planks nailed together, and it opened with a protesting groan as he unfastened the chain which held it.

He moved into a small dark room that was obviously some sort of kitchen. There was a cupboard, a rough table and a pail of fresh water at the side of the door. The living room was furnished with a table and several chairs. There were two or three cupboards, and a skin rug covered the wooden floor in front of the stone hearth on which logs burned fitfully, heavily banked by ashes.

He crouched to the warmth, spreading his hands, and a cold wind seemed to touch the side of his face. A voice said quietly, 'Easy now. Hands behind your neck and don't try anything stupid.'

He came up slowly. There was a soft footstep and the hard barrel of a gun was pushed against his back. As a hand reached for the hilt of the knife at his waist, he pivoted to the left, swinging away from the gun barrel. There was a cry of dismay as they came together and fell heavily to the floor. Chavasse raised his right arm to bring down the edge of his hand.

He paused. His opponent was a young girl, perhaps nineteen or twenty, certainly no more. She wore a heavy waterproof hunting jacket, corduroy breeches and leather knee boots and her dark hair was close-cropped like a young boy's, the skin sallow over high cheekbones, the

143

eyes dark brown. She was not beautiful and yet she would have stood out in any crowd.

'Now there's a thing,' he said softly and sat back. For a moment, she lay there, eyes widening in surprise and then, in a flash, she was on her feet again like a cat, the hunting rifle in her hands.

She stood there, feet apart, the barrel steady on his chest, and he waited. The barrel wavered, sank slowly. She leaned the rifle against the table and examined him curiously. Her eyes took in his bare feet, the shirt and trousers that were clinging to his body.

She nodded. 'You're on the run, aren't you? Where from? The chain gang at Tama?'

He shook his head. 'I'm on the run all right, angel, but not from there.'

She scowled and reached for the rifle again. 'You're no *gegh*, that's for sure. You speak like a *tosk* from the big city.'

Chavasse was aware of the enmity which still existed between the two main racial groups in Albania: the *geghs* of the north with their loyalty to family and tribe, and the *tosks* of the south from whom Communism had sprung.

There were times when a man had to play a hunch and this was one of them. His face split into the charming smile that was one of his greatest assets and he raised a hand as the rifle was turned again.

'Neither *gegh* nor *tosk*. I'm an outlander.'

Her face was a study of bewilderment. 'An outlander? From where? Yugoslavia?'

He shook his head. 'Italy.'

Understanding dawned. 'Ah, a smuggler.'

'Something like that. We were surprised by the military. I managed to get away. I think they've taken my friends to Tama.' She stood watching him, a thoughtful frown on her face, and he made the final gesture and held out his hand. 'Paul Chavasse.'

'French?' she said.

'And English. A little of both.'

She made her decision and her hand reached for his. 'Liri Kupi.'

'There was a *gegh* chieftain called Abas Kupi, leader of the *Legaliteri*, the royalist party.'

'Head of our clan. He fled to Italy after the Communists murdered most of his friends at a so-called friendship meeting.'

'You don't sound as if you care for Hoxha and his friends very much?'

'Hoxha?'

She spat vigorously and accurately into the fire.

# 11

Chavasse stood on a rush mat beside the large bed and rubbed himself down with a towel until his flesh glowed. He dressed quickly in the clothes Liri had provided: corduroy trousers, a checked wool shirt and knee-length leather boots a size too large, so he took them off again and pulled on an extra pair of socks.

The clothes had belonged to her brother. Conscripted into the army at eighteen, he had been killed in one of the many patrol clashes that took place almost daily along the Yugoslavian border. Her father had died fighting with the royalist party, in the mountains in the last year of the war. Since the death of her mother, she had lived alone in the marshes where she had been born and bred, earning her living from wildfowling.

She was crouched at the fire when he went back into the living room, stirring something in a large pot suspended from a hook. She turned and smiled, pushing back the hair from her forehead.

'All you need now is some food inside you.'

He pulled a chair to the table as she spooned a hot stew on to a tin plate. He wasted no time on conversation, but picked up his spoon and started to eat. When the plate was empty, she filled it again.

He sat back with a sigh. 'They couldn't have done better at the London Hilton.'

She opened a bottle and filled a glass with a colourless liquid. 'I'd like to offer you some coffee, but it's very hard to come by these days. This is a spirit we distil ourselves. Very potent if you're not used to it, but it can be guaranteed to keep out the marsh fever.'

It exploded in Chavasse's stomach and spread through his body in a warm glow. He coughed several times and tears sprang to his eyes.

'Now this they wouldn't be able to offer, even at the London Hilton.'

She opened an old tin carefully and offered

him a cigarette. They were Macedonian, coarse, brown tobacco loose in the paper, but Chavasse knew how to handle them. He screwed the end round expertly and leaned across the table as she held out a burning splinter from the fire.

She lit a cigarette herself, blew out a cloud of pungent smoke and said calmly, 'You're no smuggler, I can see that. No seaman, either. Your hands are too nice.'

'So I lied.'

'You must have had a good reason.'

He frowned down into his glass for a moment, then decided to go ahead. 'You've heard of the Virgin of Scutari?'

'The Black Madonna? Who hasn't? Her statue disappeared about three months ago. Everyone thinks the government in Tirana had it stolen. They're worried because people have been turning to the church again lately.'

'I came to the Buene looking for it,' Chavasse said. 'It was supposed to be on board a launch which sank in one of the lagoons in the marsh towards the coast. My friends and I were searching for it when the military turned up.'

He told her about Francesca Minetti, or as

much as she needed to know, and of Guilio Orsini and Carlo and the *Buona Esperanza*. When he was done, she nodded slowly.

'A bad business. The *Sigurmi* will squeeze them dry, even this smuggler friend of yours. They have their ways and they are not pleasant. I'm sorry for the girl. God knows what they will do with her.'

'I was wondering whether it would be possible to get into Tama,' Chavasse said. 'Perhaps find out what's happened to them.'

She looked at him sharply, her face grave. 'We have a saying. *Only a fool puts his head between the jaws of the tiger.*'

'They'll be beating the marshes towards the coast,' he said. 'That stands to reason. Who's going to look for me in Tama?'

'A good point.' She got to her feet and looked down into the fire, her hand on the stone mantel above it. She turned to face him. 'There is one person who might be able to help, a Franciscan named Father Shedu. In the war he was a famous resistance fighter in the hills, a legend in his own time. It would hardly be polite to arrest or shoot such a man. They content themselves with making life difficult for him – always with the utmost politeness, of course. He hasn't been here long. A couple of months or so. I think the last man was taken away.'

'I could make a good guess about what happened to him,' Chavasse said. 'This Father Shedu, he's in Tama now?'

'There's a mediaeval monastery on the outskirts of the town. They use it as local military headquarters. The Catholic church has been turned into a restaurant, but there's an old monastery chapel at the water's edge. Father Shedu holds his services there.'

'Would it be difficult to reach?'

'From here?' she shrugged. 'Not more than half an hour. I have an outboard motor. Not too reliable, but it gets me there.'

'Could I borrow it?'

'Oh, no.' She shook her head. 'They'd pick you up before you'd got a mile along the river. I know the back ways – you don't.'

She took down an oilskin jacket from behind the door and tossed it to him, together with an old peaked cap. 'Ready when you are.'

She picked up her hunting rifle and led the way

151

out through the front door and down towards the river. There was still no boat moored at the little wooden jetty. She passed it, moving through dense undergrowth, and emerged on to a small cleared bank which dropped cleanly into the water. Her boat, a flat-bottomed marsh punt with an old motor attached to the stern, was tied to a tree.

Chavasse cast off while she busied herself with the motor. As it coughed into life, he pushed the punt through the encircling reeds and stepped in.

Liri Kupi certainly knew what she was doing. At one point, they hit rough water where the river twisted round sandbanks, spilling across ragged rocks, and she handled the frail craft like an expert, swinging the tiller at just the right moment to sweep them away from the worst hazards.

After a while, they left the Buene, turning into a narrow creek which circled through a great stagnant swamp, losing itself among a hundred lagoons and waterways.

When they finally came into the river again, it was in the lee of a large island. The mist hung like a grey curtain from bank to bank, and as they moved from the shelter of the island to cross over he could smell woodsmoke, and somewhere a dog barked.

The first houses loomed out of the mist, scattered along one side of the river, and Liri took the punt in close. She produced the tin of cigarettes from her pocket and threw it to Chavasse.

'Better have one. Try to look at home.'

'Home was never like this.'

He lit a cigarette, leaned back against the prow and watched the town unfold itself. There were fewer than five hundred inhabitants these days, that much he knew. Since the cold war had warmed up between Yugoslavia and Albania, the river traffic had almost stopped and the Buene was now so silted up as to be unnavigable for boats of any size.

The monastery lifted out of the mist, a vast sprawling mediaeval structure with crumbling walls, several hundred yards back from the river bank.

The Albanian flag, hanging limply in the rain, lifted in a gust of wind, the red star standing out vividly against the black, double-headed eagle, and a bugle sounded faintly.

A little further along the bank, forty or fifty convicts worked, some of them waist-deep in water as they drove in the piles for a new jetty. Chavasse noticed that the ones on the banks had their ankles chained together.

'Politicals,' Liri said briefly. 'They send them here from all over the country. They don't last long in the marshes when the hot weather comes.'

She eased the tiller, turning the punt in towards the bank and a small ruined chapel whose crumbling walls fell straight into the river. At the foot of the wall the entrance to a narrow tunnel gaped darkly, and Liri took the punt inside.

There was a good six feet of headroom and Chavasse reached out to touch cold, damp walls, straining his eyes into the darkness, which suddenly lightened considerably. Liri cut the motor, and the punt drifted in towards a landing stage constructed of large blocks of worked masonry.

They scraped beside a flight of stone steps and

Chavasse tied up to an iron ring and handed her out. Light filtered down from somewhere above and she smiled through the half-darkness.

'I won't be long.'

She mounted a flight of stone steps and Chavasse lit another cigarette, sat on the edge of the jetty and waited. She was gone for at least fifteen minutes. When she returned, she didn't come all the way down, but called to him from the top of the steps.

He went up quickly and she turned, opened a large oak door and led the way along a narrow passage. She opened another door at the far end and they stepped into the interior of the small chapel.

The lights were very dim and, down by the altar, the candles flickered and the Holy Mother was bathed in light. The smell of incense was overpowering and Chavasse felt a little giddy. It was a long time since he had been in church – too long, as his mother was never tired of reminding him – and he smiled wryly as they moved down the aisle.

Father Shedu knelt in prayer at the altar, the brown habit dark and sombre in the candlelight.

His eyes were closed, the worn face completely calm, and somehow the ugly puckered scar of the old bullet wound that had carried away the left eye seemed completely in character.

He was a man strong in his faith, certain in his knowledge of that which was ultimately important. Men like Enver Hoxha and Adem Kapo would come and go, ultimately to break upon the rock that was Father Shedu.

He crossed himself, got to his feet in one smooth movement and turned to face them. Chavasse suddenly felt awkward under the keen scrutiny of that single eye. For a moment, he was a little boy again at his grandfather's village in Finistere just after the war when France was free again, standing before the old, implacable parish priest, trying to explain his absence from Mass, the tongue drying in his mouth.

Father Shedu smiled and held out his hand. 'I am happy to meet you, my son. Liri has told me something of why you are here.'

Chavasse shook hands, relief flowing through him. 'She seemed to think you might be able to help, Father.'

'I know something of what happened to the

statue of Our Lady of Scutari,' the priest said. 'It was my predecessor, Father Kupescu, who gave it into the charge of the young man who was later killed in the marshes. Father Kupescu has since paid for his actions with his life, I might add.'

'The girl who was with me was the young man's sister,' Chavasse said. 'She was the one who guided us to the position of Minetti's launch.'

Father Shedu nodded. 'She and an Italian named Orsini arrived in Tama earlier this afternoon. They were taken to the monastery.'

'Are you sure?'

'I was visiting sick prisoners at the time, one of the little privileges I still insist on.'

'I'm surprised you're allowed to function at all.'

Father Shedu smiled faintly. 'As you may have noticed, my name is the same as that of our beloved President, something for which the average party member holds me in superstitious awe. They can never be quite sure that I'm not some kind of third cousin, you see. There are things they can do, of course. We had a wonderful old church here. Now, it's a restaurant. They use the altar as a counter and the nave is crammed with tables at which the happy workers can consume *kebab* and *shashlik* to the greater glory of Enver Hoxha.'

'All things in their own good time, Father,' Chavasse said.

The priest smiled. 'As it happens, I *can* help you, Mr Chavasse. Your friends are at the moment imprisoned in the back guardroom, which is inside the inner wall of the monastery. A Colonel of Intelligence and a high *Sigurmi* official named Kapo, who brought them in, left again almost at once with every spare soldier they could lay their hands on.'

'To look for me.'

'Obviously. I shouldn't think there will be more than one man on duty at the guardroom – perhaps two.'

'But how could we get in, Father?' Liri demanded. 'There are two walls to pass through and guards on each gate.'

'We go under, my dear. The good fathers who built this monastery thought of everything. Come with me.'

He led the way out of the chapel and back along the passage to the door that led down to the landing stage. He took an electric torch from a ledge on which an ikon stood and went down to the water's edge. When he switched on the torch, its beam played against the rough walls of the tunnel, which ran on into the darkness, narrowing considerably.

'The monastery's sewage system comes down through here to empty into the river,' he said. 'Not a pleasant journey, I'm afraid, but one that will take you inside the walls without being seen.'

'Show me the way, that's all I ask, Father,' Chavasse said. 'You can leave the rest to me.'

'To require you not to use violence against violent men would be absurd,' Father Shedu said, 'but you must understand that I myself could not possibly take part in any such action. You accept this?'

'Willingly.'

The priest turned to Liri. 'You will stay here, child?'

She shook her head. 'There may be a use for me. Please, Father. I know what I'm doing.'

He didn't bother to argue, but hitched his trailing robes into the leather belt at his waist and stepped into the water on the left-hand side of the tunnel. It was no more than ankle-deep and Chavasse followed along a broad ledge, his head lowered as the roof dropped to meet them.

There was a strong earthy smell and a slight mist curled from the water, fanning out against the damp roof. The tunnel stretched into the darkness and gradually the water became deeper until he could feel it swirling about his knees.

By now the stench was appalling and he stumbled on, his stomach heaving. Finally, the priest turned into a side passage which came out into a cavern about fifty feet in diameter.

It was some three feet deep in stinking water and at least a dozen tunnels emptied into it. The Franciscan waded across and counted from the left.

'I think the eighth will be the one.'

The tunnel was no more than four feet high and Chavasse paused at the entrance and reached out to Liri. 'Are you all right?'

'Fine.' She chuckled. 'The swamps stink worse than this lot in the summer.'

They bent double and went after Father Shedu, who was now several yards ahead. A few moments later, he stopped. Light filtered down through some sort of grille and a short tunnel sloped up towards the surface.

'If I am right,' the priest said, 'we should be in a cell of the old cloisters behind the square containing the guardhouse.'

The tunnel was a good fifty feet in length, the stonework smooth and slippery, making it difficult to climb. The priest went first, Liri next and Chavasse brought up the rear. He jammed himself between the narrow walls, working his way up foot by foot. Once, Liri slipped, falling back against him, but he managed to hold her and they continued.

Above them, Father Shedu was already at the entrance, a large slab which had been carved by some master craftsman into a stone grille. He put his shoulder to it and it slid back easily. He climbed out and turned to give Liri a hand.

Chavasse clambered up after them and found himself in a small crumbling cell with a gaping doorway which opened into half-ruined cloisters, broken pillars lifting into the sky, grass growing between great, cracked stone slabs.

'Through the cloisters and you will come to the square,' Father Shedu said. 'The guardroom is a small flat-roofed building of brick and concrete.' A slight smile touched his mouth. 'From here, you are on your own. There is nothing more I can do for you. As I said earlier, I must not play any active part in this affair. I will wait here.' He turned to Liri. 'You will stay with me?'

She shook her head stubbornly. 'There may be something I can do. Something to help.'

'Father Shedu's right,' Chavasse said. 'You stay.'

'If you want my gun, then you take me.' She patted the stock of the old hunting rifle. 'That's my final word.'

Chavasse looked at the priest, who sighed heavily. 'She's got a will of iron, I'm afraid, and she hates the Reds.'

Chavasse said to Liri, 'You can come as far as the edge of the square. You watch from there while I go in. If anything goes wrong, you'll have plenty of time to join Father Shedu and get clear. All right?'

He moved out across the ruined courtyard and through the cloisters to the crumbling wall on the far side. The square stretched before him, quiet and still. The guardhouse was built against the wall halfway along the other side, just as Father Shedu had described, a difficult place to come at from the front. In the far wall, great double gates leading to the outer square were closed.

Chavasse turned to Liri. 'You stay here. I'm going to work my way round the wall so that I come in from the other side where there are no windows. If anything happens, get out of there fast and back to Father Shedu.' She started to protest, but he pulled the rifle firmly from her grasp. 'Now be a good girl and do as you're told.'

He moved along behind the ruined wall to the point where it joined the other, stepped into the open and ran, half-crouching, until he reached the side of the guardhouse. He paused, conscious of the sweat soaking his shirt, and started forward. At that moment the guardhouse door opened and someone stepped out.

Chavasse heard voices, two men talking. One

of them laughed and a match was struck. He was trapped with no place to run. If one of them took a step to the corner of the building, he was certain to be discovered.

A fresh young voice called, 'Hey, you there! Yes, you, you great ox. Come here!'

Liri Kupi strolled calmly across the square, her hands in her pockets. Her intention was obviously to attract the attention of the guards and she succeeded perfectly. As Chavasse went along the side of the guardhouse, two soldiers moved out to meet Liri.

They weren't even armed and one of them was stripped to the waist, as if he had been having a wash. Chavasse ran forward, raised the rifle and rammed it down hard against an exposed neck. As the soldier crumpled with a groan, the other swung round. Chavasse swung the barrel into the man's stomach. He keeled over, and the butt of the rifled smashed his skull.

Chavasse was already moving towards the door when Liri arrived on the run, her face flushed. 'There can't be anyone else. They'd have come out when I called.'

'Let's hope you're right.'

The outer office was quiet, papers scattering across the desk in the wind which blew in through the doorway. Keys hung on a board on the far wall. Chavasse moved across quickly and opened the inner door. There were only six cells. The first four were empty. Guilio Orsini was in the fifth, sprawled on a narrow bunk, head on hands.

'Now then, you old bastard,' Chavasse said amiably.

The Italian sat up, an expression of astonishment on his face. He jumped to his feet and crossed to the grille. 'Paul, by all that's holy! You go in for miracles now?'

'Ask and ye shall receive,' Chavasse said. 'You'll never know just how apt that quotation is. Where's Francesca?'

'Next door. We've been here ever since we arrived. Kapo took off again in something of a hurry. Presumably to chase you.'

'He's out of luck.'

Liri was beside him with the keys. As she released Orsini, Chavasse was already at the next grille. Francesca Minetti stood there, eyes like dark holes in the white face.

'I knew you'd come, Paul.'

He took the keys from Liri and unlocked the cell. Francesca came straight into his arms. He held her close for a moment, then pushed her away.

'We've got to get moving.'

Orsini was already ahead of them, following Liri, and Chavasse picked up the rifle and pushed Francesca along the passage. The Italian paused in the doorway and looked out into the square.

'Seems quiet enough.'

The noise of the siren rising through the still air was like a physical blow, numbing the senses. Chavasse swung round and saw Francesca on the other side of the room. She had opened a small metal box on the wall and her thumb was pressed firmly against a scarlet button.

He pulled her away so violently that she staggered back against the desk. 'What the hell are you doing?'

In answer, she spat in his face and slapped him heavily across the left cheek. In an instinctive reflex action, he returned the blow with his clenched fist, knocking her to the floor.

She lay there moaning softly and Orsini grabbed Chavasse by the sleeve, pulling him round, 'For God's sake, what's going on?'

A single shot echoed across the square, splintering the doorpost, and Orsini ducked, pulling Liri to the floor. Chavasse looked out through the window and saw a movement on the wall above the great gates. Another rifle shot was followed by the rapid stutter of a submachine gun, and a line of bullets kicked a cloud of dust into the air in a brown curtain.

He smashed the window with the butt end of the hunting rifle, aimed quickly and fired. There was a faint cry and a soldier pitched over the parapet and fell, still clutching his rifle.

One of the two guards lying in the square pushed himself onto his knees, an expression of bewilderment on his face. Chavasse shot him through the head and ducked out of sight as the man's comrades started to concentrate on the window.

He moved to the doorway and crouched beside Orsini and the girl. 'There must be half a dozen of them up there now and more on the way. I'm going to draw their fire. It might give you and Liri a chance. She knows the way. Just do as she says.'

Orsini opened his mouth to protest, but Chavasse was already running into the square. He flung himself down beside the body of the guard he had shot, took aim and started to fire at the men on the wall.

Behind him, Orsini and the girl emerged from the guardhouse and started to run. It was at precisely that moment that the great double doors on the far side of the square swung open. An engine burst into life and a jeep roared through in a cloud of dust. A light machine-gun was mounted on a swivel in the rear, and Colonel Tashko swung it in a half arc, a line of bullets churning the dust into fountains beside Orsini and the girl, bringing them to a halt, hands held high.

Chavasse, the heart freezing inside him, saw a detail of soldiers come through the gate, rifles at the port. In the moment that the jeep braked, slewing broadside on, Francesca staggered past him and lurched towards it. Chavasse jumped to his feet and fired the hunting rifle from the hip as he ran.

His first shot kicked up dirt a foot to one side of her and then something punched him in the left arm, spinning him round, the rifle flying from his grasp. He crouched like an animal, holding his arm tightly, blood oozing between the fingers, and heard boots crunch through the dirt in the sudden silence.

When he raised his eyes, Adem Kapo looked down at him, a slight smile fixed to the small mouth.

# 12

Rain drifted in through the bars of the window and Chavasse pulled himself up and looked out across the monastery walls towards the river. He was immediately aware of the pain in his left arm and dropped with a curse.

The bullet had passed through cleanly, a flesh wound, and the only treatment he had so far received was to have it bandaged. They were in some sort of store room on the second floor of the main building. Liri Kupi slept in the corner, a blanket hitched over her shoulders.

Orsini crouched beside her to straighten the blanket. When he rose to his feet, there was a strange expression on his face. 'Quite a girl. A pity she had to get mixed up in a thing like this.'

'As I've already explained, she wasn't supposed to.' Chavasse walked to the door and peered through the grille at the guard outside. 'God, what a fool I've been and I never saw it.'

'Francesca?' Orsini shook his head. 'I still can't believe it.'

'She said the Madonna was in the forward cabin and it wasn't, and remember we had to blast our way in. How do you get round that?' He kicked a packing case savagely. 'The little bitch. That night outside the Tabu when she was attacked. They must have been waiting for me to show. The whole thing was laid on for my benefit.'

'But why?' Orsini demanded. 'It doesn't make sense. And what happened to the Madonna?'

'That's one thing I'd like to know myself. That part of the story was genuine enough, because Father Shedu confirmed it. At least they don't seem to have laid hands on him, which is a good thing.'

A key rattled in the lock and the door was flung open. Liri came awake and scrambled to her feet as two soldiers moved into the room, followed by Tashko. He examined the girl and smiled.

'I'll come to you later.'

She spat in his face and he reached out, quick as a snake, and grabbed her shoulder. As Orsini and Chavasse started forward, the soldiers raised their machine pistols threateningly.

Tashko's face was expressionless as his thumb expertly pressed a nerve against bone. Liri's mouth opened in a cry and she crumpled to the floor. He turned to Chavasse, adjusting his leather gloves.

'Karate, my friend. You were lucky with the vodka bottle. Next time, all the luck will be mine – this I promise you.'

He nodded and one of the soldiers grabbed Chavasse by the shoulder and dragged him outside. He had a quick glimpse of Orsini dropping to one knee beside the girl, and then the door closed.

They took him along the wide stone-flagged passage and up a narrow circular staircase at the far end. Tashko opened a door at the top and led the way into a comfortably furnished office.

Adem Kapo sat behind a desk, reading through some papers. He glanced up and a smile flashed across his face. 'You'll never know just how much of a pleasure this is. We've been most anxious to lay hands on you since that little affair in Tirana the other week.'

'*Sigurmi?*'

Kapo nodded. 'My Italian front is only one of many, as I'm sure you'll appreciate.'

'So the business in Matano? It was all a fix? No Ramiz? No Marco Minetti?'

'Ramiz was just a little blood on the floor and a bribe to the young woman who lived across the hall from his room. Minetti was a figment of the imagination.'

'Which explains why Francesca was so insistent that I didn't disclose what was going on in Rome.'

Kapo nodded. 'The story was genuine enough. It was played out by a high-minded young Italian named Carveggio who tried the same trick and got his head blown off for his pains.'

'And the statue?'

'We recovered it from the wreck almost immediately.'

He nodded to Tashko, who went to a cupboard, opened it and took out a shapeless bundle. He unwrapped a grey blanket and set the statue on the desk.

She was perhaps four feet high and carved from a single piece of ebony, her robes inlaid with gold. The features carried an expression of wonderful serenity and peace. It was a supreme achievement by some great unknown artist.

'All right,' Chavasse said. 'In all its essential details, the story handed me by Francesca Minetti was true and it did what it was supposed to do – it got me back into Albania. Which means you went to a hell of a lot of trouble – why?'

Kapo selected a cigarette from a wooden box on the desk and leaned back in his chair. 'As you may know, relations between my own poor country and the USSR and its satellites have somewhat deteriorated over the past few years. In our trouble, only one friend came to our aid – China.'

'How touching.'

'We are a sentimental people, I assure you. We like to pay our debts. The report from our counter-intelligence section, which contained the information that you intended to enter our country as a member of an Italian workers' holiday group, was passed on to Chinese Intelligence

Headquarters in Tirana as a matter of courtesy. They expressed great interest. Apparently you did them some disservice in Tibet last year. Something to do with a Doctor Hoffner, I understand. We promised to let them have you.'

'And then I slipped through your fingers.'

'But not for long, you must agree, and thanks to only one person. An extremely able member of the counter-intelligence section of the *Sigurmi*. Perhaps you'd like to meet her?'

When Tashko opened the door she came in at once. She was still in the clothes she had worn on the boat, but looked different. Harder, more assured.

'Why, Francesca?' he said.

'I am as much Albanian as I am Italian,' she said calmly. 'You can't have a foot in both worlds. I chose mine long ago.'

'You mean you've been working for the other side ever since the Bureau took you on?'

'How did you think our people in Tirana knew you were coming? I only transmitted that radio warning from Scutari because the night duty officer was present when it came in.'

And then it really hit him for the first time.

Someone from the other side had been sitting at the very heart of things, with a top security rating, for two years, passing on the information men had sweated and died for, perhaps even sending them to their deaths.

Something of this must have shown on his face, and she smiled slightly. 'Oh, yes, Paul, I have accomplished great things. Remember Matt Sorley and the Frenchman, Dumont? Neither of them lasted long, I saw to that. And there were others.'

'You lousy bitch.'

'You killed my husband, Paul,' she said calmly, and a cold hatred blazed from her eyes.

'Your husband?' He frowned slightly and shook his head. 'I don't know what you're talking about. In any case, I've seen your personal file. There was no mention of any marriage.'

'Not a difficult thing to keep quiet about if one goes the right way about it. His name was Enrico Noci. You drowned him like a rat in a fishing net. No marks, no violence. Just an accident.'

'Which I must say was really damned ingenious of you,' Kapo put in.

There was obviously nothing more to say and

Chavasse turned from her to the little man. 'What happens now? A quick flight to Peking?'

'No rush.' Kapo grinned. 'We've all the time in the world and there's so much you could tell me. How on earth you managed to get inside the monastery, for example. Of course that was the idea – that you should show up. We were quite certain that a man of your resource and energy wouldn't leave his friends in the lurch, but to be perfectly honest your sudden materialization out of thin air was even more impressive than I'd figured on.'

'A trick I picked up from an old fakir in India years ago.'

'Fascinating. You can tell me all about it when I return. If you can't, I'm sure Tashko can persuade the young lady you picked up on your travels to be more cooperative.'

Chavasse ignored the threat and calmly helped himself to a cigarette from the box on the desk. 'You're going somewhere?'

'Didn't I explain?' Kapo took another cigarette, lit it and tossed the matches across to Chavasse. They might have been good friends enjoying a pleasant conversation. 'It's really rather ingenious, though I do say it myself. At this moment, your young friend Arezzi is sitting on the *Buona Esperanza* awaiting your return.'

Which didn't make sense at all. Chavasse was unable to suppress a slight frown and Kapo smiled. 'Later tonight, I shall take Francesca in the motorboat to within a reasonable distance of the launch. In the grey light of dawn, she will float out of the mist in your dinghy, in a distressed condition, I might add.'

'And with an even more distressing story to tell.'

'Of course. They'll be most upset back in Rome when they hear they've lost the gallant Chavasse and his friend Orsini.'

'And you think they'll accept Francesca back into the fold without a question?' Chavasse shook his head. 'My boss would never believe it. He'll check every step she's taken since she was six months old.'

'I wouldn't be too sure.' Kapo smiled. 'You see she'll have the Black Madonna with her, such a lovely stroke of propaganda against Albania. Everyone will be so pleased.'

And he was right. It was good. Kapo started to laugh and nodded to Tashko. 'Take him back to his friends. I'll deal with him when I return in the morning.'

Chavasse turned to face Francesca. She held his gaze for a moment, then looked away and Tashko gave him a push towards the door. They went down the stairs and back along the corridor.

Just before they reached the store room again, Tashko paused to light a long Russian cigarette. The two soldiers waited respectfully a few paces away, obviously frightened to death of him, and he glared at Chavasse coldly.

'That one up there is a big man with words, but I have a different approach. Soon you will find this out.'

'Why don't you take a running jump,' Chavasse said calmly.

Rage flared in the cold eyes. Tashko took a step forward and restrained himself with obvious difficulty. There was a door to one side of Chavasse and, quite suddenly, the Albanian's right fist shot forward in a straight line in the terrible basic karate blow now known as the reverse punch. The inch-thick centre plank of the door splintered and sagged inwards.

There was a little Japanese professor whose

class Chavasse attended three times a week whenever he was in London, who could do the same thing to three planks at once and he was half Tashko's size. His words echoed faintly like an old tune: *Science, Chavasse-san. Science, not force. God did not intend the brute to lord it over the earth.*

'Try to imagine what that would have done to your face,' Tashko said.

'It's certainly a thought.'

Chavasse moved on along the passage. One of the soldiers unlocked the door and they pushed him inside. As it closed, he looked through the grille into Tashko's cold eyes.

The Albanian nodded. 'I'll be back.'

His footsteps died along the corridor and Chavasse turned to the others. Orsini was sitting by the window, an arm around Liri, and the blanket was draped over their shoulders. It was bitterly cold.

'What happened?' Orsini demanded.

Chavasse told him. When he had finished, Liri shook her head. 'She must be a devil, that one.'

'No, *cara*, no devil,' Orsini said. 'She is like

181

all her kind, convinced that she alone knows the ultimate truth of things. To achieve it, she believes anything to be permissible.'

'Which doesn't help any of us one little bit,' Chavasse said.

He went and sat on a packing case, turning up the collar of his jacket, and folded his arms to conserve what heat was left in his body, thinking about Francesca Minetti. So Enrico Noci had been her husband? Strange that a woman so obviously intelligent should fall for that sort of man.

Orsini and Liri were talking together in low voices, an intimacy between them. What was it someone had once said? A day told you as much about a person as ten years? Pity they'd had to meet under such circumstances.

How ironic that Guilio Orsini, the man who had penetrated the main harbour at Alexandria on one of the first underwater chariots, who had sunk two British destroyers, survivor of one desperate exploit after another through the years, should end like this because he had been touched by the apparent sorrow of a young girl. Life could be puzzling, all right. After a while, his head dropped forward on his breast and he slept.

# 13

Chavasse was not certain what had caused him to wake up, and he lay for a moment, staring through the darkness, conscious of the ache in his cramped muscles, of the bitter cold. His watch was still functioning and the luminous dial told him that it was two a.m. He sat there for a moment, aware of the wind howling across the square outside, and got to his feet.

There was movement in the corridor, and when he looked out through the grille he could see the sentry standing in front of his chair, a look of abject terror on his face. Colonel Tashko confronted him, hands on hips.

'So. You were sleeping, you worm.'

His hand lashed forward, catching the unfortunate sentry across the side of the face, sending him back across his chair with a crash. As the man scrambled to his feet, Tashko booted him along the corridor.

'Go on, get out of here! Report to the guard-house. I'll deal with you later.'

Orsini and Liri, awakened by the disturbance, came to the door. 'What is it?' Orsini demanded.

'Tashko,' Chavasse told him briefly. 'I think he's drunk.'

The Albanian moved to the door and looked through the grille at Chavasse. His tunic hung open and underneath he was naked to the waist, great muscles standing out like cords.

He unbuckled the black leather holster at his hip and took out a Mauser, then unlocked the door and opened it slowly. Liri took a step forward towards Orsini, whose arm encircled her at once.

'How touching,' Tashko said.

'It's been a long day and we'd like to get a little sleep,' Chavasse said. 'So kindly state your business and get the hell out of here.'

'Still full of fight?' Tashko said. 'That's the way I like it. Let's have you outside.'

'And what if I tell you to go to hell?'

'I shoot the girl through her left kneecap. A pity to waste good material, but there it is.'

Orsini took a step forward, but Chavasse pushed him back. 'Leave it, Guilio. My affair.' He moved into the corridor and Tashko slammed the door and locked it. 'I don't think Kapo's going to like this. He's saving me for Peking.'

'To hell with Peking,' Tashko said. 'In any case, I'm in charge now. Kapo and the girl left half an hour ago.'

He sent Chavasse staggering down the corridor and followed three feet behind, the Mauser ready for action. They went down a spiral staircase at the far end, turned along a broad stone passage and descended a flight of stone steps that seemed to go down forever.

At the bottom, Tashko produced his keys and unlocked an oak door, bound with bands of iron. Chavasse moved in and Tashko flicked a switch and locked the door behind them.

They stood at the top of a flight of broad stone steps and beneath them in the dim light of a couple of electric bulbs was an amazing sight. A great Roman plunge bath, perhaps a hundred feet long, stretched into the gloom flanked by broken pillars and the stumps of what must have been at one time well-proportioned colonnades. There was a strong sulphurous smell and steam drifted up from the water.

'Amazing what they got up to, the Romans,' Tashko said. 'Of course, the mediaeval fathers who built this monastery weren't too keen on such pagan survivals. They simply built over it.'

They went down the steps and crossed a cracked tessellated floor. The pool was about six feet deep, the water very still, and the face in the brightly coloured mosaic that was its floor gazed blindly up at him out of two thousand years of chaos.

'It's fed by a natural spring,' Tashko said. 'One hundred twenty degrees Fahrenheit. Quite pleasant. They say it's good for rheumatism.'

As Chavasse turned slowly, the Albanian slipped off his tunic and let it drop to the floor. He held up the keys in one hand, the Mauser in the other, then tossed them into the centre of the pool with a quick gesture.

'There's nothing to help you this time, my friend.'

So that was it? Was it simply a case of personal vanity on the part of a man so proud of his brute strength that he couldn't bear to be beaten by anyone? Chavasse stumbled back, as if panic-stricken. If Tashko thought him an easy mark, he might still do something stupid.

The Albanian moved forward, arms at his side, and laughed harshly. In the same moment he delivered a tremendous reverse punch, a karate blow that takes the uninitiated unawares because it is delivered with the hand that is on the same side as the rear foot.

Chavasse crossed his hands above his head to counter with the X-block, the *juji-uke*, and delivered a forward elbow strike in return that caught Tashko full in the mouth.

The Albanian staggered back, blood spurting from his crushed lips, and Chavasse grinned. 'A *gyaku-zuki* and badly delivered. Is that the best you can do?'

Tashko's face was twisted by anger, but he immediately dropped into the defensive position, adopting the cat stance, arms down inviting combat. Chavasse moved in, his right forearm vertical, the left protecting his body. They circled warily and Tashko made the first move.

He pushed the heel of his palm at his opponent's face, and as Chavasse blocked it, delivered a lightning punch to the stomach. Chavasse turned sideways, riding most of the force, and at the same moment fell to one side and delivered a roundhouse kick to the groin. The Albanian keeled over and Chavasse, throwing caution to the wind, raised a knee into the descending face.

He realized immediately that he had made a bad mistake. A blow that would have demolished any ordinary man only succeeded in shaking the Albanian's massive strength, and great hands clawed across his body, grabbing for his throat.

The lights seemed to be very far away and there was a sudden roaring in his ears, and through it he seemed to hear the professor's monotonous, sing-song voice. *Science – science and intelligence will beat brute force.*

He summoned every effort of willpower and spat full in that great stinking face and Tashko recoiled in a reflex action that was as natural as breathing. Chavasse stabbed upwards with stiffened fingers at the exposed throat and Tashko screamed and staggered back.

Chavasse rolled over several times and came to his feet as the big man lurched towards him, hands extended, all science forgotten. Chavasse ducked in under the hands, delivering a fore-fist punch, knuckles extended, and it sank into the muscles beneath Tashko's rib-cage. He started to fall and Chavasse raised his knee into the descending face, throwing him back.

Tashko swayed on the edge of the pool, his face a mask of blood, and Chavasse jumped high in the air, delivering a flying front kick, the devastating *mae-tobigeri*, into the Albanian's face, knocking him back into the water.

Chavasse followed him in, twisting in mid-air, going under awkwardly, the warm water drawing him down. His hands took the shock against a bearded mosaic face and he surfaced quickly.

Tashko was about twenty feet away, lurching towards the centre of the pool where he had thrown the Mauser, and Chavasse went after him. He scrambled up onto the great back, his hands sliding under the armpits, locking together at the nape of the neck. He started to press and Tashko screamed. All pity dying in him, Chavasse maintained his relentless pressure and the head sank down into the water.

The body bucked and heaved, hands flailing the surface into a cauldron, but Chavasse strengthened his grip and hung on. The end came with startling suddenness. Tashko simply went limp, and when Chavasse released his grip, the body planed down through the water, turning on its back when it reached bottom.

Chavasse took a quick breath and went after the Mauser. The keys were perhaps ten feet away and he had to push Tashko to one side to pick them up. The Albanian's eyes stared into eternity, blood drifting in brown strings from his smashed face, and Chavasse turned and swam for the side.

He sat on the edge for perhaps five minutes, his chest heaving, drawing air into his tortured lungs. When he felt a little better, he got to his feet and mounted the steps. He had to try four keys before he found the right one. As he opened the door, he looked down for the last time at Tashko, who stared up at him, just another figure in the mosaic now. He switched off the lights, closed the door and locked it.

The corridors were quiet and he met no one on his way back. Outside the store room, the chair on which the sentry had been sleeping still lay on its side, and he righted it before slipping the Mauser into his pocket and fumbling with the keys.

As he worked through them, Guilio Orsini appeared at the grille. He glanced up and down the passage and an expression of bewilderment appeared on his face.

'What happened to Tashko?'

'He made a mistake,' Chavasse said, swinging the door open. 'His last. Let's get going.'

He turned along the passage, remembering the way they had come. A stone spiral staircase dropped to the first floor, another to the basement. All was quiet and he led the way along a narrow whitewashed corridor, pausing to reconnoitre the entrance hall at the end. There was no sentry, but then, why should there be? The building was encircled by two thirty-foot walls, the main gates in each being strongly guarded.

They had explained earlier to Orsini how they had gained access to the monastery and the big Italian followed Chavasse unhesitatingly, the girl at his side.

They kept to the shadow of the wall, skirting the square on the far side of the guardhouse where a light shone in the window, and entered the cloisters through a gap in the ruined wall. It was very dark and Chavasse moved through the pillars cautiously and turned into the passage containing the cells.

He had to try three before he found the one with the grille and it was Orsini who pulled it out, fingers fastening into the latticework like steel hooks.

'I'll go first,' Chavasse said. 'Then Liri. You follow, Guilio, and replace the grille as you come down.'

He shot down the stone chute on his back, forearms raised to protect his face, and landed in the tunnel below with a splash. Liri followed so quickly that she cannoned into him as he was getting to his feet. Orsini joined them a moment later and they crouched in a little group.

It was so dark in the tunnel that they couldn't

see each other's faces and Chavasse said quietly, 'This isn't going to be any picnic. Whatever happens, keep close together. As long as we can make it to the main channel, we can't go wrong because it's bound to flow in the direction of the river.'

'Anything's preferable to what we've just left,' Orsini said. 'Let's get moving.'

Chavasse started along the tunnel bent double, Liri holding on to the tail of his oilskin jacket. It was a strange, claustrophobic sensation, like nothing he had ever experienced before, and yet he wasn't frightened. The darkness was a friend, cloaking their flight, enfolding them in gentle hands, and he was grateful.

A few moments later, they emerged from the tunnel into the central cavern. He stood thigh deep in the stinking water, staring into the darkness.

'Father Shedu counted eight openings to the left from where we came out, Paul,' Liri said.

He nodded. 'Keep behind me, both of you. I've got an idea.'

He took out the Mauser, pointed it at the water and fired. In the single brilliant flash of light, the tunnel openings stood out like dark wounds. He fired again, counting quickly, then started across the pool.

His questing hand found the opening and he grunted.

Fifty yards further on, the passage emptied itself into the main tunnel and he could hear the splash and gurgling of the water on its way down to the river. Already the stench seemed to be lessening, and as he followed the wall Chavasse breathed deeply to clear the heaviness that weighed upon his brain.

The landing stage loomed out of the darkness, light flowing down from the candles burning at the ikon in the niche at the head of the stairs. Liri's punt was still tied to the bottom of the steps, and Chavasse sat on the edge of the landing stage and rubbed the back of one hand wearily across his eyes.

'How much juice you got in that thing? Enough to get us to the coast?'

'I think so. Most of the way, at least.'

'We still need a compass to get back to the *Buona Esperanza*,' Orsini said. 'At least if we're going to go now in the dark.'

194

'We can't afford to wait till dawn,' Chavasse said. 'That's when Kapo will send Francesca in the dinghy. If we're going to beat them to it, we must go now.'

'Father Shedu will have a compass,' Liri said. 'Wait here. I'll go and get him.'

She mounted the steps and the door closed behind her. Orsini slumped down beside Chavasse. 'Most girls would have had hysterics by now.'

'She'll have to come with us,' Chavasse said. 'She can't stay here.'

'What about an entry permit? I know what it's like for the stateless refugees.'

'Don't worry about that. I know the right people at the Ministry in Rome. We'll even find her a job. She's earned it.'

'Maybe she won't need a job.'

Chavasse glanced at him curiously. 'You make up your mind in a hurry, don't you?'

Orsini shrugged. 'You either know straight away, or it's no good. Of course, I've got twenty years on her.'

'I wouldn't let that worry you,' Chavasse said. 'She knows a man when she sees one.'

He sat there, his left arm aching like hell, his strength slowly ebbing, and after a while the door clicked open and Father Shedu came down the steps with Liri.

'So miracles can still happen,' he said as he moved forward.

'My friend, Guilio Orsini, Father,' Chavasse said. 'I'm glad you kept out of it back there. They still haven't got the slightest idea how we got inside.'

The priest poured brandy into a couple of tin mugs and handed a small basket to Liri. 'This isn't much, I'm afraid. Bread and cheese and some dried meat. The rich, full life is long in coming for the People's Republic.'

'We'll eat it on the way,' Chavasse said. He drank some of the brandy and coughed as it burned its way down his throat.

'Liri has told me what happened in there,' the priest said. 'It pains me to know this woman deceived you.'

'And she'll go on playing the same game unless we can manage to stop her,' Chavasse said. 'Liri thought you might have a compass.'

The priest held one forward, pressing a small

spring so that the lid flew open. Chavasse examined it, noting the inscription 'W.D. 1941' and the official broad arrow.

'British Army issue?'

'A souvenir from another life. Take it with my blessing.' He turned to Liri and placed a hand on her shoulder. 'And what happens to you, Liri?'

'She goes with us, Father,' Orsini said gruffly. 'I'll look after her.'

The priest gazed at him searchingly and then smiled. 'God moves in His own strange ways. Now go, all of you, while there is still time.'

They dropped into the boat and Liri took the tiller. The roaring of the engine seemed to fill the cavern when it broke into life and the boat turned away quickly.

As they moved through the dark entrance, Chavasse glanced back and saw the Franciscan still standing there watching them. A moment later, they swung into the main current and turned downstream through the darkness.

# 14

The river was angry, swollen by the rains flowing down from the mountains of the north, and it rushed towards the sea with more than usual force.

The frail punt shipped water constantly and Chavasse and Orsini took turns at bailing with an old tin basin. They ate the food the priest had provided and finished the bottle of brandy.

Chavasse sat in the prow, his collar turned up against the spray, and longed for a cigarette. He wondered what Kapo would do. Probably tie up further downriver till dawn. Then he would send Francesca in with the dinghy and Carlo would swallow every damned thing she said.

Perhaps half an hour later, the engine faltered and died abruptly. As the punt started to drift broadside-on in the strong current, Liri called,

'There are paddles under the seat. Keep her head round.'

Chavasse fumbled in the darkness and found two crude paddles. He leaned over the side and dug one deep into the water, using all his strength, and gradually the punt turned into the current.

Orsini scrambled to the stern and, after a struggle, managed to get the engine housing off. He started to try to trace the fault by touch alone, and after a while his sensitive fingers encountered a broken lead to one of the plugs. The wire was old and brittle and crumbled between his fingers, but he eventually managed to link it together and tried the starter. The engine turned over twice, faltered, then rumbled into life and Chavasse rested on the thwart in relief as the punt surged forward.

'Any chance of that happening again?' he called softly.

'I wouldn't be surprised. This must be the one they used on the Ark.'

Orsini stayed at the tiller, nursing the engine along, and Liri moved into the centre and started to bail. It was still quite dark and visibility was almost nil. Only the surge of white water against the bank gave them any kind of bearing.

The bulk of a large island loomed out of the night, and Liri called urgently as Orsini swung the tiller, taking them away towards the centre of the river.

As the current caught them, there was a sudden challenge from the left and Chavasse glanced over his shoulder and saw the motor-boat anchored in the lee of the island, a light in her wheelhouse.

He was aware of people moving along the deck, of confused voices, and then a power-ful spot mounted on top of the wheelhouse was switched on, the beam splaying out across the dark water. It followed them relentlessly, trapping them in its dazzling beam like flies in a web.

There was an incredulous cry of dismay and Francesca's voice sounded on the cold air like a bugle. 'Kapo! Kapo! Come quickly!'

Chavasse leaned over the side, digging the paddle into the water feverishly as Orsini gave the old motor everything it had. They dipped into the millrace as the current flowed past the final curved point of the island and coasted into darkness again.

A few moments later, the engine of the motorboat rumbled into life and Liri scrambled back into the stern. 'I'll take over now,' she said. 'There's a creek about a quarter of a mile below. If we can reach that, we're safe. It's too narrow for the motorboat to enter. They'll have to stay in the main channel.'

Orsini moved down beside Chavasse, picked up the other paddle and drove it into the water with all his great strength. They were passing through a narrower section of the river now and the flood waters rushed with a mighty roar, drowning the sound of the motorboat's engine. Chavasse stabbed the crude paddle into the water again and again, exerting everything of mind and will in a supreme effort, pushing the tiredness, the fatigue of the past twenty-four hours away from him.

They swung in close to the land as the river broadened, and quite suddenly, as the roaring of the flood waters subsided, the engine of the motorboat sounded close behind.

He glanced over his shoulder, saw the lighted

wheelhouse, the searchlight stabbing out towards them. There was the harsh deadly staccato of a submachine gun and then the punt swerved into the lee of a small island and started to turn.

Reeds swam out of the darkness, and as the beam of the searchlight fell across them, the opening of the creek sprang out of the night. The punt surged towards it, slowed as it slid across a submerged mudbank and then they were through. The machine gun rattled again ineffectually as the reeds closed about them.

Liri reduced speed and they coasted on, brushing against the pale fronds. Gradually, the sound of the river faded. The engine of the motorboat had stopped for a while, but now they heard it start again faintly in the distance and fade downstream.

Orsini laughed shakily. 'A close call.'

Chavasse took from his pocket the compass Father Shedu had given him, and passed it to the Italian. 'You'd better start using this. We haven't got time to hang about.'

Orsini moved in to the stern beside Liri. 'South-southwest must be our general direction. Can we do it?'

'I think so. I know this creek and where it goes. We'll come to a large lagoon soon. We change direction there. But it's possible you might have to get out and push in places.'

'When will it be light?' Chavasse asked.

'An hour, perhaps a little longer. It will be misty, one can always tell.'

'We're in your hands, *cara*,' Orsini told her.

They moved into a large lagoon as she had indicated and turned into a maze of twisting channels. The outboard motor stopped several times as trailing weeds clogged the propeller, and finally it died altogether.

Orsini examined it for several minutes and shook his head. 'That's all, I'm afraid. There's nothing I can do, not under these conditions.'

From then on they used the paddles, and after a while the reeds became so thick that the two men had to go over the side, wading through thick glutinous mud as they forced a way through for the punt, always trying to keep to their general compass bearing.

The swampy water was treacherous and had a way of changing depth without warning. Once, Chavasse stepped into a deep hole and went in over his head. He struggled back with a curse to a comparatively safe footing and scrambled back into the punt as they emerged into another waterway.

Orsini laughed grimly. 'Now this I could do without.'

It was bitterly cold and a damp mist curled from the water. Occasionally, wildfowl fluttered protestingly from the reeds as they passed through, calling angrily to each other, warning those ahead of the intruders.

There was an appreciable lightening of the darkness and a faint luminosity drifted around them. And then they could see the reeds and there was a honking of geese overhead lifting to meet the dawn.

Orsini was pale and drawn, the dark stubble of his beard accentuating his pallor. He looked about twenty years older, his hands shaking slightly in the extreme cold, and Chavasse didn't feel any better. The girl looked healthier than either of them, but on the other hand she hadn't spent the best part of an hour up to her waist in freezing water.

They coasted into a broad channel and Orsini

held up his hand. 'We must be close now. Very close.'

He stood up in the punt, cupped his hands to his mouth and called at the top of his voice, '*Buona Esperanza*, ahoy! Ahoy, *Buona Esperanza*!'

There was no reply and Chavasse joined him. 'Carlo! Carlo Arezzi!'

Their voices died away, and in the grey light they looked helplessly at each other. Liri held up her hand. 'I heard something.'

At first Chavasse thought it was the cry of a bird, but then it sounded again, unmistakably a human voice. They paddled into the mist, calling again and again, and gradually the voice grew louder.

For the last time, Chavasse and Orsini went over the side, forcing the punt through a wall of reeds and then, quite suddenly, they were through and drifting into a familiar lagoon.

At the other end, the *Buona Esperanza* seemed to swim out of the mist to meet them, Carlo Arezzi poised on top of the wheelhouse.

# 15

It was warm in the cabin. Chavasse vigorously rubbed himself down and dressed quickly in a spare pair of denim working pants and a heavy sweater of Carlo's.

There was a knock on the door and Liri Kupi called, 'Are you dressed?'

She came in carrying a mug of coffee and he took it gratefully. It was scalding hot and the fragrance seemed to put new life into him. 'Best I ever tasted. Where's Guilio?'

'He went up to the wheelhouse. He wanted to chart the course.'

She opened the little box, gave him one of her Macedonian cigarettes and struck a match for him, holding it in her cupped hands.

Chavasse blew out a cloud of smoke and looked at her shrewdly. 'You like him, don't you?'

'Guilio? Who wouldn't?'

'He's got twenty years on you, you know that?'

She shrugged and said calmly, 'You know what they say about good wine.'

Chavasse slipped an arm about her shoulders. 'You're quite a girl, Liri. I'd say he was a lucky man.'

He swallowed the rest of his coffee, handed her the jug and went up the companionway. It started to rain as he went out on deck and the mist draped itself across everything in a grey shroud. Orsini and Carlo were leaning over the charts when he went into the wheelhouse.

'What's the score?' he said.

Orsini shrugged. 'I think we should try the main channel out. It's quicker and we could stand a good chance of getting away with it. It's Yugoslavian territory on the other side and Albanian boats don't like going in too close. If we can get into the open, nothing they've got stands a chance of catching us.'

'Won't Kapo count on us doing just that?'

'Probably. I say we go and find out.'

Chavasse shrugged. 'That's all right by me, but I think it might be an idea to break out a little hardware, just in case.'

'You and Carlo can handle that end. I'll get things moving up here.'

Chavasse and the young Italian went below, opened the box seat and unpacked the weapons. There was still a submachine gun left, a dozen grenades and the old Bren. They went back on deck and laid the weapons out on the floor of the wheelhouse under the chart table, ready for action.

It was just after five a.m. when the engines shuddered into life and Orsini took the *Buona Esperanza* into the mist. Chavasse stood in the prow beside Liri and rain kicked into his face, and the wind, blowing in from the sea, lifted the mist into strange shapes.

The girl stared into the greyness eagerly, lips parted, a touch of colour in each cheek. 'Are you glad to be going?' he said.

She shrugged briefly. 'I'm leaving nothing behind.'

As the light grew stronger, the dark silver lances of the rain became visible, stabbing down through the mist, and somewhere a curlew called eerily. Once, twice, and he waited with bated breath, trapped by a childhood memory. *Once for joy, two for sorrow, three for a death.*

There was no third call, which left them with a little sorrow, but that he could bear. He turned and went back to the wheelhouse.

For half an hour, they moved slowly along the broad channel, crossing from one lagoon into the other, changing direction only once. Visibility was down to twenty yards, but the reeds were falling away now and the channel was widening.

The water began to kick against the hull in long swelling ripples and Orsini grinned tightly. 'The Buene. We're about half a mile from the sea.'

The launch crept forward, the engines a low rumble that was almost drowned in the splashing of the heavy rain. Chavasse examined the chart. The estuary was a mass of sandbanks and the main channel, the one they had used on the way in, was no more than thirty yards. If Kapo was anywhere, it would be there.

A few moments later, Orsini cut the engines

and they drifted with the current. He opened the side window and leaned out.

'We're almost there. If they're patrolling, we'll hear the engines.'

Chavasse went on deck and stood in the prow listening. Carlo and Liri joined him. At first there was nothing, only the wind and the sizzle of rain, then Carlo held up a hand.

'I think I hear something.'

Chavasse turned, signalling Orsini down, and the Italian swung the wheel, taking the boat in to where a low hog's back of sand lifted from the sea. They grounded with a slight shudder and Chavasse ran back to the wheelhouse.

'Carlo thinks he heard something. No sense in running into anything we can avoid. We'll take a look on foot.'

He stood on the rail and jumped, landing in a couple of inches of water. Carlo tossed the submachine gun to him, then followed and they moved into the mist along the sandbank.

It stretched for several hundred yards, in some places water slopping across it so that they had to wade. The noise of an engine was by now quite unmistakable. At times it faded, then a minute or two later grew louder again.

'They must be patrolling the mouth of the channel,' Chavasse said.

Carlo pulled him down into the sand. The motorboat floated out of the mist no more than twenty yards away. They had a quick glimpse of a soldier crouching on the roof of the wheelhouse, a machine pistol in his hands, and then the mist swallowed it again.

They ran back along the sandbank and the sound of the motorboat faded behind them. The mist seemed to be a little thicker and the water was rising, flooding in across the dark spine of sand, tugging at their boots, and the *Buona Esperanza* loomed out of the gloom.

Chavasse waded into the water and Orsini reached down to give him a hand over the rail. 'Are they there?'

Chavasse nodded and explained briefly what they had seen. 'What happens now?'

They went back into the wheelhouse and Orsini leaned over the chart. 'We could return to the marshes. There is a way through, certainly, but it would take many hours with a boat of this size and there is no guarantee. By that time, Kapo could have called in the Albanian Navy, such as it is. They could give us trouble if we ran into them with no way round.'

'Have we any choice?'

Orsini traced finger across the chart. 'There's a channel here. It runs a mile to the southwest, emerging at Cat Island. See where I mean?'

'What's the snag? It looks good to me.'

'As I said earlier, the river isn't used much these days because of the border dispute, and the channels, such as they are, have been allowed to silt up. There's no knowing just how much water there is any more. It's probably shoaled up.'

'Are you willing to try?'

'If the rest of you are.'

There was really no question, Chavasse knew that as he glanced at Liri, and Orsini pressed the starter and reversed off the sandbank. The launch turned in a long sweeping curve and started back up the river.

Orsini leaned out of the side window, eyes narrowed into the mist, and after a while he gave a quick grunt and swung the wheel, taking them

213

between low, humped sandbanks. He reduced speed to dead slow and the boat moved forward as cautiously as an old lady finding her way across a busy street.

Waves slapped hollowly against the bottom, a sure sign of shallow water, and once or twice there was a slight protesting jar and a scraping as they grazed a shoulder of sand. It was perhaps five minutes later that they ploughed to a halt.

Orsini reversed quickly. At first the launch refused to budge and then it parted the sand with an ugly sucking noise. Carlo vaulted over the side without a word to anyone. The water rose to his chest, and as he waded forward it dropped to waist level.

He changed direction to the left and a moment later it lifted to his armpits again. He waved quickly and Orsini swung the wheel, taking the boat after him.

The young Italian swam forward into the shoals, sounding the bottom every few yards, and behind him the *Buona Esperanza* carefully followed his circuitous trail. And then a wave lifted out of the mist, swamping him, and he went under.

He surfaced and swam back to the launch, and when Chavasse pulled him in there was a wide grin on his face. 'Deep water. I couldn't touch bottom. We're through.'

Orsini waved from the wheelhouse and gave the engines more power, swinging the wheel to take them out of the estuary to sea. Fifty yards beyond the entrance the dark bulk of Cat Island lifted out of the mist, and he turned to port. As they rounded the point, the current pushing against them, engines roared into life and a grey naval patrol boat surged out of the rock inlet where she had been waiting.

As she swept across their bows, a heavy machine gun started to fire, bullets sweeping across the deck, shattering glass in the wheelhouse. Chavasse had a quick glimpse of Kapo at the rail, still wearing his hunting jacket with the fur collar, mouth open as he cried his men on.

Carlo appeared in the doorway of the wheelhouse, the submachine gun at his hip, firing as he crossed the deck to the rail. On the patrol boat someone screamed, and Kapo ducked out of sight.

Already Orsini was taking his engines to

full power and from the for'ard deck of the patrol boat another machine gun started to fire, tracer and cannon hammering into the hull of the *Buona Esperanza*, great shudders rushing through her entire frame as she reeled at the impact.

And then they were through, prow lifting over the waves as the patrol boat faded into the mist behind them. Chavasse picked himself up from the deck and gave a hand to Liri. There was blood on her face and she wiped it away quickly.

'Are you all right?' he said.

She nodded. 'A flying splinter, that's all.'

Carlo turned, the submachine gun hugged to his breast. For the first time since Chavasse had known him, there was a smile on his face.

'I gave the bastards something to remember me by.'

Chavasse moved to the door of the wheelhouse. The windows were shattered, glass scattered across the floor, but Orsini seemed to be all in one piece.

'I got down quick,' he called above the roar of the engine. 'Did you see Kapo?'

'For a moment there I thought he'd put one over on us. We should have figured on the possibility of him having both exits watched.'

'I hope the swine's head rolls for this.'

As Orsini grinned savagely, the engines missed a couple of times, faltered, tried to pick up, then stopped completely.

The *Buona Esperanza* ploughed forward, her prow biting into a wave, slowed and started to drift with the current.

# 16

When Orsini got the hatch off the tiny engine room, they could smell escaping fuel at once. The Italian slid down the short steel ladder and Chavasse and Orsini followed him.

Carlo made a quick examination and turned. 'It could be worse. A section of the fuel-intake pipe is damaged. We were lucky the whole damned lot didn't blow sky-high.'

A jagged hole in the steel hull punched by a cannon shell was mute evidence of how the damage had been caused.

'How are we off for spares?' Orsini demanded.

'No problem there, but I'll have to cut a section to the right size and braze it.'

'How long?'

'Twenty minutes, if you all get the hell out of here and leave me alone.'

Chavasse went up the ladder and joined Liri on deck. 'How bad is it?' she asked.

'Bad enough to make us sitting ducks for the next half an hour.'

Orsini scrambled out of the engine room and nodded grimly. 'If the swine doesn't get us now, he doesn't deserve to. We'd better make ready, Paul.'

He broke open a box of cartridges and carefully loaded the submachine gun's one-hundred-round circular clip and Chavasse checked the machine gun and the half-dozen magazines which went with it. Liri scrambled on top of the wheelhouse and kept watch, straining her eyes into the mist.

When he had finished loading the submachine gun, Orsini went below and came back with an old American service-issue .45 automatic. He tossed it to the girl, who caught it deftly.

'Best I can do, but watch it. It has the kick of an angry mule.'

'I've been using guns all my life,' she said, pulling out the magazine and examining it expertly.

Orsini grinned up at her. 'I wonder what

you'd look like in a skirt and some decent stockings and shoes. The thought has great appeal. When we reach Matano, I must do something about it.'

She laughed, her face flushing, and then the smile was wiped from her face. 'Listen, I think I hear them.'

The boat lifted on the swell, waves slapping hollowly against her bows. Chavasse stood at the rail, straining his ears and, in the distance, heard the sound of an engine.

'Come down from there,' he told the girl. 'Go into the wheelhouse and lie flat.'

She did as she was told. Chavasse stood over her, the barrel of the Bren gun poking through one of the windows, and Orsini crouched beside the engine-room hatch.

'Perhaps they're going away?' Liri whispered.

Chavasse shook his head. 'Not on your life. They must have heard our engines stop and they cut their own and listened to see what was happening. Kapo must know that there are only two possibilities. Either we're being picked up by another boat or our engines have packed in.'

221

The patrol boat came nearer and nearer, obviously beating backwards and forwards through the mist. It passed very close to them indeed, its bow-wave rippling across the water, rocking the *Buona Esperanza* violently. For a moment, Chavasse thought they had been missed and then the engine of the patrol boat lifted and it roared out of the mist.

It swept across their stern, and the air was broken by the sound of violence. The main trouble came from the heavy machine gun mounted in the stern of the patrol boat, its crew couched behind a curved shield of armour plating. In the prow, several soldiers stood at the rail, firing rifles and machine pistols, and Kapo lurked behind them, a revolver in his hand.

Chavasse started to fire, swinging the barrel of the Bren in an arc, and a couple of soldiers stumbled backwards to the deck. He saw Francesca running, head down, and swung the Bren desperately, his bullets chipping the rail beside her head. As his magazine ran out, she disappeared into the wheelhouse.

He ducked, reaching for another magazine, and glass shattered above his head and the walls splintered, rocking to the impact of tracer and cannon shell. As the patrol boat swung away, Orsini jumped to his feet and fired a long burst at the crew of the machine gun in the stern. There was a sharp cry. As the boat disappeared into the mist, one of them lurched to the rail and toppled into the sea.

The sound of the patrol boat faded and Orsini shouted to Liri, 'Keep down. Next time he's really going to mean business.'

The patrol boat circled several times, invisible in the heavy mist, and Chavasse waited impatiently. When Kapo at last made his move, it was from a different quarter. As the boat roared out of the mist behind him, Chavasse frantically swung the Bren round, firing from the hip.

The heavy machine gun in the stern of the patrol boat raked them with a murderous fire, the *Buona Esperanza* reeling at the impact, and Chavasse ducked as he finished his last magazine and portions of the roof disintegrated above his head.

Orsini was still firing, the barrel of the submachine gun braced against the side of the wheelhouse. As the patrol boat veered in a wide arc, cutting across their bows again, Chavasse snatched a grenade from the box beside Liri, pulled the pin and ran out on deck.

For a brief moment, the patrol boat was so close he could see the expressions on the soldiers' faces, and as it swept by he lobbed the grenade over the railing to her stern. It started to roll, one of the soldiers kicked out at it frantically and then it exploded. When the smoke cleared, only the tangled wreckage of the machine gun was left. The soldiers had vanished.

The patrol boat ran on into the mist and there was quiet. Liri got to her feet, blood on her face, and wiped it away with the back of her hand.

'Will they try again?'

'Certain to. They'll be a little more careful next time, that's all.'

Orsini was leaning over the engine-room hatch and he stood up and came towards them. 'Not so good. At least another fifteen minutes.'

They looked at each other without saying

anything, knowing what that meant, and quite suddenly Kapo's voice boomed out of the mist. 'Why don't you give in, Chavasse? You can't hope to get away.'

Liri gave a startled exclamation and Orsini reassured her. 'Don't be alarmed. He's using a loudhailer, that's all. I wonder what the swine's playing at.'

'We're not interested,' Chavasse called.

The engines of the patrol boat roared into life and it erupted from the mist, the men at her rail raking the *Buona Esperanza* with small-arms fire.

Chavasse shoved Liri down against the deck and Orsini crouched beside them, the sub-machine gun chattering angrily. He stopped firing abruptly just as the patrol boat disappeared into the mist.

He checked the magazine, then tossed the weapon into the wheelhouse. 'What about the Bren?'

'Nothing left for that either.'

Orsini went and pulled the small box of grenades from under the chart table. 'At least we've got these.'

'If they come close enough,' Chavasse said.

Kapo's voice drifted out of the mist again. 'It's obvious that you're incapable of moving, Chavasse, but I'll be generous. Give yourself up without any further nonsense and I'll let your friends go free. I give you my word. I'll give you ten minutes to think it over. After that, we'll come and finish you off.'

In the silence that followed, Orsini gave an audible grunt and disappeared down the saloon companionway. When he returned, he carried the spare aqualung.

'Help me get into this thing quickly,' he said to Liri, and turned to Chavasse. 'You'll find some more of that plastic explosive in the saloon, Paul, and some chemical detonators. Get them quickly.'

'What the hell do you think you're playing at?' Chavasse began, but Orsini gave him an angry shove.

'Don't argue. Just do it.'

The Italian was buckled into the aqualung and pulling on his rubber flippers when Chavasse came back on deck with the bandolier of explosive.

'I'm going to have a go at fixing Kapo once and for all,' Orsini said, as he fastened the bandolier around his waist.

Chavasse shook his head. 'You haven't got enough time left.'

Orsini grinned. 'That's what they told me in forty-one when I took a team into Alex. But we got in *and* out and left two British destroyers squatting on their backsides in the mud. I know what I'm doing.'

He pulled his mask down, turned from Liri's white face and vaulted over the rail. He had only a rough idea of the direction of the patrol boat, but he knew it couldn't be far away. He swam very fast, kicking strongly with his webbed feet, and within a couple of minutes had penetrated the mist.

He surfaced gently and looked about him. There was no sign of the patrol boat, but Kapo's voice boomed over him and he saw a dark outline in the mist.

'Five minutes, Chavasse, that's all.'

Orsini went under, swam forward and the keep of the patrol boat loomed out of the water. He worked his way along to the stern, opened

the pouches of his bandolier and squeezed hand-
fuls of the plastic explosive between the propeller and the hull. He was fast running out of time
and he pushed home the detonator, snapped the
end and turned away.

He drove forward, drawing upon his final
reserves of strength, feet churning the water
into a cauldron, and then the hull of the *Buona
Esperanza* seemed to be moving towards him
and he surfaced.

Chavasse leaned over the rail, Carlo beside
him, and they hauled him up on to the deck.
Somewhere, through the roaring in his ears, the
engine of the patrol boat rumbled into life.

When the explosion came, it echoed through
the rain and the screams of the dying mingled
with it. For a long time, debris continued to fall
into the water and then there was silence.

'Holy Mother,' Carlo said in awe. 'She must
have gone down like a stone.'

Orsini slowly unbuckled the straps of his
aqualung. 'How are things below?'

'All finished,' Carlo said. 'We can move out
whenever you're ready.'

Liri was kneeling beside Orsini, her cigarette

tin open. Chavasse dropped beside them, took one and bent his head to the match as it flared in her hands.

Orsini looked at him curiously. 'You're sorry about the girl?'

'Anything she got, she asked for.'

Chavasse turned and stood at the rail, aware of the tightness in his throat that couldn't be logically explained, remembering a gay and lovely girl he had met a thousand years ago at an Embassy party in Rome.

His head was aching and he was tired, damned tired, and she was calling his name over and over again. He closed his eyes briefly. When he opened them again, she came swimming out of the mist.

She had never looked lovelier, her dark hair spreading around her in the water, her eyes large in the white face. As she drifted in, she looked up at him appealingly.

'Help me, Paul! Help me!'

He looked down at her, remembering Matt Sorley, Dumont and all the others, good friends who had gone to a hard death because of her.

Orsini said, 'For God's sake, Paul. Are we animals?'

Chavasse turned and looked at him, and the Italian shrugged. 'If you won't help her, I will.'

He started forward and Chavasse shook his head. 'It's my affair, Guilio.'

He reached down and pulled Francesca aboard and she sprawled on the deck, coughing and gasping for breath. 'Thank you, Paul. You'll never regret it, I promise you.'

As she got to her feet, her hand swung up and he was aware of the blade, shining in the harsh morning light. He tried to turn, but he was too late and it caught him in the left side, slicing through flesh, bouncing from the rib cage.

He staggered back, recoiling as much from the cold hatred in her eyes as from the force of the blow, and Orsini cried out in dismay. Chavasse was aware of the knife raised high, gleaming in a ray of early-morning sunlight which at that moment pierced the mist, and then Liri's voice was lifted in a savage cry.

She moved forward, the heavy automatic Orsini had given her in both hands, and one heavy slug after another hammered Francesca back over the rail into the water.

Chavasse was aware of Orsini kneeling beside

him, of Liri throwing the gun far out to sea. He took a deep breath, fighting against the pain.

'I'm all right, Guilio. I'm fine. Just let's get the hell out of here.'

Orsini called to Carlo in the wheelhouse and, a moment later, the engines started and the *Buona Esperanza* moved forward slowly.

They passed through a great, widening circle of wreckage from the patrol boat and Liri, standing at the rail, called out sharply and pointed to the water.

Chavasse shook his head, holding his bunched shirt tightly against his side to stem the flow of blood, and tried to hear what was being said. There was a roaring in his ears and grey cobwebs seemed to be drifting slowly across his field of vision. He was aware that the engines had stopped, that Carlo had joined Liri, and then Orsini went over the rail.

Chavasse leaned over, suddenly faint, fighting hard against the pain. When he straightened, Carlo was lifting the statue of Our Lady of Scutari over the side.

Orsini brought it across and laid it reverently on the deck in front of Chavasse. 'Look, Paul, floating in the wreckage without a mark on her. A miracle.'

Carlo went back into the wheelhouse and started the engines, and Chavasse sat there looking at the statue. He was crying, which was a strange thing and couldn't be explained, and yet somehow the dark serene face smiling up at him seemed to ease his pain.

Above his head, a gull cried sharply, skimmed low over the sea and sped away through the misty rain like a departing spirit.

# MANHATTAN
1995

# 17

In the sitting room at the Trump Tower apartment, Chavasse finished reading the file, closed it and sat back.

Vinelli said, 'Another drink, Sir Paul?'

'Why not?' Chavasse said. 'Champagne will be fine.'

Vinelli went to the bar, opened a fresh bottle. Chavasse took the glass he offered and savoured it. 'Let's have him in, Aldo.'

'As you say.'

It was quiet, only that damned rain drumming on the windows, and then the door opened and Vinelli came in ahead of Volpe.

Chavasse said, 'A hell of a story. I mean, it was really heavy stuff for you to get hold of it.'

'Like I said, those clerks at the Public Records Office aren't the best paid people in the world.'

'So all you had to do was check up on Paul Chavasse and the Bureau, and it was all there?'

'Well, you were a star performer.'

'What can I say? I'd sound modest.'

'What you did – it was better than James Bond.'

'Oh, I don't know. Just another job for the Bureau. That's what it was all about. The name of the game.'

'You may think that, but I'm truly impressed.' Chavasse said, 'What now?'

'We go to see Don Tino.'

'At the Saddle Room at the Plaza Hotel.'

'Actually, things have changed. The Don would like to see you on the family yacht. It's moored off Pier Ten at the waterfront in Brooklyn. Full crew, great chef. Don Rossi is concerned with confidentiality here.'

Chavasse picked up his rain hat, slanted it across his head and reached for his Burberry. 'So, let's get on with it.'

Aldo got to the Burberry and held it for him. Chavasse said, 'Why, thank you, Aldo.'

Vinelli appeared to hesitate and Chavasse smiled. 'I'm really looking forward to this. I love boats, Aldo.'

\*     \*     \*

Aldo drove, Chavasse and Volpe sat together in the back of the Mercedes. The rain washed the streets clean of people as they moved towards Brooklyn. Chavasse took out the silver case, selected a cigarette and lit it. He blew out the smoke.

'Yes, fascinating, that file. Of course, Bureau files are on a fifty-year hold so it would be impossible for anyone to take a look. An offence under the Official Secrets Act.'

'Amazing what money can do. People are so corrupt.'

'Oh, I agree totally, but in this case, there's one thing wrong.'

'And what would that be?'

'Bureau Case Study 203, Field Agent Doctor Paul Chavasse. You said I probably wrote it myself. Actually, I did and there's only one problem.'

'Which is?'

'It's been expanded. For instance, the mention of the death of Enrico Noci. You remember that?'

237

'Sure. Drowned in a fishing net by you and your friends.'

'No, to be correct, executed.'

'Murdered.' There was a sudden violence in Volpe's voice.

'A point of view. He was what you'd call a bad guy, his actions responsible for the deaths of friends of mine. Having said that, the manner of his death wasn't the kind of thing to put in an official report, so under the Chief's instructions, I left it out.' He took out his case and selected another cigarette. 'So how did you find out?'

'From my aunt.' Volpe was shaking a little.

'And that would be Signora Volpe, if I recall your background, Don Tino's niece.'

'Great-niece by marriage.'

'You Italians take family so seriously. So what was Enrico Noci to you?'

'My father – the father you murdered. Something I learned from my aunt's knee.'

'I see.' Chavasse's voice was gentler.

'No, you still don't. Would you like to know who my mother was?'

Chavasse waited for the axe to fall. 'I believe I know.'

'Francesca Minetti.'

'Who, as I point out in my report, gutted me with a rather large knife.'

'Never mind that. Your friend, Liri Kupi, shot her to pieces, you admit that?'

'So?'

'All my life I dreamt of revenge, but these things take time, one step after another. Your friend Orsini married Liri Kupi. Do you remember what happened to them three years ago?'

Chavasse went cold. 'They were killed in a car accident outside Rome.'

'Exactly. Faulty breaks was the conclusion of the police.'

Chavasse managed to stay very calm. 'So, now it's my turn?'

'Precisely.'

'And what will the Don say?'

'That's not important. His time is long past.' He took a Walther PPK from his pocket, rammed it into Chavasse's side and searched him quickly.

'No weapon. That's interesting.'

'I thought I was amongst friends.'

'So did the Don. The biggest mistake of your

life,' Volpe said as the Mercedes moved along the waterfront.

The pier was deserted in the rain, the large motor yacht moored at the far end, a few deck lights on.

'Don't worry,' Volpe said. 'No crew on board tonight. Usually there's a watchman, but I gave him the night off too. Just you, me and Aldo.'

Vinelli pulled in by the gangway, slid from behind the wheel and opened the rear door. Chavasse got out.

'Does this suit you too, Aldo?'

Vinelli said, 'Heh, conversation I don't need. Just get moving.'

Volpe led the way, Chavasse behind him and Vinelli followed, gun in hand. They passed along the deck and came out in the stern, which was illuminated by dim lights. There was a half canopy, rain thudding against it, the railing of the upper deck above.

Volpe turned at the stern rail, put the Walther in his pocket, took out a pack of Marlboros and lit one. 'Over here, Aldo.'

Vinelli moved towards him holding a Browning against his right thigh. Chavasse said, 'So this is it?'

He removed his rain hat and ran his left hand over his face, his right clutching the butt of the .22 Colt in its clip.

'You know what they say in Sicily is true tonight. Paul Chavasse will sleep with the fishes. Just like my mother and father, you bastard.'

A soft voice said, 'Why Mario, what's all this?'

Don Tino Rossi moved out of the shadows of the port deck and confronted him, his face shadowed by a broad-brimmed hat, Malacca cane in one hand, a raincoat draped over his shoulders.

Volpe registered cold shock, started to stammer. 'Uncle, I . . .'

'Never expected to see you here, isn't that how it goes?' Rossi shook his head. 'Foolish boy. I've known all about your plans, every conversation with Aldo here. In my home, you're even wired for sound in the bathroom – on camera – everything. I treated you like a father and how do you repay me? By killing Sir Paul, who is important to all my plans.'

'He murdered my parents,' Volpe said desperately.

'I've known about that for years. So, it was all right for them to kill others, but not to be killed themselves? A point of view, but there is the matter of your intention to kill me. We can't have that, can we?'

'Aldo!' Volpe cried.

Vinelli's hand swept up clutching the Browning, and Chavasse fired through the rain hat and shot him between the eyes. Vinelli dropped the weapon, bounced against the rail and fell on his face.

'Damn you to hell!' Volpe cried, pulling the Walther from his pocket.

There was the muted crack of a silenced AK assault rifle from the rail above, the first shot spinning him round, the second shattering his spine. There was a step on the companionway and two men came down in reefer coats and knitted caps, both holding AKs.

Chavasse said, 'You left it a little late.'

'Oh, I had very confidence in you, my friend, and as I now know you like a brother, even your trick with the Colt in the rain hat was familiar to me.' Rossi shrugged. 'If you hadn't got Aldo, my man would have.'

'So what happens now?'

'My boys will dump them out there, victims of another Mafia feud.' He smiled bleakly. 'Does it give you a problem or can we still deal on London and Eastern Europe?'

'I don't see why not.'

'Good. Then be on your way. If you look over the rail you will notice a Lincoln has pulled in behind the Mercedes. Your bags have been packed and you are booked out of the Plaza.'

'To where?'

'My chauffeur will take you to Westhampton Airport on Long Island where I keep a private Gulfstream that will have you on your way to London before you know it. Goodbye, my friend. This never happened.'

'Oh, yes, it did,' Chavasse said, turned and walked away.


As the Gulfstream climbed out over the Atlantic, Chavasse sat in solitary splendour and asked the steward for a large Irish whiskey, which he drank quickly.

He thought of Enrico Noci, Francesca, Guilio Orsini and Mario Volpe, asleep with the fishes. A long time ago, most of it, a hell of a long time ago, but was anything ever finished? Truly finished? He closed his eyes and leaned back.

# Kill Your Friends

John Niven was born in Irvine, Ayrshire. He read English Literature at Glasgow University and spent the next ten years working in the UK music industry. He has written for *Word*, *Esquire*, *Arena* and *Q*. He is the author of six novels including *The Second Coming* and *Straight White Male*. He lives in Buckinghamshire.

Praise for *Kill Your Friends*

'I loved *Kill Your Friends*. Who didn't? Scorched earth humour at its finest.'

Douglas Coupland

'Hilarious … The bile-black cynicism of Niven's writing makes this the funniest book about music for ages.'

*Independent*

'Niven's insider knowledge, coupled with the kind of headlong, febrile prose that would have Hunter S. Thompson happily emptying both barrels into the sky, results in a novel that is cripplingly funny.'

*The Times*

'Wonderfully nasty … Extraordinarily vicious, deeply cynical and thoroughly depraved, but it's also bed-wettingly funny … *American Psycho* meets *Spinal Tap* … except more evil, more shocking and much, much funnier.'

*Scotsman*

'This timely and disturbingly funny novel nails the extravagances of the Britpop era perfectly.'

'A very funny, morbid, sensationalist read, and a total page-turner.'

'The novel is furiously, filthily funny, and, I imagine, tragically true.'

'Anyone working in or trying to get into the music industry should read this book.'

'One of the evilest, most vicious, despicable characters ever. I couldn't put it down.'

'Brilliant. It made me ill with laughter. The filthiest, blackest, most shocking, most hilarious debut novel I've read in years.'

'The fickle music industry is ripe for satire and here former record-label man Niven creates a compelling and hilarious portrait.'

# Kill Your Friends

JOHN NIVEN

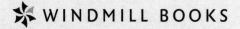
WINDMILL BOOKS

1 3 5 7 9 10 8 6 4 2

Windmill Books
20 Vauxhall Bridge Road
London SW1V 2SA

Windmill Books is part of the Penguin Random House group of companies
whose addresses can be found at global.penguinrandomhouse.com.

Penguin
Random House
UK

First published in Great Britain in 2008 by William Heinemann

First published in paperback in 2009 by Vintage
First published in paperback in 2014 by Windmill Books

This edition published in 2015 by Windmill Books

www.windmill-books.co.uk

A CIP catalogue record for this book
is available from the British Library.

ISBN 9780099592686

Printed and bound by CPI Group (UK) Ltd, Croydon, CR0 4YY

*To Helen*

'A&R (artist and repertoire): *The branch of the music industry concerned with finding and nurturing new talent.*'

I'm smoking and looking out of my office window while I listen to some guy, some manager, crapping away on the speakerphone. Five floors below me a group of black guys – probably some band – are lounging in the car park. The glass is bronzed, honey-coloured, and they can't see me. It's icy winter out there and their breath rises with the smoke from the spliff they're passing around, shrouding them in a pewter cloud. Beyond them, along the Thames at Hammersmith Bridge, is a gigantic poster of the Labour guy, Tony Blair. A slash has been ripped across his face where his eyes should have been and a pair of red eyes – hellish, demonic eyes – burn out instead.

Back down in the car park and one of the kids is actually leaning against my car now, his hands in his pockets and his back arched against the silver Saab as though it were the counter of his local KFC. I keep an eye on him as my mind wanders back to the voice coming out of the speakerphone. It's saying stuff like this:

3

'And EMI, Virgin and Chrysalis. Warner Chappell are doing the publishing and they've, well, I shouldn't be saying this yet, but . . .'

Don't tell me, they've got a major TV advert confirmed?

'They've got a major TV advert as good as confirmed.'

'Wow,' I say, sounding like nothing.

'But you know we like you,' the cretin says.

'Yeah, great, send it over.'

'It's a rough mix. Your ears only?'

'Sure.'

'Great. Bye, Steven.'

'Bye,' I think for a second. 'Mate.'

I hang up as Rebecca comes in. It's almost eleven, the crack of dawn around here. 'Good morning,' she says, placing a stack of mail on the coffee table, next to a pile of demo tapes of new bands – Cuff, Fling, Santa Cruz, Magic Drive, Montrose Avenue – which Darren, one of the scouts, has left for me to go through.

'Rebecca,' I say, not turning from the window.

'Mmmm?'

'Could you please interrupt whatever you're doing, run downstairs and tell security to get that fucking great *darkie* off of my car?'

She shrieks, pretending to be horrified, and joins me at the window.

'God, who on earth are that lot?' she says, chewing on a strand of her fine, long blonde hair.

'Fuck knows. Probably some imminent signing of Schneider's. The Jew is using the black man as muscle. Against us.'

'You're *terrible*!' She gives me a little elbow as she heads

4

for the door, pleased because I'm in a good mood. 'There's your post. Don't forget, you've got the business affairs meeting at twelve.' Rebecca is tall with full gobbler's lips. Great legs. Decent rack. But the face is beginning to go – little crow's feet creep around the eyes, grooves deepening at the corners of the mouth. She is a couple of years older than me – dangerously close to thirty – and terrifyingly single. She needs to be sorting this out and she knows it. Today she's wearing a tartan miniskirt a foot wide, trainers and a tight black T-shirt that has the word 'WHORE' picked out in little diamond studs. Like all the girls who work here – apart from Nicky, our Head of International, who is so ugly it actually makes me angry to have to be in the same room as her – Rebecca dresses just the right side of prostitution.

'Rebecca,' I say as she reaches for the door handle.

'Mmmm?' she says, turning round.

'The hotel?' I am off to Cannes next week for MIDEM and so far, depending on whom I choose to believe, either Rebecca or our worthless travel agents have failed to get me into a suitable hotel.

'I'm on it, Steven. Relax.' She turns to leave.

I believe her because Rebecca, like most girls, loves to organise things for you. She's never happier than when she's got the travel agent on one line, BA on another and copies of *The World's Great Hotels* and the Zagat and Harden's guides flattened out on the desk in front of her. It strikes me as very odd that she enjoys planning these trips for me even though she will take no part in them, will in no way benefit from them. I cannot comprehend planning something from which I will not gain anything. Something about the girl mind, I suppose – taking pleasure from knowing that the flight will arrive in time to make the restaurant reservation, that the hotel will be lavish and unexpected.

'And, Rebecca?' She turns back again, trying not to sigh. 'You look nice today.' (Carrot and stick.)

'Thank you,' she replies, smiling coyly. Well, as coyly as a girl who probably sucked a minimum of thirty cocks last year is capable of smiling. 'So do you.'

She's not wrong. I've just spent a month on holiday – Thailand–Vietnam–Australia – and I'm tanned to the fucking eyeballs. I'm wearing a black cashmere V-neck sweater, black jeans and black suede loafers, all of which are box-fresh.

She leaves and I flip through my post, mostly waxy Jiffy bags containing demo tapes, feeling the usual reflexive anger at the attempts at spelling my name – there's 'Stalefox', 'Stellfax' and one mongoloid has even gone for 'Stellarfix'. It's Stelfox. Steven Stelfox – before settling down with the new issue of *Music Week*. Some guy who works there has died. Heart attack at thirty-two. Nasty. Very fucking nasty.

As I turn the pages I feel the floor shake, concentric rings ripple in the black coffee, and I look up in time to see Waters come lumbering past the glass wall that separates my office from the rest of the floor. He's really something, Waters. Six two, six three, about eighteen stone. He's clutching a piece of paper and trying to look purposeful in a ludicrous attempt to mask a mammoth hangover. He's red-faced and pouch-eyed, with blips of sweat dotting his forehead. (Doing anything, lifting a cassette, dialling a telephone number, causes Waters to break into a filthy rapist-sweat.) He wearily flashes me a devil sign, extending the pinkie and forefinger of his giant left paw. He is trailing his rat-dog, a little Jack Russell, behind him. He thinks bringing the fucking thing into the office makes him eccentric and interesting. It makes him look like a cunt. Like the brontosaurus, his colossal frame is powered by a brain the size of a grape, and this grape-brain itself, none too dynamic to begin with, has been further buffoonerised by years of chronic chang abuse. I nod a needlessly business-like hello, just to rub his lateness in, and pick up the TV remote.

I watch VH1 for a bit – Blur, Radiohead, Oasis and the Brand New Heavies – and am about to turn it off when there's a little preview of the upcoming Brit Awards. We get Dodgy, the Chemical Brothers, the Prodigy, Longpigs, Mansun. I light another cigarette and watch as Ellie Crush is interviewed. 'Yeah,' she says, 'I know there's people out there that fink a woman can't do all the stuff I'm doing. That she's a puppet? Yeah? But, y'know, I'm here, writing the lyrics and checking on the arrangements and doing all of that stuff. Yeah? My songs come from in *here*.' She flattens a hand sincerely across her heart.

Crush, nominated for Best Newcomer, is a twenty-one-year-old east Londoner who was signed by Parker-Hall over at EMI. Her critically lauded debut LP was released last spring and charted at no. 63. And, mercifully, it looked like that was that. Game Over. See you later, Sooty. Then, gradually, horribly, it started to sell. Word of mouth. Suddenly they got a single playlisted at Radio 1 and the album went gold. I do not want to contemplate what might happen to the fucking thing, what might happen to Parker-

Hall, if Crush wins Best Newcomer. I make a note on my 'to do' list to put a matey call in to the fucker.

'Cause that's what it's all about,' Crush says to the interviewer, *'integritty.* Yeah?' I turn the sound down as she goes on to discuss gun control or something.

It's interesting, I remember being at her signing party a year ago when someone used the phrase 'artistic integrity' in her presence. Her brow knotted and she asked her manager – not rhetorically – 'Wot's "integritty"?' I mean, here is a girl who can barely read. A girl who, just twelve scant months ago, would have sucked the curdled sweat from a tramp's dimpled nutbag to obtain a record deal, and yet here she is talking about 'integrity' and Christ knows what other nonsense. When they sell no records, it's a nightmare. When they sell lots of records – it's a whole other nightmare. Because then these fools, these one-GCSE merchants, these casualties with half a fucking thought to rub together, they suddenly think that the fact that a few hundred thousand of the Great British Public (yeah, those *animals*) enjoy their ditties and respond on some primitive level to their doggerel, means that they have something of value to say about anything from the FTSE to the Middle East peace process. So, the next time you see some Mercury Music Prize/Brit Award/Grammy-nominated diva up there giving it the whole 'I am a strong independent woman with interesting ideas' bit, remember this – it is only because of the tiniest quirk of fate, a deranged quiver of serendipity, the most unlikely of miracles, that her big speeches are not climaxing with the words: 'I'm sorry, sir, this checkout is closing,' or 'Anal is an extra twenty quid, mate.'

There is talk of the Ellie Crush record starting to take off in America. Were this to happen it is conceivable it could sell millions of copies rather than the few hundred thousand it takes to constitute a reasonably big record over here. I know Parker-Hall has two points on the record because I got his lawyer drunk at a Christmas party. If the record properly took off in America Parker-Hall might well become a millionaire. He's twenty-five. Two years younger than me. Admitting the possibility of his success into my head makes me reel back. I feel faint. Sick. I take my mind off the subject by smoking another cigarette and doing some expenses, noticing with some surprise that I managed to spend nearly two thousand pounds on 'entertainment' last December.

Actually, it's not strictly true that my mind is *on* the subject, or any subject, for very long. Here's the deal with the inside of my head: picture a giant bank of screens, dozens of them, reaching high into the air, like you see at NASA, at Mission Control. At any given time many of them are simply showing hardcore pornography: banks and banks of close-ups – some so close they are pixellated to the point of image-degradation – showing troublingly large cocks punching in and out of cunts, lurid dildos violating angry rectums, cocks gliding stiff and imperious between lubed breasts. Other screens show financial stuff: graphs of London house prices, City traders screaming in their striped blazers, pie charts of record-industry market shares, bricks of cash being stacked up, balance sheets, red figures, black figures, recouped acts, unrecouped acts. A few screens show bands and singers: acts I've signed in the past, new acts we're thinking about signing, successful acts I wanted to sign and didn't (the most haunting images). A small row of distant monitors, tucked away high up in a dusty corner, randomly shows footage of colleagues and rivals being baroquely tortured.

There are guys in my head too. The technicians in their short-sleeved shirts, with the pens in the breast pocket and the little headsets on and their styrofoam cups of coffee. They sit slack-jawed in front of the monitors. They aren't happy about any of this. They know it's not good. But they can't seem to do anything about it. They run around and shout at each other. They gather anxiously around blinking computers. They shake their heads over crazily spooling printouts and mutter, '*This can't be right, goddammit*,' but the monitors just go on showing what they show.

That's what it feels like in there – like there's a Mission going on, but there's no Control.

Before I go down for the meeting I pick up my paperback copy of *Unleash Your Monster*, by the American self-help guru Dr David S. Hauptman, and open it at random: '*In every age men are born who, in their hearts, in the black of their blood, are warriors. But, for most of us, there are no longer wars to fight. What must they do, these men?*'

As I leave my office I can hear the sound of celebration – laughter and corks – coming down the hallway from the accounts department. 'What are those clowns so fucking happy about?' I ask Rebecca.

'Oh, Rick's just found out he's going to be a dad,' she says cheerfully, and I realise that she's genuinely happy on his behalf.

This astonishes me on two counts: 1) actual happiness at someone else's good fortune in which you have no personal stake, and 2) why is this guy celebrating the fact that he has terminated his life? You might as well run out of the doctor's surgery screeching with joy as you wave your positive cancer test around. The notion of children makes me ill. The thought of having one . . . when you see those guys in the supermarket, wheeling the trolley around while their brats whine and wheedle and some blundering sow questions every little thing they take off the shelves. I mean, just the fucking idea of it, the very word: *family*. Whenever I see it, on travel brochures, on house schedules ( *family holiday, family room*), I feel sick.

Also I'm thinking, Rick? Who the fuck is Rick from accounts?

So here's what I do. I listen to music – singers, bands, songwriters – and decide which ones stand a good chance of commercial success. I then arrange for them to be recorded in a sympathetic manner and we, the record company, sell them to you, the general public. Sound easy? Get fucked – you wouldn't last ten minutes.

Now, I don't have a perfect track record. No one does. But I'm pretty fucking good. On average I only get it wrong maybe eight or nine times out of ten. That is to say, if you played me ten pieces of unsigned music I might instantly dismiss three or four acts that might go on to enjoy enormous success. I have thrown the demo tapes of bands that are now megastars, bands whose records you own, across the room with tears of laughter running down my face. I have berated and insulted subordinates for having the temerity to play me tracks that have subsequently sold in their millions.

It's very likely that I'll applaud three or four tracks that will turn out to be absolute, grade-A, Bernard Matthews turkeys. We, my label, have spent millions, literally millions, of pounds signing and developing music that, as it turned out, no sane person wanted to hear.

Which perhaps begs the question, what kind of music do I like? Incredibly, you really do get asked this from time to time. Usually by some new kid, some earnest junior product manager who has tagged along to lunch or by a member of some band you're trying to sign. The new kid will be quickly dismissed with a curt 'fuck off' and the guy from the band you're trying to sign will get a sincerely delivered litany of seminal bands and songwriters; 'Yeah,' you intone sombrely, 'Dylan, Joni Mitchell, the Clash, Husker Du, the Band, Lennon.' (Delete as applicable to the musical tastes of the retard you're talking to.) What kind of music do I like? Asking a major label A&R manager this question is like asking an arbitrageur what kind of commodities he likes. Or saying to an investment banker, 'Hey, what's your favourite currency?' I have very wide musical tastes. 'Eclectic', as spastic musicians say when they're trying to sound clever in interviews. I don't care which genre something comes from – rock, trance, hip hop, Bulgarian fucking heavy metal – *as long as it's profitable*.

Finally, though, out of those ten tracks, I'd probably get at least one right. As long as I manage to do that every couple of years, then I'm doing incredibly well. I'm ahead of the curve. I mean, there are guys who *never* get it right.

Here's the important thing to say about meetings – nothing important ever got decided in a meeting. The place to get your own way is over lunch, in someone's office, in the corridor, over drinks, dinner, *anywhere* but in a fucking meeting. What meetings are very good for, however, is stitching people up – undermining, belittling and humiliating them.

This is particularly the case in gatherings where there are representatives present from several different departments. In the Business Affairs meeting I am now tooling into there are people from Legal (Trellick), Accounting (Leader-kramer), A&R (myself, Hastings and Waters, who are my colleagues, my fellow A&R managers, and Schneider, Head of A&R and our immediate boss) and International (Nicky). At the head of the curving glass-topped table sits Derek Sommers, the Managing Director. At forty-five Derek is, by some distance, the oldest person in the room. Katy, Trellick's PA, takes the minutes.

A useful trick in meetings like this is to try and have a little nugget or two about everyone else's business filed away. Something that they should have known, or that they haven't done that they said they'd do. You then slip your carefully sharpened nugget in at the correct moment – usually in the form of an innocent question or observation – and retire to a safe distance. Business Affairs is an especially good forum for this kind of backstabbing because the stakes are high. Every A&R man has his roster graphically analysed; how much you've spent on this act, how many records they've sold, what's still to be spent, how much more can we sell. There's nowhere to hide because it's like looking at a bank statement; there's credit or debit. And, believe me, we don't spend too long talking about the credits.

'Paul, the Rage LP?' Trellick says, turning to Schneider and sweeping a raft of thick blond hair back off his forehead. James Trellick is a generic toff, the end product of a lineage of fine dining and arse-fucking the poor that stretches back to the Domesday Book. He's tall and pointlessly handsome with the questing, jutting cleft chin that seems to be standard issue to his class. But it's the voice that really does it; an oak-and-gilt Etonian baritone, the sound of someone brought up to run the empire.

'Nearly done,' Schneider says, leaning back, eating a green apple. 'He wants to have a playback for everyone in a couple of weeks.' Schneider is like a weedier, discount, Jewish version of Trellick; similar clothes not filled out so well, a more minor public school, his voice a thinner, reedier take on Trellick's fruity rumble. Today his dark hair is slicked back and he has recently taken to wearing glasses, black-framed designer jobs the clown undoubtedly thinks make him look more intelligent. He will take them off and chew thoughtfully on them during meetings. Rodent-like, Schneider has a victim's face. The happenstances of time and geography surrounding his birth have provided him with opportunity, but there's no getting around it – if Schneider had been born a few decades earlier and a few hundred miles east of here, he'd have toppled off the train, blinking into the sun at Birkenau or Belsen, to find the guards falling over each other to get stuck into him. He nibbles on his apple and talks on, about release dates and lead times. He appears relaxed. He's not.

Truth be told, Schneider has signed one too many turkeys on the bounce and his position as Head of A&R is increasingly shaky. He signed 'drum'n'bass superstar' Rage two years ago and the debut album *Phosphor-essence* (fuck me) was the dance and style press sensation of last year, going gold and picking up a Mercury nomination along the way. However, a gold record means fuck all when you follow it up by dropping two million quid on signing four absolute donkeys in a row. You need platinum sales to insulate yourself from that kind of failure. Rage's new record is, Schneider hopes, his big Get Out of Jail Free card. Ominously, though, Rage has been working on the record in total isolation in a residential studio for the last four months and we haven't heard a note yet. Rumour has it (and rumour is always right, however briefly) that he is *battering* the chang. Grams and grams every day. As I brought the Rage deal in when I was a scout I'm still involved in the project. But at a safe enough distance, because Rage, I suspect, is a one-trick pony. A talent vacuum. He's also the nastiest piece of work you could imagine.

'And do we have a final tour support budget yet?' Derek asks.

'Just about,' Schneider says, tossing his apple core into the bin, 'Steven and I are having lunch with him and Fisher next week, over at MIDEM, to finalise everything.' (Schneider, in his turn, is trying to keep me close to the project, just in case the whole thing goes properly tits up and he suddenly needs an Oswald.)

'Good, good, make sure and cc me on the budget as soon as you have it please,' says Trellick, as he turns to face Rob Hastings now.

Hastings is thin as a guitar string and as nervy as a freshly released paedophile. His rabbit eyes are already shooting around the room – trying to work out where the next attack might be coming from – while his bucky little rabbit teeth wrap themselves around one of the filthy roll-ups he always seems to be smoking. He does not dress like the rest of us either; no black cashmere V-necks, no chisel-toed Prada or Kurt Geiger for Hastings. He wears untucked flannel shirts with shredded elbows, decrepit jeans and Dr Martens. I admit it, the guy is something of a puzzle to me. Someone told me that Rob told them he can comfortably live on a hundred quid a week. All he does is the odd pint, a curry here and there and the occasional lump of hash. He drives a VW. *He rolls his own cigarettes.* (Why isn't the dribbling megamongol spending his entire salary – and more – every single weekend? Why isn't he doing mountains of bugle and whores? Where are the five-star holidays and the Montecristos? Why isn't he dropping stacks of dough in Paul Smith and Armani? He earns enough. I mean, what the fuck is going on here?) He's a genuinely nice guy who has good taste in music and treats people with dignity and respect and the closest he ever comes to a hit record is when he has a wander round HMV on a Saturday. That's right, he's a fucking loser and how he ever got into A&R is completely beyond me. On one level I simply do not care if Rob lives or dies, but, on another, there have been times when I've been very glad he's here because he's made me look good. I could comfortably be lobotomised and still do my job better than Rob Hastings. All Trellick and Derek see, however, is the charcoal strip of the bottom line, which directly affects their bonuses, and consequently either of them would gladly have Rob fired. Fired? They'd have him fucking killed if they could. 'Raawb,' Trellick drawls, 'can you give us an update on the Sound Collective, please?'

There's lip-biting as Rob hauls himself upright in his chair for his weekly beating on this subject.

The Sound Collective – a loose affiliation of DJs, rappers, producers and MCs from Southend – were signed by Rob about eighteen months ago on the back of a couple of gushing articles in the dance and style press and a few late-night Radio 1 plays. Rob has been 'developing' them since then and we are no closer to releasing a record now than we were when we signed them. In fact, my mother is probably closer to releasing her debut album than the Sound Collective, who believe that our role is to shovel mountains of cash into their account and keep our fucking white mouths shut. We have now spent about four hundred grand and haven't heard a bar of music.

Rob rolls a cigarette between his fingers and goes for nonchalance, 'Update? Yeah, sure. Uh, I went down there last week. It's, ah, it's really coming together.'

Trellick: 'Aha. Good. Could you be little more specific?'

'Man, you wouldn't believe how the studio's coming together. They've painted the live room a sort of sky blue.' People look at him. I wonder if he's stoned.

'Good. Good,' says Trellick, losing patience. 'Do we have any music yet?'

'Not yet, no. The thing is MaxMan, their rapper, he had to go back to Trinidad to . . .' He blathers on about what these shiftless spear-chuckers have been up to with our money. Some people frequently dig their own graves in these meetings. Rob is building himself a fucking mauso-leum. Derek is colouring, turning from mauve to vermilion to fluorescent, the colour of his shirt.

Derek, in his turn, dresses like what he is: a wealthy, psychotic, tasteless, middle-aged queer. Grotesquely over-weight, he favours billowing shirts by Versace and Ralph Lauren – in fuchsia pink, emerald green, canary yellow and candy-striped combinations of all three – which are worn in a doomed attempt to disguise his enormous girth. His black hair and little beard are flecked with silver, the hair thinning on top now while remaining in a luxuriant thatch around the sides. His normal facial expression, the one he uses when he's 'off', when he isn't trying to present a certain persona, is really something: the hooded eyes rotate slowly, scanning, evaluating. The faintest flicker of a smile, or a sneer, trembles like an electrical current across his thin top lip while, above it, the crimson nostrils – the colour a painful reminder of the hellish quantities of cocaine and poppers he undoubtedly forced up there the night before – rhythmically flare gently or rapidly, according to his mood. I mean, he looks like fucking Caligula or something, mad and ravaged, cold and violent.

Rob is still going. 'And Massive Attack, Goldie and James Lavelle are all keen too. But the outboard equipment wasn't really up to scratch so we to had to replace most of it and –'

'Yes, Rob, I understand.' Trellick raises a hand to silence him. 'However, we're now,' he consults his notes, 'four hundred and seventy-eight thousand pounds in the hole on this act and we're no closer to having –'

'Look, James man, I know the situation is, y'know, frus-trating,' says Rob, trying to be assertive, 'but the, the creative process, man. Sometimes you can't, y'know, rush it.'

There's collective astonishment at this nonsense. I inter-rupt, directing my comments at Trellick.

'Yeah, James, hang on, it's not like nothing's happening. There's definitely a vibe for the band out there –' I manage to keep a straight face. Rob, the total cuntfuck, is nodding away, thinking I've come to his defence – 'and Rob's doing some good stuff to support it. I mean, those T-shirts look fantastic.'

Derek's head snaps up – a starving attack dog shown sirloin – 'T-shirts? What fucking T-shirts?'

Jackpot. In a misguided fit of craziness (and, I suspect, under extreme pressure from our coloured friends down in Southend) Rob had got a few Sound Collective T-shirts made up. Just a few, but spending company money on having T-shirts made for a band who are half a million quid unrecouped and who have yet to release a record is a bit like taking a full-page ad out in the *Sun* to announce yourself as winner of the lottery before you've even bought the ticket. Rob had quietly and proudly shown me one of the shirts a few days ago and I was pretty sure Derek had no idea.

Rob swallows. 'Yeah. I had a couple of T-shirts m—'

'YOU'RE MAKING FUCKING T-SHIRTS FOR A FUCKING ACT THAT DON'T EVEN HAVE A FUCKING RECORD OUT AND ARE HALF A MILLION FUCKING POUNDS IN DEBT TO US! *ARE YOU OUT OF YOUR FUCKING MIND?*' Derek's fury is so total and instant that, for a second, I think little Katy is going to burst into tears.

'But Derek, I thought if –'

'I DON'T GIVE A FUCK WHAT YOU THOUGHT! IF WE DON'T HAVE A FUCKING SINGLE FROM THIS BAND BY THE END OF THE MONTH WE'RE PULLING THE FUCKING PLUG! DO YOU UNDERSTAND?'

'But –' Rob is going down, drowning.

'*DO YOU FUCKING UN-DER-STAND?*' Derek pounds his fist on the table six times, with 'understand' getting three of them. Total silence. People admire the oatmeal carpet. Draw on their notes.

Derek is generally in a pretty bad mood. I don't know, maybe the experience of spending his entire adult life having men spray their burning jism over his face and back, of hearing them growl as they pump another radioactive load deep into his mouth or rectum, has soured him on life. I mean, it'd definitely fuck me off, being used as a human toilet for a quarter of a century.

In fact, this whole business of pumping and groaning and roaring and whatnot is really old news for hardcore queens like Derek. For ultra dark-side faggots in the nineties the idea of having some moustachioed arse-demon clad head to cock in studs and leather pummel away at you until your Gary looks like something out of a medical textbook has become a bit quaint. A Norman Rockwell painting. The bender equivalent of a married couple's Friday night, lights out, sheets over you, missionary position fumble. A few months back one of the kids from the marketing department had been up all night clubbing and found himself drinking in some hardcore after-hours place in the East End, one of those real HIV dens where the proper, certifiable queers round off their evenings. He wandered through a salty fug of amyl nitrate and GHB into a dimly lit back room where he bumped into Derek – chained to a wall, half naked and bleeding, with a couple of muscular Bethnal Green irons giving him a good beating.

Now, they say that an organisation's value systems, its

core beliefs, are shaped from the top down. Given that its Managing Director's idea of a reasonable evening's entertainment involves paying a couple of rent boys to kick the living shit out of him, it seems logical enough that greed, viciousness, duplicity, exploitation, hedonism and aggression feature prominently among the values our company encourages and rewards.

'Yes,' Rob finally whispers.

I mouth 'sorry' at him. He nods as if to say 'not your fault' and goes back to staring at the table, tears in his eyes. I nearly wet myself. Nicky shoots me a look. She is much smarter than Rob and may well have understood where my 'help' was coming from. I return her glare pleasantly, looking at her properly for the first time and noticing that today, as part of an ongoing and doomed attempt to disguise her unimaginable bulk – which the A&R department sweepstake variously puts at between sixteen and twenty stone – she is wearing some sort of muumuu, or sack, or kaftan. On some days she sports the sort of Lycra leggings you only ever see incredibly fat boilers wearing, the kind which make their thighs look like two immense black puddings. Her mouth is just a tiny little hole – a Polo mint lost in the enormous fleshy pudding of her face. The face itself is framed by lank greasy black hair and seared by angry clusters of spots, by deep ravines of acne. Most beasts of Nicky's stripe get thrown the odd break – the big tits, say, or the good complexion, or nice hair or something. Nicky got fucked out of the lot. Sometimes, when she's talking, I'll steal a glance at Trellick or Schneider as they listen to her, their expressions saying the same thing: how the fuck do you have the nerve to leave the house and show your face among decent society? Obviously Nicky was hired directly by Derek. As she has tits and a cunt she is completely invisible to the demented homo. Nicky is un-doable. You could not do her. She could not be done. If, by some chemical derangement, some alchemy of ketamine and smack, you woke up in bed to find Nicky next to you, you'd have two options: emigration or suicide. A plane ticket or an exhaust pipe.

'OK, boys and girls, moving on then,' Trellick announces, rapping his notes on the table, 'unsigned bands.' Waters starts yabbering on about some indie groups he's been to see; Ultrasound, Tampasm, Grouch, Angelica, Disco Pistol.

Later, as we leave the meeting and file down the corridor, Trellick sidles up to me and whispers, 'What is the meaning of life?' 'To drive your enemies before you and hear the lamentations of their women,' I reply automatically as, ahead of us, Hastings scuttles down the stairs.

*'The object is to find a winner. The process makes you mean because you get frustrated.'*

Simon Cowell

A couple of words for all you hopefuls out there in unsigned bands: Fuck. Off. Seriously, your parents are right. You may as well spend your guitar-string money on lottery tickets – your chances will be much the same. We receive upwards of three hundred unsolicited demo tapes every week. There are five other labels within our corporate group, all receiving about the same volume. That's fifteen hundred demos a week. There are six other corporate groups, EMI, Universal, Warner Bros, Polygram, BMG and Sony, most with several labels within them, all receiving at least the same amount as us, and probably a little more. That's over ten thousand little packages of hopes and dreams arriving every week. (And arrive is often all they do – the vast majority of these packages are never opened. They just lie in boxes and sacks around the A&R floor, where they seem to breed and multiply, spilling over the carpets and taking up sofa space until Tom, our work experience, has to lug sacks of them down to the incinerator where your hopes and dreams are – rightly – burned in the fires of hell.)

Occasionally, if it's a rainy afternoon and we're really bored and want something to do, a few of the A&R staff will gather in someone's office, roll ourselves a couple of thick spliffs, uncork a bottle of red, and go through one of the sacks marked 'UNSOLICITED DEMOS'. These sessions usually end with two or three of us on our hands and knees on the floor howling, gasping for breath, ribs and facial muscles aching.

To this ten thousand we should add (conservatively) another couple of thousand to cover the demos received by all the independent labels. That makes roughly twelve thousand demos a week received by the whole industry – well over half a million a year. In any given year my company will maybe sign something like ten to fifteen acts. The whole UK industry probably signs – at most – a couple of hundred artists every year. Out of these two hundred, in a very good year, you might have twenty or so who break through to some degree, who get their records on the radio, their pictures in the music press, and who fill decent-sized venues. Out of this twenty maybe half will eventually recoup the money invested in them. That's right – ten acts out of over half a million hopefuls will make themselves some real money. And yet a lot of aspiring musicians really believe that getting signed means they've made it, that the physical act of signing a recording contract means they're on the way to fame, riches and drinking Bono's Cristal at the Grammys.

Here's what's more likely to happen: on the back of a spurious 'buzz' from the music press, a few packed gigs in tiny clubs and a couple of late-night radio plays, some idiot like Rob Hastings offers you a record deal for, ooh, let's say, a hundred grand. Great! (You now owe us 100K.) You pack your job in *Quadrophenia*-style and take your parents out to the local Chinese for a slap-up feed where you tell them you'll 'never work again'. You leave Bolton (or wherever) and get off the train at Euston thinking to yourself, 'I am the fucking king.'

You're keen to get cracking on that debut album. However, the odds are that it will take Rob – or some cretin like him – months to make up his mind about a producer. He will then, inevitably, choose the wrong one. This guy will spend two or three months destroying what little talent you had to begin with and you're back to square one. Not content with getting the wrong producer the first time, Rob will pick the wrong guy a couple more times. By the time you've gone through this process three times it's a year down the line, the record still isn't finished, and your initial recording budget has tripled to about three hundred grand. (You now owe us 400K.)

By the time we finally get a single released your great mates over at press and radio could no longer give a good drop of spunk if you're dead or alive. They liked you a year ago. They've got new bands to play with now. In fact, I'll go you one further – the music press *hates* you now. You've gone from being the next Sex Pistols to the last Black Lace in twelve short months. So you get zero airplay and just a tiny smattering of reviews in the likes of the *Aberdeenshire Gazette* and the *North Wales Chronicle* (both of whom love the record; unfortunately no one who reads these papers is under sixty-five or lives within a hundred miles of a chart return shop).

In an attempt to rebuild your profile we send you out

on the road. But you've got a record company behind you now. Why would you travel in a Transit van like in the old days? So you get a fucking great tour bus the size of an aircraft carrier, six totally superfluous roadies, an outlandish catering company run by a pair of titless Notting Hill dykes and a light show with the equivalent power of the sun. Of course, you're still selling zero records and playing tiny venues so you're only getting paid about five hundred quid per show. However, the roadies/aircraft carrier/titless dyke/sun combo is costing something like five grand *a fucking day*. But – hey – we still believe in the band, man, so we underwrite the shortfall. You play twenty dates losing thousands every night, bringing your debt to us up to something like half a million quid. Oh, and by the way, your hundred-grand advance is now long gone. Where did it go? Well, let's see: tax, 20 per cent to your manager, and huge legal fees (your lawyer – some utter lowlife like Trellick – spent a lot of time arguing about pointless clauses in order to line his own pockets) leaves maybe twenty grand. You pay yourselves the princely salary of two hundred quid a week each. Alas, thanks to hanging out with animals like me and Waters, you all now have chronic chang habits, so this doesn't go far. Assuming there are four of you in the band, this means a monthly wage bill of about three grand. You're broke in a year. So we start advancing you extra money to cover the wages. A few months of this and you soon rack up another twenty Gs.

Finally we release your debut album. The *NME* expends a hundred words – and no photo – to call it 'undiluted piss'. We optimistically press five thousand copies. We sell seven hundred in the first week and two hundred in the second. Then, well, that's it. No more. Not another copy troubles a chart return machine anywhere in the world. Ever. Thanks to a combination of your mediocrity and our gross incompetence your debut LP – the crystallisation of all the energy, insight and ambition of your young life – has sold nine hundred copies. With retail discounts you have generated maybe four thousand pounds' worth of income. You are finished. Game fucking over. You are twenty-two years old and six hundred thousand pounds in debt to us – a bunch of subhuman demons who were your best friends a year ago but who would now gladly slit your throat and dance in your blood if we thought it would help us claw back a penny of your debt.

But sadly that's not an option. We take the loss on the chin, chalk it down as a write-off, and you get the coach back up to Bolton where you lie around your parents' house drinking lager and crying for a few weeks until you go crawling back to your old job painting houses, stacking shelves, frying chips or whatever the fuck you used to do up there. Until the day you die – probably at age fifty-five through a combination of abysmal Northern lung cancer and thirty-odd years of back-breaking work – you will bore your friends rigid with stories about your twelve months on top of the world, snorting lines in the toilets of London nightclubs and getting your dick sucked by some skanky monster on a tour bus parked behind Northampton Roadmenders. The time you spent with us playing at being pop stars will probably be the high-water mark of your entire life. Someone like me will probably be somewhere among your dying thoughts.

So, y'know, just don't do it. Go and become an accountant, or an IT guy or something. *Get a fucking job, you stupid cunt.*

*'I love sports because I'm a total competitor. If we're playing tennis and you're winning, I'm going to get my cock out and piss on the goddam net.'*

Don Simpson

'Ladieez an gennelmen, we are now beginning our descent into Nice. Please return to your seats and fasten . . .'

She goes on. I look out of the window as the plane continues to bank left, falling out of the sky towards the runway that juts out into the Mediterranean. Dusk is hitting the sky over to our right, the sky above Africa, and turning it incredible colours – purple and gold and orange and red. We yawn and quickly turn back to our copies of *Loaded, NME* and *Music Week*. 'Ze local time is now five twenty pee em.'

'All righty!' says Trellick in the seat next to me. 'The cocktail hour!'

MIDEM. Sometime in the middle of the swinging sixties a couple of Frog fruits decided it would be cool to have a little convention in the South of France for the music industry. Thirty years on, last week of every January, something like ten thousand freeloading madmen descend on Cannes from all corners of the globe and go crackers.

Champagne is drunk, lobsters are chomped, coke is honked and expense accounts are wildly abused in a week-long orgy of networking and deal-making. The Palais des Festivals on the Croisette houses hundreds of stalls where record labels, publishers, CD manufacturers and merchandising companies – everything central and peripheral to the music business – hawk their wares and ply their trades.

The plane is *rammed* with industry. Had this flight gone down, London's cocaine, prostitution and private members' club industries would have been devastated.

With a comic, a cartoon-strip 'EEEK!' the wheels rubberise the tarmac and we're already popping buckles and reaching for bags. (Hand baggage only for us on these trips. If you were to check a piece of luggage in our company you might as well be caught on your hands and knees in the bathroom blowing one of the stewards.) The major-label guys favour luggage by Mulberry and Prada while the indie boys all have record bags with their label logos stitched or transferred on them: Soma, Talking Loud, Nova Mute, JDJ, Rising High, Moonshine and lots more. These guys will also have checked hulking great boxes of records, the promos and white labels they'll be hawking around the stalls for the next few days as they desperately try to license some piece of shit track for a couple of hundred quid to help cover the cost of the trip. This is how the indie boys do business. Those of us higher up the food chain will take meetings in the chill, air-conditioned suites of the big hotels.

I look around as my fellow A&R men – all smudged with champagne, spangled with vodka tonics – begin braying at each other. This is the sharp end of the record industry. The front line. We're the SAS. Fucking Delta Force. Our jobs involve making fast decisions with hundreds of thousands, often millions, of pounds at stake. These decisions are often predicated on no more than a hunch or a rumour and are often made under the influence of drugs, alcohol, peer-group pressure and fear.

The fear is constant because, and you must understand this, *no one really has a clue what they are doing*. There is no training programme. No manual. To say that the job (the art of predicting why husky-female-singer number 3 will sell more records than numbers 1, 2 and 4 through to 99, or why loutish-group-of-youths-with-guitars C will, six to twelve months from now, bewitch the nation's youth to a greater extent than groups A, F, P or Z) is an inexact science is like saying that Fred West could probably have been a better father. Here's what we, the A&R community, put our money on last year. This is what we reckon you're going to be buying and enjoying in the coming year or so: the Beekeepers, Luna, Feline, Proper, Lower, Arnold, the Dub Pistols, the Hybirds, the Aloof, Spookey Ruben, Sally Burgess, Ragga & the Jack Magic Orchestra, Genaside II, Hardbody, Finley Quaye, Jocasta, Old Man Stone, Ajax Disco Spanner, Gus Gus, Vitro, Travis, Agnes, Monkey, Tiger, Don, the Nicotines, Mantaray, Laguna Meth, Symposium, Deadstar, Foil, Peach, Manbreak, Ether, Charlotte Kelly, My Life Story, Robbie Williams, Aquasky, Code Red, the Driven, Dust Junkies, Silversun, Alistair Tennent, Kenickie, 1st Class, Ryan Molloy, North & South, Olive, Blue Amazon, Nash, Kelly Lorena, Belvedere Kane, Horace Andy, Ariel, Craig Armstrong, Kavana, Lilacs, One Inch Punch, Kings of Infinite Space, Mandalay, the Stereophonics, Akin, Amar, DJ Pulse, Snug, Eboman, M Beat, Slipmatt.

Go on then, *you* pick the change out of that lot. How many of those chancing spunkers will be kicking back in their country pile with a shelf full of Brits and Grammys in ten years? No one knows what they are doing and everyone has to live with the knowledge that they will – one day – be fired.

Right now you can hear fear rattling around the taxiing aircraft in her socially acceptable disguise: bravado.

'Oi! Oi! Oi!' someone shouts.

'Stelfox! You queer loser fool!' shouts another.

'We're larging it, mate!'

'Bollocks, you cunt!'

'Hello, tolers!'

It is the bravado of soldiers in a landing craft about to crunch onto a hostile shore. The few civilians on the plane – mostly rich Frogs with permatanned alligator skin – sigh and shake their heads. Needless to say, the last two hours have not been pleasant for them.

'What time we got this meeting, Steven?' Darren asks me.

'Nine.'

'Coolio.' Darren has been quiet on the flight, nervous. It's his first MIDEM. When he started here as an A&R scout a little less than two years ago, straight from running his own indie fanzine (called something like *Big Growling Pop Thing!*), he actually looked puppyish. He'd never taken cocaine in his life. Wide-eyed, he'd scamper from office to office with his stack of 7 singles and demos, a constant ball of teenage enthusiasm. Well, we soon knocked that out of him. He looks like fucking Methuselah now: his skin dry and flaking; his eyes bloodshot and sunken; his hands forever trembling as he lights a fresh Silk Cut with the butt of the last one. He stumbles from office to office, nursing a constant hangover and a three-gram-a-week habit, and being shouted at for playing us some crappy record, or not playing us some crappy record, or whatever. When he isn't being shouted at in the office he's standing at the back of some festering indie gig until three in the morning. His glossy mane of tyre-black hair is already streaked with grey fissures. He has just turned twenty-one. I'm taking him into a few meetings with me. He's got good ears.

Parker-Hall stands up and stretches in the seat in front of us. 'Gawd blimey!' he says, yawning. 'Dis is a bit more blahddy like it! Nice an 'ot. Fackin' tayters in London!'

Parker-Hall is about five foot four and looks like an unruly, mischievous child, like one of the fucking Bash Street Kids. He comes from Hampstead. He went to Wellington. His parents own a couple of *streets* in north London. His surname involves a hyphen, for fuck's sake, and yet he often chooses to talk like a kind of blacked-up Dick Van Dyke – the splayed vowels, the vanished consonants – because somewhere around the age of fifteen he heard a hip-hop record and decided that Kaffirs were cool. But Parker-Hall is hot at the moment, very hot. So I laugh and clap him on the back and ask him, 'Where you staying then?'

'Facking Ritz Carlton, innit?' he says and I immediately wish I hadn't asked.

*

The door swings open. 'SCHTEEVEN! FAANTAS-CHTICK! FAANTASCHTICK! COME IN! COME IN!' Rudi Gertschlinger embraces me as he ushers us into his suite at the Martinez.

It's tacky-impressive: a huge lounge with chintzy furniture and floor-to-ceiling bay windows overlooking the Croisette and, beyond it, the sea. It is dark now and the lights of dozens of huge yachts twinkle here and there in the blackness.

The suite is almost as tacky-impressive as Rudi himself. In his late forties, with silver hair pulled back into a ponytail, he has the face of a well-fed concentration camp commandant, a role I am sure a couple of his direct ancestors probably filled.

We take a seat on the floral sofa and a minion fixes drinks as Rudi continues his spiel, his volume going down a notch to the simply unbearable level he uses for normal conversation. 'How have you been, my friend?! It has been too long! I must thank you for what you did with our last record! And thank you for sending the gold discs from the UK! We're trying to get them up but – you know – there is so little space left on our walls. Eh, Günter?'

'*Ja.*' This will be Günter's sole contribution to the meeting. He hands Darren and me tumblers of Buck's Fizz. Fucking Germans. Darren, nervous, knocks back half of the sickly orange jism in one go.

'When did you get here?' I ask looking around. Rudi looks pretty well ensconced; a tower of gleaming black hi-fi equipment is set up in the corner.

'Ach, just this morning. I had Günter and Anna fly ahead yesterday to get things set up. You know me, Steven. Time

34

is money! I am – what did you call it – hardcore? I AM FUCKING HARDCORE!' He laughs his tits off and we cackle along with the mad bastard.

Rudi's company DMG (Dance Music Group. Yeah, must have taken him a while) has a huge building on the outskirts of Hamburg. On the top floor are offices housing his three record labels, artist management and video production companies. (He diversified into music from pornography.) Below that is a floor with several small recording studios and below that, on the ground floor, is Das Technotron, Rudi's nightclub. It works like this: he has teams of writers, engineers and producers working twenty-four/seven in all three studios. They're young kids desperate to break into the music business, so Rudi pays them a minuscule wage and they get free studio time to work on their own tracks. They get next to no income from record sales and Rudi's name appears as co-writer on every track that comes out of there. (In Rudi's defence here he will, occasionally, charge into one of the studios and scream at these guys to make it 'HEAVIER!' or 'FASTER! or 'CRAZIER!') Amazingly most of them think this is a good deal. Well, for a while anyway. Inevitably they will get wind of how royally Rudi is fucking them and will ask for what's coming to them. At this point Rudi will show them a) the bit of paper they signed when they joined, and b) the fucking door.

And how do you write a song? Well, in the words of a hero of mine, the late, great Morris Levy, you 'get some kids in a room, you get a beat going, you get a few words together. Boom. You got a song.' This was Levy's statement to the judge when he was being cross-examined about his role in the creative process behind the many hit records his name had appeared as co-writer on. He had, of course, written absolutely jack. A bunch of spear-chuckers – on breadline wages but kept perfectly sweet with the occasional (leased) Cadillac and the odd chicken dinner – wrote the actual songs of course. Levy simply told them that, if they ever wanted the record to see the light of day, then they'd better be putting his name in the brackets too, and cutting him in for a goodly slice of the publishing. Levy was a music-industry mogul back in the fifties and sixties – the good old days. The Wild West. When artists did whatever you told them to and thought it was fucking Christmas when you paid them a royalty of half a pence in the pound. (Not like now, when every toerag with a demo tape has their lawyer in tow, some lowlife who, when he's not banging on about royalty uplifts, or trying to skank you for a few extra points, is trying to make everything non-recoupable and threatening you with an audit every fifteen minutes.) Back then you could really make some money. So, while Rudi's tactics might seem draconian to someone who dabbled in, say, ethics, they're hardly innovative.

When one of Rudi's kids has a track they are particularly enthused about they will charge downstairs to Technotron on a Friday or Saturday night – when the place is rammed with two thousand gurning, pilled-up Krauts – and get the DJ to give it a spin. If the crowd go uber-ballistic then they know they've got something and the tune will be pressed onto white labels, whacked up to the third floor, and mailed to key club DJs. It is as sure-fire a way to road-test pop-dance records as has ever been invented and has made Rudi one of the most successful producers in Europe and a millionaire many times over. I have licensed several of his tracks for the UK, earning Rudi's undying love by scoring top-five hits with the last two 'My Baby Wants to Come' and 'Doof! Doof! (This Is House)'. (Those titles. Again, fucking Germans.)

'Anyway,' Rudi is saying, 'let me make you happy, Schteeven. Günter.' He nods to his muppet who hits 'play' on the DAT machine. The room fucking *explodes* as a bass drum louder than the march of a thousand Waffen SS crunches out of the speakers. Rudi and Günter nod along. My fillings thrum. After a moment a flummoxing bass line kicks in and then a female voice joins it. It rumbles along like this for maybe a minute as a second, male, voice creeps in, insistently repeating the words '*Why don't you, why don't you, why don't you, why don't you . . .*' before the chorus drops: 'WHY DON'T YOU SUCK MY FUCKING DICK!'

I look up; Rudi and Günter have their eyes shut, completely lost in music. I glance left towards Darren but he won't meet my gaze, clearly too terrified of collapsing in hysterics. Or perhaps just plain terrified. The chorus is continuing to build, tribal drums pounding and a pack of guys yelling 'WHY DON'T YOU SUCK MY FUCKING DICK!' Except . . . they're not just yelling, the fucking thing is actually incredibly tuneful; a nagging keyboard riff twines around the vocal line, sweetening it.

There's a breakdown about halfway through where the inevitable rapper tells the girl to do stuff like lick his balls and stick her tongue up his ass and stuff, and then the chorus comes back in and it all builds to a deranged crescendo before the track stops abruptly and a single, passionate, soulful voice cries out, '*SUCK IT!*' Then it's over.

Rudi sits there for a moment breathing heavily, his

nostrils flaring, his eyes closed in rapt silence. Before I can say anything he leaps to his feet and thrusts his arms in the air as though he's scored the winner in the World Cup final. 'DIDN'T I TELL YOU!' he screams. 'A SMASH! OUR BIGGEST HIT YET!'

A few things are instantly apparent: 1) Rudi is off his fucking chanks (but we knew this already), 2) obviously no radio station in the civilised world will go anywhere near the record, and 3) the tune is insanely catchy.

'Wow,' I say, 'have you played it at the club yet?'

'Last Friday we dropped it for the first time. Schteeven, I cannot tell you. You have been to Technotron, *ja*? You know what they are like in there, they know their music. Well, they went FUCKING INSANE!' He always says this.

'Wow,' I repeat.

'Who's the singer?' asks Darren redundantly, for something to say.

'Michelle. She is, what do you call them, Schteeven, a moose?' He waves a hand dismissively, 'Ha ha! But this is not a problem. We will find someone else to front it.'

'It's fantastic, Rudi. It's just . . .' I spread my palms.

'The lyrics?'

'Exactly, Rudi.'

'Ach, you English! So schquare! It is no problem, we have a radio edit almost finished.'

'Yeah? Wow. Really? How, er, what did you do?'

'We have changed the chorus to "*Why don't you slap me on the ass!*"'

Holy shit. If this isn't the tackiest, stupidest, most unworkable idea I ever fucking heard then it's definitely in the top five. 'Great!' I say. 'That could work.'

'So, what do you think, my friend? You know I will offer this to you for the UK.'

What do I think? The record is absolutely, off-the-scale, demented, tacky, cheesy, single-entendre garbage. But, and never forget this, this is exactly what 99 per cent of the Great British Public enjoy. It is also properly infectious and stranger things have happened. However, I must also be mindful that while Rudi has as good a track record as you can have with this type of crap, he has also shafted a few labels for hundreds of thousands of pounds for records that have charted at 41 before disappearing without trace. (Last year Virgin paid a fortune for a record of Rudi's called 'Happy Song!'. I remember being in Trellick's office when the midweeks came in showing it at no. 46, with a strontium fucking anchor. Laugh? We nearly needed oxygen masks.)

'How much, Rudi?'

'Ach, Schteeven, I do not know. You paid us, what, twenty-five for the last one?'

'Twenty.'

'Whatever. I could not take less than thirty and eighteen points.' (Percentage points – his royalty rate from us.)

I nod. 'That doesn't sound unreasonable.' Like fuck it doesn't. By the time we pay this Nazi paedo thirty grand for the record, commission some remixes, do artwork, promo the record to club and radio, manufacture the stock, take out print and street advertising and make a video, it will cost us maybe a hundred grand to try and have a hit with this piece of shit. This is what is involved every time you say 'yes'.

'Schteeven, it is a fucking bargain. Where are your ears? It's a smash.'

'Tell you what, let me talk to business affairs, crunch some numbers and I'll come back to you tomorrow. OK?'

'OK,' he shrugs, 'but don't hang around, my friend. I want you to have this, I am playing it to you first, but you know what this place is like!' He gestures out the open window towards Cannes. Several floors below throngs of industry people are heading out for the evening, their laughter and chatter drifting up towards us.

'I'll call you,' I say as I get up.

'Good! Good! Will I see you tonight? Where are you eating?'

'I'm not sure yet. What are you guys up to?'

'I will be in the Barracuda! Getting my *FUCKING DICK SCHUCKED*!' he roars, punching me playfully on the arm.

As soon as the lift doors close Darren bursts out laughing. 'Christ, he's off his tits.'

'No shit. But what did you think?'

'It's a fucking tune, mate, no question, but those lyrics, man.' He shakes his head. 'Would this edit work? I don't know. What are you thinking?'

What am I thinking? I don't know. It's my job to know, but I don't. 'I'm thinking . . . two world wars and one World Cup,' I say.

He cracks up. His laughter contains just the right amount of hysteria and reverence due to a superior and benefactor.

Later, looking through some crap in my hotel room (a decent enough, sea-facing room at the Majestic – Rebecca came through), I noticed that there were delegates from no fewer than ninety-one countries attending this year's convention. Apart from the obvious – the Krauts, Frogs,

Shermans, Japs and Brits – there's a raft of the less obvious – New Zealanders, Mexicans, Russians – and a clutch of the downright crazy – Ugandans, Romanians, fucking *Tanzanians*. I mean, I don't know much about the domestic affairs of Tanzania, granted, but I'd have imagined they had more pressing concerns back there – and better uses for their cash – than sending some witch doctor to Cannes at incredible expense so he can watch a load of drunk, chang'd-up fools shout abuse at each other and vomit hundred-quid dinners down the toilets of nightclubs. How high can music be on their agenda?

But everyone gets along. Oh yes. Background and ethnic origin form no barrier to trade here. If there's a deal to be struck, if there's dollar, yen, rouble or franc to be made then differences will be put aside. Diversity tolerated. Look over there – the Arab contingent is uncorking the Cristal to celebrate a potentially lucrative licensing deal for *Ultimate Bar Mitzvah Classics*! In another corner the staunchly Catholic label boss is snapping up the exclusive distribution rights for an exciting new label called Red Hand: Kill All Fenian Bastards. Music really does cross all barriers. Greed is so incredibly inclusive.

The following afternoon, and Schneider and I have a table on the glass-encased veranda of an insanely expensive restaurant at the far end of the Croissette, overlooking the harbour. There's lead crystal, thick, starched table linen and heavy silver cutlery. Personally I think it's an own goal bringing Rage into a place like this, but Schneider, anticipating a disagreement (because, with someone like Rage, there is only ever disagreement), wanted somewhere off the beaten track, somewhere that wasn't going to be rammed with industry. Which this place isn't – there's just lots of chic lunching Frogs, cracking open the rust-red exoskeletons of big lobsters and scraping the creamy flesh from the softer, mottled-white shells of the langoustines. Rage and Fisher, his manager, are so late that we've ordered: huge tureens of thirty-quid bouillabaisse sit steaming in front of us. We spoon and sip Sauvignon and make small talk about deals and rumours. Schneider is nervous, his foot tapping away beneath the table. He knows he is on ultra-thin ice with this record. Below the ice, waiting to tear him to pieces, are the sharks. Terrible, ravenous sharks with rusted hypodermics for teeth, the chambers of the syringes filled with plague, anthrax and AIDS. They swim in fast circles, coming nearer and nearer to the surface as the ice begins to creak and splinter beneath Schneider's gleaming Patrick Cox loafers.

Suddenly we sense the pulse, the heartbeat of the place, change and we look up to see Rage and Fisher come swaggering in.

Fisher is impressive enough in here – a bald, twenty-stone East End hooligan with a heavy, gold cord around his neck, dressed in billowing, baggy sportswear topped off with dodgem-sized paper-white trainers – but Rage . . . fuck me.

Forget the fact that he's wearing shades, a baseball cap and a T-shirt that says 'NIGGER', it's the *jewellery*. Half a dozen gold studs are punched into each earlobe. Three thick cables of gold hang around his neck. On every finger of each hand is at least one, often two, huge gold rings, all studded with rocks – diamonds, rubies, emeralds. On his right wrist is a custom-made gold Rolex so encrusted with gems that to try and read the time on it might induce a brain haemorrhage. From his left wrist dangles a half-kilo platinum-gold bracelet. Just to take a step must be like a half-hour workout. He looks like he's covered himself in glue and charged headlong through an outlet called Rich Black Bastard.

'All right, boys?' he says, simultaneously slapping my shoulder, pumping Schneider's hand, aggressively tugging a chair out and casting an imperious glance around the place. The rest of the clientele suddenly find things of great interest in their soup bowls and among the dismembered sea creatures on their plates.

Rage's success is recent and he's not used to being in places like this. Consequently he's on red alert, Defcon 3, ferociously on the lookout for any sign of being patronised, any flicker of condescension. He doesn't even look at the menu proffered by the swallowing waiter. 'Burger and chips, mate, yeah?' he says.

Burger and chips. Steak and chips. Always ordered 'well done'. These are the staple restaurant foods that will be ordered by every filthy working-class toerag you will ever sign. (Until they get saddled with some Hampstead girlfriend – some Millie, some Sophie – who starts civilising them, teaching them about wine and telling them what a fish is. Then you've got to put up with the bastards ordering Rioja with Dover sole and talking about fucking restaurants.) The waiter backs away, looking sick and uncertain, and, after the briefest of 'How's tricks?', Fisher gets straight to making his point. It's basically the same point he makes in every meeting: how we should be paying them more money.

'We gotta go out on this fucking tour, right?' he says.

'I don't wanna do it in the first fucking place,' says Rage.

'Easy,' says Fisher, placing one of his massive wanking paddles reassuringly on his client's arm but not taking his eyes from Schneider, 'we're gonna do the fucking tour . . .' he says benevolently. I wonder how thoroughly they've rehearsed this.

'Great,' says Schneider.

'But we ain't gonna dismantle the studio to take it on the road . . .'

'No way, man,' says Rage, shaking his head solemnly, as if we're asking him to sell one of his – surely many and illegitimate – children into sex slavery.

'So we need to rep, repli . . .' Fisher has a quick pop at pronouncing 'replicate', then changes his mind, 'buy all the gear again, you know? To have a touring rig.'

'How much are we talking about?' Schneider asks.

'Sixty,' says Fisher with a straight face, but his left hand goes automatically to his lobe to finger a big gold stud. This tour – with backing musicians, lighting, transport, hotels, crew, catering, sound, etc. – is already costing us something like eight grand a show in tour support.

'Mmmm,' says Schneider.

'Excuse me, sir?' The manager is standing there, our waiter hiding behind him. Rage swivels around, already, always, angry.

'Yeah?'

'I'm afraid, with your order, we are a zeefood restron and –'

'For fuck's sake,' Rage says.

'Peraps sir would like to shoes another dish?' The guy

offers him the menu again. Rage doesn't even look at it.

'Look, you can make me some fucking chips, man. You got potatoes in the back, ain't you? All you do is fry 'em up in . . .' Rage thinks, 'stuff.'

'There are potatoes on the menu, sir, oven-roasted in oleeve oil, thyme and zee salt?'

Rage clenches his fists together, black skin banding white around gold rings. Here we go.

Every time I have been in a public place with Rage there has been an angry, dramatic scene – a walkout, a storm-off, physical violence on more than one occasion. I'm not of what you'd call a 'cheery' disposition myself, but these guys, guys like Rage, you wonder how they do it. What does it take to wake up every morning already furious, and for that anger to increase steadily during the course of *every single fucking day*? He lives in a world where every possible encounter – from parking the car, to buying a pint of milk, to eating dinner, to having a business meeting – is fraught with the potential for real or imagined 'disrespects', which must be immediately, viciously, avenged. How *does* he do it? Then you remember his childhood: the foster-homes, the beatings. His actual conception: a radioactive wad of angry nigger-rapist semen getting pumped into some gibbering crack whore to produce the 'drum'n'bass superstar' sitting opposite me.

Here's the thing. When Rage was a little boy his mother drove them from London up to Manchester for the day. She pulled up in the city centre and made him get out of the car. Then she drove back to London. He never saw her again. He lived on the streets – crying and begging – for a couple of days before the cops got hold of him. They slung him in and out of a bunch of care homes for the next ten years, where he was doubtless constantly beaten and fucked in the ass. Let's face it, that'd fuck you off, wouldn't it? That'd about do it for you with regard to the notion of unconditional love.

But today, surprisingly, he decides to be benevolent. Graceful even. 'Whatever,' he says airily, somehow managing to wave an ingot-heavy hand, 'just bring me some fucking food. Yeah?'

'Couldn't we just hire the gear for the tour?' I say.

Rage shakes his head, sucking air in through a mouthful of chrome teeth. 'Can't work with no hired gear, man. No way.'

'Look,' says Fisher, 'do you guys believe in this fucking guy,' he jerks a pudgy thumb at Rage, 'long term?'

'Yes,' we both lie.

'Then this ain't gonna be the only tour we ever do. It's an *investment*.'

'I just don't think we can justify the additional expense,' Schneider says, nervously. 'The tour support's high as it is.'

'Right,' Fisher sighs as he lays down his last card, 'we'll have to pull the tour.'

We laugh. They don't.

'I ain't fucking doing it,' says Rage. There's a long silence.

'But,' Schneider says, realising they're perfectly serious, 'we've already paid for advertising, we've —'

'Not our problem,' says Fisher.

Would they pull their own tour out of spite? Of course they fucking would. When your own mother tells you to go and get fucked at the age of seven, telling the rest of the world to go and get fucked on a daily basis holds no terrors. I wonder why they bothered with lunch. Why didn't they just walk into the boardroom with stockings over their heads, wielding shotguns and demanding sixty grand?

Schneider pretends to think for a long time. There's nothing to think about.

'Thirty grand,' he says, 'recoupable.'

'Fifty,' Fisher says.

'Forty.'

'Deal, man.'

They shake hands. At some point we'll see a *Fantasy Island* budget from Fisher's management company with a bunch of fake receipts stapled to it for silly money they never spent on gear they do not own. Essentially Schneider has just agreed to give them forty grand, no strings attached. We might get it back if – and it's a continent-sized 'if' – Rage's album ever recoups all of its costs.

Neither Rage nor Fisher really had any formal schooling, but, in their own ways, their backgrounds prepared them thoroughly for a successful career in the music business. There was a visa problem for a trip to the States last year and the legal department had to sort it out. Trellick got to see the rap sheets.

Yes, you guessed it. Back in the day Rage and Fisher were both muggers.

'So,' Schneider says pleasantly, 'how's the album coming?'

'Mate,' Rage says sombrely, slowly removing his Oakley's for the first time and making eye contact with Schneider. His irises are so brown as to effectively be black. A shark's eyes. 'It's gonna blow your fucking tits off.'

'When can we hear it?'

'Soon, mate. Soon.'

The waiter glides into view. With a triumphant '*Voilà!*' he sets an enormous platter of *fruits de mer* in front of Rage. Rage looks at it – at the spines, tendrils and tentacles, the claws, wobbling antennae and glistening jet eyes of dozens of dead crustaceans. He looks up and says to the beaming waiter, 'Are you having a fucking giraffe, cunt?'

Midnight in the lobby bar of the Martinez. There must be at least three hundred people in here – a boiling scrum of booze and noise and networking. Business cards are constantly exchanged, phone numbers scribbled on napkins and punched into mobiles. People hold imaginary receivers up to their ears and mouth 'Call me' across the room while others throw their heads back and unleash torrents of horrible laughter. The roar of forced bonhomie is deafening. Massively outnumbered, a handful of melting, white-jacketed waiters squeeze through the crush with silver trays, bearing bottles of Krug, Cristal, San Miguel, Budweiser, Heineken, Stoli and Johnnie Walker. A beer costs about eight quid. To have a bottle of Scotch or vodka left on your table will cost you about three hundred. Plenty of people are happily paying that rather than trying to tag an exhausted, near-fainting waiter every fifteen minutes.

Dinner had been the usual deal you fall into over here, with fourteen of us sharing a table at a seafood place on the Croisette: Chardonnay, champagne, cognac, cocaine and untouched food. Swearing and shouting and braying laughter. Elderly customers asking to be moved then the tightly smiling maître d' and the trio of harassed waiters hunched over the metre-long bill and the stack of credit cards and francs we've flicked onto the ruined tablecloth.

Trellick and I have shouldered our way in at the bar, passing close to Parker-Hall and Marty Kersch, a senior Vice President at Capitol in LA. Parker-Hall – as I knew he would – nodded politely but made no move to introduce me or bring me into the conversation. In fact, I watched as he quickly thought of some detailed, urgent question he had to put to Kersch and leaned in close to yell it until I passed by. This is SOP; if you are engaged in a visible, centre-of-the-room, high-profile conversation with someone very powerful then you must jealously protect that conversation from interlopers of your own, or lower, stature. Conversely, had Parker-Hall been talking to some muppet – some guy who works in marketing for some tiny French dance label whom he had mistakenly fallen into conversation with – he would have greeted me like a long-lost brother, brought me into the discussion, and then fucked off leaving me with the muppet. And I would do the same to him in a heartbeat.

'How was Rage by the way?' Trellick asks me.

'The usual.'

'And the album?

'He reckons it'll blow our tits off.'

'Mmmm, odd that.'

'I know. Pompous cunt. Just out of interest,' I say, lowering my voice, 'for argument's sake,'

'Go on.'

'Let's assume the new Rage album is a pile of shit. Unsellable.'

'Assume away.'

'What's that going to do to Schneider's position?'

'Death row. Game over.'

'So if, when, Schneider goes . . .'

'Who's in the frame for Head of A&R?'

'Yeah.'

'Well, it's not fucking rocket science. It's either you or Waters, or they go out of house.'

'Do a Duke of Wellington on Waters.'

'Pros: a couple of years older than you, a little more experienced in making albums, the rank and file think he's a nice bloke. Cons . . . he's a lazy, brain-dead, cocaine addict with the attention span of a fucking gnat who hasn't had a hit record in donkey's.'

'So he could get the job?'

'Definitely.'

I try to run a few Waters-as-my-boss scenarios through my head: Waters shouting at me because we've missed out on some deal. Waters calling me into meetings, locking me out of meetings with important managers and heads of departments, Waters sending me off to, I don't know, fucking Stoke on a Saturday night to see some band. But I don't get very far with picturing any of this, because a crimson mist keeps closing in, a skull-charge of blood keeps dimming my vision. I feel faint. Sick.

Trellick looks at me and realises exactly what I am thinking. 'You know what they say, young Steven. It's not dog-eat-dog around here . . .' He drains his glass.

'I know,' I say, finishing the aphorism for him, 'it's dog-gang-rapes-dog-then-tortures-him-for-five-days-before-burying-him-alive-and-taking-out-every-motherfucker-the-dog-has-ever-known.'

'Any more for any more?' Trellick says, pointing at my glass, signalling with a drinking motion to Darren and Leamington behind me.

'Wifebeater,' I say.

'Rockschool,' say the other two.

Trellick gets the Stella and the Jack and Cokes in.

Three a.m. and we are *ruling* this fucking place.

We're in a big, tasteless nightclub somewhere on the outskirts of Cannes. It must be 120 degrees in here. We've commandeered our own chunk of the packed dance floor right in front of the DJ booth and we are going bonkers.

Underworld's 'Born Slippy' pounds at festival volume from the massive sound system. There are about fifteen of us now, with waifs and strays. I'm leaping around with an ice bucket on my head, Trellick is down on his knees on the dance floor, playing air guitar, Darren is spraying champagne all over the place, Ladbroke is stretched out against a pillar, nearly unconscious.

Schneider and I split another pill and we're all shouting along to 'Born Slippy', which gets mixed into something else which gets mixed into something vaguely familiar – tribal drums, lolloping bass – and we're all grooving along to it for a minute before – *whump!* – the chorus drops: *'WHY DON'T YOU SUCK MY FUCKING DICK!'* The entire room goes absolutely fucking nuts. By the time it gets to the second chorus everyone is singing along. Holy. Fucking. Shit.

I'm staggering off the dance floor, pushing my way through dancing, singing idiots, trying to find an exit, pawing in my hip pocket for the Nokia. Someone puts an arm around me and shouts, 'Hey, Steven! Is this the record you're signing?'

'Yeah. Done deal.' The lie is automatic.

'Congratulations, mate! Fucking tune.'

Darren looks like he doesn't know whether to laugh or cry. I pull him close and – still smiling – scream in his ear, *'We verbally agreed the fucking deal today. OK?'*

He nods and I stumble off towards an exit, dialling Rudi's number. It rings a few times before going straight to message. 'RUDI!' – I bellow over the roar of a thousand people screaming *'WHY DON'T YOU SUCK MY FUCKING DICK!'* – 'IT'S STEVEN. JUST TO CONFIRM – WE DEFINITELY WANT THE RECORD! "SUCK MY DICK"? WE WANT IT! CALL ME WHEN YOU GET THIS!'

I hang up and lean against the wall, catching my breath. The door to the main room opens and some kid I know from EMI wanders out, gurning, with sweat pouring off him and some sour-faced stick-insect cow dressed in nothing but a thong and some duct tape over her nipples on his arm.

'All right Steven?' he says. 'Fucking tune this, ain't it?'

'Yeah, fierce.'

'Graham was quick off the mark, eh?'

'Uh?'

'Graham at Sony. He signed this record tonight.'

'Yeah?' I swallow.

'Yeah, he was cracking the champagne in the Barracuda with Rudi Gertschl—'

'Excuse me.' And I'm off.

This is the problem with chasing hit singles – it's such hard fucking work. And you have to chase them all the time. If you're going to rely on singles to perk up your bottom line then you have to have a lot of them; four, five, six every year.

This is why I must soon find an act that will sell albums. Smack an album into the top ten that stays there for a year or two and you start generating proper turnover. Making real money. You can start to do less work. (You've been watching, you know I'm overworked.) This is why a little fucker like Parker-Hall is revered in A&R terms: he has signed a bona fide platinum albums act. Who are cool and credible to boot. The mother lode. True, the fluky, chancing prick just happened to be in the right place at the right time but who gives a fuck; he is respected as a 'music guy' – the ultimate A&R accolade.

I'm not. Which is why I'm pulling myself out of bed at ten in the morning and, pausing only to throw up, dialling the Martinez with trembling fingers. Some rude, inefficient French switchboard bumbling goes on for a couple of minutes before the receptionist comes back with, 'I am sorry, sir, that line is engaged.' I tell her – with some emotion – that it is a matter of life or death that Mr Gertschlinger rings me back as soon as he is off the phone.

I crawl across the room and rack up a twelve-quid bill in forty seconds by swallowing three mini-Cokes from the minibar. Everything is mini except for my hangover, which is most definitely fucking maxi. I struggle to place the hangover on my personal Richter scale. Eight? Nine? I try to remember how the previous night ended, but it's like I fell asleep watching some movie and I'm trying to recall where I saw it up to. Then I throw up again.

Breathing hard, I rub my pulsing temples and look around. There's a pool of vomit on the floor, a rusty streak of blood on the white sheets, pieces of glass from a broken champagne bottle scattered all over the place, and a woman, a hooker I guess, looking at me from the bed. Other than that the room seems to be completely normal.

The hooker – who is black and fat – starts talking to me in French. I don't get all of it, but the gist seems to be that I still owe her money from the night before, for some unspeakable extra I must have made her perform. I ignore her, lost in wondering exactly how I'm going to pin the blame for us not signing Rudi's track on Darren. The phone rings and I snatch it up.

'Hello?'

'Schteeven? It is Rudi.' He sounds formal, almost stern, and immediately I know it is bad.

'Rudi, listen, I –'

'I know. I got your message this morning. I am sorry to tell you this, but I have done the deal with Sony.'

Fucking Nazi cunt fuck shit. 'But, Rudi, I told you I –'

'Come on, Schteeven, we are big boys. These things happen.'

I close my eyes and ask him, 'Have you signed the contract yet?'

'As good as. We have a verbal agreement.'

Thank Christ. 'How much?'

'Schteeven, it doesn't matter now. I shook hands on it with Graham last night. As you know, I am a gentleman. A man of my word.'

'Come on, Rudi, how much?'

'There will be other records, my friend.'

'*How much?!*'

'Sixty,' he says, almost sounding embarrassed.

'I'll see you in half an hour,' I say, hanging up.

The hooker gets to her feet, wincing, and tiptoes gingerly towards the bathroom. She's clearly having some trouble walking, and I notice a couple more streaks of dried blood on the backs of her legs and buttocks. Her tone of voice is properly angry now and it dawns on me that I must have been going absolutely bananas last night.

The Barracuda is a Cannes institution. You go into the main bar – a black, windowless hole just off the Croisette – and drink yourself senseless for a few hours, ordering bottles of champagne at two hundred quid a pop, before asking for the 'special vintage'. Your credit card is whisked through the machine and you are charged for another bottle that doesn't appear. Instead, you get ushered through to one of the little back rooms where one of the waitresses hunkers down and slides your balls into her mouth, the waitresses being, in fact, top-notch ostros. Hookers. The Barracuda is the music industry in microcosm: the guys are out front dancing around with champagne glasses on their heads while the girls are chained up in the back, gargling with spunk. The best part of it is that the credit-card receipt still reads 'champagne', rather than 'vicious blow job'. Consequently, every MIDEM there is a steady flow of company plastic over the Barracuda's bar. Last year, when Trellick finally left the place after a seven-hour session, staggering into the dawn clutching a bottle of bubbly and a sheaf of Amex slips totalling three and a half grand, the only people left were the cleaners and a few 'waitresses' rubbing their aching jaws. As the madame held the door open for him she playfully thrust her hand between his legs, grabbed the aching, drained raisins he had instead of balls, and huskily intoned, *'Sexos machinos!'*

'I am sorry for the, ah, mix-up, Schteeven,' Rudi is saying.

'Hey, don't worry about it. We got it fixed.'

'I know. You know I always want – ach! Softly, baby, softly!'

'I understand, Rudi, Graham made you an offer and, ah . . .'

*'Ja, ja!* I was only trying to . . . ach, ah *gut!'*

Rudi and I – both paralytic – are sprawled on facing sofas in one of the back rooms drinking champagne. I take a long swig and look down: an absolutely gorgeous French girl of maybe twenty-one is trying to take her tonsils out with my cock. She looks up and makes perfect eye contact with me for a second or two before her dark brown eyes flip upwards in their sockets and she moans softly, as though my sour prick tasted like cherries and ice cream. Through the beaded curtains that serve as a door we can hear the roar from the bar drifting down the hallway.

I lie back and shut my eyes. We closed the deal with Graham Westbourne calling Rudi's suite the whole time going nuts and upping his offer. Trellick has the signed contracts in his briefcase and Darren has been comprehensively briefed on the need for utmost secrecy as to why my indecision has cost us thirty thousand quid.

Actually, we're now in kind of scary territory – a proper bidding war and a sixty-grand deal for a one-off single means you have to have a proper hit. Number 18 is no use to anyone. This stupid, dreadful, novelty record will have to be top five, minimum, for me to walk away with any kind of aplomb. Top five and we'll make the cash back purely from licensing the utter piece of shit onto dozens of *Now That's What I Call A Total Insult To Fucking Humanity, Vol. 32* type compilations.

But this is all to come. Right now, tonight, we got the record and the competition didn't. This can be savoured for a day or two before you have to worry about turning the fucking thing into a hit.

I become aware of Rudi, only a few feet away, chanting *'Ja! Ja! Ja!'* as he starts to come. I sit up and watch him roar a final *'JA!!!'* as he blasts a jet of hot Teutonic semen into the bobbing French head, which flies back as though a shotgun has gone off in its mouth: 'Ahhgroooughh!' she says.

After a moment Rudi gets up and zips up. We chink flutes over the head of my girl and I watch him – this gentleman, this man of his word – tooling off through the beaded curtains, wiping his forehead with a handkerchief, while his waitress crawls to the corner where, retching and coughing, she spits his cum into a wicker waste-paper basket.

Going home in the morning, I think.

# February

*Thanks to the Spice Girls, Virgin has an 88.9% share of the singles market. Mark and Lard are confirmed as the new hosts of the Radio 1 breakfast show. EMI's share price is in the toilet. BlueBoy and Vitro are hot new acts. No Doubt have a no. 1 single. Alan McGee is preparing to launch the debut album by 3 Colours Red. He says, 'By the second or third record we'll sell five million. I'm serious. They're going to be huge.' Some guys get done for killing that black kid, Stephen something. The Brit Awards happen.*

*'A woman's two cents is worth two cents in the music business.'*

Loretta Lynn

Everyone is up and out of their seats and table-hopping now. The thrum of conversation is rising and no one is listening to the Bee Gees, who, incredibly, are *still* onstage about thirty yards away, cranking out the greatest hits for the tolers watching at home. Their nerve-shredding harmonies keen out over the disinterested crowd of executives and flutter up into the darkness, disappearing into the steel-and-concrete roof of Earls Court. It'll probably sound fine on television though.

I lean back in my chair, away from my cold, untouched dinner – salmon, broccoli and new potatoes – and pinch the bridge of my nose. I inhale hard and there's a pop in my ears as the rock of coke dislodges and shoots down the back of my throat, pleasingly strong and bitter. I loosen my tie and wash the glob of chang down with lukewarm Chardonnay and pretend to listen to Desoto while I scan the crowd for someone better to talk to: Lucian Grange from Polydor, Keith Blackhurst from Deconstruction, Nancy Berry from Virgin, Colin Bell from London Records and Matt Jagger.

Ferdy Unger-Hamilton from Go! Beat is talking to Derek, Pete Tong and some guy from Island. Unger-Hamilton has his arm around Gabrielle, her statuette for Best British Female Artist on the table in front of them. Rob Stringer is laughing his head off as he talks to one of the guys from the Manic Street Preachers, their awards on the table next to them. Frank Skinner, Vinnie Jones, Simon Cowell from BMG, some soap star, one of the *Trainspotting* guys and Geri Halliwell. The singer from Kula Shaker and Sony's Muff Winwood. Geri from the Spice Girls totters by, a bottle of champagne in one hand and the cheeks of her (massive) arse spilling out of the bottom of the ludicrous Union Jack minidress she wore for their performance. I wave to some girl I vaguely recognise, Anita or something. I think she's an A&R coordinator over at BMG. She's wearing a tight black dress, kind of Chinese-style with gold patterning, split right to the top of her thigh and slashed deeply between her breasts. Her hair is cut in a short bob. Normally she dresses kind of indie, I guess – T-shirts, trainers, jeans. She waves back, blows me a kiss. Hello.

'Oi, loser!' Trellick claps me on the leg, shouting over the music. '*Listen*. This is good.' I turn back and lean in between Trellick and Desoto. Behind them Ross – our Head of Marketing – and Waters are heckling the Bee Gees. Ross is in his early thirties, tall with a businesslike crew cut.

'Right. Strap yourself in,' Desoto says, leaning forward. Desoto – a lawyer, a friend of Trellick's – is coke-sweating, his rugby-player bulk straining against the seams of his suit. His fine brown hair is shorter now than it used to be. Until a few years back he kept it pretty long but he felt, rightly, as he approached fifty, that it was getting a bit undignified.

Desoto went to Harrow, then the Bar, then, briefly, the City. When he figured out that life in the square mile meant that you had to get up in the morning and actually work for a living he soon gravitated towards music industry law. He made a fortune. Then he lost it.

'A couple of weeks ago I put an ad in *Music Week* for a new PA.'

'You're firing Sophie?'

'No. *Listen*,' Trellick says.

'I put the ad in and made it non-specific,' Desoto continues, 'it just said "major music industry lawyer seeks PA blah blah blah". The response is Off. The. Fucking. Scale. I get something like fifty replies in forty-eight hours.'

'Sen-say-shunal,' says Trellick.

'So I go through the CVs, checking out the dates of birth to make sure they're all under thirty, and ring six of them back.'

'But you're flying blind at this point, no?' I say.

'Correctos, but you have to figure that out of six at least one of them is going to be doable, no?' We both nod. 'So, I arrange for them to come in for interviews, different days, all at the close of business, around five thirty. Now,' he pushes his glass towards Trellick, who is pouring the three of us more champagne, 'I kick off by saying to them that I'm *really* sorry but it looks like I won't have a job to offer any more.'

'Why not?'

'Oh,' he waves a hand, 'because my original PA just decided that day to stay on.' A bit of bread flies past me. Ross.

'But,' I intone slowly, beginning to see where Desoto is going with this.

'You've got it. *But*, she's probably going to leave in about six months, so if they'd still like to have a chat, then in the future who knows?'

'Good work. Continue,' says Trellick, emptying the bottle and upending it in the ice bucket.

'By this time it's after six so I –'

'Sorry,' I interrupt, 'what's the quality like?'

'*Astonishingly* high. Out of six there's only one monster, two are doable and three of them are sen-say-shunal.'

'Fucking result.'

'So, it's after six now –' Suddenly, thankfully, the Bee Gees finish playing and Ben Elton walks back on and starts crapping away. Desoto lowers his voice a little. 'It's after six, so I play the "shall we go over to the pub for a chat?" card. Not one of them, *not one*, says no.'

'So, how many did you fuck?'

'Three. Two of them played the boyfriend card early on. The others, it was four or five vodka tonics, back to my place – bosh. Thank you very much and see you later Sooty.'

'You didn't even have to buy dinner?' I ask, genuinely impressed.

'Once. One of them wanted dinner.'

'How much was the ad?' asks Trellick.

'Couple of hundred.'

'And you got laid three times?'

'Correctos,' says Desoto, trying to hail a waiter.

'Bargain of the fucking millennium,' Trellick says.

'Couldn't you get sued?' I ask.

'Bollocks. What am I going to get sued for?'

'Fuck knows. Misrepresentation?'

'Listen, clown, I told them very clearly, upfront, "I'm really sorry, *there's no job*." They're not doing me thinking it'll get them anywhere. In fact, one of them actually *thanked* me for "being so honest"!' The idea of a girl existing somewhere who is dense enough to believe that Desoto is honest is so lunatic that Trellick and I both burst out laughing. 'Two hours later, I'm doing her up the fucking Gary.' Desoto drains his flute and thumps it down, looking very pleased with himself

'Did you wear a condom?' I ask.

'Oh yeah,' says Desoto, with no sincerity whatsoever as he leans back in his chair to survey the room.

Desoto only got divorced last year. It was a blinder. He'd packed the family off to Italy for a holiday, telling the wife he had to stay on in London for a few days. Work. He'd meet up with them. The wife, nanny and kids fuck off out of it and Desoto gets stuck into a forty-eight hour crack bender.

He hadn't got the wife's messages – the unacceptable hotel, the lost luggage, the heat, the kid's illness – because he'd lost his mobile somewhere along the line. Nor did he check the home messages. He was so cracked up and the music was so loud, that he didn't hear the front door, then the feet on the stairs.

Desoto's wife opened the bedroom door and the children – aged five and seven – burst out from behind her, laughing at the thrill of surprising Daddy. Daddy gradually came into focus through the children's watering eyes; watering first chemically from the rubbery stench of burning bicarbonate of soda, then watering naturally through tears of confusion and anguish: Daddy was naked with a jutting, Viagra-fueled erection. Daddy was propped up against the headboard, almost in crucifix position with a Coke-can crack pipe in one hand and a shit-streaked dildo in the other. Daddy had a dreamy grin strung across his face as he watched two young Latvian girls – hired cheaply from an agency he favoured – furiously 69ing each other across the foot of the bed, their heads coming up, their mouths both slick with cum as the scream began to rise from Mrs Desoto.

The divorce was swift and financially close to ruinous. Among many other things she sought, and secured, an enormous monthly payment towards the cost of post-traumatic stress counselling for the children.

We sit and scan the room and gossip and bitch. It's very easy – everyone falls neatly into one of two categories: winners and losers. People on the up and people on the down. The winners are 'fucking cunts' and the losers are, well, 'fucking losers'. At a nearby table Schneider is talking to Nick Raphael, an A&R guy, recently installed at BMG with Christian Tattersfield. Raphael, in his turn, is monitoring the room over Schneider's shoulder, casually yet fiercely casting about for an upgrade. He doesn't need to be caught having a high-profile conversation with a loser like Schneider. Like being caught cracking jokes with a rabbi in downtown Berlin in 1938. Desoto nods towards Schneider and says, 'Dead man talking.'

Trellick, catching the drift, waves a hand in the air and says 'Waiter? A bottle of *Schadenfreude* for my friends here.'

A few yards away Ellie Crush is interviewed by some TV girl. '*Very* exciting,' the interviewer gushes breathlessly to the camera, 'twenty-one-year-old Ellie Crush taking home Best British Breakthrough Artist tonight. Ellie, just quickly, what does winning this award mean to you?'

'Oh God,' says Ellie, hefting the silver statuette into view, 'I'm speechless, Jo! Honestly, I can't even begin to tell you how much this means to me.' She glances around the babbling throng. 'I'm going to have to find a safe place to put it, mind you!'

'Thanks, Ellie.'

'Cheers!'

'Doable,' Trellick says thoughtfully. 'Very doable.'

'Mmmmm,' I say as Crush comes towards us through the crowd, the statuette cradled against her chest, a bottle of champagne and lit cigarette dangling from the other hand. 'Hi, Ellie,' I say as she passes.

'Oh, hi . . . there!' her face explodes into a ludicrous smile. 'Mwwwah, mwwwah.' She smacks the air either side of my cheeks.

'Congratulations.'

'Shit, I can't bloody believe it! Will you pinch me? I feel like I'm dreaming!' Her face is just an exclamation mark.

'Nah, you deserve it.'

'Aww, thanks, love.' She tries to take a swig of the champagne but burns her hair with the cigarette, dropping her award in the process. Her press officer steps in to help manage the crisis as, right on cue, Parker-Hall emerges from the throng, accepting handshakes, his features a picture of benevolent indulgence. It's always worse when they're magnanimous. 'OI! OI!' Ross shouts in greeting.

'All right, lads? Steven,' he says, shaking my offered hand. 'What a fucking result that was, eh?' he says, rubbing his hands together briskly and accepting a cigarette from Trellick. 'Done them other cunts up like kippers, didn't we?'

Remember, Parker-Hall comes from Hampstead.

'You fluky cunt,' I say.

'Suck my root,' he says, lighting up.

'What you up to later?' Ross asks.

'We got a party on. Up West, innit?' Parker-hall says, reaching into his pocket and handing out a brick of laminates to his after-after-party. 'Right, better do one. Ellie's got to meet the press while she can still fucking speak. C'mon, love.' As he ushers her off Crush turns to me and says 'Bye . . . um, Alex.'

Trellick is still laughing when we reach the green-and-white EXIT sign which glows in the distance on the other side of the auditorium, showing us the way to the after-party.

After the awards ceremony proper finishes the floodgates open and the cannon fodder pours in: the secretaries, marketing assistants, junior PRs, make-up artists, runners, stylists, hairdressers, accountants, legal assistants and friends-of-friends who could only get after-show tickets. Clearly you or I would, upon being told that these were the only tickets available to us, simply climb into a warm bath and open up our veins. However, these losers consider themselves lucky, fortunate even, to be able to get within two bouncers of Robbie or Liam. To be allowed to pay for their own drinks. The secretaries in our building spend *months* planning for tonight. They buy new clothes, they get haircuts and facials, and they pool their miserable salaries to buy a few grams. It's a boiler-fest in here.

Now, you keep reading things — in magazines, in newspapers — about how the nineties are turning out to be, well, nice. According to these articles, men in the sharing, caring nineties have rejected the hollow materialism and sexism of the eighties and embraced women as equals. Partners. You read these things and you wonder – where the fuck are the people who write this stuff hanging out? Primary schools? A rural Greenpeace office?

My industry, always resistant to change (in the fifties we hated the idea of singles, in the seventies cassettes were the enemy, initially CDs were the Antichrist in the eighties – boy, we soon got our heads around that one), hasn't really bought into all this nonsense yet.

Thankfully, very few women seem to have understood it either. There are lots of them already here and thousands more clamouring to get in. Every day piles of CVs tumble into the office. Fresh-faced young girls with excellent qualifications, all hungry to get a job where, in return for working twelve-hour days, being sexually harassed from dawn till dusk, having to cope with all manner of coked-up, coming-down, hung-over, flaky, irrational, abusive, demanding behaviour from people like me, they will be rewarded with maybe fifteen grand a year, the odd backstage pass and occasional glimpses of pop stars in the building.

In toilets, offices, broom cupboards, hotel stairwells and on the chill leather seats of BMWs, Saabs and Mercedes coupés, they will suck cocks and take it up the arse. Their twenties will flash by in a holocaust of parties, hangovers, semen and bad champagne until, one fine morning some-where down the line, they wake up to find themselves thirty-five years old with sagging tits, a cancerous, shrivelled womb, tired, fucked-out eyes, and a complexion battered by late nights, drugs and cocks. A lucky few of these girls will, through a combination of low cunning and viciously skilful fellatio, manage to marry one of the executives they serve and hang on to him for – at best – a decade, raising his children and decorating the house while he works late at the office pumping his way through her successors. Eventually, either she will put her foot down or (more likely) he will upgrade to one of the Sophies or Samanthas who replaced her. They will get divorced somewhere in their mid-forties and she will find herself standing in the kitchen of a big house somewhere in Buckinghamshire with two nasty, pre-pubescent monsters whingeing at her as she haplessly uncorks her second bottle of white wine at half past four in the afternoon.

A very, very few of these girls will manage to marry one of the pop stars. The Meg Matthews deal. This is the record-industry boiler equivalent of winning the lottery – the *Pretty Woman*, rags-to-riches story that surely keeps so many of these girls choking down warty cocks, swallowing spunk and throwing themselves down on all fours like it's going out of fashion for the best part of twenty years. It. Could. Be. You. For the tiny minority of Cinderellas who pull off this incredible coup the life pattern will be much the same as it is for the ones who marry the executives, although the time frame of the marriage will be greatly truncated and the remuneration significantly enhanced.

We're hunkered around a corner table in another cavernous room. Billowing white drapes have been hung, candles lit and carpeting laid down. There are blackjack tables and roulette wheels but, here and there, you can still see the cement floor, the steel poles and corrugated metal of the roof and the gloomy dark above the canopies. You remember that the hulk of Earls Court looks down impassively on everything from car and boat shows to international widget manufacturers conferences – all of them filled with the same kind of guys trying to figure out if Susan from accounts is really up for it or not. Echoing behind the crack of champagne corks, the supercharged laughter, the crackle of suits and sparkling dresses, there is a tinny, reverberating sound. It is the sound of people trying to have a really good time in a lightly decorated underground car park.

Pete Dunn rocks up to our table, arms raised, a bottle of Perrier Jouet in each fist. 'AHHHHHGH! Wahey the lads!' he screeches. He's a big guy, Dunn. Once chunky and, back in the eighties, ponytailed, he's now bald and running, sprinting in fact, to fat. His broad Geordie face is ruddy, the stubble greying and the eyes puffy, set back in little pouches. Dunn is our Head of Radio and TV Promotions. He has spent his adult life wheedling and begging radio DJs and programmers and kids' TV producers and presenters to put our acts on their shows. I'm sure he loved his job when he was twenty-six: falling out of nightclubs with Radio 1 DJs and flying to the south of France with pop stars. Now pushing forty-six his every waking moment is a nightmare. Told to fuck off and die on a daily, hourly, basis by TV and radio executives, he must then drive back to the office where he is – far more robustly – told to fuck off and die by Derek.

How much better his job would have been back in the good old days of the fifties – the golden era of payola and 1 per cent artist royalty rates. Now payola was a genius idea, wasn't it? Tell me that wasn't a winner for everyone involved? You didn't have to take anyone out to dinner and suck their dick. You didn't have to laugh at Chris Evans's jokes. You just paid the cunts. Here's the money, now play the record and fuck you. *Fuck you.*

Not too bright to begin with, a decade of grovelling and sucking dick has turned Dunn into a sort of failed light entertainer with a melancholic streak. He pours champagne into all our glasses, singing, 'Here we go, here we go, here we go.' Shouldn't he be at home with the wife and kids? Then you remember – he went upgrados and left the wife and kids two years ago, to go balls-deep in a twenty-year-old dancer he met at the taping of some Saturday-morning kiddie moronathon. She, in her turn, left him for some photographer's assistant six months later. His upgrade upgraded him.

Dunn actually raises his glass to propose a toast – something only the truly suicidal ever do. 'To the lads!' he shouts.

Waters joins in like a retard, pathetically clunking his plastic flute against Dunn's. Leamington from Virgin materialises through the crowd and sidles over to me.

'Oi oi,' he says.

'All right, mate? Two awards for those cows?' I say, nodding across the room towards Mel B, 'You're having a laugh, aren't you? They must think it's fucking Christmas.'

'Nah, I think Geri's off crying somewhere.'

'Ah, fuck her. Congratulations.'

'Nothing to do with me, mate,' he says shrugging, 'but cheers.' We clack tumblers. 'Here,' Leamington says, 'is it right what I'm hearing about your old mucker Rage?'

'What are you hearing?'

'That it's all gone Colonel Kurtz – he's upriver, gone fucking native. Off his nut on the nosebag, months in the studio, no contact with anyone.'

'Fuck knows. Schneider's problem.'

'When's the record due?'

'Three months ago.'

'Could be Bad News Bears for Schneider.'

'Mmmm,' I say. As we drink and gossip and bitch I look over at the recently clean and sober Robbie Williams, who is sitting at a table a few feet away. He's fiddling with the label on a bottle of mineral water, smoking two-handed, and nodding while some guy I don't know – some manager, some lawyer – explains something to him. Williams periodically turns away to stare hard – a hard stare I know well – at the glittering rump of some boiler standing near him. Poor bastard, I guess that's all he's got now, isn't it? The pumping. Can you imagine it? You're not even thirty and you can't do *anything* any more. No nose-up, no pills, no frosty beers, no warming shots of Jack or Rémy. You're just sitting there, completely sober, in your fuck-off mansion, dressed head to foot in all the finery you spent the morning trawling New Bond Street with some stylist for, you've just given up trying to read some book for the umpteenth time, because it's too *hard*, you're turning on Sky Sports again, or forcing some underling to drink fruit juice and play cards with you, and you're thinking – another forty years of *this*? You're just some stage kid, some poor song-and-dance spastic with a cheeky grin who fate threw a whole bunch of sevens. And now you're staring down the wrong end of four decades with just your own thoughts for company when you don't really have two fucking thoughts to rub together. Nasty.

Danny Rent sidles up. He's a scumbag, a real rapist of a manager, one of those old-school Tin Pan Alley guys that you just don't see much any more: late forties, stubble, well-worn Armani suit with hash burns all over it, heavy *gold* Rolex (so wrong) on his right wrist. He looks like a down-on-his-luck nightclub owner from *Miami Vice* and smells like he just went on a four-day Scotch binge and then jumped into a vat of aftershave.

'Hey, Stelfox, how's tricks?' he says.

'Oi oi,' I say.

'Listen, I been meaning to call you. Got a bit of a band coming together just now that's right up your *Strasse*, mate.'

'Yeah?'

'Fucking yeah. Four birds. Girl power. Innit.'

Christ, I bet no one else is thinking that, the week the Spice Girls go to no. 1 in the States. 'Any good?' I say.

'Fucking useless at the minute, mate, but you'd do the lot of them. We're working on it. One of em's got sumfin.'

'Yeah? What they called?'

'Get this – Songbirds. Gerrit?'

'Yeah.'

'Right, do you want a fucking nose-up or what?'

Girl power. Do me a fucking favour. However, there's going to be a bunch of these whores having it away over the next couple of years. No question. One thing you learn when you're in the business of selling utter shite to the Great British Public is that there's really no bottom to where they'll go. Shit food, shit TV, shit bands, shit films, shit houses. There is absolutely no fucking bottom with this stuff. The shittier you can make it – a bad photocopy of a bad photocopy of what was a shit idea in the first place – the more they'll eat it up with a fucking big spoon, from dawn till dusk, from now until the end of time.

It's too good.

Come the early hours we wind up at the Met Bar and then up into the hotel above, to Parker-Hall's suite for his 'after-after-party'. We're all chang'd up to the eyeballs by this point and listening to a chang'd-up Parker-Hall go through a variant of his 'How-I-Did-It' speech for, surely, the billionth time tonight. Now and again Chalmers, Crush's Product Manager, will boringly interject details about the marketing plan, how big the TV ad spend is going to be, the increased poster campaign, who they're getting to direct the next video. Chalmers is just one of the thousand fathers suddenly lining up to stamp their parentage on Crush's success. 'We're looking at doing thirty thousand albums a week from here on,' he says.

I'm trying not to hear this. The expression on my face is pleasant while, inside, I feel like the village girl as she stares at the face of the tenth soldier in the raping queue – blood on her thighs and half a pint of semen already up her. *I'm not here*, I tell myself. *I'm walking in a forest. I'm walking in a forest* . . .

The room is crowded – industry, random girls and a few fairly well-known musicians. Trellick is sitting on the ledge of the tall windows which overlook Hyde Park, arms folded, nodding earnestly as some girl talks shit to him. A few feet away from Trellick, Damon Albarn is engaged in exactly the same sort of conversation. I tune back in. Parker-Hall is telling us, '. . . the fucking mixes were all over the shop. I says to Flood and Moulder, "Listen, cunts . . ."'

'Excuse me,' I say.

In the bathroom I sit down on the toilet, put my head between my legs, and take deep, steady breaths. I'm sweating. *Thirty thousand a week. That fluky little prick. That chancing mockney wanker.* In Mission Control there's a red wash of colour, alarms sounding, the screens all flashing deranged, bloody images of Parker-Hall and Chalmers being forced to gobble and bum each other before a shotgun is slipped in each of their mouths and, simultaneously, their heads fly apart in a pinkish mist of viscera. The technicians are thumping their monitors, twiddling knobs, but they can't shake the pictures.

I splash some water on my face and hold my wrists under the cold tap for a long time and finally I start to feel better. I'm scraping some powder out from the wrap and carving out a heart-stopping elephant's leg when I become aware of a gentle tapping at the door. I open it a crack and squint out, trying to focus into the dark hallway. 'Steven?' a girl says.

'Yeah?'

'It's Anita. From BMG? Can I come in?'

I pull her in and point her towards the coke.

Maybe fifteen minutes later, as we're leaving, I take a quick look around for Trellick. I wander along a hallway and try the door to one of the bedrooms. It opens silently and I hear a girl's voice breathlessly chanting a mantra of *'oh fuck, oh fuck, oh fuck'*. I peer in. A huge bed is lit by soft halogen spots. On the bed Ellie Crush is naked on her hands and knees. There is a black kid — one of the singers in this new boy band Leamington has signed — crouched behind her, doing something to her with his fist. As I softly close the door something silver flashes under the amber halogen glow.

Yes, twenty-one-year-old Ellie Crush had definitely found a safe place to put the statuette for Best British Breakthrough Artist.

'The thing is,' she says, 'no one over there takes my opinion seriously.' Anita and I are at opposite ends of my sofa, an oversized number from Heal's in heavy caramel cloth. A gold disc for some dance record I signed, flecked and streaked with cocaine, lies between us. Jeff Buckley warbles soft in the background as we discuss her career prospects in A&R. Given that she has none it is a remarkable tribute to both my patience and the focusing power of the drug that we've managed to keep the conversation on the rails for a good three hours. Outside, horribly, dawn is beginning to crinkle through Maida Vale. The clock is ticking, but there's still some crap I have to listen to.

'Oh, I'm sure they do,' I say, standing to pour cold shots of Stoli and then flopping back down a little nearer to her. When we got back, remembering that she's really an indie kid, I quickly washed and changed my shirt and tie for a Radiohead T-shirt.

'No they don't. I was the first one saying we should sign Mansun the other year. Look at what that turned into.'

'Really?' I say.

'Oh, there's been loads,' she says and goes onto reel off a list of bands she loves, all either total or demi-turkeys, while I chop more lines out.

'Well,' I say, handing her the furled twenty, 'what are your plans? Where do you want to go from here?' She stands up and bends over right in front of me to snort her line. Her rump – which is near perfect by the way – strains against the tight, shiny dress. I wonder – knickers? thong? nothing? The slit falls open to the top of her thigh, laying bare a yard of brown flesh. 'Ahh . . . thanks,' she says, throwing her head back. She sits down beside me and passes the gold disc. 'I've been A&R coordinator for three years now,' she continues, snuffling, 'I could do it in my fucking sleep. I mean, I'm nearly *twenty-three*, Steven. What am I doing?' She looks at me with sad, damp eyes. Her breasts – which are pushed tight together by one of these new superbras I've been reading so much about, some triumph of geometric wiring and tit-engineering – are straining hard against the gold-speckled satin of her dress. She's really packed into it. I am so thick, so angry, with lust that, just for a moment, I think I may attack her.

'Well, listen,' I say, 'off the record?' She nods, wide-eyed, and I realise that I have absolutely no idea what I'm going to say next. But it's no problem. I lie constantly, I lie all the time. The very fabric of my daily existence from breakfast until bedtime, from toast until tranquillisers, is a finely woven torrent of utter shite. So I know, I'm reasonably confident, that when I start speaking the words, the lies will tumble from my mouth and arrange themselves into a convincing sentence that will take me nearer to what I want. 'Well,' I say, 'we're about to promote Darren to Junior A&R. He doesn't know that yet so you can't tell anyone.' She nods solemnly. 'So we're going to be hiring one, possibly two, new scouts sometime in the next few months. I think you'd be perfect, but the thing is,' I say, completely free-forming now, 'it'd probably mean a drop in salary.'

'I don't care about the money,' she cuts in quickly, leaning towards me, smelling of perfume, sweat, cigarettes and vodka, 'I mean, you only get one life and you have to make sure that whatever you do makes you happy. I've always loved music and I know that, if someone would just give me a shot at it, I'd make a brilliant scout. I spend half my life going to gigs anyway. You couldn't name a new band in London I haven't seen in the past twelve months. The Audience, Bellatrix, Cuff, AC Acoustics, Basement Jaxx . . . Even when I was a kid, I'd listen to the *Top Forty* every Sunday because I wanted to hear what records were going up, what was going down and all that. I've got my own account at Rough Trade. I pay for it myself. BMG won't let me have one because I'm not technically A&R staff – hey, I've got perfect pitch too, did you know that? – and I'm so sick of it there that I've been thinking about just packing it all in and going travelling. A couple of my friends are out in Goa right now and sometimes I just think, "Fuck it, why spend the winter here? You're worth more than this." I mean, what am I doing? Booking studio time and booking cabs and biking bloody tapes around London and all that crap. My dad died last year and we never really got on and that really made me take a look at things because at the end of the day if you're not happy then, basically, what's the point? Do you know what I mean?'

'Anita,' I say hoarsely, 'can I suck your tits?'

*

Fucking cocaine.

Two hours later and she's *still* trying to mangle my cock into something in the vicinity of a hard-on. We're both naked, slick and salty with sweat, and she's going at it like a *demon*: flicking at the tip with her tongue, nibbling the shaft with her teeth, blowing on the helmet gently, viciously gobbling up and down the whole thing, kissing it as softly and tenderly as a mother soothing a crying infant, biting and gnawing on it like an angry pit bull, spitting on it, greasing it with baby oil, making direct eye contact and moaning with pleasure as she sucks, rubbing my cock greedily against her clit, pussy-lips and arsehole, and sliding it between her heavy, lubed breasts. At one point she crams the entire package – prick, balls, the lot – into her mouth and churns them crazily like an overdriven washing machine. Finally she goes absolutely bananas and simply begins furiously wanking me off. For a long, sorry time – teeth gritted, sweat flying from her – she pounds her clenched fist up and down on the melted ribbon of plasticine I have instead of a cock. Somehow, somewhere into about the fifteenth minute of this (by which point she's emitting random screams of pain, her arm just an insane blur, like one of those machines they use to shake paint in DIY shops), my cock stiffens minutely, going from the consistency of – say – jelly into Play-Doh. As she eagerly, desperately, swivels a leg across my chest in an attempt to mount me, I shudder, moan, and ejaculate.

Well, 'ejaculate' is probably over-egging it. 'Ejaculate' is like using 'explosion' to describe what happens when you pierce the foil lid on a jar of instant coffee. What actually happens is that I scream and a drop of semen the size of a grain of rice seeps out the end of my cock. It's not enough to even dribble down onto her hand, the hand which is – still! – frantically trying to guide me into her.

I roll over and gratefully pass out.

When I wake up she's gone. Horribly, inevitably, I have a raging, titanium erection. I roll the sheets back and look at it. My relationship with my prick is beginning to resemble the kind of friendship you have with an old, alcoholic college pal – completely unreliable, always turning up at the worst possible time and costs you a *lot* of money. Yet you're stuck with him. I stare him down. 'What the fuck do you want? You're *late*,' I say. I want to punch him out.

But, with heavy heart and thick blood, I root around on the floor, pluck my wallet from my trousers, and begin dialling the number of a local escort agency. '*Aww*,' I think, folding a cool, soothing fist around my radioactive helmet, '*how could I stay mad at you?*'

A couple of weeks after The Brits we have an emergency marketing meeting, to get a plot in place for Rudi's record. Present are Ross, one of Ross's product-manager muppets, Dunn, the TV promotions girls Hannah and Clare (fucked them both), Barry and Alex, the club promotions kids, who will try to get every DJ in every filthy, tacky toler-infested nightclub in the country playing the record, Bill, who deals with manufacturing, Suzy the press officer (nearly fucked her, blow job) and Nicky. As always I find myself angry at how fucking ugly Nicky is. Usually Ross would chair this meeting, but Derek, sensing a big hit he wants to get his fingerprints on, has decided to sit in.

'Now,' Derek booms, gesturing grandly towards me, 'Steven has recently come back from MIDEM where, I'm pleased to say, he signed the hottest club record of the whole convention.' There is a round of applause and some whooping from Barry and Alex, who already know the record, Barry even implying he had tried to play it to me before Christmas. I move over to the stereo. 'This is the club mix,' I say cueing the track up, 'I'm working on a radio edit.' I am, of course, doing fuck all. One of Rudi's boys will do the radio mix, but these clowns don't know that. Once the thing is a huge hit it will be, naturally, 'my' radio mix that saved the day. I crank the volume all the way to the right, hit 'play' on the CD, and bass flattens the gold discs and posters against the walls. Everyone nods along.

You'd think you wouldn't have to bother with all this, wouldn't you? The process of selling the fucking record to the people in your own company. But you do. Yesterday I picked off Dunn and Ross – playing each of them the record in their offices and telling them both only they could make it a hit. I mean, if you worked at Baked Beans Inc and your job was marketing beans and the guy who made the fucking beans came in with some hot new beans, he wouldn't have to do a sales job on you, would he? He wouldn't have to take you out and get you drunk and slip you a taste of the beans and really try to convince you they were good beans, would he? He'd just say, 'Here's the new beans I've made – which is my job – now sell the fucking things. Because that's your job.' But not in the record industry, oh no. Everyone's got a fucking opinion, everyone wants to be an A&R guy and – most importantly – *everyone wants you to fucking fail*. Do any of the poor cunts around this table (some of their faces – Hannah, Nicky – now twitching with horror as the chorus unfolds) really need to be seeing me striding around the office with a no. 1 record going on? Do they fuck. I'm kind of unbearable when I'm having a hit.

*'SUCK IT!'* reverberates around the boardroom and then it all goes quiet.

Ross breaks the silence – 'It's a smash!' – and then we're all talking about practical stuff; release dates, lead times and artwork.

Derek loves the record. The marketing department love the record. The club promotions department love the record. The radio department love the record. I love Rudi. I have tooled back from Cannes bearing the cure for cancer.

# March

*Lucian Grange becomes Head of Polydor. The single 'Local Boy in the Photograph' by hotly tipped new act the Stereophonics stiffs at 51. Cast release their second LP. The Manic Street Preachers album goes double platinum. Lots of people want to sign the Audience, an indie band with this girl singer who's the daughter of the boiler who used to present* Blue Peter. *Steve Allen, an A&R guy at Warner Brothers, says, 'I see her developing the way Madonna has. This is probably the dance album of the decade.' He is talking about Gina G.*

*'I don't know anything about music. In my line you don't have to.'*

Elvis Presley

'. . . very much like the early Jam, but more *angular*, and you'd need to find a producer who was sympathetic to that. I don't think . . .' Waters craps on about the band we've just watched in the Dublin Castle as Parkway at closing time creeps past – the Spread Eagle, a kebab palace, three drunk girls in short skirts, another gigantic poster of Tony Blair, the Labour guy, his red devil eyes burning out of the tear across the poster, scaring the shit out of me.

Waters and I are both coked up in the back of a hot stinking minicab, on our way to the Falcon to see some band called Kidnapper, who are meant to be a bit like Elastica. There's the usual gibbering Paki at the wheel, the usual distorted ragga fizzing out of the tiny plastic speakers behind us. Waters is still talking. '. . . his mixes are just too . . . middle-y . . .' I turn to look at him for the first time in a while. He's just a madman with double-glazed pebbles for eyes. He's talking to the air. He may as well be talking to Abdul in front. 'Too middle-y?' I repeat.

'Yeah. You know, not enough top or bottom end . . .'

I nod slowly. 'Sorry, who are we talking about?'

'Mike Hedges.'

'Right. Too . . . middle-y?'

'Yeah.'

Waters is saying that one of country's most respected producers – a guy who has been making records since Waters was a child – is incapable of turning out a mix with the necessary levels of bass and treble. Waters is not saying this because he believes it or because he has given the matter any serious thought (an endeavour he is, in any case, incapable of). He is just saying it to have a *view*. Views are very important. You should always have one.

I say, 'Shall we fuck off this band at the Falcon? Go back to yours and have a think about producers? Draw up a shortlist? Get some more bugle in?'

He grins. Well, he gets as close to a grin as his coke-blasted features will allow, like he's trying to eat his top lip with his bottom teeth. Actually, he looks like he's having a fucking stroke. But he's nodding.

Waters leans forward, causing a fresh torrent of sweat to pour off him, and gives the driver his address in Notting Hill. We make an illegal left up Camden High Street, past the tube station, the Brassiere, teenage goths outside the Electric Ballroom, a woman tramp with a filthy bandage around her arm rooting through a rubbish bin.

By one we're well into the third gram. Waters is still talking – I don't think he's stopped talking since we left the Dublin Castle – and pouring drinks while I root through his record collection. He has about twenty-five CDs – mostly major label promos and a few Greatest Hits collections: Fleetwood Mac, Japan, the fucking Doors. For some reason

– some inexplicable, haunt-you-to-the-grave-unfathomable reason – he has a copy of *Nuisance*, the debut album by Menswear. I also see an advance copy of the new Jam box set Polydor are bringing out and a copy of the Gang of Four's *Entertainment*. My copy of the Gang of Four's *Entertainment*, the one that went missing from my office a couple of weeks ago. This explains Waters earlier, mystifying, spastically inappropriate use of the word 'angular'. I put disc two of the Jam set on. 'Thanks,' I say, taking the tumbler of vodka tonic he hands me and sinking into his ludicrously oversized sofa. 'Right, where were we?' says Waters, tapping his teeth with a biro and staring at the piece of A4.

We've been 'brainstorming' for nearly two hours now. There are two names scrawled in Waters' mutated handwriting on the grimy sheet of paper: Ed Bueller and Dave Eringa, both my suggestions. Waters' dog lies sleeping on the sofa. On the coffee table between us is the coke-flecked mirror, the heaped ashtrays, the empty bottle of Stoli. Copies of *Music Week* are scattered all over the floor, all opened at the album charts where we've been scanning the producers' names for ideas. Waters thinks hard. Or rather he makes the expression he imagines humans use when thinking – furrowed brow, gaze focused somewhere in the mid-distance – while whatever goes on in his mind goes on. I picture the inside of his head as a sleeping donkey, a 747 exploding on the tarmac, a nuclear winter. 'How about . . .' I say sitting forward, picking up his Amex, scooping some powder towards me, pausing dramatically as Waters looks up hopefully, '. . . Guy Stevens?'

I wait a few seconds while his brain turns, as swift as a container of near-set concrete tipping over. There's the vaguest light somewhere in his eyes, the tiniest hint that something like a mind lives and functions in there. 'You know,' I say helpfully, 'he produced *London Calling*. Mott the Hoople.'

'Oh, Guy *Stevens*!' the clown exclaims, as though I'd said Guy Stephen*son*, or Guy Simons or something. 'Yeah, great idea,' he says, enthusiastically writing down the name of a man who has been dead for nearly twenty years. 'I'll get the drinks,' I say.

Waters' kitchen is chrome and marble, clean-lined, halogen-lit and never-used. An aluminium baseball bat with a navy leather grip leans against the fridge. 'Home security,' Waters had said casually when we came in. I grab his mortar and pestle and quickly grind up three more Valium, two Es, a tab of acid, and a scoop of ludicrous-strength, Trade-certified, hardcore-queers-only ketamine. 'Fuck it,' I think, breaking open two big, egg-shaped temazepam with my thumbnail and squeezing the viscous, gluey liquid into the chalky powder. I dump the lot into his glass and fill it to the brim with neat vodka, adding a splash of tonic as an afterthought.


'I'm a bear! I'm the dancing bear!'

We were both dancing to some rave compilation when the furious cocktail of class As kicked in and Waters started tearing his clothes off. I suggested to him that he might like to pretend he was an animal of some sort. Now, an hour or so later, I'm lying back contentedly in Waters' huge leather beanbag, watching him capering naked around his living room pretending to be a circus bear. He is fucking *deranged*.

I shout instructions and encouragement to him, making

the most of the short window I have before he collapses. 'Bear eat CDs?' I suggest, chucking a handful at him.

'Bear eat CDs!' Waters shrieks delightedly and stuffs a copy of Pulp's *Different Class* into his mouth. He crunches right through it – jewel case, sleeve, CD, the lot. 'Mmmm,' he says, turning to me and rubbing his naked belly happily, bits of paper and plastic falling from his bleeding mouth. A worried expression crosses his face. 'Bear need . . .' He's trying to say something, his eyeballs flipping back in their sockets, as though he's trying to look at whatever is left of his brain.

'Bear need what? What does bear need?' I say encouragingly, like you would to a confused child.

'Bear need –' Abruptly he squats down and unleashes a torrent of foul shite all over his nice sea-grass carpeting. Then he loses his balance and falls into his own effluent.

The stench is incredible, arousing the sleeping dog. I lock him in the bedroom.

I check my watch – four a.m. Enough's enough. 'Here, thirsty bear,' I say, lifting his head up – being careful not to get shit on me – and holding a mug to his lips. It's filled with Evian in which I've dissolved a further two dozen of his Valium. Waters greedily gulps it down. 'Good bear,' I say, patting his head, 'good bear . . .'

An hour or so later I watch him sleeping – dying – while I snort the last of the coke and listen to the Menswear album. What the fuck was he thinking with this? 'Roger! What the fuck were you thinking with this?' I shout, slapping his face with the CD case.

'Mmmmmm?' he mumbles, face down on the carpet, death nuzzling up close by, putting his feet up.

I turn the TV on and watch VH1 for a while – the Cardigans, Radiohead, Texas, the new Blur single – as Waters' breathing goes from loud, laboured snoring to a rattling whisper to absolutely nothing. Satisfied he's dead I get my cock out and piss all over him.

Then I go and root through his bedroom drawers, hitting pay dirt when I find a sex-trove of porn mags, videos, toys and lubes at the back of his wardrobe. I pull out a butt-plug. It's about the size of a champagne cork and is attached to the handle/battery compartment by a grey wire about four feet long. I click it on. It thrums feebly so I replace the batteries with the ones from the remote control for the flat-screen TV in Waters' bedroom. Much better – it's like holding a small, angry frog. I get rubber gloves from beneath the sink.

Before I leave I flip through the channels until I find *Red Hot Amateurs*. Some spotty-bummed housewife in cheap red underwear smiles coquettishly into the camera as she fingers a dildo, like a flautist preparing for a tricky recital. I leave the TV on, bluish light flickering across Waters' piss-spattered, shit-flecked corpse, the empty bottles of Valium and vodka atop the cokey mirror, the cord for the butt-plug trailing out from between his cheeks, a faint, muffled hum audible beneath the moans and groans from the TV.

I walk home to Maida Vale, the sun coming up and 'Beetlebum' in my head as I cross the Harrow Road. The long, festering strip studded with fried-chicken shacks and everything-a-quid emporiums – a greying London wound which gentrification will never reach – is deserted except for a solitary double-decker bus. It slams past me, rattling the pavement. It is full of tolers: poor people, their faces as grim and stark as pornography, as blunt as final demands.

They flash by me on their way into W1, where they will do whatever they do all day for no money. Yellow letters glow feebly on the front of the bus, telling me that these people have come from Kensal Rise, Cricklewood, Wembley and other places, poorer, more terrible places, that I don't even know about.

'What do you think? Honestly?' one of them – the bass player? the singer? – asks as the last blips of feedback fade out.

I look around my office. The four musicians (early twenties, thin, anaemic, torn clothes) sit on the sofa and the floor while their manager (a couple of years older, a little better dressed) sits in the chair across the desk from me.

Waters' non-appearance in the office this morning caused . . . nothing. I guess that, in most workplaces, it's unusual, reprehensible even, when people just don't turn up. Or turn up so hung-over all they can do is vomit and cry. But not here. Not in the record industry. ('Industry'. That's blinding, isn't it? *'Diligence or assiduity in any task or effort.'* I look through the glass wall of my office at all the diligence and assiduity going on around here: Rebecca, laughing her head off as she feverishly types a gossip-laden email to some whore she knows; Darren and Stan, our scouts, chasing each other around with water pistols; Schneider berating Nancy for failing to secure him a necessary restaurant reservation.)

What do I think? Honestly?

I picture the expressions which would appear on these earnest faces if I even *began* to tell them what I was thinking while we listened to their demo. '*Well, kids, during the ludicrously overlong intro to the first number I started wondering if those fucks in the car department had finally gotten around to installing the new CD changer in the boot of my car. By the time your clichéd, long-overdue first "chorus" was finally dropping, I was mentally re-enacting a recent coke- and E-fuelled gang bang I had with a pair of cheap Eastern European prostitutes. Then I started worrying because I realised I'd forgotten to drop a suit that I want to wear to the Music Week Awards tomorrow night into the dry-cleaner's and could they do it same day or should I have Rebecca pop by my flat at lunchtime and take it in for me? Or should I just buy a new suit? I saw one in Paul Smith I liked the other day, but could I possibly have any alterations done in time? Then Lisa from finance walked past the window wearing her low-cut jeans — the piano-wire of her thong just visible above the denim — and I started working her into the East European hooker gang bang, having her being fucked by one of them with a huge strap-on while I'm ejaculating an astonishingly large payload into her gagging mouth and blinking, grateful eyes while the other ostro eats her out from beneath. By the time I was standing there in my mind's eye, sweat-glazed, panting and triumphant, over the three tearful, naked semen-encrusted bodies, your last overwrought ballad was spiralling to a close and I hadn't really heard a fucking note. Sorry.*'

What do I think? Honestly? I think I would like to see you and the rest of your band die screaming in agony from something like testicular cancer. I think that last week I spent a hundred and eighty pounds on a necktie and lost it a few hours later, drunk in Soho. I think about telling these hopeless, penniless cunts this. But instead, pointlessly, I say, 'Great guitar sound.'

'Yeah,' the manager says, and he starts crapping on about how Doug – or whoever – has been playing guitar since he was a fucking foetus or something. Doug looks up from the floor and smiles bashfully. It's about all I can do not to punch his stupid, talentless face in. To stand up, run the length of the room, and boot him full-force in his pasty, pimply, stinking indie chops. But – ever reasonable – I just nod and listen and say things like 'yeah?' and 'yeah' and 'great' and 'really?' for a long time.

I *hate* indie music. Until a couple of years ago you didn't really have to think about it. It was just a couple of hundred losers fucking around in Camden. Then a pair of Mancunian losers rock up clutching a Beatles songbook and suddenly you've got to listen to all this shite and take all these meetings in case you miss the next one. It's a fucking nightmare.

I'm tired. I got home from Waters' place and managed just a few hours' fitful, cokey sleep before I had to get up and drive over to the new house, where there was another problem.

I've bought a toilet at the top of Ladbroke Grove. Desoto hooked Trellick and me up with a bent estate agent, one who specialises in finding 'undervalued development opportunities'. What this means is that he convinces derelict pensioners (ideally ones without immediate families) who have been in their derelict houses since the dawn of time that the place is worth a lot less than it really is. You buy it, gut the place, lick of paint, couple of real fireplaces, do the floors up, and flog it a few months later for a sickening profit.

I pulled up at the place and walked through a trio of builders on the front steps – astonished-looking Albanians, buckled over tea and tabloids, smoking like lab beagles – down the hallway, where a couple more Albanians are hunkered down either side of a tea chest savaging a stinking parcel of vinegar-sodden fish and chips, and into the living room where Murdoch, their boss, my builder, stood in a large pool of water gazing thoughtfully at a wall.

A section of plaster around six feet in diameter had been hacked away leaving a black, gaping wound, exposing the guts of the old house; a hydra's head of ancient wiring, rusted copper pipes. One of the pipes had been hastily bandaged, but a thin trickle of water still ran from it down into the wall cavity. 'You're joking?' I said.

'Dinnaeworry,' Murdoch replied cheerfully, 'Plumber's-cummin'rooninnaminnut.Jistasweelwefunoutthenoo.'

'Found out what?'

'Thonpipe'sbinleakin'furdonkey'san'it'sweekendyer halewathere.'

Murdoch was saying that the pipe has been leaking for a long time and has caused damage to the entire wall. It's taken three agonising months but I'm now fluent in the kind of horrible, guttural Scottish Murdoch speaks. It's like I've been forced to learn a language I will never use again.

There's no point getting angry at Murdoch. He just talks more. You just have to ask the question. 'How long and how much?' I said.

'Well . . .' He fired up one of his unspeakable cigarettes

– a Raffles, a Mayfair, a Concord, a Savoy – and started talking.

I didn't listen – it's not worth the effort. It really isn't. Whenever a problem comes up with the building work – which it does on a weekly, sometimes daily, basis – Murdoch will crap on for eternity, giving me several options. He'll then tell me why the cheapest option isn't worth bothering with. And then why the mid-priced option isn't really what I'm after either.

It's all good for Murdoch though. No matter how tits up anything goes – he just keeps raking in cash. He has squadrons of crazed Albanians all over north-west London. Some of them do very well, Murdoch's Albanians. Strong work ethic. You come over here and you work your balls off from dawn until dusk – plastering and painting and bodging and fucking up – while the wife (or sister, or mum) does her bit across town, ankle-deep in spunk in some massage parlour off the North Circular.

I say Murdoch gives me options, but he doesn't really. He just talks shit for a while until I wind up spending more money. But what can I do? What do I know about this stuff? Murdoch could lift up some floorboards and show me a pair of elephants, chained to a tandem and frantically pedalling, and tell me that the building is, in fact, elephant-powered and that we need to replace one of the beasts. I'd display irritation, but only mild surprise, as I scribbled out a cheque for the most costly house-powering elephant on the market.

'Abootseevenoreightthoosanahreckon . . .' he finally said.

'Fuck me.'

'Ayeit'sbadnewsrightenuff.'

'Right, whatever. Do it. And will you please tell your guys to stop eating that stinking fucking takeaway food in here?'

'Ayeah'lltellthemtaewatchitbuttheboayshuvgotaeeatlike.'

I'm now three months and a *lot* of money into this nightmare. I've reached the point where just the sight of Murdoch's mobile number popping up on the screen of my Nokia makes me feel sick.

Murdoch went on, talking about skylights and RSJs and supporting walls, about hardwood flooring and cornices. About new windows and planning permission. And it's all expensive. None of it is cheap.

The funding for this whole farce is, of course, borrowed. Just a few years back it would have been impossible to do this at my age and income. To obtain the financing you'd have needed guarantors, collateral and accounts going back to the Stone Age. I just told them a mad pack of utter crap – I'm Senior Vice President of A&R for the Fucking World – and I earn a billion quid a minute. Bosh. Done Deal.

I drove back to the office, for this meeting. Crawling along Ladbroke Grove with the top down I got stuck in traffic across from a pub; until very recently a crunchily carpeted pit of bitter, satellite TV and boil-in-the-bag pies. Now there are polished oak floors and pan-fried, line-caught Scottish trout. Frosty bottles of champagne and Sauvignon gleam in glass-fronted coolers. An ancient local, baking in his tattered overcoat and cap, stands on the pavement outside, frowning at the braying laughter and the Propellerheads pumping from the jukebox. He's easily eighty and squints through thick glasses at the chalkboard menu, which is telling him that today's special is seafood linguine with Irish lobster, scallops and prawns. The chalkboard may as well read 'go home and die, you fucking old cunt'. I smile. What wars and depressions, what hardships and indignities has this poor bastard lived through, coming of age as he did during unarguably the worst stretch of the twentieth century, to end his days having to witness this shit?

I think about money. I'm running two mortgages, a bridging loan, an overdraft and six credit cards, as well as all the usual monthly outgoings: large and regular tabs must be settled with west London's cocaine dealers. Drinks, fine dining and regular exotic holidays must be factored in. Monthly, it seems, I must write cheques (or rather, Rebecca must before I sign them) to various London parking authorities for hundreds of pounds' worth of fines. There are clothes, gadgets and impulse buys in Heal's and Harvey Nicks of a Saturday morning – last weekend a pair of cherrywood bedside cabinets, snapped up for just twelve hundred quid when I was hung-over and showing off in front of Trellick, four hundred quid the week before on a set of Japanese butcher's knives which sit gleaming and never-used on the black granite breakfast bar. There's the cleaner, a witless Colombian demi-hooker whose efforts in the flat seem to diminish in direct proportion to the wage increases she regularly demands. Some days I bowl through the door and the only significant difference to the place is the fact that she's lifted the money from the kitchen counter. I jump into Sainsbury's for a pint of milk and stumble back to the Saab three hundred quid later, juggling bottles of champagne and Ecuadorian kiwi fruit, foie gras, fresh Loch Fyne oysters, Jerusalem artichokes, Belgian chocolates, sushi and dinky miniature vegetables. The champagne is drunk and the food is tossed straight into the bin from the fridge by the cleaner a couple of weeks later after it's started to fester and turn incredible florid colours.

Because I'm never home, of course. I sometimes think I am buying all this stuff solely to impress the monosyllabic retards who work the supermarket tills. I smoke three packs of Marlboro Lights every day – my tabs tab is approaching four hundred quid a month. An average night out with the lads – drinks at the Atlantic bar, dinner some-where new and ludicrous, more drinks at Soho House or the Groucho, coke, cabs and boilers – clocks in at about eight hundred quid. It's no wonder I'm trying to keep it down to two or three nights out a week. Even though a fair chunk of this can be punted onto expenses, it still takes a lot of fucking dough to keep the wheels on the wagon. My bank manager stutters in disbelief as every month brings the same request to maintain, or increase, my overdraft. He knows what I earn. (About five times what he does.) He can't believe I'm getting through it either. On the plus side my hooker expenses do seem to be steady and manageable at around a grand a month these days. Maybe it's the cold weather. Sometimes, in the feverish months of spring and summer, I have to admit I go a bit bonkers.

Anyway, the answer to all of these problems is simple enough: Big. Fucking. Hit. Records. Have a few of those and – bosh – no more problems.

I edge along Ladbroke Grove – at one point ecstatically managing to get into third gear – and I keep seeing them; hunched on doorsteps with their tabloids and their tea, smoking their Raffles or Coliseums as they heft rolls of seagrass matting and lengths of hardwood flooring in and out of the dusty old houses. The builders. You see? *Everyone's* doing it. It's like you can look along the road, through the leafy trees towards Holland Park, and see the fireball of cash come flaming down the hill, burning out all the tolers: the Kaffirs, the old people, the welfare families. They've had it around here. Finished.

Finally, blissfully, the meeting is ending and I'm saying things like 'let's do some demos' and 'see you soon'. They hand me a flyer – a picture of Malcolm McDowell from the movie *If*, presumably a totem of cool in whatever sorry universe these jizz-rags inhabit – for their next gig as they leave.

I flop down on the sofa and start rolling a spliff. There are days at work, whole days, where nothing seems to happen. All morning long there is coffee and cigarettes and phone calls where I say things like 'send it over' and 'in last week's *NME*' and 'shipping a hundred thousand' while I watch MTV – Foo Fighters, Daft Punk, the Chemical Brothers – and think about lunch. Somewhere in the mid-afternoon I'll have a spliff and a belt of Scotch, or a line of gak, and the day will look a little brighter, sharper. I'll make the same calls and watch the same videos with a little more enthusiasm. Or sometimes I'll just crawl behind my sofa for a nap after lunch, the blinds drawn against the outer office and music whumping from my stereo. Later I'll start to drift up, suspended in that sweet honey-drop between waking and sleeping, to see that the street lights have started to come on along the park across the road.

Darren comes in and starts banging on about new bands

he wants me to listen to; Athletico Strip, Dragdoll, Magoo, Starfish.

I flip through *Music Week* while he talks and slips cassettes and CDs into my machine. Lucian Grange has been promoted to MD at Polydor. He is only a few years older than me. This news mixes with my simmering hangover and fills me with a depth, a profundity, of sorrow I cannot adequately describe.

'What the fuck is this?' I say to Darren, nodding towards the stereo at some tuneless pile of shite he's stuck on the turntable.

'Ah, the Lazies, American band. Fucking cool.'

'It's an insult. Take it off.'

The racket stops and he rummages through his pile of 7 and CDs for something else.

My mobile chirrups. 'Hello?'

'Christ, big night or what?' a thick, hoarse voice says.

It takes a few seconds for me to register it, to believe it.

'I . . . how do you feel?' I manage finally.

'Bit rough.' He goes on for a while, talking about a gig we're meant to be going to tonight, some band called Bellatrix at the Bull and Gate and finally I hang up, numb.

I'm thinking a couple of things. 1) Fucking worthless Thai Valium. 2) From the sound of things it is not that unusual, it is not completely out of the normal run of things, for Waters to wake up naked and covered in his own shit with a thrumming butt-plug up his arse.

Like Freddie, or Jason, or Michael Myers, he is probably unkillable.

The greenery of Oxfordshire blurs past the tinted windows

of our people carrier. Derek is shouting on his mobile, ranting about some artwork he's unhappy with. Ross taps away at his laptop while Dunn, Nicky, Waters and I read the trades. Schneider has headphones on, listening to Christ knows what on his Discman and trying to act relaxed.

We're all headed to the Rage playback. No one's heard a note yet, but the album will be a key summer release for us among what is a pretty thin-looking release schedule and expectations are running pretty high.

We bowl through the studio – where wine, beers and nibbles have been laid on – and into the control room where Rage, Fisher and two engineers are waiting. Rage sits in a huge leather chair at the centre of the mixing desk.

The first thing I think as he swivels round to greet us is – *fuck me*. His nose is dewy and leaking, his eyeballs vibrating marbles, his left leg stutters and pumps uncontrollably, his jaw is locked forward and set hard, frozen by cocaine. Ross and I exchange a quick, incredulous look.

'Right,' Rage says once we're all seated on two huge leather sofas at the back of the room, glasses of warm Chardonnay in hand. An engineer hits 'play' and Rage moves a trembling hand towards a fader, pushing it all the way up.

Forty minutes into the thing I sneak a look around at the expressions on display. Most people just look blank. Ross is fighting laughter. Derek looks like he might burst out of his seat and kill someone at any moment. Schneider's face is harder to read. It is buried in his hands.

The first five or six minutes of the song were simply annoying – a hi-hat pattern and some abstract tweeting sounds. Somewhere around the fifteen-minute mark a bass line arrived and Rage began conducting the music with his hands, his eyes closed, lost in some mad rapture over this abortion he's created. People cross and recross their legs, sip their wine and pray for it to end. But it doesn't. It just keeps on going – drum loops clattering randomly, snatches of vocals, jarring keyboard stabs.

As the track approaches the one-hour mark and *nothing* has emerged that vaguely resembles a hook, or a chorus, or a recognisable melody, it collectively dawns on us that we're listening to the sonic representation of someone's mind coming apart. On a positive note I'm thinking that I must get the name of Rage's dealer, because the chang the cunt is getting his hands on is clearly fucking phenomenal.

In the end I simply stare at the red, digital numbers on the tape counter, watching the minutes, the money, Schneider's career, tick away. The counter reads '64.33' when it all finally ends in a mad, juddering flourish, like the crescendo at the end of 'A Day in the Life', played on broken computers by mongoloids. Rage has his hands extended, trembling, his forefingers pointing skywards as he wrings the last notes out of his cocaine-induced hallucinatory mind-orchestra.

I look over at Schneider. He has tears in eyes. He is finished and he knows it.

Rage swivels around in his chair to face us. 'It's called "Birth",' he says.

Of course it fucking is.

It gets better when Rage corrects our assumption that we've just heard the whole album, segued together in its entirety. No, he tells us that this will be a *single*, the first single to precede the album in fact, that he *will not* allow an edit of any sort, and how pleased he is that we've been the first witnesses to the world's first drum'n'bass opera. Then he runs off to the toilet. There's a lot of polite nodding and words like 'interesting', 'radical' and 'challenging' get thrown around.

The second we're all inside the people carrier and the driver slams the door shut Schneider turns to Derek and says, 'Look . . .' It will be his longest contribution to the conversation for some time.

'WHAT HAVE YOU DONE? *WHAT THE FUCK HAVE YOU DONE!* THREE AND A HALF MONTHS IN ONE OF THE MOST EXPENSIVE STUDIOS IN THE COUNTRY AND WE DON'T HAVE A FUCKING THING! I'M TELLING YOU RIGHT NOW THAT THERE IS NO WAY ON EARTH THIS LABEL WILL EVER RELEASE A FUCKING NOTE OF ANYTHING WE HEARD TODAY! HOW COULD YOU LET IT GET TO THIS? HOW?'

Schneider tries to speak but Derek's already on the phone to Trellick at the office, telling him to get Rage's contract out and firing questions at him. What's the unrecouped balance? How cheaply can we get out of the deal? Can we, in fact, make any case for suing Rage for breach of contract for delivering material which is so blatantly uncommercial? Is there a sanity clause?

Janette from press leans forward and pats Schneider comfortingly on the knee. 'Actually, I quite liked it,' she says quietly, but he doesn't reply. He just goes on looking out of window as we thread our way back along country lanes towards the M40. Dead Man Staring.

*

Danny Rent brings his girl band, Songbirds, in for a meeting.

The four of them sit bunched up on my office sofa, scowling and chewing gum, looking like they've been kept back in class. Three of them are white and one black, but the white girls all act like Kaffirs – they kiss their teeth and click their fingers and say things like 'seen?' They're all aged between seventeen and twenty, all lookers – one of the white girls in particular (Denise? Sonia?) is stunning – but with that working-class whore look. They're genetic time bombs, DNA-Semtex. Every one of them will explode into monsterism the minute they hit twenty-seven. They're all dressed the way these girls dress, tits busting out of T-shirts made for newborn babies and low-slung combat pants which allow their thongs – pink, black and lemon – to jut way up above the waistlines. I mean, they look like they'd let you do *anything* to them these girls; fuck them in the arse and punch them and stuff.

We're watching a 'video' Danny has had made, to try and sell them to record companies – the four of them, dressed in cheap, nasty, high-street clothes, grind their way unsteadily through a really tacky R&B number.

The video finishes.

'Mmmm,' I say, 'who are your influences then?'

Silence. They shift uneasily. I realise they do not understand the question.

'Steven's saying,' Danny butts in, 'what music do you like?'

Another gargantuan pause. ''Ip op?' says a brunette, uncertainly.

'Madonna,' says the blonde.

'Good,' I say, nodding, 'good.'

'Ere, mate,' the black boiler says, 'Danny says you signed Rage. Yeah?'

'Yeah,' I lie and they all murmur approval.

'Wot's e loike?' one asks.

'Rage? He's great. Really clever guy.'

Another long silence. 'So,' the blonde one, the really attractive one says, fingering a trainer lace and nervously looking up, making eye contact with me through her fringe, 'what chew fink of our stuff then?'

What do I think? I think you look like the worst sort of sink-estate, single-mother, benefit-fraud trash imaginable. I think that your 'music' is about the biggest insult to humanity since a roomful of Nazis first cooed over the blueprints for Auschwitz.

But I'm also thinking that, if we bring in real songwriters, session musicians and a decent producer, if we throw suitcases of money at stylists and hair and make-up artists, if we hire world-quality photographers and video directors, if we get personal trainers in and manage to keep you all off the KFC and the vodka for a few months, if we can find someone to teach you how to speak properly, if we spend eye-popping sums on retainers for press officers and pluggers, and if they can somehow convince enough journalists, radio programmers and TV producers that you're not really talent-free sluts who would gobble a donkey just to meet Chris Evans, that you are, in fact, 'the real deal', then maybe, just maybe, with the wind behind us and a couple of breaks, I think we could probably sell a few fucking records.

'I think it's great,' I say, getting up and showing them out. I mean, it might be worth a pop.

Girl power, innit?

Rebecca is holding a phone towards me. 'It's Barry from club promotions.'

'Barry?'

'Steven, hi, I got the club reactions in on "Why Don't You . . .".'

These are A4 sheets, like little report cards that all the club DJs fill in to tell you what they reckon to the track.

'Well?'

'Ah . . .' In a nanosecond my blood turns to antifreeze.

'Barry?'

'Yeah, they're all right. They're all right.'

All right? Just *all right*? This is bad. This is very fucking bad.

We have a second 'Why Don't You' marketing meeting. It is markedly different from the first. Dunn kicks off.

'Sorry, Radio 1 don't think it's for them. If the record had been bigger at club then we'd have some ammunition. As it is . . .' He spreads his hands.

Barry pipes up, 'It just seems to be the kind of record that . . . we'll need a bit of radio before we can get a lot of the commercial club DJs to pick up on it.'

Hannah: 'MTV quite liked the video. But they're not going to playlist it until we get some radio.'

Through all of this Derek just glares at me. With the video (hastily shot, at my insistence) we have spent well over one hundred thousand pounds on this turkey. Turkey? That's an insult to turkeys. It's a fucking dodo.

Ross: 'No point in doing much advertising or a big poster campaign until we've got some awareness at radio and TV . . .'

Suzy: 'Not much interest at press, I'm afraid. We're getting reviewed in *Mixmag*.'

Nicky: 'I'm afraid there's not much I can do with this at the moment.' She tries to look sympathetic but the bitch can hardly keep the smile from creasing her fat fucking face in half.

Finally Derek hits critical mass: 'ARE YOU TELLING ME WE'VE SPENT OVER A HUNDRED FUCKING GRAND TO GET A FUCKING REVIEW IN FUCKING *MIXMAG*?! JESUS CHRIST!

I stare at the glass table – through the glass table and onto the carpeting where I uselessly notice that Dunn is wearing the same Prada shoes as I am – and say nothing. There is nothing to say. If there was something to say I'd be saying it.

Derek hates the record. The marketing department hate the record. The club promotions department hate the record. The radio department hate the record. I want to kill Rudi, that Nazi-scumbag-fucking-child-molester-fucking-animal. In a bizarre alchemic process perhaps unique to the entertainment industry the cancer cure I brought back from Cannes has mysteriously morphed into something closer to the cause of AIDS.

Finally Derek looks around the room and says, with absolutely no enthusiasm, 'So where do we go with this record now?'

'Lourdes?' Ross suggests, unhelpfully.

Sure enough it comes to pass. Schneider's contract, due to expire later this summer, will not be renewed. They pay him off and he clears his desk out. I go for a drink with him on his last day. It is three in the afternoon and the pub is empty. Outside, rain falls lightly across Hammersmith. It's warm though; the pub doors are open and cars sizzle by on the wet tarmac. Schneider sluices the ice around in his vodka tonic and tries to be upbeat, giving it the whole 'best-thing-that-could-have-happened-in-a-way' type shit. 'What are you going to do?' I ask.

'I've had a couple of interesting offers,' he lies. I mean, fuck. He hasn't had a proper hit in years. He's *thirty-nine* — wife and two kids — and suddenly — bosh! — it's Goodnight Vienna. At best he might land a sympathy job with some reissues label, hawking back catalogue and farting about trying to secure the rights for Eddie and the Hot Rods live LPs. As he craps on about the non-existent offers he reckons he's had, Alisha's Attic, then Kula Shaker, then Mansun blare from the jukebox. It dawns on me that they are all bands that Schneider (and, by extension, me) either turned down or failed to sign in the past year or two. All of whom are having hits now. Any one of them might have saved him. But he went with Rage. The man who put it all on red . . .

'For what it's worth,' he says, 'I told Derek they should make you Head of A&R.'

Fuck. Support from a loser like Schneider can probably only weaken my case right now. 'Really? Thanks. What did Derek say?'

'That they're probably going to give it to Waters.'

He drains his glass, bangs it down on the wet mahogany, and signals wearily for another. 'Sorry,' he says, not looking at me, 'bad timing there with that record of Rudi's.'

\*

Sometimes you need to act fast. You really do. 'A good plan today is better than a perfect plan tomorrow,' and all that crap.

The celebration for Waters' promotion began in the fifth floor bar at Harvey Nicks at lunchtime with the whole of the A&R department plus Trellick and Derek. From there onto Quo Vadis for dinner and then Soho House before Waters and I – absolutely smashed beyond human belief by this point – ducked out and caught a cab up to Camden, to see some useless band who are playing at the Dublin Castle. We last two songs before we hail another cab on Parkway and – stopping briefly outside the house of a dealer we both know in Chalk Farm, where we score three more grams – head back to Waters' flat off Westbourne Park Road.

'You know how much I respect you,' Waters says, sniffing and screeching out big lines on the big mirror while I pour the vodka. 'I don't want you to feel that you're suddenly working *for* me. We're working *together*.'

I close my eyes and swallow about a quarter-pint of neat Stoli.

'I want to try and build the kind of culture where . . .' Waters goes into an idiotic rhapsody about his 'vision', about the kind of A&R culture he plans to establish at the label. Words like 'organic', 'Chris Blackwell', 'synergy' and 'John Hammond' are freely tossed around. His stupid fucking dog snoozes at his feet while he snorts and sweats and theorises. The conversation drifts and rambles, landing on the subject of Great British Songwriters, the kind of people Waters wants us to sign. Waters is struggling for actual names. I mention Paul Weller.

'Uh, yeah. He . . . he writes most of his own stuff,

doesn't he?' Waters says, his head thrown back as he sucks a gooey wad of snot and gak down his throat.

CDs are scattered all over the place; on the low coffee table, the sofa, the floor. I pick one up at random, to have something to read while Waters craps on – he's now literally talking about how his daddy laughed when he fell off his bike when he was nine, or some fucking thing – and find I'm holding a copy of the last Prodigy album, *Music for the Jilted Generation*. I open the gatefold inner sleeve and stare at the painting which covers both panels. Or rather 'painting'. The crude piece of artwork depicts a raver – long, straggly hair, trainers, sweatshirt, etc. – who is standing on one side of a dark chasm. On the other side of the chasm a huge group of riot police are wielding truncheons and Perspex shields. Their faces are obscured by the black visors of their helmets. On the raver's side of the chasm is an idyllic green field with a sound system, a DJ and other ravers dancing around blissfully. The sun is shining. Back on the other side, behind the coppers, is a dark industrial city: hulking tower blocks, ominous skyscrapers and factories retching sulphur into the blackened sky. The two sides of the chasm are connected by a rope bridge, which the coppers are preparing to cross, clearly in order to give the raver a good fucking beating. But hang on, the raver is holding a sabre to the rope bridge, about to sever it and thwart their plans. He is also giving the coppers the finger. The quality of the actual painting is *appalling* – like some handicapped kid's O-level art project.

Waters looks up from shaping more lines and peers over my shoulder. 'Good that, isn't it?' he says.

I stare at the picture, dumbfounded, for a long, long

time. All I can think about is how much – if you were somehow forced to live in the world depicted on the Prodigy sleeve – you'd want to be on the coppers' side of that chasm; in the filthy city with its casinos, hookers and petrol stations. Its five-star hotels, sex shops, nightclubs and banks. I am also filled with a great and unexpected affection for Britain's riot police.

I look up at Waters. 'How?'

'What?'

'How is this picture good?'

'It's . . . y'know. It's got a message.'

'What fucking message?'

He craps on with some anti-Establishment balls for a while as I sit there getting angrier and angrier. To calm myself down I try and think of all the words I know for cocaine – gak, chang, nose-up, bag, beak, charlie, krell, powder, chisel, bump, posh, bugle, sniff, skiwear, schniff, Bronson, Bolivian, toot, junior (crack is called senior), chas, nonsense, bounce, blow, Vim – but it's not working.

'Oh fuck off. You know what I mean,' Waters says huffily. 'Anyway . . .' he tries to change the subject.

'Excuse me,' I say as I get up and leave the room.

It's hard to say what does it. Whether it's his views on the Prodigy sleeve, or the fact that that dismal spunk-worshipper Derek could choose to make this guy Head of A&R over me, or the fact Waters doesn't even know that Paul Weller is primarily known for being a songwriter. I mean, don't get me wrong, I don't give a good drop of spunk about the Prodigy, or about Weller or his music – although it was certainly impressive that Go! Discs managed to resurrect the fossilised mod cunt and grind a million albums out of him – it's just . . . the indignity of the situation suddenly hits me. No one knows what they are doing, yes, granted. But Waters . . . Waters really doesn't know *anything*. And now he's my boss. For a second I almost experience sadness, a sense of loss, regarding Schneider.

I walk into the kitchen. There, still in the corner by the fridge, is the blue-and-steel baseball bat.

Home security.

I come back in. He's sitting on the floor with his back to me, hunched over the mirror on the low coffee table, already – always – shaping more lines. I check my watch. It's almost 6 a.m. A dance compilation plays softly. Waters is still talking, gibbering. To me? To the sleeping dog? To the wall? Who knows?

I walk up behind him. I start the bat back, swinging it so far over my head that I'm sure I feel it touch the heel of my right shoe. Then I bring it down with humming force. I can hear the air being moved aside. Waters is saying the word 'crossover'.

Sound of Impact.

Now, I expected there to be some crunchy give as his skull caved in and he slumped forward. Goodnight Vienna. But no. There's a loud clear 'thwock' – like hitting a very hard piece of wood – and Waters immediately *howls* in agony, grabs his head, and starts staggering to his feet, knocking glasses and ashtrays noisily onto the polished wood floor. The bastard dog explodes into life and starts yelping and growling. Stunned and shaking, it takes me a second or two to recock the bat, by which time he's on his knees, halfway up. I swing down again, this time the bat glances off his forehead, which is already slick with blood, and sends him reeling into the middle of the room. He looks up, right at me. Then he looks at his trembling hands, which are covered in blood. The expression on his face . . . he looks confused, horrified. Like when you open your bank statement thinking you've had a quiet month, and scan down the tumbling debits, to the unthinkable figure at the bottom with the letters 'OD' beside it. The dog is barking its tits off, going crackers.

For a second I think he's going to charge at me, and he's a big guy, Waters. Then the force of the blow, the shockwave, hits him, his eyes start vibrating, his legs spastic about and he wobbles onto his knees, making a terrible 'ohhhh . . . urrrr' sound. Blood is pouring down his face now and it looks like oil under the soft halogen spots. I run towards him. He manages one actual word – 'please' – as I bring the bat down for the third time in a massive, terrible arc. He's on his knees, at around waist height to me, and I connect right in the centre of his dome. This time there is *lots* of crunchy give and his skull caves in. A jet of blood sprays out of his nose and he goes over, falling onto his side and twitching on the floor.

Bear eat CDs!

'You stupid fat cunt!' I scream. 'Paul Weller writes *all* his own songs! *He's one of the foremost singer-songwriters of his generation!*' Just to be on the safe side, because the anger is fizzling out now, the adrenalin going, my blood clotting, becoming thick as tarmac in my veins, I smash the bloody bat down once more, onto the side of his head this time. With the sound of a loud, wet fart, a mess of grey-white 'brains' spurts out of the crack in the top of his head. The dog stops barking and growling and starts licking and nibbling at the spreading puddle of blood and brains which is oozing out of his master's broken head. Disgusted, and with about the last of my strength, I smash the Jack Russell incredibly hard over the head. Its skull just explodes, the eyeballs both flopping out and dangling down its face and then it's nice and quiet, the only sound that of the house compilation, Frankie Knuckles' 'Your Love' playing softly.

There's something small, pink and bloody on the floor next to Waters' mouth and I realise he's bitten the tip of his tongue off. It's just lying there, a few inches away from a bloodstained paperback copy of *Fever Pitch* by Nick Hornby.

# April

London Records terminate their deal with Tony Wilson's label Factory Too. R. Kelly is no. 1 for a fucking month. XL spends a lot of money signing some band called Stroke. Whispers start to circulate that the new Radiohead LP is off its tits — an unlistenable prog-rock nightmare. Andy Thompson's label VC Recordings prepares to launch an album by dance act D*Note. Thompson says, 'I can see D*Note at the Royal Albert Hall. The sky is really the limit for them.'

*'Lemme tell ya something — if a guy's a cocksucker in his
life, when he dies he don't become a saint.'*

Morris Levy

The day after I kill Waters I have to go to Dublin to see a
band.

I *hate* the cab ride into Dublin. It's a bitch. I mean, it'll
soon be the twenty-first century and these worthless Paddy
tramps can't even get their diseased, potato-ravaged arses
into gear and build a fucking motorway. You have to sit for
eternity on some two-lane B-road that winds through
housing estates, high streets and Christ knows what, all the
while with some lobotomised fucking Mick asking you all
manner of crap about yourself.

'AndwillthisbeyerfirstvisittoDublinnow?' the horrible
tip-scrounging cunt has the balls to ask me.

I just groan and crank up my Discman, turning to stare
silently out of the window at the dreadful shops, bars and
inbred mutants that crawl past in the rain-streaked grid-
lock. But the guy, the cabbie, swings round from the wheel
again and keeps asking me something. I slide the headphones down.

'Andwhichhotelwasityewereafternow?'

'What?' I sigh.

He says it again, slower.

'The Clarence.'

'Ohverynicenowyeknowit'syermanfromyewtoowho . . .'

But I don't hear the rest of this because I slip the headphones back up over my ears and Richard Ashcroft's singing 'You're a slave to money . . .' as I return to staring out the window through cracked, stinging, hung-over eyes: a big Guinness poster, a dirty child on a mountain bike, an old man bawling in the doorway of a pub, and a bright red butcher's shop with carcasses hanging from hooks and gleaming entrails piled in plastic trays.

I check in at the Clarence.

I go to my room, masturbate, and fall asleep.

I wake up and realise I've missed the gig.

I go back to sleep.

I get up the next morning and eat a late, expensive breakfast.

I lie in bed and watch a film called *Outbreak* starring Dustin Hoffman on pay TV.

I fly back to London.

I tell Derek the band were 'promising'.

He nods, like he understands something.


I waltz into the office around lunchtime the next day, sucking on an ice lolly and wearing shorts and sandals – London's having one of those early-spring mornings where it thinks it's summertime. As I round the corner towards my office I see Rebecca and Pam. They're huddled over Rebecca's desk, their faces red, both clutching wet, shredded Kleenex.

'Oh Steven,' Pam says, a catch in her voice, 'it's terrible . . .' She bursts into fresh hot tears.

'What?' I say.

'It's . . . Roger . . .' she manages between sobs.

'WHAT?' I say.

'He's dead!' Pam says.

'No!' I say. (I thought about saying 'NO!', but then I thought, *no*.)

She just nods, blubbing, shoulders shaking, crinkly tissue pressed to her face. I like girls' faces when they've been crying – hot, soft and pulpy. I wonder if Pam – in her grief – is recalling the night after the Ivor Novello Awards last year when she rashly went home with Waters and he tried – at length from what I heard – to cajole her into anal sex. She pulls herself together a little, sweeping wet strands of hair out of her face and taking a deep breath.

'A neighbour found him this morning. It looks like someone broke into his flat, a burglar, and Roger must have disturbed them. Or he tried to stop them or something.'

The idea of Waters being confronted in his living room at 3 a.m. by a couple of big, angry tooled-up niggers and doing anything other than begging for his fat, sleazy life is so laughable I have to bite my cheeks. Pam collapses forwards again into me, shuddering and sobbing as she buries her face in my neck. As I comfort her, and quietly enjoy the press of her (decent) rack against my chest, Rebecca and I look at each other. Rebecca's eyes are red like Pam's, her cheeks slick with tears too, but she's looking at me strangely, with an expression on her face I can't quite place.

Hastings comes out of his office. 'Isn't it terrible?' he says. I put a hand over my face and say, 'Excuse me, please.'

I run into my office, slamming the door behind me, and throw myself face down on the sofa, my shoulders shaking and my whole body convulsing. I can feel Hastings, Rebecca and Pam watching me through the glass partition. I can feel their buffoonish concern upon me.

It must really look like I'm *crying*.

Later, seven o'clock, after everyone's gone home and the place is empty, I go and sit in Waters' office. It is strange to sit there as it slowly gets dark, surrounded by the things he saw and touched every day – his computer, his diary, phone and stereo – and think about how he said 'please'. On the wall is a framed gold disc from the one (almost) successful act Waters signed. (They're 'bands' or 'groups' when you're trying to sign them, and 'acts' once you have. I don't know why that is.) Scattered around his desk and perched on his shelves are various *Star Wars* products; little X-Wing fighters, a Millennium Falcon, a big R2D2 that's actually a phone. Like many men in the record industry in their late twenties/early thirties Waters thought *Star Wars* was cool. Just looking at his dismal toys feels like justification enough for killing the cretin.

I'm bound to get a few of his acts dumped on me. But that's not so bad – most of them are so fucked that they're beyond rescue. 'It was broke when I got here' stuff. I plan to suggest we drop pretty much all of them.

A Jiffy bag, with an EMI address label on it, is propped up on his keyboard. I feel inside and pull out a promo CD. I squint at it in the half-light: Radiohead. Their new single, which isn't out for a month or so and which I haven't heard yet. Dunn says most radio stations are giving it the fuck off.

I slip it into Waters' machine and a strange, terrible noise fills the room. I turn it down.

I open the top drawer of his desk and have a root: taxi and restaurant receipts, half-completed expenses claims, cassettes and CDs, pens and pencils, a couple of empty cocaine wraps. One half-full wrap . . .

I do a line off his mouse mat. The mouse mat is a picture of Hervé Villechaize, the midget actor who played Nick Nack in the James Bond film and Tattoo in *Fantasy Island*. (Like many men in the record industry in their late twenties/early thirties Waters thought that shit TV shows from the seventies and eighties were cool.)

Hervé was three foot ten and weighed four stone, but the mad dwarf cunt fell in love with, and married, a fully grown woman. When she divorced him and took all his cash he went mental; he hit the painkillers, the Scotch and the chang and wound up topping himself. He taped his own suicide too. Honestly. He got hold of a tape recorder, pressed 'record', put a pillow against his chest, held a big fuck-off gun up to the pillow, and he said, *'Goodbye, my darling. I could not satisfy your love,'* and shot himself through his tiny heart.

Or rather, he tried to. Somehow he missed everything vital and had to cock the gun again and shoot himself a second time. Apparently the tape ends with him moaning and groaning, saying, *'Ohhh it hurts, it hurts. I am dying . . . I am dying now.'*

The Radiohead track, which is called 'Paranoid Android', has built through an appalling crescendo of arty noise into a kind of washed-out coda with Thom Yorke, bleating and warbling the words 'rain down' over the top. What the fuck were they thinking with this nonsense? They're finished. Surely no cunt's going to be having this?

I turn it off and just sit there in Waters' office in the quiet dark, doing the last of his chang and thinking about Hervé Villechaize, until it's time to go to the Borderline, to see some band called the Hitchers who Lamacq has been banging on about.

The car from the airport seems to take a long time and we pull up at the church already – always – late. While Trellick winds up a call on his mobile I get out the car and look around: grey skies, windy, brutal. Down the hillside, off in the distance, is a big, dismal city. Sheffield or something, I suppose.

Christ, I hate being out of London.

The cabbie is saying something to us but he's Northern and none of us understand a word. Ross slips the guy a fifty and tells him to wait for us. The cabbie blinks at the big, unfamiliar, strawberry-coloured note and carefully folds it into his shirt pocket, like it's an old, delicate parchment or something. 'Pay your mortgage off, mate,' Ross says as we walk away. We go through the gate and up the path towards the grey stone building, towards soft, horrible organ music.

Inside it's busy – a couple of hundred people – and we have to stand at the back. A minister, a vicar or something, is crapping on about Waters: '. . . in London, in the music industry, where he enjoyed great success and made a great many friends, so many of whom have travelled here to be with us today. As a boy Roger was always a huge fan of music and it was because of this . . .'

It's been a far easier ride than I ever imagined. Two policemen came to interview me as I'd been out with Waters on the night he died. I told them we'd gone to see some bands in Camden and I'd dropped him off in a cab before going home. They'd nodded away, made some notes and that was that. They reckon it was a burglar. Then again, perhaps this isn't so odd:

Schneider had his mobile and wallet taken from him at knifepoint on Hammersmith Broadway a few months ago. The Kaffir doing the mugging even let him finish his call.

Darren was knocked off his bike in Kentish Town. He got up, dazed and bruised, to find himself surrounded by a mob of teenagers, who proceeded to kick the shit out of him, dip his pockets, and ride off on his bike.

Leamington got back from holiday and walked into his basement flat in Fulham. Everything gone and the proverbial smoking log in his bed.

Rebecca was waiting for the bus in Shepherd's Bush. They punched her in the face and grabbed her handbag.

Nicky from International was sitting at the lights on the Cromwell Road when the car door burst open and the kid – a snarling mess of gold teeth and sportswear – took her bag, phone and a handful of CDs. ('I thought he was going to get *in* the car. I thought he was going to rape me,' she said, telling the story in a meeting. Trellick and I looked at each other, both thinking the same thing – *you're fucking dreaming, love.*)

Daily, it seems, you walk out to your car in the morning to find your feet crunching on the tiny pebbles of glass, then the brick on the passenger seat, the wires hanging like guts from the dashboard, and your Blaupunkt being flogged for a tenner's worth of rocks in some local ragga den.

It serves me well, London: the streets crawl with suspects. The houses and the cars gleam with motive.

I look around the church at the people who I guess Waters grew up with. The girls, apart from the industry whores who made the trip up, are all utter fucking monsters. I'm guessing that most of them are around thirty, Waters' age, but Christ, they look like pensioners – lined, wrinkled faces, massive sagging teats, arses like busted sacks of gravel. The kind of working-class sows who stop being doable around the age of twenty-one. You look at the guys who are with them, guys around our age (but poor guys, failures) and they look innocent. They look like they don't know what's going on. Like they're unaware that they've married some disfigured atrocity. I mean, you look at these guys and you'd expect to see a little shame. Self-consciousness at the very least. If I was one of them I wouldn't be able to look a stranger in the eye without gesturing to my monster and saying, 'Sorry, mate, I don't know what I was thinking.' Maybe they don't. Maybe they look at these women and see the girl they met at school. Is that even possible? That kind of . . . well, love, I suppose you'd have to call it. I shudder at the word, at the thought. No wonder Waters got the fuck out of here as soon as he could.

It occurs to me, not for the first time, how strange it must be not to come from London.

After what feels like a long, long time it's over and we all bow our heads as what I presume is Waters' immediate family file out behind the coffin. There's two girls (his sisters?) who look bad, they're shaking and crying and holding onto each other and stuff, and, behind them, the parents. The father looks like he isn't quite there – red-rimmed eyes set in a thousand-yard stare – but the mother. Jesus wept, *the mother*. She's this tiny woman crumpled into a ball, half clinging to her husband's arm, half being carried along by him. She's clutching a soaking handkerchief in each fist and is making this noise. It sounds like the noise ghosts make in old horror films, a sort of wobbly moaning, whining 'woooo-aahhhh-ooohh'. I mean, she looks fucking insane.

The guys holding the coffin have to pause, to get something out of the way, and she comes right up against the coffin. She starts screaming – *'No! No! My son! My son!'* type stuff – and this triggers off loads of the girls in the crowd crying even harder until a couple of old hags calm her down and they get her out of there.

Going outside a few minutes after this we have to pass in a line by the family. I shake the dad's hand and tell him how sorry I am, that I knew his son through work and all that, and he just nods and doesn't really say anything. The mother isn't in the line-up, it's just the dad and the sisters, one of whom looks doable: big tits strapped tightly into a black dress that's a little too small for her and bright red lipstick on. I hug her quite hard and then I'm out on the steps of the church, lighting a cigarette in the hateful Northern air.

Ross goes off to try the office again, to see if they've got the midweeks yet. Trellick has to get hold of Fisher and I call the office to speak to Rebecca, to make sure she's booked me a cab to Heathrow in the morning. (I am off to

Miami in the morning, for the Winter fucking Music Conference – which is like MIDEM, but with just dance music – and then onto Texas for South by South-fucking-west – which is like the Winter Music Conference, but with indie music. They're all the same thing: a tide of net-working cunts going bananas.) The three of us stand off to one side smoking and talking on our phones as more people file out of the church and the coffin is carried out.

So. Much. Fucking. Respect.

I listen to Rebecca reminding me about connection times and check-in baloney as the coffin is rolled into the big hearse. People are scattered around crying and hugging each other. Waters' mother is sandwiched between the two old girls on a bench. She twitches like some bar-rattling inmate from a Victorian asylum, literally *demented* with grief.

Wow, I think to myself, remembering the expression on Waters' spastic face when he died, it really is something to kill somebody and create all of this.

*'You can't spell "star" without A and R.'*

Ronnie Vanucci

'Maybe we should go out,' someone says.

'No . . . I . . . that would be bad,' someone else says. It might be me. It's hard to tell who is saying what because all our voices are the same now – all cracked, ghosted whispers, static crackling across the room. Fragments of several different conversations ricochet around, over-lapping, out of sync, at cross-purposes.

The suite is dark, the curtains drawn, the only light coming from a couple of table lamps and the gently strobing pornography on the TV screen.

'We'll need more coke soon.'

'The guy's bringing it.'

'The black guy? Oh fuck . . .'

'Go in the bathroom.'

'And we need more fucking booze. *I need a whiskey.*'

'Have you heard that Stardust bootleg?'

'I can't face him . . .'

'Get room service to fill the minibar again.'

'Hide in the fucking bathroom.'

'Fucking tune.'

'Oh God. I can't face room service. I think I'm having a heart attack.'

'*Hide in the bathroom, you cunt.*'

'I think we should go out.'

'Fuck off.'

'Right, you cunts. I'm calling room service!' Leamington says this.

We've been in Miami for thirty-six hours now and I have yet to leave this room. I move across the darkened, fetid suite (we're in the hotel, where they filmed some of *Goldfinger*, as someone uselessly points out every five minutes) to the window and very nervously pull the curtains a couple of millimetres apart. A thin band of intense toxic sunshine lasers across the room and, just for a second, I glimpse sky, green palms and, beyond them, the beach and the ocean before everyone is screaming for me to shut the fucking curtains. 'Just . . . um, checking,' I say. It is around thirty degrees outside, but we have the windows all sealed and the air con on full crank. I reach behind the curtains and open a window. Ten floors below you can hear the roar of chattering delegates intercut with splashes as people dive into the pool.

I walk about the room swinging my arms, kicking my legs, my chin tucked tight into my chest. I'm beyond wired – pure current.

'I think if I did a couple of pills I could go out,' someone says.

'That's not totally crazy,' someone replies.

'Fatboy Slim tonight,' someone else says.

'Roni Size.'

'Where?'

'At the Cameo Theatre?'

'Fuck that.'

'We *have* to go out tonight.'

'Size at the Cameo?'

'Maybe we should get some hookers in.'

'No Fatboy.'

'He's at the Delano.'

'Or strippers anyway.'

'Do you mean where he's staying or where he's playing?'

'Eh?'

We started on the chang somewhere over Ireland. When we landed – having raped the Virgin Upper Class bar for ten hours straight – we were met by this dealer someone knew. We got a limo and continued with the chang on the drive into town. I don't know everyone here. There's some guy from some indie (XL? Mo Wax? Rising High?) and a publisher kid (Warner Chappell? BMG?) and a couple of ex-pat Brits, drug-dealer types, who someone vaguely knows who've attached themselves to us. Darren hasn't spoken for five or six hours. He just sits there, rocking back and forth. At one point I made an attempt to go downstairs and register at the convention, to pick up my delegate pass, so I could attend the showcases and discussion panels (where gak and pill-lobotomised fools will ruminate on worthy topics like 'How Will Internet DJing Affect the Economies of Former Soviet Bloc Countries?' and 'Is the SuperClub Killing Club Culture?'). The lift doors opened and way across the lobby I could see some of the Brit contingent – Dave Beer, Kris Needs, people like that. I glimpsed a sober, businesslike Parker-Hall striding up to reception. I pressed the button for our floor again and *ran* back to the fucking room. 'You don't want to go down there,' I told everyone. That was, I think, sometime yesterday afternoon. The outside world now looks like an abstraction; a dream you had when you were a kid. Intangible, a few blurred images, the faintest tang of an aftertaste.

'Ritchie Hawtin,' someone says.

'Dimitri from Paris.'

'Get the Yellow Pages.'

'He shit his pants in CentroFly.'

'More coke.'

'Peanut Butter Wolf.'

'Todd Terry.'

'Carl Cox.'

'Basement Jaxx.'

I think someone is crying.

'Grooverider.'

'A case of fucking Cristal.'

'Maybe sushi.'

'Ritchie Hawtin.'

'Double-ended her.'

'Propellerheads.'

There's a fierce, copper-style rap at the door.

'Oh fuck.'

'Jesus fuck.'

'Who's that? *Who is it?*' someone asks in a whisper.

'It's room service, you clown,' says Leamington – incredibly the only person seemingly in control – as he heads for the door.

'Fuck that. You're kidding, aren't you?' I say.

Three or four of us hurdle furniture, elbowing each other out of the way, as we scramble into the bathroom. We bolt the door and crouch down in the milky plastic light.

'Oh God, oh God, oh God . . .' someone keeps saying.

'It'll be all right, it'll be OK,' someone else says soothingly.

'Is this your first time in Miami?' some bloke whispers to me. I shake my head. I'm off my nut, but I'm vaguely aware that this isn't a reasonable way to earn a living.

A long time passes. You can hear everyone's heart beating. The tap drips.

There's a knock on the door, Leamington's voice, the all-clear. We open the door and creep out.

Christ.

A black waiter – a young guy, tall, thin – is standing in the middle of the suite unloading cocktails from a tray onto the coffee table. He turns and sees us. We all freeze.

'Have you got the coke?' one of the bathroom idiots says to the waiter, just seeing a Kaffir and mistaking him for the dealer, despite his tray, and his purple-and-black tunic and the gold name tag on his chest. And the fact that he's *clearly a fucking waiter*.

'I'm sorry,' I say, 'I'm so sorry.' The black kid takes his unloaded tray, and the proffered twenty-dollar tip, and fucks off out of it, looking scared.

'You cunt,' I say to Leamington, who is laughing his head off.

'Oh God, we're finished now,' Darren says.

'Have a drink,' Leamington says.

'Don't you understand, *it's over!*' Darren is actually becoming hysterical. 'He's going to go back downstairs and he's going to tell them what's happening and they're going to come up here and they're going to come in and –'

'Shut up and have a fucking cocktail, you twat. Here, have a Cosmopolitan.' Leamington hands Darren a gigantic Martini glass full of thin, pale blood. He seems to have ordered every cocktail on the menu.

'Do we have any fucking pills?' I ask.

'Yeah,' someone says.

'Should we switch rooms?'

'Maybe if we take some pills we could go out.'

'Have you heard that Stardust bootleg?' someone asks.

'Here.' Someone presses an E into my hand and I suck it back with a gulp of Tequila Sunrise.

'Hey, did you know they filmed *Goldfinger* here?' Leamington says, still laughing.

That evening and the next day become what they always become: a series of blurred snapshots, random shreds of CCTV footage, shakily pixellated stills from a bootleg video I don't remember starring in. I was dancing in the DJ booth to 'Praise You', clinking pills with Leamington as we both double-dropped, vomiting out of a moving cab on the Strip, throwing an ice cube across the lobby of the Delano at some DJ (Rampling? Oakenfold?), being thrown out of a DJ booth somewhere, an alleyway behind the Strip, buying glass vials of coke, buying an E that came individually wrapped in its own cellophane bag, wanking in a private booth at a lap-dancing club, the Propellerheads onstage, lying on the floor of someone's hotel room watching a stripper do herself with a beer bottle, dawn on the beach – Leamington and I looking out to sea dumbstruck as an oil tanker the length of the Westway slunk across the horizon – a breakfast pint of rum and Coke at that bar in the middle of the hotel pool.

The next morning and early afternoon are fine. I sleep right through both of them, missing both my original flight to Texas and the rebooked flight. I finally make it to the airport late in the afternoon where, of course, the flight I've made is delayed.

I find a quiet corner in the BA exec lounge and crumple into an armchair. The screen hanging from the ceiling silently wipes itself and unrolls the revised flight times: AA157, MIA to Houston, Texas, is now leaving at 6.10 p.m.

I settle in and inhale a long chain of Bloody Marys. I thoughtfully chew half a Quaalude and try to place my hangover on my personal Richter scale. Twenty minutes later, when I still haven't come with an answer, when I still don't understand the question in fact, it dawns on me why I can't properly evaluate my hangover. I'm not having it yet. I'm still completely off my fucking nugget.

'Sir, excuse me, sir? Are you OK?'

I look up – he's about my age, airport uniform, concerned expression. 'Uh, yeah,' I cough. Urine-temperature drool flecks from my chin. Outside, sunny Florida has vanished, there's just darkness and lights; lines, grids and blocks of them. 'What time is it?' I ask, my voice a tramp-rasp produced by broken piping, blocked air passages. There's a modulating whine in my ears, a rising note, searching for its rightful, most painful, key.

'It's just after six, sir.'

'Shit.' I swing into action, swivelling up and onto my feet, grabbing my jacket and scooping up my bag. The guy helps me up from the floor. 'Sir . . . *sir?*'

'Which way to Gate . . .' I'm fumbling for my boarding pass.

'Sir, it's six in the morning. Six a.m.'

I look at him. The whine in my ears finally finds its pitch and something pops somewhere deep in the centre of my face, some blockage behind my nose clears as a small dam bursts.

'The next flight to Houston isn't for a few hours.'

Fucking Quaaludes. The Shermans know how to put a tranquilliser together – you have to give them that.

'Uh, sir, you've got a . . . Christ.' He's fumbling in his pocket.

But I can already taste the blood, sharp and salty in the back of my throat, as it begins its warm, oddly pleasant, cascade across my top lip and spatters down onto the T-shirt I'm wearing. The T-shirt has a picture of Al Pacino as Tony Montana. He's holding a huge fuck-off gun. *'Say hello to my leetle fren.'*

Sometimes, when they're trying to understand what A&R means, people who don't know anything about the music industry will say, 'Ah, so you're talent spotters?' This is inaccurate. Madonna, Bono, the Spice Girls, Noel Gallagher, Kylie . . . do you really think any of that lot are *talented?* Don't make me fucking laugh. What they are is ambitious. This is where the big money is. Fuck talent. Forget Rock and Roll, if he'd just turned the other way out of the schoolyard Bono could have been a very successful

CEO of a huge armaments manufacturer. The Spice Girls? How driven are those boilers? You get these fucking indie bands moaning about having to get up before lunchtime once every three months to appear on some kids' TV programme. In return for her fifteen minutes I guarantee you that Geri Halliwell would have risen at the crack of dawn every morning for a year and swum naked through a river of shark-infested, HIV-positive semen – cutting the throats of children, OAPs and cancer patients and throwing them behind her as she went – just to be allowed to do a sixty-second regional radio interview.

This is the kind of person you want to sign. You've got a shot with that kind of attitude. Talented? Fuck off. Go and work in a guitar shop with all the other talented losers.

'I'm telling you – Pawl? Steve? – there are piracy issues involved that we're only just beginning to understand. The long-term implications could be catastrophic. Cat-a-stroff-ick.' Some cunt from our American label has been dribbling on for a fortnight about the impending devastation the Internet will wreak on the record industry. I can't see it myself.

The stench of burning flesh fills the air and it's hot. It's like being in hell. We're in the grounds of one of the big hotels, attending a barbecue some publisher is throwing. Whole hogs – basted in barbecue sauce thicker than melted chocolate – are crackling and spitting over flaming pits. Steaks the size of babies sizzle on hotplates. A slaughter-house of ribs is piled up next to rows of silver dishes containing refried beans, coleslaw, fries, chicken wings, cornbread, mashed potatoes, chilli and gravy. Now and then the warm, feeble breeze changes direction and I get a whiff of this lot and nearly throw up. Everyone of the English contingent here is either coked up or hung-over. Either way, we're not eating a fucking thing. You look around at these things and you can spot the Yanks a hundred yards away. They're the ones who actually look like they've been to bed in the past year. They look tanned, fit and rested and they want to talk business. Players – or thinking they are – they came to play. We – the Brits – look like we've just staggered off the set of a snuff film after a meth-driven four-day shoot: blood in the eyes, skin cracked and yellow, nostrils inflamed and blood-caked. We look like ghosts. We came to play too.

'Mmmm,' says Trellick nodding to the Yank like he gives a fuck, 'it could be problem.' I nod solemnly too and drain my fifth glass of cold white wine.

As we leave, the Mexican busboys are shovelling tons of uneaten food into plastic garbage bags. I see one of them pocket a steak.

Later we're all at one of the hundreds of gigs taking place across the city. There's a band on the stage, some four-piece punk rock kind of thing called the Lazies, I think. The very doable girl singer is screaming over a splintering tower of glassy feedback. There's a couple of rows of kids going crackers at the front, like there are at every gig. Abortion, I think to myself. Derivative, tuneless abortion. I start polishing and sharpening a few caustic phrases to toss off later. She's on the floor now, the mike lead wrapped around her body, sweat pouring down her face as she screams something like 'fuck me in the ass' over and over.

She's wearing fishnet tights that are shredded to pieces, half an arse cheek is bursting out. Very fuckable, but still a derivative, tuneless abortion.

Finally, mercifully, they finish. I walk through a crunchy sea of plastic beer mugs to the bar. Leamington, Trellick, Parker-Hall and Simon Tench, Parker-Hall's scout, are all at the bar. I also see Miles and Dan from Parlophone, Steven Bass from Go! Beat, and a few others. Someone hands me a drink. A tequila shot.

'Capitol just offered two hundred, US only,' someone is saying.

'What did you think?' that weasel Tench asks me.

I think I want a nose-up. I think my hotel room isn't big enough.

It really gets tedious sometimes – being paid primarily for your opinion when you very rarely have one. Or frequently have the wrong one.

'You'd do the singer,' I say, sagely. Everyone nods. 'And I liked the "fuck me in the ass" song. You ain't getting it on the radio though.'

'Which song?' says Leamington.

'The one where she says "*fuck me in the ass*".'

Leamington laughs. 'It's "*love me, make it last*". It's the single.'

'Haven't you got it?' Tench asks.

'Yeah, whatever,' I say airily, knocking back the oily, bitter spirit, 'fuck them.'

Trellick sidles up to me as we leave the venue to look for cabs. 'I don't know,' he says quietly, 'they all seem to like it. Should we be in on this?'

'I was downgrading it, you clown. I've already got a

meeting set up.' The lie slides softly out of the corner of my mouth. The lie itself is effortless, but, sadly, it means I'll actually have to do some work.

'Good boy,' says Trellick, his hand in the air as a canary-yellow taxi comes towards us out of the jungly Texas night.

'Best live band I've seen in a long, long time.'

'Yeah?' The manager – a stringy, indie, vegetarian-looking anorak cunt – doesn't look up from spooning pulpy melon into his mouth. He couldn't look less enthusiastic if he tried, which is fucking cheeky considering the effort, the time, I've put into arranging and preparing for this lunch.

When I got back to the hotel last night – tramp-drunk at 3 a.m. – I rang Darren. While I should, by rights, have been snorting inhuman amounts of chang and trying to negotiate the local ostros down to a hundred bucks for uncovered oral, I was on the phone, working. After berating Darren for not already being on to the Lazies (the lying prick claimed he tried to play me the single) I told him I needed to know who managed them, I needed his phone number, I needed a potted history of the band, and I needed him to find a record store in Austin who had the band's records and then he had to buy the records over the phone with his credit card and have them cabbed to my hotel.

Then I passed out.

I woke up five hours later. The fax with all the info was in an envelope that had been pushed under my door. A package containing the band's slender catalogue – one single and an EP – awaited me behind reception.

I rang the manager, the kid Jimmy now sitting opposite me, and here we are. I gave the music a cursory listen earlier – it's all right. I don't know really. Who knows? But enough people seem to be interested. We're having lunch in the restaurant at the hotel. Good PR for me to be seen lunching with the manager of a hot band.

'What was your favourite track on the EP?' he asks.

Shit. 'Track three,' I say, 'definitely.'

'Yeah? That's interesting.' Is it?

'Are you going to be playing in England soon?' I ask.

'Uh, yeah. In a month or so. Glastonbury. We're doing some warm-ups first. At the, uh, is it the Borderline?'

'Yeah. Good venue.' Stinking fucking toilet.

He finishes his fruit salad and surprises me by lighting a cigarette. 'So, man,' he says, leaning back, pushing long, unkempt hair from his face, 'what's your favourite album of all time?'

The fucking nerve. I pretend to think for a moment, then say, '*Marquee Moon*.' With a certain type of indie loser you cannot go wrong with *Marquee Moon*.

The clown nods and says, 'Cool.'

He starts talking about how hard the band work, how little they're willing to compromise, how great their debut album's going to be. All the usual shit I've heard a billion times before. I nod away, looking like I'm listening, generally doing a reasonable impression of a normal human being.

Across the restaurant I see Parker-Hall and Tench walking towards us. 'All right, lads?' I say magnanimously, chewing on a toothpick, 'this is J—'

'How you doing, Jimmy?' says Parker-Hall. Jimmy's

already on his feet and they're embracing warmly. 'Hey, Tony! My man! What's up?'

'Me and Si are just going for a bit of a stroll. Catch some rays.' Jimmy, the Yank cunt, is lapping up Parker-Hall's Dick Van Dyke schtick. I cannot believe he gets away with this shit. 'We still on for later?' Parker-Hall asks him.

'For sure. I've just got this meeting to finish up with . . .' the manager has forgotten my name, '. . . ah, with Steve here. Then I'll be back at my hotel.'

In the background I'm sure Tench is smirking as they say their matey goodbyes and tool off.

'You know Tony then?' I ask.

'Yeah, we talk on the phone a lot. He was a big fan of the first single.'

'Right.' Cunt. Fucking fuck.

'Hey, Steve, I've really got to run too. We're playing again tonight at this thing, it's a little way out of town . . .' he writes the address down on a napkin.

'Yeah, great. How far along are you? You know, in terms of other companies.'

'Well,' he says grinning, shaking his head, 'I've got to tell you, we've got a couple of really interesting offers on the table already. I wouldn't want you to get your hopes up.'

I laugh. 'Another offer wouldn't hurt though, would it?' I am going to fire Darren. Why weren't we on to this fucking band earlier?

'Maybe not, maybe not. Thanks for lunch.'

We shake hands and I watch him fruit off through the restaurant, stopping halfway to shake hands with some girl.

A waitress appears. She's cute, huge rack.

'You're finished?' she says.

No, I think. Not completely. Not yet.

With the indie kids you have to remember this: they really think that what they do matters in some way. They reckon that history will care. (They don't know that history will have other shit to be getting on with.) The indie kids figure that they're passing on the torch or some fucking thing. That, just as they were influenced by someone – the Velvet Underground, Jonathan Richman, the Stooges, whoever – then, in the future, young bands will be influenced by them. Maybe so. Maybe a few thousand malnourished cockless freaks scattered around the globe will give a shit. So what? Real people don't care, do they? Real people put stone cladding and UPVC double-glazing on their council houses, they buy four albums a year and they want to be able to hear all the words. And there are fucking *billions* of them.

That's why I like it when you deal with a genuine pop act. It's so refreshing and honest. Some greasy demi-paedo of a manager flops down in your office with three fit fifteen-year-old sluts on his arm. Half a GCSE between them, they say, 'We want to be famous and make a lot of money.' You know what? No problem. *Let's fucking rock.* I might thereafter have to have the odd conversation about, for instance, do we need to Photoshop someone's jugs to make them look bigger or firmer? What I *won't* have to do is sit in some toilet flat at three in the morning, listening to tuneless B-sides and talking about, I don't know, Tom Verlaine's guitar solos. Because, really, who gives a fucking shit?

Here – you want to say to these indie kids – have a *steak*. Let's go to Harvey Nicks and buy you some decent clothes.

Here's three hundred quid – go and get a hot boiler to suck your dick properly for the first time in your life. *Live a little, son.*

# May

*Talk of EMI/Seagram merger. Spice Girls do massive Pepsi deal. Lots of interest in Ultrasound now. The Jamiroquai LP goes triple platinum. Audioweb's single 'Faker' charts at 70. Deconstruction signs this girl singer called Sylvia Powell. The label's MD Keith Blackhurst says, 'I'm sure her songs will make it onto TV and radio and that the album will be huge.' Echo and the Bunnymen look like making a comeback. Labour wins the election.*

> '*The nature of show business means that people within the business feel that if someone else fails, they move up a notch.*'

> Tom Arnold

A few days after I get back from Austin I go on a *date*. Yeah, I know.

The thing is, if you just fuck an awful lot of whores all the time then you kind of need to go on a date now and again, if only to prove to yourself that you can still do boilers without a fistful of grubby fifty-pound notes changing hands. Also, sometimes I'll look at people who have girlfriends and I'll think, 'That doesn't look so crazy.' Who knows, maybe it's worth a pop.

I've been listening to this girl (she's literally called Sophie, for fuck's sake, a friend of a friend, works in international at . . . Warners?) crapping on about something – an argument she had with the singer from some band about, I don't know, maybe the quality of cheeseburgers at Oslo airport, or the purity of bottled water in Auckland – for what feels like a decade. This is the thing. You're expected to make conversation, aren't you? Beyond the level of 'here's your money, now suck this, you rancid fucking slut'.

'Hey,' she says, waving a hand across my vacant face as a fawning spic plonks her dessert in front of her, 'what are you thinking about?'

*Gak, chang, nose-up, bag, beak, charlie, krell, powder, chisel, bump, posh, bugle, sniff, skiwear . . .*

This is the thing about girlfriends. They'll say to you: 'What are you thinking?' I am always thinking about cash and fucking, but you can't really say this, can you?

But people do it, don't they? You see it all the time. There seem to be definite upsides, financially and health-wise at least. I mean, you're unlikely to come in from work of a Friday evening and – during the course of a quiet weekend with your girlfriend – spend nearly two grand on coke, crack, booze, Viagra and hookers. I don't imagine that's how it goes, is it? Your girlfriend is unlikely to suggest the kind of evening out that will terminate sometime the following afternoon in an Albanian knocking shop in Brixton, up to your nuts in an illegal immigrant. You don't do that nasty stuff with a girlfriend, do you? You . . . What do you do? You go to, I don't know, the cinema? Or maybe for a walk? Stuff like that?

But then I think about the downsides. The talking. They're really into the whole talking thing, girlfriends. Ross has a girlfriend. He tells you about the things they do, the stuff they say. They try and talk to you about complicated weekends away in three months' time over breakfast. About wallpaper colours. They ask things like, 'How was your day?' and 'How did your meeting go?' What do you care how the meeting went? *I* don't fucking care how the meeting went and I was there.

Why? Why would they ask these things? What can they

possibly have to gain from the answer? At least with hookers I find the banter, the discussions, manageable: *bend over . . . put your leg there . . . good . . . suck harder . . . faster . . . lick my balls . . . piss on me.*

I mean, I can just about manage that.

I tune back into the present, into the restaurant, the date. She's saying, '. . . and anyway, these days BA's business class is *almost* as good as first.'

You're wrong, I think. But I don't correct her. I just listen, wondering how much more of this I will have to sit through before she will be drunk enough to let me fuck her. Tiredly I reach for the Pinot Grigio and refill her glass.

'What are you thinking?' Well, I'm thinking about having some big hit records and then upgrading your pock-marked arse for someone younger and fitter. Now, what film did you want to go and see? Shall we get a takeaway? Do you really want to go for a fucking *walk*, you horrible cow?

I'm lying on the sofa in my office, half listening to demos, mostly playing Fifa '97 on the PlayStation, when Rebecca, ridiculously serious-faced, pops her head around the door.

'Steven?'

'Yeah?' Just the defender to beat, if I . . .

'There's someone in reception who wants to see you.'

'Tell them to fuck off.' That's it, scoot along the edge of the box . . .

'Actually, I don't think that's a good idea.'

'Why not?' He shoots . . .

'It's a policeman.'

. . . he hits the post.

The guy comes in. Plain clothes, a nasty-looking Next/ Marks and Sparks type suit on. He's young, maybe just a couple of years older than me. 'Mr Stelfox?' he asks needlessly, extending his hand. Rebecca hovers in the doorway.

'Steven,' I say.

'DC Woodham. Thanks for seeing me without an appointment. I could come back another time if this is inconvenient?'

'No, no. It's fine. Can we get you anything?'

'No, thank you.' Rebecca shuts the door and Woodham folds himself awkwardly into the chair opposite me. He's tall and gangly, all limbs and angles in his nasty, ill-fitting suit. He's fair-haired, but it's not the thick Aryan blond you see on someone like Trellick. This is pauper's hair – thin, pale and frayed into a cheap, bad cut which (surely unusually for a copper) touches the collar of his shirt here and there. His face is thin and pinched, kind of sad-looking. But that's fair enough. If I had to tool around in a Next suit dealing with the world's sewage for – what? twenty grand a year? – I'd be looking fucking sad too.

'Wow,' he says, eyeing up the pile of gold and platinum discs stacked beside my desk, 'shouldn't they be up on the wall?'

'Oh, I'll get round to it,' I shrug bashfully. 'I'm sorry, is this about Roger? Because I already spoke to –'

'Yes, I know you've given a statement. I just had a couple of questions about the – hey –' he breaks off, pointing to the pinboard on the wall behind me – 'is that . . . is that you and *Joe Strummer*?'

I turn. He's pointing to a photograph of me and Strummer – arms around each other, both in wellies and macs covered in mud, both out of our poor minds – standing behind the Pyramid Stage. I'd been looking at signing him last year but the demos were a pile of shit. But young bands often respond well to that photo. Good ice-breaker. 'Yeah,' I say chuckling, 'backstage at Glastonbury last year. We'd had a few.'

'Wow. What's he like?'

A washed-up cunt. 'Joe? He's a sweetheart. Are you a fan?'

'God, not half. I saw the Clash live when I was fifteen,' he beams proudly.

'Really?' Jesus wept, what a waste of fucking semen this cunt is. 'Bit before my time I'm afraid.'

'Oh, best live band in the world, I reckon.'

'A few people say that. Sorry, Officer, I do have a meeting starting shortly.'

'Of course. Sorry. What it is, I'm following up with a few people and . . . I believe you told one of my colleagues that you,' he consults a notebook he's pulled out, 'you were with Mr Waters on the night of his death?'

'Yeah.'

'You'd been to . . . the Dublin Castle in Camden?'

'That's right. Then we shared a cab and I dropped him off.'

'See anything good?'

'Anything good? Oh, the gig. Band called Rape Squadron I think. They weren't bad.'

'Bit of an old toilet the Dublin Castle, isn't it?' he grins.

'Oh, you know it?'

'Yeah. Well, I played there a few times. Back in the day, you know.'

'Really? You were in a band?' Mother of fucking uncontrollable God. 'What did you play?'

'Guitar. And songwriting. We still play a bit as it happens, in our spare time and that. We've all got jobs now. Wives and kids and all that.'

Fuck me. 'Yeah, it can be tough.'

'Tell me about it,' he says, shaking his head. 'Anyway, I really wanted to ask you about Mr Waters' state of mind that night.'

'In what way?'

'Well, did he seem worried about anything? Did he have any enemies that you know of? Debts? Money problems?'

I pretend to think for a moment. 'No. Nothing like that. He's unlikely to have had any money problems.' The fat overpaid spastic.

'Yeah, I didn't think so. Expenses all the way in this racket, isn't it?' Woodham laughs.

I laugh too. 'Yeah, we've been known to claim a few beers back.'

'You'd been drinking?'

'Yeah, we'd had a few. He'd just been promoted. We were celebrating.'

'Drugs?'

'No.'

'Really? The autopsy showed considerable levels of cocaine in Mr Waters' bloodstream.'

'It must have been after I left him. I don't take cocaine.'

'I thought all you guys . . .'

'Oh, that's a myth. It's not the eighties. You have to work too hard these days.'

'But you knew he took drugs?'

'Well . . .'

He writes something down and goes on to ask me a few more vaguely Waters-related questions before getting onto what he really seems to want to talk about: what kind of bands were getting signed these days? How many demos did we get a week? How many gigs did I go to? Who have I worked with? What kind of music did I like? (The Clash, Bob Dylan blah blah blah . . .) Finally I email Rebecca telling her to come and get me for a non-existent meeting.

She pops her head around the door. 'Sorry to interrupt,' she says, leaning in, giving Woodham full cleavage, 'but you've got that meeting starting now, Steven.'

'Thanks, Rebecca.' She ducks back out.

'Well, thank you, Mr Stelfox,' Woodham says, getting up.

'Steven's fine. Sorry I couldn't be more helpful,' I say walking him to the door.

'No, you've been very helpful. Just one last thing. This is a bit awkward.' He reaches into his jacket.

Fuck. Here it comes, the fucking Columbo bit. He's almost out the bastard door when he turns round and produces the smoking gun. 'Could you tell me what you think of this?' he says, holding something towards me.

Oh God. I look down.

It's a CD. 'It's just some rough mixes we did at my mate's home studio, but I'd really like, you know, a professional opinion about the songs. If you could spare ten minutes to have a listen sometime . . .'

I look at him for a moment.

'Sure,' I say, taking the CD. 'Is your number on here?'

Seconds after he leaves Rebecca comes in to find me

standing up at the window. 'Is everything OK?' she says, sounding genuinely anxious.

'It's nothing. Just some questions about Roger.' She joins me at the window and we watch Woodham walk to his car – a shitty Ford of some description.

'Quite cute for a policeman,' she says.

'Mmmm.' We stand there for a moment in silence.

'Are you all right, Steven?'

'I'm fine.'

She raises her hand, as if to stroke my arm, then thinks better of it and leaves.

I often wonder what sort of life people like Woodham end up having. I don't mean policemen, I mean guys who toiled away in pointless bands for years, never getting anywhere, until they got some hag up the duff. Are you one of them? How do you get through it? You turn round and – bosh! – you're nearly thirty and standing in line at some fucking B&Q at nine o'clock on a Sunday morning, a giant monster holding your hand while your five-year-old runs around smashing the place up and another brat howls in a papoose round your neck. You've maybe got two hundred and fifty quid in your current account until the end of the month. I mean, what keeps the noose from around your neck, the razor blade from your veins? Love? Don't make me fucking laugh. Look at how you're *living*.

Without warning, with no warning at all, winter just becomes summer somewhere in the middle of May. There is no spring. The heat does what it does to London; cars become boiling torture boxes as – and everyone is surprised about this, no one thought it possible – the traffic slows even further. *Everywhere* seems to be under construction; the navvies, stripped to the waist, or wrapped in fluorescent yellow and orange vests, scratch their heads as they stare at some mad coil of piping they've dragged up through the broken bubbling tarmac. They stand on the hard shoulder, on the pavement, in the middle of the road, chewing gum and insolently holding up their circular red 'STOP' signs, or – rarer and briefer – their bright green 'GO' signs. All the slip roads lead to despair. In their torture boxes the people sluice Evian, light cigarettes, drum their hands on the wheel and fiddle with the radio and all the time you hear the sampled string loop and Richard Ashcroft singing 'Bittersweet Symphony' and you punch through the stations and you hear 'Things Can Only Get Better'.

The summer does something else to London too. You've noticed, haven't you? How could you not? Look at them appearing; pouring from the tubes and buses, emerging from doorways and office blocks, chattering and stretching out in wine bars and at wooden tables outside the pubs: the fucking boilers.

I mean, girls, where do you all *go* in the winter? Fill us in. October rolls around and you all vanish underground. Or you fly off to some island somewhere, some girls-only paradise where you work on your tans and leaf through lingerie catalogues, planning the summer attack. From October until May the female population of London is composed entirely of octogenarian Polack hags wearing carpet-thick tights and growing beards. You look around Oxford Street and you think – what the fuck is going on? It's just blokes, benders and beasts. Then the sun comes back and – bosh – it's a boiler-fest, a sea of silicone-jugged teenage porn stars in micro-skirts, sawn-off tops and thongs. Taunting midriffs, heckling arse-cheeks and abusive nipples all over the fucking shop. Even Nicky has abandoned her traditional fat-chick black leggings and has taken to parading around the office in some kind of condom-thin kaftan, her gigantic, nightmare paps sloshing around beneath it like a couple of carrier bags filled with glue.

It gets worse every summer. It fucks us up. It interferes with work. The needle of my libidometer, which is generally nudging 'RAPIST' at the best of times, is jumping off the scale. The other night, stumbling through Soho, I became so enraged with lust that I had to dive into one of those festering doorways off Berwick Street to spend fifteen minutes and fifty quid having my pulsing balls drained by an East European teenager in a grubby satin slip. (In London after midnight, as in many capital cities, it is far easier to get your cock sucked by a pair of terrified fourteen-year-old immigrant twins with a gun at their heads than it is to buy a bottle of Chardonnay. And there are lots of young fit Bosnian and Kosovan chicks on the game at the moment – a pleasing by-product of the recent punch-ups over there.) And, yes, of course I feel guilty about contributing to the sum total of this kind of human misery and all that. But, come on, what are we meant to do? I mean, have a heart. Put some fucking clothes on.

It gets hotter and things happen.

Rage is arrested for attacking a British Rail employee who asked him to put his cigarette out. We still have no plans to release his album.

It looks like Seagrams will buy EMI.

Ellie Crush's record goes gold – half a million – in the US. Parker-Hall is officially the industry fucking wonder boy.

I have a couple more meetings with Danny Rent about Songbirds. A couple of other labels are interested in them now, which is always good news as it means I'm not completely off my nugget, but . . . I just don't know. They're so fucking bad. Having said that, apparently Tracy Bennett over at London Records has just signed some cobbled-together bunch of sows called All Saints, so it looks like a few people will be having a pop with the Spice Girls cash-ins. I need to be signing something soon.

Neither Waters nor Schneider has been replaced yet and I am de facto running the department, although there is no official recognition of this and no extra remuneration. If 'Why Don't You . . .' was shaping up to be a hit I reckon I'd have been offered the job by now.

Trellick gets some girl from Sony pregnant. But he does the decent thing and forks out for a top-drawer abortion, an overnight-stay job at the Wellington near Regent's Park.

The Lazies fly into the country soon. They're doing a short European tour, playing a few warm-up dates for Glastonbury and meeting record companies. No less than seven labels are now trying to sign them. Apparently Parker-Hall is all over them. With the possible exception of Ultrasound, they are now the hottest unsigned band on the planet. I have managed to convince Jimmy, their indie-manager loser, to let me take them to dinner while they're in town.

I quadruple-park the car on Parkway across from the Spread

Eagle, which is already rammed with summer drinkers, and run into the off-licence to buy cigarettes and whisky. Waiting for my change I happen to glance along the top shelf, at the glut of hardcore: *Cum Sluts, Anal Housewives, Fifty-Plus, Suck. Pump. Grinder.*

My eyes settle on a pair of brown cheeks, thrust high in the air, a red satin G-string splitting the cleft, barely covering the faceless boiler's gleefully proffered anus. The strapline reads: *'She Wants You Up Her. Now!'* I am immediately overwhelmed by a sickening rush of lust so powerful as to be indistinguishable from total rage. The shopkeeper – a toothless, octogenarian Paki – doesn't bat an eyelid, doesn't register a flicker of alarm or interest as I add an armful of the most hardcore titles to my purchases, even though the top magazine is called *Asian Whores* and features one of his Sikh or Hindu sisters naked and fingering herself while sucking greedily on a huge orange plastic prick.

'Sorry, sir. No bags,' he says.

I stagger out to the car, teetering with fags, Scotch and hardcore, and there he is: a hulking Nigerian monstrosity in serge blue uniform, frowning at my licence plate as he punches numbers into his little machine. 'Come on, mate,' I begin.

'No parking,' he grunts, not looking up.

'I was only in there a minute.'

He just repeats the two words. The only two words of English he knows.

I mean, Jesus Christ. They bowl over here, straight out of some boiling HIV cauldron, some genocide-rape-famine meltdown entirely of their own making, and are they grateful? Are they fuck. They go to some language class (probably at the taxpayers' expense) to learn how to say 'no parking', and then they march around London fucking you up.

'Look,' I say reasonably, 'fuck off, cunt.'

'No parking.' The ticket whirrs out of the machine.

He holds it out to me. I throw it on the ground and spit on it. He shakes his head and starts writing something in his notebook.

'Oh yeah?' I say. 'You can *write*, can you, you fucking animal? Why don't you –'

'Hi, Steven.'

I turn. It's a girl called Charlie, or Chrissie or something. She's a scout somewhere. Sony? EMI? 'Ah, hi there,' I say.

'You going to see Ultrasound?' she asks me brightly.

'Ah, yeah. Trying to.' I shift the magazines, trying to huddle them in towards my chest, but it's too late, her gaze is already ambling down towards the glossy pile of total disgrace.

'Right . . .' She says uncertainly, already backing away, 'maybe I'll see you in there.'

'Yeah, see you there.' I turn back, but he's already across the street and the spittle-flecked ticket has been fixed to my windscreen.

The Ultrasound show is rammed: A&R people from Virgin, Island, Warner Chappell. I see Nick Mander, Andy MacDonald, Andy Leese and Malcolm Dunbar from Mother, Leamington, Dave Gilmour. No Parker-Hall, who is already on record as saying the band are 'pony'. Across the room I see Rebecca talking to some girl I don't know. I wave hello and she smiles back. You often see Rebecca out at gigs. Why the fuck does she bother? I mean, I wouldn't be here if I didn't have to be.

I'm in a filthy mood, lounging at the bar sipping a triple Rockschool when someone taps me on the shoulder. 'Hi, Steven,' this guy says. He's in his late twenties, a bit old to be in here. I've no idea who he is, probably some manager, some agent. 'Hi,' I say shaking his offered hand, no light of recognition whatsoever in my eyes. He senses this and says, 'It's Alan Woodham.'

Nothing.

'DC Woodham? I came to interview you about Roger Waters?'

Fuck, the copper. 'Oh, hi! Didn't recognise you, you know, in civvies.'

'What do you think?'

'About what?'

'Err,' he looks confused, 'about the band,' he gestures towards the stage where the singer of Ultrasound, who must weigh twenty fucking stone by the way, is screaming over an angry fizz of noise.

'Oh them.' I pretend to think. Maybe I actually am thinking. I don't know the difference any more. 'Not bad. Angular.' He nods, like this means something. 'What brings you here?' I ask.

'Oh, I'd heard some good things about them. Thought I'd check it out.'

Christ, what a fucking loser. What the fuck is he doing here watching some poxy unsigned band? Shouldn't he be out cracking crime?

'So,' he says grinning, 'what did you think of our demo? Be frank, I can take it.'

'Actually,' I say, putting my drink down on the bar for emphasis, 'I was going to call you about this, but I couldn't find your card. I have to say . . .' His face is doing a good impression of passive, professional disinterest but you can see the ticks and judders of fear and apprehension in the way his eyeballs flicker and dart, the way his lips squirm and quiver. They all look like this just before you tell them what you think. Obviously I have no idea what I am about to say. I listened to about half a song of his demo – worthless sub-Oasis drivel – before I pegged it into the bin. So I say, 'I was really impressed.'

'Really?'

'Yeah. Great songs. Honestly.'

'Any song in particular stand out?'

Fuck. 'Track three.'

'"Time Keeps Moving"?'

'Yeah. That's the one.'

'Yeah, I like that too. I was trying to . . .'

He starts to crap on about whatever influences he was trying to merge in the song or something. It's good because I can stop listening now. It's just a bunch of self-serving toss requiring no comeback, no specific rejoinders. I nod away, looking across the room at some girl's arse and thinking about an Asian boiler being smacked repeatedly in the face by a very stiff cock. I catch Rebecca's eye across the room and she looks away quickly. Finally Woodham finishes speaking so it's my turn.

'Listen,' I say, 'the only thing that's letting you down is the production.' He nods eagerly. 'What if I spring you a little demo money? Put you in the studio with a decent engineer for a couple of days?'

'Really? Shit, that would be great.'

'Give the office a ring and ask for Darren, yeah? I'll get him to sort it out. Have you made any progress on finding out what happened to Roger?'

'Not really. None of the neighbours saw anything, we don't have any witnesses. It was most likely a disturbed burglar.'

'Fucking bastards,' I say, draining my glass and plonking it on the bar. 'Well, keep me posted, won't you?'

'Of course. And thanks, Steven. Thanks for the chance. I mean, obviously with the job and the kids and everything and being, well, *nearly* thirty, I'm not still harbouring any illusions about being a rock star . . .'

No shit, mate. You look like a fucking copper. No – you *are* a fucking copper.

'. . . but I thought,' he continues, 'with the songwriting, maybe I could get a publishing deal? Write songs for other people?'

Fuck me. *Fuck me.* 'Yeah, definitely,' I say instantly, 'I mean, don't give up on it just yet, Alan. Noel Gallagher was, like, twenty-eight or something when he got signed. And Mark Knopfler. And Sting was old *and* he was a fucking teacher!'

We share a laugh and I can see he's thinking the same crazy shit that they all think. It goes something like this: *'Yeah. It happened for them, it could still happen for me. Why not? I'm talented. You just need the break. Right place at the right time. It's not* what *you know, it's* who *you know.'*

They really do think like that these people. They think that Dame Fame and Lady Fortune are going to loaf into the room and single them out. You wouldn't fucking believe it.

I'm making my way through the crowded bar towards the door when, for the second time that evening, a heavy hand falls on my shoulder. Wearily I turn round – straight into a snarling mess of burnished fangs, a pair of burning devil's eyes. Tony-Blair-poster eyes.

'Oi, cunt, what the fuck is going on?' Flecks of spittle hit me.

'Ah, hi, Rage.' What the fuck is he doing here?

'Don't fucking give me that. What the *fuck* is happening with my album?' There's a couple of big darkies with him. One of them carries a record box. Rage must be DJing somewhere later.

What is happening with the album is nothing. We're sitting on the abortion until the cretin speaking to me writes something approaching a hit single.

'How do you mean?' I say innocently.

'Are you trying to be fucking funny?'

'No.'

'Schneider gets fired, that fucking queer Sommers ain't returning our calls, I ain't got a release date, I ain't been fucking paid, I . . .' he goes on and I see now that he really is angry.

'Listen,' I say, interrupting, 'can we go somewhere quieter and have a chat? I need to speak to you. Alone, yeah?' One of his boys glares at me and kisses his teeth but Rage waves them away and leads me off towards the dressing room, managing to get into only two serious arguments with security guards on the way there.

Soon enough we're hunkered down over the nosebag and, once he's got a thick line of my chang into his greedy fucking face, I hit him with the truth. Schneider *hated* the record. Derek's on the fence. I think it's a masterpiece. I tell him that I have some strong ideas on how to market it properly. That we *have* to get it released.

'That cunt of a fucking Jew-boy,' Rage says.

'I mean,' I say incredulously, 'he wanted you to fuck about writing some pop single! The fucking cheek. I kept telling him, you're an *albums artist*.'

'Yeah. Fucking straight up, blood.'

'We'll get great press and build it from there. Fuck Radio 1. *Fuck them.*' I smack a fist into my palm. I'm getting into it myself now, almost believing the utter shite I'm spewing.

'Yeah, fuck radio,' Rage says.

'Listen, when we came to the studio, to that playback, that track you played us, "Birth", yeah?'

'Yeah.'

I shake my head solemnly. 'I had tears in my eyes,' (this much was true) 'fucking goosebumps, mate. I mean, who gives a fuck if its sixty-four minutes long? It's a classic.'

'Yeah? Cheers, Steven.'

'Look, everything's fucked right now with Schneider going. But it ain't gonna be that way for long.' I have started to speak like Rage, a trait I have when talking to bands. If this conversation goes on much longer I'll be breaking out the fucking boot dubbin. 'I'm not saying I've got the job yet, but when – if – I do, I want you to know you'll be a priority act, mate. A priority act.'

Rage looks at me for a long moment, the silence dripping with cocaine. Finally he points a finger at me. The finger has three heavy gold rings on it. 'I always said to Fisher that you fucking understood what I was doing,' he says.

'Yeah? Cheers, Rage,' I say raising my glass.

'I'll tell you what I was trying to do with that track . . .' He starts talking about the piece-of-shit song in mind-frying detail, but it's OK because I don't have to listen any more. It's fine. I can just stand here, nodding, and moving frozen shards of coke around the roof of mouth with my tongue while saying over and over to myself *you black bastard, you black bastard, you black bastard . . .*

The following morning, in business affairs, I whole-heartedly add my vote to the unanimous landslide as we decide to drop Rage from the label. 'All righty,' says Trellick rapping his notes on the table '. . . moving on, boys and girls. Unsigned bands . . .' Within a few months Rage will probably be back to whatever he did before – chiselling stereos out of dashboards, holding Stanley knives to the throats of terrified pensioners, and filling council flats with half-caste babies.

Darren and I take The Lazies out to an insanely expensive Russian restaurant on the Embankment – caviar and thirty-seven different kinds of vodka and private dining rooms where you can do nose-up right off the table without being seen.

'Jimmy! Good to see you again, man,' I say, getting up and slapping him on the arm, trying to remember what we talked about over lunch in Austin the month before. 'How's things? This is Darren,' I say as Darren gets up and extends a hand.

'Uh, hi, guys. Darren? Yeah. I'm good man. This is Greg, and Adam and Kevin . . .' He introduces a shy, gangly, six-legged tangle of pimples, torn jeans and BO. The musicians.

We shake hands and do the 'hi, how are you' stuff. None of them makes eye contact. It is probably blowing their minds to be ordering a meal somewhere you don't just put the handbrake on and speak into a grille. '. . . and this is Marcy.' The singer comes out from behind them. She's tiny, stunning. Skin white as a fridge and perfect features half hidden under thick black, bowl-cut hair.

We do the small talk – how was your flight? Been to London before? Bish, bash, bosh. What you're trying to figure out here is: who am I talking to? Whose band is it? You can usually – not always – forget the drummer and the bass player. It's normally a guitarist/singer deal. I make sure I'm sitting next to Adam, the guitar player, and across from Marcy. Darren gets plonked with the rhythm section, the Muppet Show.

A waiter appears in full Cossack rig and dispenses menus. 'May I get you some drinks?' the fruit asks.

'Yes,' I say, 'can you bring us the vodka menu? You have to check this out, guys, they've got over thirty –'

'Could I just have some water please?' Marcy says.

'Yeah me too,' from Adam.

'We got an early start tomorrow,' Jimmy explains, 'gotta drive to . . . Dover?' (he pronounces it 'Daw-ver') 'to get the ferry.'

'No problem, water's good for me.'

Water. Waters. He *liked* the Prodigy artwork.

It's a fundamental – if they drink, you drink. If they don't . . . dear sweet mother of teats-blown Jesus. I am going to have to spend a couple of hours with these cunts sober.

The drummer – Greg? Kevin? – orders a beer and they fall to frowning over the menus.

'So,' I say, 'are you looking forward to Glastonbury?'

'Shit, man,' Adam says, 'it'll be . . .'

'Wild?' one of the other guys suggests.

'Yeah, wild.'

'We are going to rock that motherfucker.' The drummer. Obviously.

Marcy doesn't say anything. She stares at a hole in her shoe, a chunky, scuffed DM boot. I try to visualise her in heels.

We order and I make a big show of ordering nearly everything on the menu – beluga, sevruga, blinis, smoked salmon, chops, goose, baked fucking pike. Ominously the band order mostly salads.

'What's the vibe like at Glastonbury?' one of them asks. *Vibe?* It is a fucking insult that I am sat here having to live through this. For the umpteenth time today I lament the fact that I am not more successful and above all this.

'Oh, Glastonbury? It's just the most incredible . . . atmosphere.' (If you reckon that the atmosphere in medieval England – plague, filth, disease and billions of mud-spattered tolers everywhere – would qualify as incredible, then Glastonbury is indeed incredible.) With an upward surge of nausea I realise that, if we're going to have any chance of signing these clowns, I will probably have to go to Glastonbury.

The food starts to arrive. Darren talks indie with Adam. I watch Marcy pick at her salad. 'You must have had a bellyful of those record company dinners by now?'

She smiles for the first time – nervously, hesitantly, but still a smile – revealing a row of gleaming teeth whiter than her skin. A shred of purple lettuce is stuck between the front top two. Nice lips too. I can't make out the jugs because she's wearing a baggy sweater but, if I remember rightly from the gig in Austin, she's well stacked for a boiler her size. I don't remember any of the fucking songs, but I remember that.

'Nah,' she says, removing the strand of lettuce, 'it's nice, y'know? People being interested.'

'Have some caviar.' I push a dish of beluga towards her.

'No thanks. I don't eat fish.'

'So . . . tell us about your label,' Jimmy says.

'OK . . .' I clear my throat.

But what is there to tell really? We'll manufacture your records and put them in the fucking shops. We'll try our best not to spend a red cent unless we're sure we'll get it back with interest. We'll second-guess you and interfere at every conceivable stage of the artistic process. We'll edit and remix tracks without your permission. We'll force you to appear on appalling, degrading kiddies' TV programmes where you will shake hands with Dobbin the Donkey and have to explain yourself to a teenage VJ with the attention span of a Ritalin-fuelled infant. We'll work you until you can't stand up. In collusion with your publishers we'll try and license your music to TV adverts for everything from banks to multinational petrochemical companies. (We'd license it to whaling fleets and arms dealers too if only they advertised on TV). We'll under-account to you and charge you for every recoupable expense from the staples used to knock your horrendous contract together to the Coke you had from the fridge in my office. And if it doesn't all work out, you'll be dropped faster than a Plymouth hooker's knickers when there's a big ship in town.

Howzat, you pasty-faced vegetarian hippy cunts? Strap that on for a fucking laugh.

But, sadly, you can't say that these days. So I sip water and talk and they all nod away as I drone on about 'artistic freedom' and 'creative control' and 'long-term artist development' and all the usual balls until I'm nearly crying with boredom. Finally, when I can stand it no more, I get up and say, 'Excuse me.' I head for the Gents, leaving Darren to continue his part of the conversation – B-sides and the guitar solos of Tom Verlaine.

On the way to the toilet I stop at the bar and drink three double bison grass vodkas. In the toilet I deftly roll a fifty, lean close into the cistern lid, and snarfle up a heart-stopper. 'Right, you cunts, *let's fucking rock . . .*' I say, before – pausing only to vomit about a kilo of black sturgeon roe down the toilet – I'm striding manfully back to the table, sweat breaking out on my forehead and clear bubbles popping and exploding in my brain.

Well, things livened up after that, I can fucking tell you. I order a massive round of vodkas and a couple of the band even join me. I crack a few jokes. One contains the punch-line, 'No, that's my flask.' I talk about making them 'bigger than U2'. I get more drinks in . . .

Things get blurry and I find myself sitting next to Marcy, pressing myself closer and asking about her childhood and shit like that. Christ, she's fit. Maybe if I . . . no, must remain professional.

I get the Russkis to turn the music up and I drag one of the waiters in and make him Cossack-dance for us, throwing twenty-pound notes at him and laughing my head off. I start singing Clash songs with the drummer but I keep getting all the words wrong. I start Cossack-dancing myself, trying to drag Marcy up but she's not really into it. I order more vodka and then Jimmy is turning to me and saying, 'Hey, thanks for dinner, man. We gotta run.'

'Fuck off. It's only eleven.'

'No really, we've got an early start.'

'Come on . . .' But they're all getting up now, pulling jackets on, gathering bags.

'Right, no problem. I'll give you a call. We'll send our offer to your lawyer.'

'Sure.'

'Thanks for dinner, man,' one of them – Adam? Doug? – says and they're gone. I mean – who fucking farted?

'That went all right,' Darren says, not convincingly.

'Yeah. Fine. Fucking Shermans.'

'You got any bugle?'

I toss him the gram and he heads for the bogs. I get up and duck out into the hallway. Marcy is pulling her jacket on. 'Hey, you're not really going back to the hotel, are you?'

'Yeah,' she smiles, 'I'm beat.'

'Bollocks. Come for a drink. I know this place. Members only.'

'No thanks.'

'Come on, love, you know you –'

'Are you, like, hitting on me?'

'Am I . . . ?'

'Look, thanks for dinner. Goodnight.'

I wander back into our room and neck a stray vodka. A grinning waiter appears and a silver dish with a long strip of paper on it is plonked down in front of me.

The bill is just over seven hundred quid.

When I get into work in the morning there's a message on my machine from Jimmy. In a flat tone he says:

'Uh, Steven . . . I just called to say thank you for last night. We, uh, as you know we've still got a few other labels to meet so . . . you could have your guy send your offer to our lawyer if you like and I . . . I'll try and give you a call and let you know what's happening. OK. Bye.'

So that's over, then.

# June

*The Ivor Novello Awards are held at the Grosvenor House Hotel. Ken Berry becomes Head of EMI. 'MMmm Bop' by Hanson is no. 1. A lot of people are talking about Basement Jaxx. The Ultrasound deal is really heating up – Simon Williams, Head of Fierce Panda, says, 'It is clear that this band will be around a lot longer than eighteen months . . .'*

*'A lot of people are singing about how screwed up the world is. I don't think that everybody wants to hear about that all the time.'*

Mariah Carey

The tailback is long and we're surrounded by tolers – goths, ravers, punks, hippies, everything – carrying their back-packs, tents, huge plastic bottles of cider, cases of cheap lager, acoustic guitars, ghetto blasters, all that crap. They stumble along the sides of the road, pressing around the cars, all of them soaking wet and spattered with mud. Through the softening quartz of the windows of Trellick's Range Rover it feels like watching a CNN bulletin about an evacuation, a refugee trail somewhere. Incredibly enough it has stopped raining for a few minutes. The sun filters through weakly and all the losers cheer.

I pull the handbrake on just enough to allow me to turn on the dashboard TV. Trellick, in the driver's seat, is patiently arguing with *another* security guard ('We're from the record company. One of our acts is playing in fifteen minutes. We need to get in *now*'), while, in the distance, the boom of the festival shudders around the hills and vales of Somerset. In the back Ross and Darren – already drunk

– are 'ironically' singing 'Here we go, here we go, here we go . . .'

A guy suddenly bangs on my window. He's stripped to the waist, tattooed, crew cut. I press the button and the window hums down a few inches, admitting a reek of lager. 'Fucking hell!' he says to some people behind him, pointing at the dash, 'There's a fucking telly in there!' I just look at him. 'All right, mate!' he says cheerfully. 'What you watching then?'

I make sure the door is locked before replying. 'Dole office is that way, mate,' I say, pointing back down the road as I hit the button and the window slides efficiently back up. The guy pumps his fist, wanking an imaginary cock off at me, as he falls back into step with the other losers.

Finally the security mutant, having examined our VIP tickets and backstage parking pass for an hour or so, seems satisfied and waves us out of the queue and towards a closer, more discreet entrance. 'Thank you *very* much,' Trellick drawls, then, when we're a few yards away, he adds, 'you fucking loser.' There is a banner over the main entrance – the entrance where thousands of weary, footsore tolers are being herded in – which reads 'Greenpeace Glastonbury Festival 1997'. 'It should read "*Arbeit Macht Frei*",' Ross says sourly.

We come to another gate, endure more tedious negotiations, and then we're on the site proper, driving past rows of tents. Scumbags and jizz-buckets sit around their tents drinking Stella and Woodpecker and Christ knows what. I see a guy drinking fucking *Newcastle Brown*.

I do not understand the festival experience. These people, these disgusting lowlifes we're driving through, they *fought* to get in here. They think they're *lucky*. They spent hours on the phone trying to get tickets, happily paying hundreds of pounds for a pair when they managed to find some. Now they're *celebrating* being here, celebrating the fact that they can lie around in urine-flavoured mud drinking warm lager and eating burgers prepared by some syphilitic gyppo while fucking Cast knock out their greatest hits in the distance.

I turn round in my seat and give Darren a playful slap.

'Get the fucking pooey open and rack 'em out then!'

He pulls another bottle of Mumm's from a cooler at his feet while Ross digs the corner of his Amex into a huge bag of chang and we all do a quick card-edge.

'All righty!' Trellick shouts, thumping the wheel. *'Let's fucking rock!'*

Darren hands me the champagne and I shake the bottle up a bit before I fire the cork out of the open window of the Range Rover 'Oi! Oi! Oi!' we shout in delighted unison as a few scumbags look up from their cups of piss and tinfoil barbecues to give us what they imagine are withering looks. 'We're larging it, mate!' Ross shouts into the uncomprehending face of a passing middle-aged hippy.

The champagne cork sails up in a high arc over a row of filthy tents and disappears into the sun, finally, one hopes, hitting some filthy toe-rag right in the fucking eye. We roll off, clanking along the metal vehicle path towards hospitality parking.

The backstage beer tent is *rammed*. We elbow our way into the crush at the bar. Ross, viciously drunk by this point, says, 'It's like fucking Hillsborough in here,' to the clear disgust of Tony Crean, who literally *is* a fucking Scouser. Debbie Harry from Blondie walks by, dressed head to foot in crimson – topped off with a bunch of red roses for a hat. She looks shocking, like an old hooker who's fallen on hard times and gone crazy. 'Oi, love, how much for unprotected anal?' Ross shouts after her.

Across the bar I see Dean Wengrow, recently moved from London Records to Island. He waves and then mimes bending over and slapping his arse while giving me the thumbs up and pissing himself.

Last week, after I put the release date back four times in the demented hope that something, *anything*, positive might happen around the record, 'Why Don't You Slap Me on the Ass?' was finally released. It sold 1,112 copies and charted at no. 68 for a week before disappearing forever. We spent about a hundred quid for every copy of the record we sold. We might as well have made the sleeves out of jewel-encrusted platinum.

Finished. Game over. See you later, Sooty.

I mime wanking an imaginary cock in Wengrow's direction.

We get absolutely fucking *mullered* at the bar and then someone's saying that the Lazies are about to go onstage in the new bands tent.

'Hang on,' Trellick says as we finish up our drinks.

We huddle in a corner of the muggy, crowded bar. Darren – who has been deputised to carry the bulk of the drugs – produces a bag of Es and we all bosh one, washing them down with a swirl of flat, sour lager. Ross produces a bottle of Jack Daniel's, we buy a load of Cokes, tip the last of our lager out of the paper cups and improvise pints of

Rockschool. We lean in for another quick card-edge and we're ready to go.

Walking from the backstage area at Glastonbury into the main arena is like stepping from a drug-addled village fete into the Holocaust. Or from a field hospital onto the battlefield itself. The mud, the devastation, is incredible. It's only Friday afternoon but already, everywhere you look, you see the casualties: tripping, wall-eyed Scousers who haven't slept in three days; Jocks who've been living on speed and lager and who have, somehow, even with the downpour, *still* managed to get sunburned; and crying teenage girls. Unconscious bodies (corpses?) lie broken in the mud and hooded Kaffirs stand by the walkways, muttering their '*speed? 'ash? aceed? coke?*' mantra out of the sides of their mouths. You see forty-five-year-old blokes with their faces painted; accountants and estate agents off their nuts on mushrooms, having their one big weekend of the year.

Clean and shining, bright with coke and bourbon, it all looks very funny to us. 'Hello, tolers!' we chirp as we pass by. '*Arbeit macht frei!*' we say brightly to their red, confused faces.

The Lazies are on early, it's only four o'clock in the afternoon, but there's an incredible surge into the tent. It takes us forever to crawl around the side and then push our way in at the front. Steam is rising in great clouds off the crowded bodies at the crash barrier. I count no less than fifteen other A&R people around us as the band walk onstage. No Parker-Hall in sight. Got to be good news. (Or is it? What if he's changed his mind? Maybe the Lazies are actually shit. How can you tell?)

Marcy runs out last. She is wearing a black catsuit as tight as a surgical glove and now, elevated by the stage, italicised by the lights, she looks about twelve feet tall.

'Sen-say-shunal,' says Trellick. People start yelling and screaming.

'What's she like?' Ross asks me.

*Are you hitting on me?* 'Bang up for it,' I reply automatically.

Marcy grabs the mike from the stand, 'Hey, Glastonbury!' she yells over a deafening squawk of guitar, two ribcage-moving thumps on the bass drum, 'are you motherfuckers ready to fucking rock!'

'NO!' shouts Ross.

'FUCK OFF, YOU SHERMAN CUNTS!' some wag shouts and then the drumsticks click together fast – one, two, three, four times, the wooden slap echoing through the huge walls of speakers in front of us – and they pile into the first song. The place goes *berserk*.

Two songs in and people are being pulled out of the crowd unconscious. People are stage-diving. For a band just two singles old, it's an incredible reaction.

Ross: 'They are going to be fucking massive.'

Trellick: 'We have to get this deal. We should up the offer.'

Me: 'I'm all over it.'


Later in the evening I find I can't remember much about their set because I was so traumatised by what happened at the end of it.

What happened was this: the last song was grinding and juddering to a climax, the E was kicking in so I was actually, incredibly, just enjoying the music. I had my eyes closed, swaying, when Trellick tapped me on the shoulder and pointed to something. I followed his finger woozily, looking along it like a gun barrel towards the stage where the band were flouncing off, waving and blowing kisses to the baying, ecstatic crowd. I watched as Marcy skipped offstage and jumped delightedly towards someone standing at the side of the stage, someone with a stage-laminate dangling around their neck, the only pass greater than ours.

With gut-pummelling agony I recognised the shaved head and grinning features of Parker-Hall, as Marcy embraced him.

Outside the tent the rain has stopped again and a weak purplish sun is setting over the fields. Time to spend the summer's evening experiencing all that the biggest, most diverse music festival in the world has to offer. We stomp sulkily backstage to someone's Winnebago where we pull the blinds and spend the next five hours angrily drinking brandy and snorting cocaine.

It's all broken, out-of-focus snapshots from there. We're in the backstage bar; we're walking across the site, through lakes of mud and along rattling metal paths; we're buying mushrooms (mushrooms?) and pints of cider (cider?); and we're walking, walking, walking and then I'm tripping my nut off in the middle of a huge crowd *are you hitting on me* and the rain is falling lightly on us as we strain to see something in the distance, something far away in the dark, glowing red and blue and gold and green and there's music and *fucking Parker-Hall* it's getting louder and there are people singing something I can't make out and hugging each other all around us and *120 grand unrecouped* this music is building and building and then suddenly it all pulls into focus *crossover* and brilliant white light washes over the crowd and you can see the raindrops – billions of them – suspended in the light above us and I realise we're watching Radiohead and he's singing '*Rain down . . .*' everyone's singing '*Rain down . . .*' and I don't like Radiohead because I don't know what they *marketing spend* want but it's really beautiful and Darren turns to me and I think he's crying and maybe you are not alone in the universe *sound of impact* and for a moment there I lose myself.

But then we're off again. We're dancing in some packed, steaming rave-tent and I'm kissing some rave-boiler, then I'm pulling her zipper down, freeing her breasts and trying to suck them right there on the heaving dance floor and there's a slap and some rave-guy wading in and then we're heading somewhere else and I'm high on a Ferris wheel with Ross, snorting poppers and roaring with laughter as the cold black air swirls around and around us, and there's thousands of orange fires and coloured lights stretching off into the night, and then there's an argument with the owner of an ethnic foods stall, who goes lunatic after I career into his falafel wagon or tofu cart, smashing it to pieces and simply thrusting a bunch of fifties into his hands in lieu of an apology, and all the time I'm thinking '*fucking Parker-Hall, fucking Parker-Hall, fucking Parker-Hall*'.

Now the dawn is coming up and a bunch of us are stretched out up in the Green Field. For some reason I can't remember we're all wearing hats – huge felt jester caps in grape, canary yellow and red. How did we get them?

I'm lying flat on my back and listening to a three-way

conversation between Darren, Ross and Leamington that goes something like this:

'How long do you reckon it takes to clean this up?'

'Wimbledon?'

'The hats?'

'No, I mean . . .'

'On the centre court?'

'Hats?'

'Cheese?'

'I want to know what's happening at Wimbledon . . .'

I don't know who's saying what and it doesn't really seem to matter much.

'Oh God . . .' I moan quietly and I sit up and survey the field in the chill dawn mist. It's an almost clichéd post-apocalyptic landscape. Doomed, lonely figures wrapped in tattered blankets stumble through the cold mud. Bodies are littered all over the place. The smoke from all the thousands of fires has created a battlefield pall over the place. It's like someone dropped the bomb.

'Is this the Green Field?' someone says.

'Who gives a fuck?' says Trellick, pulling his Nokia out, the screen already glowing a beautiful civilised green, like it's the only piece of technology to have survived the epicentre. In the context of where we are Trellick's mobile looks like the black obelisk from *2001*, gleaming in the desert among the apes.

'Shall we do one back to the hotel, boys and girls?' he says, dialling calmly.

Barely an hour later Ross and I are neck-deep in hot, bubbling water, clinking brimming flutes of Bollinger. A few feet away, Trellick, snugly wrapped in one of the hotel's thick, white towelling robes, chops out some lines and bellows at room service for more, colder, champagne. Burt Bacharach purrs smoothly from the Bang & Olufsen.

'Oh, I *love* Glastonbury,' Ross sighs contentedly.

Trellick's phone rings. He picks it up and looks at the screen. 'Shit, fucking Derek.'

'What the fuck can he want at this time?' Ross says.

'An AIDS helpline?' I reply before slipping down under the surface, my temples throbbing as the hot water loosens the grime of the festival from my skin.

Trellick is gone for a while. When he comes back he looks stunned. It takes a lot to stun Trellick.

'What's happened?'

'Strap yourself in, matey boy,' he says, looking at me, allowing a dramatic pause.

'For fuck's sake, James . . .'

'Listen! It looks like we'll be signing the Lazies after all.'

'*Go on!*' I yell, leaping up in the tub and pumping my fist. I am the King. I am the King of fucking Rock. Fuck Parker-Hall. *Fuck him.* Ross starts clapping and whooping.

'Hold your horses,' Trellick says, starting to laugh now, 'Parker-Hall is actually signing them.'

Eh? 'What do you –'

'The band want to sign with Parker-Hall. No one else. It seems Derek's been talking to Parker-Hall for a while now and, well . . . he's our new Head of A&R.'

'I don't under . . .' The words dribble off because my mouth isn't working properly. I am just standing there – literally up to my knees in hot water.

'Derek, our Managing Director, has just hired Anthony

Parker-Hall,' Trellick says, speaking simply and clearly, as you would to a child. 'Parker-Hall is coming to work for us as Head of A&R, effective immediately. He is bringing the Lazies with him as his first signing.'

They both look at me, standing there in the middle of the hot tub, my mouth hanging open.

'He's your fucking boss,' Ross says.

They both start pissing themselves.

Parker-Hall – younger than me – chewing me out in meetings. (*'Gawdnbennet, Steven, wot da fuck's appening wiv dem poxy remixes?'*)

Parker-Hall parking his car so much closer to the building than me.

Parker-Hall questioning my expenses.

'How much?' I say in a strangled whisper. I'm trembling now too. 'How much are we paying him?'

Trellick: 'I've been told not to discuss it and, trust me, you don't want to fucking know.'

I am Hervé Villechaize.

It hurts.

I am dying now.

# July

Simon Cowell signs a boy band called Five. For reasons I can't quite work out there is a lot of interest in this Paki band called Asian Dub Foundation. (Who the fuck is Satpal Ram?) Sony are about to launch a pop singer called Jimmy Ray, who is managed by Simon Fuller who manages the Spice Girls. Sony's marketing guy Mark Richardson says, 'I dare anyone to listen to the single "Are You Jimmy Ray?" and tell me it's not going to be a hit. It's both retro and contemporary.'

*'After you've finished being smart in the record business you've also got to be lucky.'*

Dick Asher, MD of CBS Records

'As you all know,' Derek announces, standing up at the head of the big conference table, his eyes – predatory eyes, queer's eyes – flickering around the boardroom, 'it's been a very difficult year so far for the company, what with Roger's tragic death . . .' Everyone nods sadly. I look around the room. Pretty much the whole company – about thirty people – are crammed in here, for this miserable 'celebration'. I catch Rebecca's eye and she looks away. '. . . and Paul Schneider's decision to move on,' ('Move on'? Yeah, right), 'we've been missing . . .' he searches for the right word, not wanting to put the boot in on me and Hastings too directly, but wanting to put it in a bit no doubt, 'leadership in the A&R department. Well, I'm very pleased to say that's all about to change.' He drops his hand onto Parker-Hall's shoulder, who has been sitting next to him throughout this, looking embarrassed. 'As I'm sure you all already know Anthony signed his contract last week and is officially our new Head of A&R.' Derek leads the applause as Parker-Hall squirms in his chair, gesturing for people to stop. The applause goes on for a while. In Stalinist Russia, if you were the first person to stop clapping after one of old Joe's speeches, they came and got you in the night. A few weeks of solid dawn-to-dusk beatings with a car battery permanently hooked up to your shaved nuts, and then you were off to the salt mines for the next forty years. Top lad, Stalin.

'I won't embarrass Anthony any further by listing his résumé here but, as I'm sure you all know, he's just had an incredibly successful run over at EMI where he signed – among others – Ellie Crush whose album has now gone double platinum in the UK and sold over a million copies worldwide.'

But everybody knew this. Last week it was the front-page story on *Music Week.* There was a big photo of Derek, Parker-Hall, Trellick and Marcy from the Lazies and an accompanying story saying how Parker-Hall's contract had expired at EMI (he'd let it run out), how he had been unable to agree new terms, how we'd come in just at the right time, with the right offer – (*How much? How much are we paying the little bastard?*) – how excited Parker-Hall was to be able to make the Lazies his first signing . . .

The story went on to list Parker-Hall's A&R achievements, focusing on Ellie Crush's continued US success, and stressing the fact that he has just turned twenty-six. It concluded with a horribly magnanimous and ominous quote from Parker-Hall:

'I'm really looking forward to the challenges of my new role. The label already has a vibrant A&R culture, one I'm aiming to take to the next level.' ('The next level'! One of those spastic music-business phrases – like 'does what it says on the tin' and 'it's not rocket science' – that spill from your mouth in meetings. Meaning absolutely fuck all.)

After I read the story I spent forty-eight hours in bed.

Parker-Hall stands up and does a bit of awkward shuffling, really laying on the 'I'm not worthy' crap. 'Thanks, everyone. I'm not much for big speeches, so I'll just say how excited I am to be here and how pleased I am to have a fantastic band like the Lazies to bring to the table . . .'

More applause, led now by Dunn. The next Lazies single is already recorded and Dunn is convinced that it's going to stroll onto the Radio 1 playlist. Consequently he's been licking Parker-Hall's Ronson like it's going out of fashion.

'Obviously I already know Steven and Rob,' he indicates me and Hastings, the broken men, 'and I'm looking forward to getting us all pulling in the same direction so we can get stuck in and sign a few more great bands for you all to work on. Thanks very much.'

Cue applause and cheers and Derek nodding as though he's just negotiated world fucking peace.

*I'm walking in a forest. I'm walking in a forest.*

Later, on the stairs, I pass Nicky. Normally the most I ever get from the monstrous diesel is a tight little smile but today she's beaming, I mean fucking *beaming* at me. Her smile says: 'End of the line for you and your turkey acts, loser. There's a real A&R guy in town now. How can you even stand to come into work?' The urge to kick her down the stairs, to jump on her head, to pummel her gloating dyke-face into an unrecognisable porridge of blood and bone, is tremendous. But, using incredible reserves of willpower, I manage to ignore her and continue on towards marketing.

Rebecca comes in. Today she's wearing leather trousers. I'm not kidding. Leather. Fucking. Trousers. If I had any self-respect left I'd fire her.

'That policeman's here to see you again,' she says in what she imagines is a meaningful tone of voice. I just yawn and click the mouse to close the window on my laptop. A graphic close-up – too close in fact, I'd zoomed in until the image was just a smear of pixels – of a bull ejaculating a ludicrous payload of glutinous semen into a Latino girl's grateful face vanishes. A Mexican website Trellick turned me onto.

'Send him up,' I say, pushing the screen down, the laptop closing with a snick.

I knew Woodham was coming. I've finally agreed to see him to talk about the tracks he recorded for us a few weeks ago. I'd been dodging his calls.

Basically, figuring there was no downside to keeping him sweet, I sprang five hundred quid from the demo fund and he went into the Stoneroom in Acton with his band where the mad cunt managed to bang down something like fourteen songs in two days. I've managed to listen to two or three tracks and they are *appalling*. You couldn't have got arrested with them even last year, when any scavenger from north of Watford with a fucking giro in one hand and a semi-acoustic guitar in the other was getting on the cover of the *NME*. Woodham's demo is so bad that there can be no prevaricating, none of the 'lots of potential' crap. I'll just have to be honest and tell him straight out to forget it.

He comes in and we do the hey-how-are-you-can-I-get-you-anything stuff before I say, 'Look, Alan, about your demos.'

'Actually, before we get onto that, I need to talk to you in connection with Mr Waters.' His tone is different. Formal. Less matey.

'Roger?' I say.

He takes out his notebook and flips to a page. What the fuck is going on here? 'There's something that's been puzzling me. You said that the last time you saw him alive was when you dropped him off in Notting Hill around 11 p.m. before you took the cab onto Maida Vale.'

'That's right.'

He consults his notebook and taps his pen against his leg. 'You were at the Dublin Castle on Parkway, weren't you?'

He looks up at me. He looks like a different guy now. He's suddenly older, more serious. He's suddenly very fucking serious.

'Yeah . . .'

'And you caught a cab on Parkway?'

'Um, yeah. I think that's right.'

'It seems a long way round, doesn't it?'

'How do you mean?'

'Parkway's one-way. You'd have had to head up further into Camden and then up towards Chalk Farm.'

'Sorry, Alan, I'm not quite following you.' But I'm beginning to.

'Well, you said you dropped him off. But you live in Maida Vale. To Maida Vale from Chalk Farm via Notting Hill? You pretty much have to go through Maida Vale to get to Notting Hill from there, don't you? Why didn't you get dropped off first?'

'Ah . . .' I am dying here. My head is pounding. Think. 'Why didn't I get dropped off first?' I repeat while, in my head, Def Con 3 goes on. A long time passes. Woodham says nothing, looks straight at me. The silent close.

'Ah!' I say, and I actually snap my fingers together. Jesus Christ, this is like a fucking masterclass in bad acting. 'Sorry, we were going to drop me off first but neither of us had any cash,' this is so *lame*, 'and I'd left my wallet in the office, so we went onto Roger's place, he had some cash in the house and, yeah . . .' he continues to look at me evenly, 'that was it. Sorry, I'd had a few.' I laugh. He doesn't.

'So – you dropped him first and then went back to Maida Vale?'

'Yeah, that's right. Sorry.'

He writes something down. Jesus Christ. Jesus fucking Christ.

'OK,' he says, snapping the notebook shut, 'so what were you going to say about the demos?'

I clear my throat. 'I have to be honest with you . . . I think the songs are incredible. Some of the best material I've heard in a long, long time.'

'Really?'

'Yeah. What we should do, what I think we can do, is we should look at trying to get you a publishing deal.'

'Seriously?' he says, smiling now for the first time since he came in. 'Well, that'd be great, Steven,' he says getting up.

'Yeah, let me look into that. Make a few calls. And, sorry about the confusion there, with the Roger stuff.'

We shake hands. 'Don't worry about it,' he says and he leaves.

I close the blinds, avoiding Rebecca's concerned gaze on the other side of the glass. I cross the room to my little fridge, chug a bottle of Beck's in one go, and open a second one. I sit down and torch a Marlboro Light with a trembling hand and I try to work out if what I think was just happening was actually happening.

So, on top of everything else, on top of Parker-Hall, on top of the hundred-grand dance single that stiffed at 68, on top of the bridging loan for a ruined house that a gang of speed-fuelled Albanians are busy dismantling, on top of the American Express and Visa bills totalling six and a half grand I received this month, I now looks like I'll have to find a publishing deal for a copper who thinks he's Noel fucking Gallagher.

Cheers.


Meet the new boss.

Parker-Hall takes me and Hastings to the River Cafe for lunch. A sort of getting-to-know-you combined with 'here's my vision' deal. We have pasta and Hastings fidgets and looks uncomfortable the whole time, probably wondering why there's no chicken fucking tikka on the menu. We're all drinking Evian. 'Bottle of still water, mate,' Parker-Hall had said when the waiter rocked up and I looked up from the wine list I was examining and said, 'Same.' If they drink . . .

'The way I see it,' Parker-Hall is saying, 'there are two categories of acts; there are entertainers – Robbie Williams, Spice Girls, what have you – and there are artists

– Radiohead, Weller . . . Ellie . . .' *You pompous little cunt.* 'Now –'

'What about the Beatles?' I interrupt. 'Weren't they both?'

'Well, if you wanna split hairs, Steven, they were entertainers who later became artists. Anyway,' he waves it away, *you pompous smart-arsed little cunt*, 'a label needs both. You need the entertainers in the short term so you can develop the artists for the long term. Now you guys both have different strengths; Rob, you're coming from an indie guitar-band area,' Hastings nods enthusiastically, 'and, Steven,' he indicates me, 'your roots are more in the pop-dance area of the marketplace. So . . .'

He goes on, but I don't hear much more of it. I get lost in a rapturous fantasy vision where I'm grabbing the steak knife from the table in front of me, I'm vaulting across and burying it in Parker-Hall's jugular vein and throwing him to the floor, then I'm jumping up and down on his head, slipping and sliding in his blood as I pound his stubbly, shaven little elfin head into fucking jelly, the other diners looking on in horror as I scream, *'Shut the fuck up! What the fuck do you know about anything, you jammy, fluky chancing little prick? Ellie Crush? You won the fucking lottery with that cow. Fuck you. Fuck you. Fuck you.'*

'Do you know what I mean, Steven?'

'Umm, yeah. Definitely,' I say, tuning back in, having no idea what I'm replying to.

'Good. Because there's rumours doing the rounds that I'm going to poach so-and-so from Island, that so-and-so from EMI is going to come over with me. All the usual bollocks. I just want you two to know that your jobs are safe. I'm gonna have complete faith in you until you give me a reason not to. Right?'

'Yeah,' Hastings says, 'thanks, Tony.'

'No problem, Rob. Steven, I hear you've been looking at signing Songbirds, them girls Danny Rent's managing?'

'Yeah, I've been thinking about it. What do you reckon?'

'I didn't reckon much to any of the songs on the demos.'

'Me neither, but –'

'But that ain't necessarily a problem with that type of band, is it? And they're lookers, the girls. Trashy, but lookers.'

'Yeah.'

'What kind of advance is he looking for?'

'Fuck all really.'

'So, do we wanna be doing the deal or what?'

'What do you think?'

He laughs. 'I'm asking you, mate. It's your call,' he says, signalling for the bill.

Do I want to sign them?

I really don't know. It's so much easier not to sign bands. Signing bands can cost you your fucking job. Also, I must be mindful of Parker-Hall's intentions here. He could be privately convinced that Songbirds are grade A, oven-ready turkeys with lead wings and hobnailed boots on. He could be cheerfully doling me out enough rope here to hang myself properly once and for all. What does he care about the advance? It's not his fucking money. Having me sign a pop act also makes practical and political sense for him.

Practical sense because he's just signed a three-year contract and you can break a pop act in six months to a year. As for breaking a 'proper' band . . . the Manic Street

Preachers were signed in 1991 and only started properly selling records last year. Same kind of time frame with Radiohead. Do you really want to be fannying about for five fucking years trying to break something like that? Chances are they'll be a billion quid unrecouped and you'll be clearing out your desk before they sell one record.

Political sense because, if Songbirds are huge, he looks the King of Rock because he authorised the deal and supervised the project. If they go down like the *Titanic* with boulders strapped to it he'll say something about how he had to allow me the autonomy to make my own mistakes, how he always had his reservations, etc., etc.

However, on the other hand, I've got fuck all else going on at the moment. If I don't sign Songbirds and some other fucker does and then they're huge, then I'm dead anyway. You're the guy who passed on the Beatles. It's a fucking nightmare. Poisoned chalices and loaded dice all over the shop.

My call. What do I want to do?

'Yeah,' I hear myself saying, 'I think we should sign them.'

'All right then. Get Trellick to put an offer in.'

The bill arrives and Parker-Hall nimbly presses his plutonium credit card down on top of it. His card is from Coutts and I am raped by envy.

The last one of the girls puts her childish uncertain signature on the contract (the 'i' in 'Debbie' is a little balloon), 'That's your career over then,' says Trellick, cracking his usual gag and the cork cracks out of another bottle and goes flying across the boardroom as the other girls – Annette,

Kelly and Jo – shriek piercingly for the umpteenth time.

I hate signing celebrations. You get drunk and do coke and have to listen to some manager, some singer, some *drummer* even, crapping on about how great you both are and how you're going to rule the world. I often think back to these moments when we're dropping the cunts a year later.

Crammed into the boardroom along with the girls and Danny Rent are Trellick, Derek (who, perhaps thinking/ hoping that this bunch of dogs are doomed from the off, kept his ludicrous 'we're going to rule the world' speech mercifully short), Ross, Darren, Rebecca, a couple of junior muppets from press and radio and Parker-Hall. Dunn isn't here but should be. Where is the Geordie cunt?

Everyone is smiling and laughing, but, to the trained eye, to the practised ear, there is a marked difference in the quality of the happiness: that of the band and the manager is of a genuine, top-of-the-world, time-of-your-life quality. They're thinking that they've won the lottery. The laughter and smiles of the executives is brittle and plastic; we've done this so many times, often for bands and singers who turned out to be about as commercial as tooth-kind drinkable HIV for children. Ours is the forced jollity of the whore, cracking a joke as she tiredly addresses herself to the fifth or sixth cock of the evening. Everyone is thinking something like 'What are the chances of this piece-of-shit band actually happening? How can I position myself so that if – when – they go down screaming in flames I don't get burned, *but,* at the same time, if by some miracle, some unforeseen quirk of taste and radio play they actually sell a few fucking records, then how can I have some of the glory spatter onto me?'

Parker-Hall gives me a wink from across the room and raises his glass. Congratulating me? Or congratulating himself on letting me trowel a few more bricks onto my DIY mausoleum? I smile back at the lowlife and take a seat next to one of the girls. Jo, I think. 'Congratulations,' I say clinking her glass.

'Oh fank you, Steven,' she says all breathy, her eyelashes fluttering and her hard little peasant's eyes glittering, 'we won't let ya down, mate.' She smiles at me from under her fringe, tracing her finger around the rim of her champagne flute. I suppose she's being as subtly and classily flirtatious as she can be, given that her teenage sexual 'awakenings' probably consisted of hiking her jeans down in a car park under some tower block and bending over while a trio of thugs lined up behind her.

The door bursts open and Dunn strides into the room looking incredibly pleased with himself. 'Hi there!' he brays, shaking a few hands. 'Sorry I'm late, just got back from Radio 1.' There's a hush of anticipation.

'The Lazies single?' Dunn continues, looking around the room, savouring the moment. 'Straight on the fucking B-list, *six weeks upfront!*' he says, punching the air. The room explodes – Nicky shrieks, literally *shrieks* with joy – and Derek is immediately by Parker-Hall's side, clapping him frantically on the back as everyone whoops and cheers.

Fucking. Shit.

'Nah,' Parker-Hall says, stretching back in his chair, 'that's pony. Take it off, Darren.' Darren, manning the stereo, takes whatever demo is playing off and slips something else in. I'm sitting on one of the sofas in Parker-Hall's office

(Schneider's old office), Hastings is on the other sofa, Parker-Hall sits at his desk reading emails, and Darren and Stan are on the floor with a pile of demos and records.

'This is Coco and the Bean,' Stan says, getting up, 'Edinburgh band, a few people are talking about this.'

A&R meetings are now weekly under Parker-Hall, rather than whenever we felt like it under Schneider. They are also driven by a new focus and clarity: he's right up every lawyer, agent and manager in town. He's on everything early and he has a sharp idea of what he likes and what he doesn't like. What he thinks will work in the marketplace and what won't. One and a half songs into the Coco and the Bean demo he says, 'Next,' and we listen to Polar Bear, Earl Brutus, Catch, the Low Fidelity All-Stars and many more. Parker-Hall tells us why none of them will sell records.

In the last couple of weeks I have sent Woodham's demo over to a few of the big publishers; Island Music, Sony, BMG, Warner-Chappell. I struck out everywhere. I put a call in to Woodham and told him I've been getting some good reactions, people like the songs, but it'll take some time. I'll get back to him. He's perfectly pleasant.

Maybe I was being paranoid. Maybe he doesn't . . .

A further indignity. The Lazies signed their deal and we had a party at the Halcyon in Holland Park. The night before the party Parker-Hall shuffled into my office and said he thought it'd be a good idea if I didn't come. 'I can't come anyway,' I lied, 'I've got a gig to go to. But, just out of interest, why the fuck not?'

'No offence, mate,' he said, 'and I don't know what happened, but Marcy says she gets a bad vibe off ya . . .'

'Right,' Parker-Hall says after we've listened to all the new music kicking around this week. 'I've been thinking about producers for the Lazies album and wondered if any of you lot had any bright ideas . . .'

Fortunately this week's *Music Week* is open on the floor next to me at the top hundred albums and I hastily run my eye down the page, over the names of producers, which are listed in brackets after the albums themselves, while Hastings craps on.

'Steven?' Parker-Hall says, swivelling in his chair to face me.

'Bird and Bush? Bacon and Quarmby? Gil Norton? Dave Bascombe? Langer and Winstanley?' I say, reeling them off.

'Why?' Parker-Hall says, looking blank.

'Why what?'

'Steven, mate,' he sighs, 'it sounds like you've just stuck a fucking pin in the *Music Week* directory and come up with a list of people who've produced a few records that are in the charts this week.'

'No, I . . .' My face is colouring. This answer would have worked fine under the old regime. 'Well, who are you thinking of?' I say.

'Steve Albini,' Parker-Hall says.

Hastings nods solemnly. I do too, while thinking, 'Who the fuck is Steve Albini?'

'He produced *In Utero*, the last Nirvana record. He rocks up with a box of microphones and records the band live. Don't take points either.' Eh? This guy Albini must be out of his fucking mind. 'The way I see it,' Parker-Hall continues, 'we're gonna have enough of a buzz on the band to have a gold record with this one whatever it sounds like.

Let's make an extreme record, establish credibility, and then we can look to make something more commercial with the second one. Yeah?'

He's thought all this through. He isn't really asking our opinions on anything.

It is just some horrible test.

I go into the studio with Songbirds.

Now, I hate going to the studio. (Unlike Parker-Hall who seems to love it. Also – and check this out, you won't believe it – he goes away for the weekend *with his artists*. Honestly. Picture it, if you will. They sit around and get stoned and talk about . . . I don't know. I guess they talk about chords and middle eights and B-sides and stuff. I've tried to imagine doing this myself but, come on. There's a limit.) In the studio nothing happens for four days and then they play you something and ask for your opinion and you pretty much tell them to make it shorter and make the vocals louder. I mean, there's not a lot to it. But I need to fill the days somehow, so here I am. (*'How do you write a song? Well, you get some kids in a room, you get a beat going . . .'*)

On the other side of the glass the girls have been trying to record some harmonies for the past four hours. I'm reading the *FT* while Allan, the producer, fucks around with the Autotune – a studio device that, in theory, should allow a tramp gargling with razor blades and spunk to sound like Pavarotti.

The Dow hit a record high the other week. People I know are making money and I'm sinking in a quagmire of delays and debt. I had another heart-caving conference with Murdoch at the new house last week. Another wall may have to come down. I am haemorrhaging cash I do not have and if I do not turn this bunch of whores around soon it is possible I will be finished before the building work is. I take some comfort from the fact that Trellick bought a load of EMI shares recently, thinking they'd hit the floor. He was wrong. They're still going down. Every morning he's waking up to find his dough has been gang-banged over night. *Schadenfreudes* all round.

'Shall we see if that's any better, Steven?' Allan says after a while. 'Yeah,' I say sullenly, swapping the *FT* for *FHM*. He hits a button somewhere on the huge desk and music fills the room.

The girls' harmonies . . . it's hard to describe. Imagine you'd got four fishwives together, filled them full of Special Brew, and told them to scream random, primal abuse at each other. It sounds absolutely satanic. Allan turns it down and looks at me sadly.

'I don't see that we have any other option,' he says.

'Fine,' I say getting up and slipping into my suit jacket, 'let them fuck around a bit more, tell 'em it's great and send them home. Then we'll get some singers in and get it done properly tonight.'

'Right,' he says with visible relief.

As soon as he kills the track shouting can be heard coming from the live room, even through the phone-book-thick glass. I squint through. Two of girls, maybe Annette and Debbie, are screaming and pushing at each other. Allan hits the talkback and the sound of the playground comes out of the speakers.

'FACK OFF, YOU FACKING SLAAAG!'

'YOU'RE THE FACKING SLAG, SLAG!'

'At least they're taking it seriously,' I say to Allan as microphone stands and sound baffles get knocked over.

'I'M WEARING THE FACKING GREEN ONES!'

'YOU LOOK LIKE A FACKING FAT COW!'

I realise as they really go for each other – nails flailing, feet lashing out – that they are actually fighting over a consignment of shoes a stylist has brought down for a photo shoot. I swivel round in my chair to Rent who is stretched out on a sofa at the back of the control room reading *Billboard*.

'For fuck's sake, Dan,' I say wearily.

'All right, all right,' he says getting up and slouching off towards the sliding glass door to go and break it up.

'And talk to them about the fucking cab accounts.'

'OK. Christ.'

Since the stupid whores got signed – sluts who had never seen the inside of a taxi in their lives – they've been using company cabs for *everything*. Going to the corner shop for a pint of milk seems to involve a people carrier on wait-and-return. Fucking bands always do this. Us too. Every few months a memo will go round vetoing all cab use without the signature of a head of department. Then, gradually, it slips back to the old ways. This climaxed a couple of years ago when a secretary in the marketing department used company cabs *for her fucking wedding*.

And then the cretins wonder why they don't make any money. Let's see, your album sold eight copies and you spent fourteen thousand quid a month on cabs.

Later that week, sitting at the traffic lights off Shepherd's Bush, staring at the blue water in the huge ornamental syringe they've stuck in the middle of the roundabout, I hear the Lazies single for the third time that day on Radio 1 and I come to a painful conclusion about Parker-Hall. He's actually very good at his job and – unlike Schneider – is not going to simply destroy himself through incompetence.

So, the following night, I drive across London to a seedy Internet café in Whitechapel: filthy, slow, old computers and a few Pakis scattered around scrolling through search results for cheap flights.

Although the place is almost empty I still make a point of choosing a screen in a far away corner. I log on and start doing some research, prepaying for my user time with cash.

I do not want to leave any sort of paper trail.

# August

*Epic trumpets the launch of the new Echobelly LP. MD Rob Stringer says, 'What a fine act they are. I was very involved in the signing.' Andersen Consulting and Sun Microsystems are to spend 50K hosting a Music Industry Trust dinner in honour of Jonathan King. All the time you hear Will Smith singing 'Men in Black' and you hear 'Tubthumping' by Chumbawumba.*

*'It's a mean industry — especially when you're on the outs.'*
Richard Dobbis, former Sony Music President

By the time the Reading Festival and Carnival roll around the Lazies single is shaping up be a proper hit – possibly top ten – and they're getting ready to record their debut album, which is already being freely talked about around the office as being 'a landmark', 'a classic' (Parker-Hall) and, from a coked-up Derek, as 'the best debut album since *Nevermind*'. (And nevermind that the homo-fool doesn't know that *Nevermind* wasn't a debut LP.) Meanwhile, over in the Songbirds camp, I'm onto the second producer, third studio, and fourth or fifth lot of songwriters – and well into six figures' worth of recording costs – and I still don't have so much as a B-side.

It's Sunday morning and everyone's in the bar at the Ramada, a few miles from the Reading site.

Cigarette smoke and hoarse laughter in the air and groups of people buckle over their Bloody Marys. The place is packed with scouts, journalists, press officers, managers, agents, A&R guys, guys from bands – all talking about bands they saw the previous day: Symposium, Kent, Pavement, Remy Zero and Les Rhythms Digitales. They enthuse about

Cha Cha Cohen, Chicks, Space Raiders, Delgados, Smog, Seafood, the Webb Brothers and Dawn of the Replicants. About Rosita, Seafruit, Cinerama, Skinny and Indian Ropeman. We have opinions about Lit, Black Box Recorder, Cornelius and SubCircus. Now, most of that lot will probably end up going down the tubes for a small fortune, probably taking a few people like me out along the way. This is why you have to watch it with signing bands – they can literally cost you your fucking job. One minute you're nodding away at the back of some indie gig. A rash wave of a recording contract later and you're down the dole office, shouldering your way between a couple of stinking tolers and a bunch of teenage mothers.

I see Darren, Leamington and a couple of people at the bar. As I make my way towards them Jon Carter passes me. 'All right, mate,' he croaks, his voice a shredded bark – a dog who has been in kennels all night, howling and yelping along with his cell mates. I nod hello.

'Large Bloody Mary,' I say to the bartender, who looks crippled with exhaustion, like a soldier who's been left too long on his own to guard some remote outpost of the empire.

'Who are we seeing today?' I ask, lighting a Marlboro and taking a swig of Leamington's beer.

'Cornelius,' Darren says.

'Arab Strap,' someone else says.

'Buckcherry later,' Leamington says and he starts singing, '*I love the cocaine, I love the cocaine.*'

My drink arrives and I gratefully sink a third of it in one go. The guys are all talking about what Carnival parties will be worth going to. Christ, Carnival. It's Bank Holiday weekend and there's still another two days to go. I had two hours' sleep last night, none the night before. I pull myself up onto a bar stool. It's already hot and bright outside, the sun filtering through the slatted blinds, smoky beams and bars falling across the sofas and tables, trying to land on the vampires and the damned. In a room full of people who've been up all night, it's like the air itself is sweating, grimy and tired.

I run a quick mental feasibility study on just fucking off out of there: concierge gets me a cab, back to London in about an hour, hit the sack for a bit, shower, food, then over to Notting Hill for Ross's Carnival party. Doable. Very doable. Sensible shoes option.

'Oi, Stelfox,' says Leamington, clapping a hand on my shoulder, 'do you want a fucking nose-up or what?'

'Yeah,' I say. And then I'm following him to the toilet, my hands on his shoulders as I bounce up and down, both of us singing, *'I love the cocaine, I love the cocaine,'* and the girls on reception can hear us and everything but we don't give a fuck. As we barge into the toilets Brett Anderson from Suede and Justine Frischmann from Elastica come staggering out looking fucked out of their skulls. She gives Leamington a sloppy kiss and then follows Anderson off towards the elevators.

The world is much brighter – sharper and clearer – as we jump out of the taxi and crunch our way through a wasteland of plastic glasses towards the backstage bar. It's pretty much a freak show in there. We say hellos and hit the bar and then a cubicle for another bump. Darren and I split an E and then we bowl off across the site towards the Evening Session stage because a couple of people want to see Ultrasound again for some fucking reason. Why? They just signed to Nude for fuck's sake.

'Hey,' I say as we make our way there through a sea of broken tolers, 'I've got an idea . . .'

We root through a few stalls, people selling T-shirts, hash pipes, Rizlas, soft drinks and crap like that, until we come to a fifty-year-old hippy with a shameful tray tucked among his flea-bitten merchandise – a few rows of tiny brown bottles with names like 'Bolt' and 'TNT'. (American poppers have far better names. In direct acknowledgement of the huge faggot market for the popular quasi-legal heart stimulant, they're called things like 'Locker Room', 'Cruising' and 'Rectal Trauma'.) As I hand over the money I notice that the guy has a little sign up advertising his amyl nitrate. 'Room Odorizer' it says.

'Hey, cunt,' I say as the guy hands me two bottles of Liquid Gold, 'who do you know whose room smells *so fucking bad* that drenching it in amyl is actually going to be an upgrade?'

Early evening and it's still hot and clear and sunny and I'm stretched out in the back of a chauffeured company people carrier with Leamington. Darren sits up front with the driver, the windows down and the M4 sizzling by outside. The only other sound is the soft hiss of the radio. We are all fucking destroyed. I tilt back in the leather seat and look out of the back window, at the sun sinking behind us as we speed towards London. The sun seems huge. I mean it looks fucking enormous; a scarlet ball that's about to touch the ground. It looks like Armageddon falling over Bristol, over Reading.

Energised by a knuckle of coke as the driver pretends not to notice we pass a bottle of Maker's Mark back and forth and talk random industry gossip: Who's going to win the Mercury? Beth Orton? The Chemical Brothers? Are Nude going to have it away with Ultrasound? Will Kylie's new indie stuff work? Are the Prodigy going to sell records in America? Money. Will London have a hit with All Saints, this new girl band they've signed? If they do will it clear the pitch for Songbirds? (Unlikely. Remember — there is no bottom to this crap.) It looks like Ray Cooper at Virgin is signing this new band Catch, who are managed by Hall or Nothing. My head starts swimming, that last pill kicking in. 'Martin Hall reckons the singer kid, Toby, is a star . . .' Darren says. 'Yeah?' I say. Or maybe I just say, 'Yeah.' I don't know. I feel funny. Leamington craps on, he's telling some story I already heard the night before, about something that happened at Tracy Bennett's wedding the other week. (Subtext from Leamington: I went to Bennett's wedding.) I nod and just stare through my Aviators — we are all wearing sunglasses — at the back of the driver's head, at his cracked, seamy neck. I need to make more money. It occurs to me — and the realisation is in no way an epiphany, it just dawns on me in the same way you might idly realise one day that you really prefer linguine to spaghetti — that, were I forced to choose between Leamington's life and my own career success, then I would happily watch Leamington die. I am now experiencing auditory hallucinations. I can hear feedback and the beating of helicopter blades. Watch? I would kill him myself. And I quite like Leamington. 'They sound like the fucking Police,' Darren says, talking about some band. The Police.

Woodham. Fuck. Money. Waters. I think I am going to be sick. A helicopter chops right by my head. I flinch and whisper something.

'What?' Leamington says, turning.

'What?' I reply.

'Did you just say,' he lowers his sunglasses, 'kill them all?'

'No.'

I feel this volume continue to build and swell behind me, beneath me, the sound of chopper blades and feedback shimmering up through the car, and I think I may be losing my mind. Then I see that, in the front, Darren is dialling the volume way up on the stereo, Leamington's hands are shooting up into the air, he's flicking his fingers Manc style and they're both laughing. I lean forward and squint through the windscreen glare and I see a sign appearing out of the dusk: the comforting forestry green with white lettering which says 'NOTTING HILL' and now the Westway is opening up in front of us and the driver floors it and the feedback and helicopters resolve themselves into drums and guitars.

'*Turn it up!*' I yell at Darren. He cranks it all the way and then the three of us are singing, screaming, '*All my people right here right now . . .*' and I've ridden it out and everything is OK again.

I fucking love the new Oasis album. Masterpiece. Three hundred and sixty thousand over the counter sales on day one? You can't be arguing with that, can you?

We edge along the pavement. You can actually feel the heat of the pavement through the soles of your Birkenstocks. All you can move is your head, your arms are jammed down by your sides, your legs crushed together as everyone sways from side to side, rotating from the feet up, like one of those inflatable kiddies' toys with a weighted base. Like a Weeble. Looking up the hill, all the way along Kensington Park Road, all you can see is bobbing heads. I'm trying to keep my hand in my right pocket – the pocket with all the drugs and cash in it – because we're surrounded by greedy, shifty-looking darkies. As the crowd moves, as the breeze changes direction, you get hit by different smells – dope, beer, vomit, frying chicken. The shrill *rakka-ta-takka-ta-tak* of calypso drums meshes with the subsonic whumf of dozens of sound systems cranking out dancehall, drum'n'bass, two-step and ragga, creating a chesty slur of noise. All around us grinning, sunburned middle-class losers – Rorys and Camillas – bop up and down cheering and blowing their stupid fucking whistles while they clink Red Stripe cans with the indulgently smiling brothers. (Who, in their turn, are wondering if they can get Millie's handbag away without being caught.)

Whose bright idea was all this? I picture a bunch of old Rastas, hunkered on a doorstep on Ladbroke Grove on an August afternoon a long time ago. 'Leroy,' says Winston, passing across the dachshund-sized reefer 'suppose we be holding dem carnival and all dem white batty boys be spending dem money?'

'Righteous,' says Leroy, shivering under the weak London sun as he takes a big, Jamaican toke. Half a century later on the Portobello Road some student hands over a tenner for a burnt piece of plantain and a couple of warm lagers and steps around the corner to be mugged.

You've gotta hand it to them, Carnival is definitely one—nil to the Kaffirs.

I'm wired from the coke, taut and angry, on the verge of going nuts and smashing an elbow into somebody's face, doing anything to bust out, when there's a change in the pulse of the crush, something weakens and opens up on my left. I grab Darren's arm and manage to pull both of us through and out onto Talbot Road, where it's quieter, where the crowd is just insanely – as opposed to life-threateningly – big. A few mounted policemen trot around smiling benevolently, their horses braying, their hooves clipping on the cement. Carnival's a PR job now for the filth; you're in shirtsleeves, you get your picture taken with a big fat mama who's wearing your helmet. I even see a young constable taking a matey swig of Red Stripe.

But now and again, on the faces and in the eyes of the older coppers, you see flashes of how it used to be. Some young ragga will flounce by, nonchalantly billowing clouds of ganja smoke, his gold teeth shining and his trainers gleaming in the sun, and there'll be a tightening of the jawline, a contracting of the pupils, and you can see these old boys thinking, *'Come on. Come on, you fuckers . . .'* High up in the saddle they glaze over as they reminisce about the Perspex shields and the baton charge, the pleasing give of black skull beneath lead-tipped truncheon, and then a leisurely hour in the cell with the rolled-up phone book and the rubber hose. The good old days.

'Fucking hell,' says Darren as we press on, edging our way along the Portobello Road towards the Earl Percy.

Shouts of 'Oi! Oi!' rend the air as we shoulder our way into the pub. Trellick stands on a chair, his arms outstretched, a bottle of champagne in each fist. Behind him, crouched down, Ross is furtively doing a bump off the back of a girl's hand. Tench is sprawled across a row of seats, his face buried between the miniskirted thighs of some shrieking boiler. Parker-Hall is holding court at a corner table with a couple of girls, what's-his-name from Chrysalis and one of the guys who writes songs for Ellie Crush. Rebecca and Katie and Sophie and Pam and a bunch of other girls we know all dancing in the corner. Someone throws an E at me. That guy Richard Bolger from London Records pours a drink over himself. Derek DahLarge is talking to the wall.

Thank Christ, I think. Civilisation.

Ross's party at his place on Colville Terrace goes on until Tuesday morning. At some point, somewhere into the early hours, I turn round and realise I am crapping away to Parker-Hall. I don't know what we're saying or how long we've been talking. We're both off our tits but he's clearly in better shape than me. In a moment of pilled-up, cracked-up, coked-up, boozed-up, sleep-deprived, woolly false-bonhomie, I put my arm around him and say, 'I'm really enjoying us working together.'

'Me too, mate,' he replies, smiling as he pats me on the knee, untangles himself from my arm, and waltzes off, disappearing into the smoke and music.

Granted, I'm off my fucking head and might be paranoid, but even so, I'm sure there's a terrifying lack of sincerity in Parker-Hall's voice. I watch as across the room he talks and laughs with Ross. It's important for A&R to have a good relationship with marketing.

I'm not sure I like the way all this is going.

*

The following Monday, having slept through all of Sunday, I stroll into the office late, hung-over and grouchy. Rebecca and Pam and a couple of the other boilers are sitting around in tears. Nothing unusual there – I figure that Derek has just blazed through the department on one of his scorched-earth rampages, a search-and-destroy mission because of an errant bar code on a single, or a wrong release date on a poster. However, it is unusual that *all* of them are crying. Then Rob Hastings comes towards me. The clown looks genuinely shaken.

'What's up?' I say.

'Haven't you heard, man?'

'Heard what?'

He pulls me into Waters' old office where a few wet-faced secretaries are gathered round the TV. Paris, an underpass, a mangled Mercedes, Kensington Palace, crowds of wailing tolers.

I hit the phones and make a few calls. Radio playlists are being suspended and reconfigured, release dates are being put back and cancelled. BMG are in trouble – the new Kylie LP, titled *Impossible Princess*, will have to be pulled, retitled and re-artworked. Death in Vegas have had a record hauled off the radio because of their name. The new Prodigy single is fucked because the sleeve featured a crashed car.

It is a fucking nightmare. Thank Christ I don't have a record coming out in the next few weeks.

Parker-Hall and I go along to Trellick's office. Ross is already in there and we join him on the sofa as Trellick flips between CNN and BBC. Peasants all over the country are losing their fucking minds. In Newcastle, Milton Keynes,

Coventry, losers are crying in the fucking streets. A fat toler appears on the screen. Tears are pouring down her face. Her face. Fuck me – it's a real forty roll-ups and a bottle of cheap vodka a day monstrosity, honeycombed with broken blood vessels, fucked in from not having enough cash or sense. 'She . . . she . . .' the mad cow stammers, hardly able to get the words out, snapped with grief, '. . . she done *so much good* for people.' We fucking piss ourselves. It's happening here too. Along the corridor in accounts the secretaries are all snuffling and comforting each other. It takes my breath away – genuine grief, upset, over something which does not directly affect you in any way whatsoever. But, a golden rule of showbiz states, whenever there is a massive outpouring of collective emotion among the lower classes – Christmas, the World Cup, summer holidays – there are records to be sold and money to be made.

'Surely we want to be cashing in on all this?' Ross says. 'A tribute LP? A charity thing?'

Trellick thinks for a bit. 'Nah,' he says finally, 'too much scrutiny. It'd be impossible to skim any cash off. Maybe in a year. Anniversary thing . . .' He's probably right, but it's a pity because in the past, thanks to a little creative accounting, we've been very successful at skimming cash off of a couple of other charity records we've been involved in.

'Yeah, not worth the grief,' I say.

'I dunno,' Parker-Hall says, lighting a cigarette, 'the sales would still count towards our market share, wouldn't they?'

'Good point,' Trellick admits, nodding.

'Yeah, but,' I start to say, but Parker-Hall has the floor. He's talking about licensing, about appropriate tracks for a nation in mourning, about marketing. Trellick and Ross are nodding away, swept up with him. I sit there and read *Music Week* and get angrier and angrier.

Trellick makes a few phone calls, but it turns out that it looks like Elton's doing something and he's signed to Mercury so the project will probably happen over there. 'Fuck it,' Parker-Hall says, 'worth a pop. Wanna get lunch, James?'

'Sure,' Trellick says. I wait for Parker-Hall to extend the invitation. He doesn't.

'I've got to go,' I lie, 'meeting in town.'

'Oh, Steven?' Parker-Hall says as I leave. I turn round and without looking at me, not taking his eyes off the TV, he says, 'Can you make sure you get them demos off Coalition for me? That band Rob was talking about? Thanks.'

I nod, turn, and walk on down the hallway. There is a roaring noise in my ears, a metallic taste in my mouth, and I cannot see properly.

I drive through Stratford and Leytonstone – cancerous high streets choked up with PoundSmasher! shops and AlabamaFriedChicken dives – and take the M25 South.

I come along a flyover and, for a moment, the Saab is suspended so high in the air that it feels like you are in a video game. On my right, stretching back towards Docklands and the City, and on my left, oozing out into Kent, is the nuclear winter of east London – hundreds of square miles of power stations and freight yards, pylons, construction sites and chemical plants, motorway and flyover, ring road and tunnel, endless miles of red tail lights, yellow headlights and sodium street lights. The air outside the blue-tinted windows of the car is smoke, dust and dirt. Out in that air, in grids and blocks, the lights are coming on in houses.

*Houses.*

You realise that people actually have to live in among all this and that east London is the bill, the tab that these cunts are picking up so that you can live in west London.

I take a left onto the M20 and drive on towards Dover in the dark. The guy – 'Charlie' – meets me, as arranged, in the lounge of an unbelievable pub on the Dover Road. He's in his forties and unshaven with stains (egg? curry?) on his cheap, bobbled sweater. It has taken me several weeks to meet Charlie. Weeks of furtive emailing – from a dummy Hotmail account, set up under a false name and accessed only from the computers in a random, disparate chain of internet cafés – to get to this point.

After the briefest of drinks and a minute of the most innocuous conversation (literally 'Wot about them Arsenal then?'), we exchange envelopes. The one I hand to Charlie contains an awful lot of fifty-pound notes. The far slimmer envelope he hands me contains only a computer disk.

I will not look at what is on the disk until later – again, in a remote corner of a remote Internet café – and even then I will only do so for a split second, just to make sure. After that I will never look at it again.

The contents of the disk are, as I'd been promised, beyond description.

# September

Roni Size wins the Mercury Music Prize. Dave Gilmour leaves Island Records to become Head of A&R at Independiente. Lots of interest in some Jocky band called Idlewild. Phil Howells over at London Records signs Asian Dub Foundation. He says, 'I'd have to be mad not to have signed them.' Mercury launches this pop singer called Thomas Jules Stock. And 'Candle in the Wind', 'Candle in the Wind', 'Candle in the fucking Wind' . . .

*'I'm basically in the David Geffen business.'*

David Geffen

It was Bournemouth last year, so it's Brighton again this year.

The TV set in my room says that the Grand Hotel welcomes 'Mr S. Stalefox'. I pull back the net curtains to check the view again, to check that it really has happened.

It has: brick walls, heating ducts, pipes. This is my 'sea view'. I am overcome by another seismic jolt of fury. How could Rebecca have allowed this to happen? I try her mobile again and it just goes straight to message for the umpteenth time. Hatefully I picture her; on the train down here, or in the bar at Victoria, drinking wine and gossiping with the other sows while I am forced to live through this.

They'll be excited, of course, all the PAs and marketing assistants love the company conference. It's an excuse to spend a couple of days wallowing in a five-star hotel, getting manicures and facials and fuck knows what by day, then agonising over what to wear in the evening before spending the early hours of the morning sweating over some guy's coke-broke prick.

My rage only increases the moment Trellick – wearing a

dressing gown, his hair wet, his mobile cradled in his shoulder – opens his door. The chinless bastard has lucked into some kind of suite, with double French windows opening out onto a balcony overlooking the seafront. 'Fuck you,' I say, taking two Scotches from his minibar.

I take a seat by the open window, the chill September breeze filling the room as Trellick strides around, simultaneously talking on his mobile, smoking a cigarette and putting on his suit. I'm wearing a suit too, by the way. I flip through Trellick's copy of *Music Week*. As has been known for a couple of weeks now, Neil Ferris, recently installed as MD over at EMI, has been hiring and firing people like a madman. He's made Tris Penna Head of A&R. Incredibly Nick Robinson, the previous Head of A&R, has not been fired. He's been demoted. He's going to work under Penna. I mean, where's your fucking self-respect? Wouldn't you just top yourself?

'What's your problem, loser?' Trellick asks, hanging up.

'Nothing,' I say. 'When did you get here?'

'Just now.'

'Anyone around downstairs?'

'I saw your mate,' ('your mate' is now the official euphemism for Parker-Hall), 'in the bar, talking to Derek.'

'Oh yeah?' I say casually. The networking little prick.

The objective of the annual company conference is straightforward enough: you gather together all the sales reps from all over the country – along with key players from retailers like Our Price, Virgin, HMV and the like – and everyone from the label above the rank of janitor, you bang them all up in some five-star atrocity by the sea for a few days, and bombard them with speeches about how great we all are and show them videos and presentations of your new acts.

Some of the acts, the priority acts, will play live at the conference. If you are in a band this must be your worst nightmare. Imagine striding onstage to belt out your heart-felt anthems of youth and alienation to a hotel conference roomful of sales reps: a roomful of Mondeo-driving, Next-suit-wearing, pebble-dash-semi-and-two-kids cunts. Some bands have kind of an existential meltdown about playing at conference. It's too funny. It's like they know it's the antithesis of rawk and roll, playing for a roomful of 'suits', but they all want to sell records too, so they fret and moan for a while before, inevitably, agreeing to do it. They're all good little capitalists at heart, bands. Even Thom fucking Yorke, when he's not crying and wringing his hands about what kind of coffee beans you should be using so some cunt in Outer Mongolia can afford to put an inside toilet in his filthy gaff, even he's wondering what the marketing spend is looking like. He's wondering about venue sizes, about playlists. He'll tell you – with a straight face no less – that he thinks about all this stuff because he wants to 'get the message across'. He wants to 'reach as many people as possible'. That's what he'll tell you.

But it's bad news for us too, conference. In the evening, at dinner, in the hotel bars, you have to mingle with the reps; the retards who pound up and down the motorways in their two-litre Vauxhall mongol-wagons, desperately trying to get some cunt at Bob's Records in Ipswich to take a few more copies of the new Mansun LP. You stand with an aching fake smile strung across your face as you listen to their stories about how many Celine Dion records they sold in a week, about what local bands from up North they reckon are going to be big next year, to their dismal, Chardonnay-fuelled views on the way the music industry is going.

Finally Trellick is dressed so we do a quick line and hit the bar.

I decided not to have Songbirds appear at conference. True, we finally have a single ready to release, a fizzy slab of pornographic dance-floor baloney called 'Fully Grown' (the lyrics rammed with near-the-knuckle plays on how close to the legal age for fucking the girls are), but if anyone actually heard them sing live, the jig would be up in a nanosecond. Derek, desperate to fill out the upcoming releases roster, begged, nearly demanded in fact, that they do a mimed PA instead, but I held out. This too would have been fraught with danger because it would have involved the girls dancing in public.

I'd assumed that, like most teenage girls, they'd be able to stomp and bomp around in some sort of coordinated fashion and that eventually, with the aid of some pricey choreography and dance gurus, we could knock together a couple of routines. I was disabused of this notion when I attended one of the dance rehearsals. It was like watching . . . carthorses won't quite cover it. Annette and Kelly at least had a basic move they could execute, a sort of running up and down on the spot while grinning their heads off kind of routine. Jo had this whole other thing going on – it was like watching a baby horse, a five-minute-old colt, still gloopy from the womb, trying to stand up. Her legs, absurdly too long for her body (like all the girls in Songbirds she has freakishly pronounced sexual characteristics: their arses jut out like ledges, the tits are gravity-insulting miracles, even through baggy combat pants you can make out Debbie's pussy lips) twanged and skittered away from her as she tried to keep her balance while she shadow-boxed, furiously thrashing the air with her tiny fists. Dance? Jo could barely fucking walk.

All this, however, was prologue to Debbie. Perhaps having already realised and come to terms with her inadequacies as a dancer she abandoned all pretence at the choreographed routine and chose instead to concentrate on the sexual angle of the performance. All the time rocking epileptically to the music, she slid her hand down her pants and worked two fingers in her crotch. She massaged and tweaked her own breasts so hard that the choreographer (who by this point was watching the whole thing from behind his clipboard, a clenched fist in his mouth, salty tears of anguish running down his face) thought she might perform a half-arsed mastectomy on herself. She started dry-humping the microphone stand. As the track climaxed, she dropped onto all fours and swivelled round to present her rump to us, shaking it madly while she tugged her G-string up and down her butt crack in wild frottage. The whole time, all around her, Annette and Kelly jogged resolutely up and down on the spot with idiotic fixed grins on their faces and Jo skittered around like a Glaswegian drunk on ice.

It was like watching CCTV footage of the tail end of a twelve-hour hen night in Liverpool.

But we should be able to cobble some kind of video together . . . and I still have this feeling. Instinct, I suppose you'd have to call it. I instinctively know that I'd love to fuck every one of them (particularly Debbie) in a vicious and degrading manner. I am nothing if not resolutely populist in my tastes, so I have no reason to believe that any other guy in the country would feel any differently. If we can just get them to put one foot in front of the other and then throw in some nice ditties and some cool clothes for the little girlies to like, we might just have a chance. We might just have it away with this piece of shit.

A guy I vaguely know, some marketing guy from some other label in the group, comes up to us in the crush at the bar. 'Hi, Steven, how's it going with those girls you signed?'

'OK,' I tell him. 'It's going OK.'

Dinner is hell. I get sat next to some rep who talks to me for a long time about the new GPS system in his car. I'm not making this up. He really talks about it. Derek gets up and makes a ridiculous speech in which he actually singles out Parker-Hall for praise, for 'injecting a new energy and focus' into the company's A&R. Jesus Christ. Parker-Hall acts embarrassed, pulling his sweater up over his head, but you can tell the little fucker is loving it.

As soon as it's respectable – i.e.: the moment a waiter holding a dessert plate walks into the ballroom from the kitchens – I'm out of my seat and heading for the toilets.

Derek has a party in his suite – a massive lair on the top floor – and, in the early hours, I find myself in the bathroom with Ross. I'm sitting on the edge of the huge circular tub, sipping Jim Beam straight from the bottle, while he racks them out on the counter. For some strange reason we're reminiscing about Waters.

'Remember conference last year? In Bournemouth?' he asks me. 'When everyone ran out of coke and he had that guy drive halfway down from London with about twenty grams and he drove halfway up and met him at a Little Chef or something?'

'Christ,' I laugh, remembering Waters' reappearance a few hours later, when he'd literally been attacked by a coke-ravenous mob. 'Yeah,' I say, 'he was a proper fucking gakhead, wasn't he?' (A proper gakhead: someone you do not like who does exactly as much coke as you do.) Ross snorts a line and sits down on the toilet, passing me the note. I reroll it carefully.

'Yeah,' Ross says, almost wistfully, 'that was a shitty way to go, wasn't it? Getting your head caved in by some fucking burglar?'

'Yeah,' I say, leaning into the powder, remembering the expression on Waters' face as he turned, after I'd hit him the first time, the tiny tear of black blood appearing at his hairline. How he just looked shocked, his eyes wide, his mouth a tiny little 'o', like the blow hadn't hurt him. Like it had just really . . . surprised him. 'It might have been, I don't know . . . drugs?'

'Drugs?' Ross says.

'Yeah. You never know. Drug debts, some mad dealer . . .' This is all pure malicious invention, but I quite like the sound of it. Might be worth putting it out there, it might well gain some credibility.

'Fuck,' Ross says.

I perch up on the counter and tip my head back, sniffing, feeling my throat constricting and numbing, feeling the trickle of cold, bitter froth. I stare into one of the spots sunk in the bathroom ceiling until it hurts my eyes and then, blinking, I turn to face Ross. 'Hey,' I say, 'I know you shouldn't speak ill of the dead and all that, *but*, Waters *was* a fucking idiot. All we ever did was bitch about the fat cunt.'

'Christ, Steven,' Ross says, laughing, 'you *are* fucking hardcore.'

There's a knock at the door. Ross unlocks it and Rebecca pops her head around. 'Room for two little ones?' she asks mock sheepishly. 'Quick, shut the door,' Ross says as Rebecca hops in trailing this girl Grace, who we know a bit. She's a press officer or something. Rebecca goes to get a gram out of her purse but I motion her towards our pile as Grace hops up on the counter beside me. Rebecca has a short skirt on and I'm wondering if it's tights or stockings. I have to admit it, she can look pretty doable sometimes. 'So,' Grace says, 'what are you freaks talking about?'

'Waters,' Ross says, climbing fully clothed into the tub.

'Oh please don't,' says Rebecca, already scrubbing her room key against the back of a fifty-pound note, 'it's too horrible . . .'

There's another knock at the door. 'Fuck off!' I say.

'Stelfox?' Derek asks gruffly through the door. Shit. Ross is already scrambling for the lock. 'Ah,' Derek says brightly as he comes in, 'making yourselves at home? Like everyone else he's coked up, sweating like a fucking rapist.

'Yeah, sorry,' I say.

'Do you want a line, Derek?' Rebecca says, pointlessly, as he's already squeezing greedily around her towards the pile. He claps me on the leg as he passes. I try to imagine the number of cocks his hand has closed around in its time, but it's unimaginable. 'How are you, Steven?' he asks, genuinely friendly for some reason.

'I'm good, Derek. Great,' I say unconvincingly.

'Ross!' Derek says abruptly, looking in the huge mirror and seeing Ross sprawled in the bathtub behind him. 'Tell me, what's the projected marketing spend on the Lazies LP up to?'

Derek has left the bathroom door half open and out in the darkened hallway of the suite I can just see Trellick, smiling and nodding as he listens to something that black girl from finance is saying.

I wake up the next morning – just, it's 11.58 a.m. – to a ringing phone. 'Hello?' I groan.

'Wakey-wakey!' Parker-Hall shouts brightly (he doesn't really do coke). 'Get your arse in gear! I'll see you downstairs in ten.' We're flying up to Glasgow together, the idea being that we can catch up on the flight, discuss progress on various acts on the roster, and generally 'review A&R strategy'. I was clearly off my fucking nut when I agreed to this nightmare.

I hang up and look around the darkened room at the usual debris – suit trousers and jacket strewn across the floor like a police outline, clutch of bottles and glasses on the table, coke-spackled CD case on the bedside table next to a bottle of Valium and a half-full whisky tumbler. There is a G-string on the lampshade.

I sense the extra warmth as I turn over and lift the covers a little. A naked back. She's well tanned, just the white 'T' that runs around the waist and down the crack of her arse. I prop myself up on my elbow as she rolls over to face me.

'Hello you,' Rebecca says.

Doing your secretary is a shocker. Worst-case-scenario shit. Here's how it happened:

We went back to my room in the early hours, to have a chat about 'a few work things', or some such nonsense. We lay on the bed drinking and nosing, getting closer to each other, and the conversation turned into what it always turns into in those situations.

'What's your favourite position?' Rebecca asks me, giggling coyly.

Bitch tied up with a knife at her throat, I think, but, ever reasonable, I say, 'Doggy,' then ask her, 'Do you masturbate?'

'Of course I bloody do! Come on, it's *the nineties* for Christ's sake! Have you ever done a hooker?'

'No.' (Tip: never tell the truth here.) 'Have you ever done two guys?'

'Ummm . . . pass,' she says, hiding her face.

'Really?' I say. What a fucking spunk bucket.

'Have you ever done two girls?'

'Yeah. How about anal?'

'What about it?'

I raise an eyebrow.

Rebecca reaches into her handbag and rummages around. 'Do you want one of these?'

I look down at her hand. There, in the middle of her outstretched palm, is a big, blue triangular pill.

'What is it?'

'Viagra.'

Well, I don't mind telling you, I got greedy. Very greedy. Greedy? I went fucking berserk – pumping, sucking, grinding, fisting. Rebecca, as it turned out, is a *demon* in the sack. I got the fucking mother lode – soup to nuts. At one point as I was viciously doing her from behind, she reached down and – unprecedented this – began to guide my cock towards her arsehole. Bosh! I started furiously pummelling her up the Gary and the next thing I know she's screaming, 'No! No!'

I stop.

'What are you doing?' she asks, looking back over her shoulder, breathing hard and still pushing back against me. I am up to my nuts in her dung funnel.

'I . . .'

'Please keep fucking me up the arse.'

I resume. 'No! No!' she starts screaming again, really enjoying it now. Wow, I think, sometimes when they say 'no' they really do mean 'yes.'

'Talk dirty to me, Steven.'

'You nasty bitch.'

'Yes . . . oh God . . . fuck me.'

'You dirty fucking whore . . .'

'Oh God, I'm . . .'

'You slut . . . you whore . . . you . . .'

But that's the problem with talking dirty. You're hardly going to start out with 'you very badly behaved girl' and gradually crank it up, are you? No. You go straight in at the deep end with 'you dirty fucking slut' and stuff like that. And then there's not a lot to move onto later. I pump her harder and try for a bit of variety.

'You fucking . . . idiot.'

'Don't call me an idiot!' she says, stopping her thrusts, sounding genuinely hurt.

'Sorry. You fucking . . . cow?' This restores order and she pushes back onto me again. Bit close to the bone there possibly.

Well, things degenerated from there. I mean they really went downhill – coke, Valium, more Viagra and amyl were all relentlessly produced from Rebecca's handbag and the minibar was thoroughly emptied as we got off our chanks and went properly crackers. Somewhere around dawn, even with the cock-pills, my prick is destroyed. It's a cautionary tale – a bloody, red-raw, still-erect slab of disgrace. And still Rebecca wants more. She's lying back, eyes closed and a couple of pillows underneath her as she busily works the index and middle fingers of her right hand over her pussy. 'Please keep fucking me,' she moans.

Fuck her? *Fuck me*.

I root around on the floor of the bedroom. Nothing – I thought there might be a champagne bottle, but we've been drinking the mini-splits of Moët from the minibar. And I don't think a mini-split is going to do it here. I mean, she wants a fucking battleship up there. She wants the Death Star.

With Rebecca still moaning and writhing on the bed I charge into the bathroom and still find nothing. There's no deodorant cans, no big bottle of shampoo, not even a bog brush – nothing which could make for a reasonable facsimile of a functioning cock. In desperation I throw open the wardrobe. Coat hangers. 'Hang on a minute . . .' I say.

A few grunts and twists and turns (and in my memory

I'm not sure what Rebecca's up to during all of this, whether she's aware of what I'm doing or not. I think she's wanking herself off. Or doing coke. Or both). I manage to fashion a strange cock-like contraption from a wire coat hanger. I mean, it looks exactly like a long, thin, cock. The only real drawback, I suppose, is that it is flat and two-dimensional. But we give it a go anyway, both of us mad and sweating and naked; me kneeling on the floor at the foot of the bed, frowning – tongue between my teeth in concentration – as I grimly work the contraption into her, looking for all the world like a backstreet abortionist on an emergency call-out.

After a while, as her moans decrease, I said, 'It's not really working, is it?' and, shortly after that, thankfully, we both passed out.


'Hello, you,' she says and leans in for a kiss. Mindful of all the utter disgrace her mouth was put through just a few short hours ago – at one point it felt like she was trying to get her whole head up my arse – I manage to just graze her lips before blurting out, 'Shit, I'm late,' and running for the shower.

I lean tiredly under the stinging needles and think about how quickly I can have Rebecca fired. Fired? No, not these days, you're joking, aren't you? You'll be up in front of some tribunal before you can say, 'She loved it, Your Honour.' With a sigh I get a foreboding glimpse of how very badly I am going to have to treat Rebecca in the coming weeks and months in order to get her to quit.

I tiptoe back into the bedroom, praying she'll have fallen asleep. She hasn't. She's propped up on one elbow on the pillow watching me carefully. 'I've got to go,' I say, 'Glasgow.'

'I know,' she says, tonelessly. I bend down to pick up my trousers. There, on the floor next to them, is a strangely bent coat hanger. The contraption. Queasily I kick it under the bed. 'Steven?' Rebecca says.

'Mmmm?'

'You killed Roger. Didn't you?'

Total silence. Somewhere outside the window, a seagull squawks. I blink at her, too hung-over to think, to lie. I manage a hoarse, feeble laugh as I say, 'What?'

'I don't care,' she goes on, matter-of-factly, 'he was an idiot.'

I sit down and we look right at each other for a long time, neither of us saying anything. It is like I am really seeing Rebecca for the first time, seeing some reserve of strength, of will, that I never knew she had.

'Why do you think I killed him?'

'I follow you sometimes. I go to all these stupid gigs because I know you're going to be there. I was parked across the street from Roger's house the night he died. Just watching the flat because I knew you were in there. I saw you leaving.'

'Why would you . . .'

'I love you, Steven.'

I sit there basking in this fresh hell while I allow myself time to register the new information: *Rebecca is insane*. It's a long time before I speak.

'What do you want to do?' I say.

She tells me. I can't believe I've heard her properly so I ask her to repeat it.

'I want us to get married,' she says for the second time.

'OK . . .'

'And then we'll never talk about Roger again.'

'OK . . .'

A few traumatic hours later (I lost my car keys so we have to get a cab to Gatwick while the Saab stays in Brighton; squatting in the NCP, racking up thirty quid a day in charges) I'm standing at reception at the Glasgow Hilton trying to check in. There's a braying mob five-deep in front of me, all waving credit cards, travel vouchers and confirmation slips. The girls behind reception look like the last few Redcoats left at Rorke's Drift, trying to front out an angry mob of spear-chuckers with two bullets and a tattered Bible.

Behind me the bar, lobby and reception area have all merged into one drunken scrum and Parker-Hall is already working the crowd. ('All right, geezer! Nice one! Fack orf, you cant!') I just want to get up to my room. To think. To try and plot some way forward through the chaos.

Parker-Hall and I were late getting up here because of our conference. Some people, a lot of the scouts, have already been here a couple of days. Pete Tong says hello. Nigel Coxon from Island strides by. Matthew Rumbold from Food waves hello. A bunch of publishers are huddled at the bar; Mike Smith from EMI is talking animatedly to Bruce Craigie from Deceptive and that lawyer from Russell's, the one who is handling the Idlewild deal. Rob Stringer is listening, angrily, to his mobile phone. Ian

Brodie from the Lightning Seeds shuffles by. People are talking about bands. They're talking about Idlewild, the Lanterns and the Smiles. They're talking about Magicdrive and Dawn of the Replicants. They're talking about the High Fidelity, Tam and Fat Lip as 'Candle in the Wind' is piped through the lobby, swirling beneath the roar of conversation.

In The City again. In The Fucking City.

In The City is an annual music industry convention that was knocked together in the early nineties by Tony Wilson, who used to run Factory Records – until those cretins the Happy Mondays skanked the whole label down the shitter for a bag of rocks. Then Wilson somehow chiselled a deal out of Tracy Bennett and Roger Ames over at London Records for a new label, the hysterically named Factory Too, which also recently went under, having produced zero hits in three years. Laugh? I nearly bought a fucking round.

Anyway, it seems that all this wasn't quite enough to fill Wilson's days for him so, a few years back, he decided that what the music industry really needed more than anything was *another* fucking convention. Hundreds of bands playing in dozens of venues all over the city, networking opportunities (have Hans from Düsseldorf palm you a 12 of some mad techno you will never listen to), and discussions and debates on things like 'Is the Remix a Valid Artform?' 'Will the Internet Engender a Pan-Global Dissolution of the Record Industry?' and 'Darkies: Have They Been Ripped Off Over the Years, Or What?'

Every year now you have to sit through this shit. (And

have you ever tried to get hold of a decent hooker up North? Fuck me. A couple of years ago, desperate in Manchester, I pulled this toothless pig into the cab off the street. She started undressing in my hotel room and, for a second, I thought she was wearing some artful, designer bodice. It turned out to be a lattice-work of stained, seeping bandages. The AIDS, I supposed, literally leaking out of her. I threw her a tenner and kicked her into the elevator rapid-style.)

The whole thing would be just about tolerable if they had it in Soho but, no, every September we all have to troop off to Manchester, or Dublin, or Glasgow. You check into the Holiday Inn, or the Ramada, and bowl around a skanky Northern city – getting in and out of taxis in the rain, standing in drizzly guest-list queues, having damp business cards thrust into your hands by stinking amateur hour 'managers' and indie label 'bosses' – for a few days, seeing a load of unsigned bands. They're unsigned for a reason, of course. Every single one of them is fucking shit. Cheers, Tony.

Leamington comes over to us through the crush. 'Oi oi,' he says.

'Oi oi,' I reply.

'Did you hear about your boy? Well, former boy.'

'Who?'

'Rage. He was DJing here at this thing last night. Gets into an argument with some bouncers, starts giving it all the "do-you-facking-know-who-I-am" business – the usual – anyway, they beat the fucking shit out of him.'

'Good on them,' I say.

'Nah, mate, I mean they *properly* beat the shit out of

him. They're talking about fucking brain damage and the like.'

Wow, I think. How can they tell?

When I get into the room the message light is flashing on the phone. I hit the button and put it on speaker while I get a drink from the minibar. As I rummage among the cool shelves I get this:

'Hi, Steven, it's Alan Woodham. I gather you're up at In The City.' Woodham's tone is flat, neutral. 'Listen, you said you'd get back to me about this publishing deal before the end of August. It's now the middle of September and I haven't heard anything. I've tried ringing you several times now. I left a couple of messages on your phone. I need you to call me back because . . .'

I cannot bear long phone messages. You want to kill, don't you? What's wrong with 'Call me back?' Why crap on for a fortnight? It's like directions, as soon as someone gets past the third 'and then a left at that roundabout and then –' you just want to cut their tongue out and fucking feed it to them.

The Woodham situation: after striking out with all the big publishers I actually sent his miserable demo round some of the smaller independent publishers – Complete, Rondor, Notting Hill Music – and got told to fuck off there too.

'. . . there's something else I need to talk to you about. In connection with the Roger Waters murder.'

Hang on a fucking minute.

'So please call me back as soon as you get this.'

I pick up the receiver and drop it back down, cutting the

message off, and start scrolling through my mobile for his number. Outside, the sky is the colour of smoked glass and it is starting to rain. Christ, I hate Scotland. What a nation of fucking losers.

I twist the caps off of three tiny bottles of Johnnie Walker from the minibar, pour them into a dirty glass and neck the lot. I start smoothing the coke out, covering the powder with a fifty and then scrubbing my room key up and down the note. I snort the line and sit back and give my problems free rein to strut and preen in my head.

As problems will, they soon settle themselves into a swirling, but definite, hierarchy. At the bottom level, coughing and grumbling and looking for attention, are all the constant, normal, low-level issues to do with work and money: Who can I get to remix the Songbirds single? How big is the Lazies LP – and subsequently Parker-Hall – going to be? How much more cash will the house haemorrhage? I must do my expenses. I should be getting paid more.

Floating above all this, sharper, clearer, more insistent, are the newcomers: My car is still in the NCP in Brighton. It is possible that Parker-Hall thinks I am a loser and will soon fire me. Does Woodham really know anything? And – straight in at no. 1 with a fucking bullet – Rebecca has been stalking me. She's gone round the bend, figured out I killed Waters and yet she wants to marry me regardless. (On reflection perhaps this isn't quite as crazy as it seems – didn't Ted Bundy get inundated with marriage proposals? And he was properly hardcore. He killed and raped dozens of women. Top lad, Bundy.)

I glug a belt of Scotch, honk a stupefying line of chang, and dial Woodham's mobile. He answers on the second ring. 'Alan? Hi, it's Steven. Listen, sorry for not getting back to you sooner. It's been mental recently. I –'

'Mr Stelfox,' (no 'Steven', 'Steven' is long gone), 'can you tell me why one of your neighbours claims that they saw you entering your flat at 5.30 a.m. on the morning of Roger Waters' murder when you already told me you'd arrived home around 11.30 the previous evening and gone straight to bed?'

He just rattles this off, staccato, machine-gun style. The blood in my head starts pumping so hard behind my eyeballs that I think they're going to burst out of my skull. 'I . . . I got up early and . . . went for a paper?'

'Where?'

'What?'

'Where did you buy this newspaper?' This is a different guy I'm talking to.

'At the newsagent . . . on the corner of Shirland Road and Elgin Avenue.' Fuck, fuck, fuck – are they even open at that time? This will be so easy to check.

'Alan, is everything OK?'

'I don't know,' he says, 'is it?'

I think hard, and then I'm talking. 'Listen, Alan, I'm sorry I haven't got back to you, about the demos. It's . . . it's looking good. It's just taking a little time. We'll get there. '

'Whatever you can do would be great.' He hangs up.

Woodham's new voice is clipped and formal, so much older-sounding than his indie-kid-down-the-Monarch voice. His new voice is the leathery whisper of gloves coming off, the hard-edged crack of cards being slapped on the table.

I'm shaking. It all comes crashing in and the precariously balanced hierarchy of problems comes tumbling down. The mortgages, the credit cards, Woodham, the coke, the never-ending building work, the whores, the overdraft, the bridging loan, the holidays, the private members' clubs, the coke, the whores, the restaurants, the airily picked-up four-hundred-quid bar tabs, the coke, the whores, Rebecca . . .

I just make it to the bathroom before I jackknife over, spewing a torrent of searing broth over the floor and down the toilet for a long, long time until I collapse onto the soothing tiled floor. I stare at the sour orange-brown puddle, recognising a few things; a bit of potato, peas, a chunk of what looks like chicken that I can't remember eating. Then I lie on the floor crying for a long time.

Much later – it is dark outside – I am sitting at the little desk up by the window of my hotel room multitasking. I am simultaneously drinking Scotch straight from the bottle, smoothing out another line, and scanning through the *Music Week Directory*.

Publishers. I'm looking for publishers.

Currency begets currency. We all know that Parker-Hall is a useless mockney twat; however, he has just signed the coolest band in the country and has also had a big commercial hit with a half-arsed soul/pop diva that he's somehow managed to hoodwink everyone into thinking is hip. So people want to meet him. People listen to what he has to say. As we make our way from elevator to pavement people stop him to talk. 'What do you reckon to them?' they say. Or 'I hear you're looking at . . .' or 'How's the album going?' or 'Hi, I sent you a demo of . . .' I stand there nodding while he pontificates.

This is what I've become. I am Parker-Hall's muppet.

We're just about out the revolving doors when we run into Derek. I look pretty rough, Derek looks . . . insane. Hitler-in-the-bunker insane. He clearly hasn't been to bed.

'Anthony! Steven!' he barks. 'Come with me.'

Back up in the elevator and we walk into his suite behind him. Little Stan, one of junior scouts, is in there. He's sitting at a coffee table in the lounge. In front of him is a gigantic pile of rocky cocaine which he's attempting to chop into finer powder. He looks up as we enter and we see real fear in his eyes. He can't actually speak, but with his eyes he's begging us to help him, to get him out of there. 'Stan!' Derek barks. 'A line for Steven and Anthony.' Stan, chained and shackled in Derek's mad gak factory, immediately begins drawing out a couple of fat lines for us. 'So,' Derek says, sitting down and motioning for us to do the same, as though everything is perfectly normal, 'what's our strategy here this week?' For the first time since he's joined the company I see that Parker-Hall is getting the true measure of Derek. I think up until this point he thought all the Derek stories were just that: mad stories. But here he is looking like death whacked out of his fucking mind on chang and asking us, sincerely, what our 'strategy' is.

Parker-Hall begins mumbling a response, some bunch of shit about 'A&R culture', while Derek nods and tightly rolls a fifty-pound note. He passes it first to Stan, who leans towards the powder and then stops. He looks up at Derek, fear and shame colliding across his face, and says, 'I'm sorry, Derek. I can't do any more.'

There's a pause.

Magnanimously Derek dismisses him with an airy wave of the hand. Passing the note to Parker-Hall, Stan gets up and timidly asks Derek, 'Do you have a hairdryer?' Stan's hair is perfectly dry.

Derek, confused himself now, says, 'In the bathroom.'

Parker-Hall and I quickly split one of the elephant-leg lines between us, tell Derek we're running late for a gig, and fuck off out of it.

As we leave we can hear the whirring blast of the hairdryer coming from behind the bathroom door.

'What the fuck was all that about?' Parker-Hall says after the lift doors close.

'Weird scenes inside the gold mine,' I say.

We go out and rattle around the freezing Glasgow night, climbing in and out of cabs (where the suspicious Jock bastards expect you to pay them *before* you step out onto the pavement) and seeing pointless band after pointless band.

We return to the Hilton and hit the bar where we drink and do coke before I finally slope off upstairs with some girl – some publisher – just before dawn.

I hold her hand as we cross the lobby, take the lift, and stumble down endless corridors of halogen and beige, seeing only old people at this hour – pensioners driven from their beds at 6 a.m. by the death fear, sleep becoming too close to the real thing for them now, what with the real thing snuffling right outside the door.

Back in my room she talks about girl power for a while and then I'm ripping her Wonderbra off and fucking her from behind. I spit into her arse and try and stuff my cock up there but she's not really having it and I think I remember punching her in the back of the head a few times (playfully but not really) and when I wake up she's gone and it's *still* raining outside.

# October

*Virgin Records' Ray Cooper and Ashley Newton move to LA to run Virgin America. The Verve album is no. 1. Daniel Miller at Mute Records, talking about the new album by an act he's signed called Peach, says, 'It is a timeless record. The album is packed with hits. I'm so confident.' Gary Glitter is honoured by the MCPS with a lunch at the Savoy.*

> *'Artists and executives come and go. Record companies are forever.'*

Anonymous lawyer

Friday night on Regent Street and I light the fourth cigarette of the tailback and engage second gear for the first time in forty-five minutes. This has to stop. We can't go on like this. You can't drive anywhere any more. You can't park anywhere. In central London now you can't even *walk* anywhere. For a mile radius in every direction from Oxford Circus it's like being down the front at Glastonbury. The shops are all rammed with filthy tolers, every last one of them wielding a sweaty handful of tacky credit cards – their Bank of Toytown Gold Card, their DSS Mastercards – as they hurl themselves at the counters, desperate to cram their blubber into another new and lurid outfit. I mean, I hate to sound like a killjoy, a party-pooper, but it's Tuesday afternoon, for fuck's sake. What do these losers all do? *Where's all the fucking dough coming from?*

Because everyone reckons they're a player nowadays. Everyone thinks they're big time.

You live in an eighteen-foot-square toilet in Dagenham with your eighteen-foot-square girlfriend. You work as a crate packer in a warehouse and she's part-time behind the till at Iceland. Effectively the two of you earn about a millionth of a pence a year. Your net worth is zero. Yet you think it reasonable – perfectly acceptable – to stroll down to the George & Dragon dressed like some bad-acid version of Tom and Nicole at the Oscars, matching his and hers Rolexes on your wrists and freshly tanned from your four-star week in Ayia Napa.

The clothes are on the plastic.

The holidays are on the plastic.

The plastic is on the plastic.

I'm having drinks at Momo with Paul Dex and Terry Del Mar, a DJ/producer duo who I am going to commission to remix the Songbirds single. We're in a booth downstairs, an ornate Eastern lamp dangling above our heads. There are patterned rugs on the walls, some of the walls themselves appear to be made out of mud, and somewhere I think incense is being burned. Dex and Del Mar are about my age, 'geezers' who've been through the whole acid-house thing, and they use expressions like 'massive tune' and 'it drops big time'.

Deafening hip hop plays and, were I remotely interested in anything these clowns have to say, I'd have to really strain to hear it. Thankfully I'm not. None of the A-list DJs we approached could remix the tune in time. These mongo-loids were top of the B-list, available and – relatively – cheap. They're hired, this meeting is a formality.

'Massive props,' Dex is saying.

'An underground vibe,' Del Mar chips in.

I nod and sip my vodka tonic.

Earlier today, at lunchtime, I waited until Parker-Hall

strolled downstairs for a meeting I knew he had scheduled. I slipped across the hallway into his office and hurriedly got to work on his computer. I uploaded the contents of the Dover disk onto Parker-Hall's hard drive. I buried the disk in a file I named 'Personal', then buried that file in a deep, remote corner of 'My Documents'. There are hundreds of files in there and I'm sure he won't notice one tiny new addition. The whole thing took less than two minutes and then I was back in my office flipping between MTV and VH1.

I drift back into the conversation. Del Mar is saying, 'Soma, Basic Channel, Peace Frog . . .'

Dex says, 'Hooj Choons.'

'Lads,' I say, getting up and peeling a fifty from my wad to cover the drinks, 'I gotta run.'

Upstairs as I leave I see Paul Oakenfold sitting in the restaurant. Coincidentally he was one of the DJs who turned down the Songbirds remix. On the table in front of him is an ice bucket containing a bottle of Dom Pérignon. Beside it is a Dictaphone, its red light glowing. A young guy faces him, chewing on a pen, nodding. An interview, then. As I pass, Oakenfold stabs the table with a pudgy finger, looks the journalist right in the eye, and says, 'I am the biggest DJ in the world. *In. The. World.*' His teeny little legs dangle over the banquette seating, his feet – kiddie's feet – barely touching the ground.

Yeah, beware the small man, I think to myself. Always beware the small man. He'll fuck you every time. Because they never forget, do they? All that grief they got at school. Over and over, and for the rest of their miserable short-arsed lives, someone's got to pay.

*

Autumn really gets going and things happen, mostly bad.

An entire wall in the house will need to be replaced. Weeks – months – and thousands and thousands of pounds before I can sell the fucking place for anything like a decent profit.

'Fully Grown', Songbirds' debut single, is taken up to Radio 1 for playlist . . . and swiftly rejected. Even *Music Week* – usually a publication that gives every record released in Britain a little gold star – describes the single as 'somewhat lacklustre'.

The Lazies are offered the cover of *NME*. Demand for their debut LP is at such a pitch that it is sure to go straight into the top ten. There is a passing reference to Parker-Hall in the *Sunday Times* where he's described as an 'A&R guru'. After I read this – at eleven o'clock in the morning – I drink half a bottle of vodka and cry for a while.

Rebecca bustles around the office jangling with happiness. We went out for a drink and a long talk after I returned from Glasgow. She doesn't see the point in a long engagement. While telling her I agree I also point out that I want to do things properly, ask her father's permission and all that, and that this will take a little time. I manage to get her to agree that we will keep our 'engagement' under wraps for the time being.

Incredibly, this strict *omertà* seems to be holding fast. Had she confided in anyone it would most likely be Katie, Trellick's PA, in which case it would have been around the business affairs department in seconds and Trellick would immediately have hauled me down to Full and Frank's. In the normal run of things asking Rebecca – asking any secretary – to keep quiet about something like this would be about as effective a silencing tactic as taking out a full-page ad in *Music Week* to announce your engagement.

Because that's what they do. That's *all* they do. They talk to each other about the shit we do. Over salads and Diet Cokes, around photocopiers and water coolers, across wine-bar tables littered with Chardonnay bottles and packs of Marlboro Lights, they talk and they rant and they dissect the shit that we do to them. If you removed the phrase 'and *then* he said' from the language every one of these fucking sows would have a hard time kick-starting a conversation. And then – I guarantee it – the ones who have boyfriends go home at night and some poor bastard will have to hear the whole thing again, with whatever refinements and embellishments they've dreamed up on the tube thrown in. I mean, the sheer fucking *arrogance* of it, to think that anyone wants to hear about your miserable day.

Infuriatingly, when no one is around, she twirls into my office and gives me a peck on the cheek. On the plus side I have had her over to the flat once or twice, late at night, when I've been off my tits. Like many crazy girls she is truly gifted at fucking.

Rumours abound that Derek is going to leave the company, to move into management or something. Up until recently the only possible internal successor to him would have been Trellick, which would be an incredible result for me. But, the way things are going, Parker-Hall might just get offered the job. A nightmare beyond description. Managing Director by the age of thirty? Could it happen?

How in the seven names of fuck am I going to get

Woodham a publishing deal? Does he really know anything about Waters? What's he going to do?

Out of all this crap the most pressing problem is the Songbirds single. We've got the Dex and Del Mar remix in, which we're going to 'put out to clubs'. Is it any good? I haven't a fucking clue. I should know, I suppose. I'm paid to know these things. But I'm tired. It's so *tiring*, not knowing anything the whole time. You're meant to listen to your 'gut instinct'. 'Go with your gut instinct,' they say. But I don't know . . . all I hear from my gut are vague unhappy rumblings that I should be making more money, fucking more, and cuter, boilers, eating in better restaurants, getting more respect from quarter-wits like Dunn.

Dunn. The spastic was almost cheerful when he told me Songbirds didn't get playlisted. Like everyone else at the label he is in love with Parker-Hall and thinks the Lazies are going to be the next Led Zeppelin.

He will pay. They will all pay.


As requested Ross calls me the minute he gets the midweeks in. 'Sitting down?' he says. Jesus, this must be bad. 'Three,' he says bluntly. I don't think I've heard him right.

'Thirty?' I say, hopefully.

'*Three*,' he repeats, 'it's number three.'

Numbly I hang up. The midweek chart prediction for the Lazies single is number three. A stupendous result for Parker-Hall and a disaster for me. Well, anywhere in the top ten would have been a disaster for me but this . . . it's terrible, a living nightmare I am praying to awaken from. I only really have two options: 1) slink out of the office, take the rest of the week off with a mysterious illness and wait until all the fuss dies down a bit, or 2) go along to Parker-Hall's office, right now, and congratulate him. Play the magnanimous card.

His door is open. I take a deep breath, will my features into an idiotic grin, and pop my head around. 'Hey!' I say. 'Congratulations on . . .' Derek and Dunn – horrible success vampires – are both already in there, the three of them are deep in conversation.

'Yeah, cheers, mate,' Parker-Hall says breaking off in mid-flow. 'Can you just give us a minute? Thanks.' Neither Derek nor Dunn even look at me.

I turn to go but – 'Sorry, Steven, hang on a minute.' I turn back. Parker-Hall is holding a piece of paper up. 'Have you spent four and a half grand on club promotion on this Songbirds single?'

Dunn and Derek look at me coolly now. Can this really be happening? 'Umm, yeah,' I say shrugging, 'what's the problem?'

'In future,' Derek says, aggressively, 'anything like this will have to be signed off by either Anthony or myself.'

'Right . . .' I say.

'Just run it by me, mate,' Parker-Hall says airily. I nod. They resume their conversation – Derek literally turning his back on me and saying 'Anyway' – and I stumble off along the hall, numb, beginning to realise just how far I have fallen.

The tiny file squats on Parker-Hall's hard drive, inert and unnoticed, waiting for me to push the button.

Not yet, I think. Not just yet.

*

I somehow manage to add a new, alarming vice to my already jam-packed roster. In addition to the chang, the booze and fags, the ostros, the online dog and pony shows, the sex lines and whatever else opportunity, cash and technology throw my way, I am now compulsively overeating. In the car on the way to the office, idling in fogbound traffic, I cram buttery croissants into my face, washing them down with litre-and-a-half vats of full-fat latte. Standing at my office window, listening to demos and gazing at the bend of the Thames, I follow triple-decker BLTs with a couple of rounds of chocolate brownies. At lunch with Trellick and Ross, with Darren and Leamington, I bulldoze through plates of gnocchi and pasta, covered in oozing tomato sauce and hidden under drifts of Parmesan. I tear apart side portions of heavily buttered bread and inhale gallons of Diet Coke. ('I see they're working,' Ross commented one lunchtime, patting my burgeoning paunch as I drained a third silver-and-red can.) The other night the normally inscrutable kid from the Thai takeaway did a slight double take as he set the groaning bags (tom yam gai, green curry, special rice, spring rolls, three orders of dumplings) on the kitchen counter and realised I was eating alone. It's the cold, I suppose, I reflect as I wait impatiently for the evening's second tub of Belgian chocolate ice cream to complete its twenty-second thawing in the microwave.

With all this going on New York is probably the worst place on earth for me, yet here I am, sprawled on my bed at the Soho Grand – a tub of minibar M&Ms in my left hand, my softish prick in my right, and some hardcore on the TV. I'm tiredly watching some brick-shithouse darkie slide his horse-prick (the vein running down it is like a section of garden hose) in and out of a traumatised arse when the phone rings, its tone soft, purring, apologetic, like it doesn't really want to disturb you. Still half-heartedly masturbating, I pick it up. 'Band's on at half seven,' Parker-Hall says, 'then we got dinner with the American label, yeah?' He's not asking me.

'See you downstairs,' I say and hang up.

We're here for CMJ, which is kind of the same deal as In The City, which was very much like Sound City, as was Pop Komm, which bore a stunning similarity to South by Southwest, which merges in my head with the Winter Music Festival, which wasn't all that different to MIDEM. New York, Glasgow, Cologne, Bristol, Texas, Miami, Cannes: you shout at waiters and sign credit-card slips and all that really changes is the quality of the porn.

Parker-Hall really does work. I don't know that he actually likes going to gigs, but he certainly sees it as a necessary part of the job – which is why we're enduring a forty-minute cab ride to some venue way uptown, where we'll watch some fucking band for twenty minutes before another forty-minute ride back downtown to meet some people from the American label for dinner at a restaurant five minutes from our hotel. Had Parker-Hall not been here the chances of me going to this gig would have been . . . minimal.

He strides into the lobby, flipping his mobile shut. The hotel – the city – is rammed with Brits. In the bar I can see a couple of guys from Virgin laughing and drinking beer with the tall blond-hair-and-specs guy from the Chemical Brothers, Ed, I think. The Chemicals are on the verge of actually taking off properly over here – half a million albums or so, about the same as Ellie Crush. That's the thing about America. It's shit or bust. Fuck all or a couple of million albums. I physically have to shake my head to knock out a vision of Parker-Hall having that kind of US success.

'Should we be signing these cunts?' Parker-Hall asks as an opener as we clatter down the hotel's ludicrous industrial-metal stairwell.

'Who?'

He holds up a CD of some band.

'Nah, pony,' I say.

'It's OK. Like the new Radiohead with some tunes. Can't see it being good for more than a hundred thousand though. Do you wanna see if we can get a meeting? Just for a laugh, fuck every other cunt up?'

'Yeah,' I say as the doorman hails us a cab.

Parker-Hall turns to me as we edge into traffic. 'What's happening with the Songbirds single?'

'Starting to get some good club reactions in,' I say. This means fuck all. Without radio play it means absolutely nothing, unless you have a *monstrously* huge club record, the kind that can become a hit with minimal radio. 'Good reaction at club' is the kind of thing you say when there is nothing else to say. I know this and Parker-Hall knows this, but he chooses to nod and say, 'Yeah?'

'Yeah, still early days,' I say. Too right it fucking is – I have already put the release date back twice.

'And the album?'

'Still writing. Trying a few different writers.'

'What's the recording budget again?'

'One twenty.'

'Gonna come in at that? Be realistic.'

'I should think so,' I say with a straight face. I reckon, once everything is in, I'll have spent that on the fucking single.

'Coolio,' he says in a completely neutral tone. What to read into it? It is just about possible that he's backing me here, being supportive of my instincts in an area of the market – pop-dance – that isn't really his field. It's also possible – it's far more likely, it's practically a fucking banker – that he's doling me out a colossal amount of thick, oily rope and watching with amusement as I coil it over my arm and climb the steps towards my shaky, home-made gallows.

Outside, the brownstones of the Village give way to the wide, loud cord of Broadway as we whip uptown through light rain and suddenly, without warning, we're in the open space of Times Square, which squats neutralised, bereft, in the daylight. Off to our left 42nd Street snakes down towards Chelsea and I experience a sudden, intense pang of pornography, a yearning for fisting, for lurid plastic dildos and ben-wa balls, to see someone other than myself being defiled and degraded.

Parker-Hall's mobile trills, interrupting my reverie – 'All right geezer!' he says delightedly – and then he's talking to someone back home, his affected, brutalised vowels flouncing off some satellite miles above us and passing silently through cold, cold space before they flutter out another chunk of plastic somewhere in London, where it will be bedtime.

*

Having managed to drink pretty heavily at the gig (four double Rockschools and a couple of beers in less than an hour), I continue drinking heavily in the bar at the restaurant – some place called Balthazar, a recently opened pseudo-French shithole that seems to be the toast of every flaming virus carrier in the fucking Village – before we sit down to dinner with the American record company, which is where I *really* kick things up a gear.

Refreshed by repeated hops to the bathroom I begin double-fisting red wine and Scotch as well as popping back stinging tequila shots whenever I (frequently) swing by the bar to smoke another cigarette. I'm not eating and food – seared foie gras, steak frites, a salad of asparagus and fennel – builds up in front of and around me. Along from me Parker-Hall is having the *fruits de mer*; two sparkling tiers of iced crab, crayfish, clams, oysters, mussels and shrimp tower in front of him. 'Are you having a fucking giraffe, cunt?' I think and I briefly wish that someone who would appreciate the Rage anecdote – Trellick, say – was here.

Because the dinner is mind-numbing. Parker-Hall sits between Ashley Werner, chairman of the American arm of our company, and Russ Koppel, Head of Promotions, the guy who gets your signings on the radio over here. He's like an even more game-show version of Dunn. There's a couple of junior A&R guys from the American label beside me and, across from me, some woman manager – in her forties, well heeled, big glasses, serious – and a couple of other boilers I don't know. All the Shermans are drinking water and eating salads and the conversation consists of listening to Werner and Koppel pontificate away and waiting for your turn to nod. They're all Ellie Crush fans and treat Parker-Hall as though he were the young Ahmet fucking Ertegun. Parker-Hall, in his turn, drones on about how much he values their input or something.

I lean across the table to the cutest girl here – a blonde in her mid-twenties, denim jacket, small tits perky beneath a tight vintage Rolling Stones T-shirt – and whisper 'Hey . . .'

'Mmmm?' she ducks towards me, smiling uncertainly.

'Wanna do a bump?'

'Sorry?'

'A bump? You wanna do a bump?

'Uh, whaddya mean exactly?'

'Do you want some bugle?'

'Huh?'

Fucking hell. 'Gak? Racket, chang, beak, bag, nose?'

Nothing.

'Charlie?'

'Do you mean coke?' she says, her face scrunching, starting to look like someone's farted.

'Oh yeah.'

'No thank you.'

'Ah, come on . . .' I say playfully.

She shakes her head and resumes listening to one of her bosses who is talking about 'Madge'.

Fucking Shermans. They hit the Stairmaster, make a quick stop at Tofu World to pick up their lunch, and are at their fucking desks by 8 a.m. It makes you sick. Fuck you then, you dyke cow, I think.

By the time dessert appears I'm translucent with booze and coke and I'm drawing the odd glare from Parker-Hall. Leaning across the table to squeeze the last few drops from a bottle of Rioja, I tune into the old manager chick's conversation. She's talking about some slag she looks after – Marianne Faithfull? Joni Mitchell? Kate Bush? Some ancient munter or other – and how hard it is to get exposure, press or radio, for them in this day and age. What a disgrace this is, living legends that they are and all. 'It's a different story,' she says, 'when it's Clapton, or Rod Stewart, but for the women . . .' she trails off, shaking her (big) hair sadly.

'Well,' I say, reasonably, 'it does get harder for women as they get older.'

She turns towards me and through the booze and gak I see properly the angles of her spectacles, the sour, rock-critic cut of her dish.

'I beg your pardon?' she says, as if I'd just said, 'I've done your mother up the coal-hole, no lube.'

'Come on,' I say addressing the table now, 'it's a tough break in general, being a chick and getting older. Being a pop star? It's gotta be a nightmare.'

'Why would you say that?' she asks, genuinely curious. A bunch of people are listening now, out of the corner of my eye, shimmering, I see Parker-Hall looking my way, his cutlery suspended over his tart. (My entire meal has, of course, gone completely uneaten.) Fuck him. Why does he care what this miserable spunk-bucket thinks?

'Why on earth,' she continues soberly, 'should things be any different for a female musician than they are for a man?'

'I don't know,' I say, 'but they are.'

'Are you saying,' the dyke in the Stones shirt chips in, 'that older women in music should be afforded less opportunity for exposure and respect than men?'

'I'm not saying they should, but,' I gesture with my glass, suavely throwing red wine across the tablecloth, 'they fucking are.'

'Why do you think that would be?' The horn-rimmed spectacled sow asks patronisingly.

'Well,' I say, marshalling my argument, 'it's like, you don't mind seeing Jagger, or Bowie, fruiting about at fifty, do you? There's a certain . . . charm there. Or Clapton, he's just a muso, isn't he? You don't give a shit what he looks like. But, say, Debbie Harry at sixty?' A couple of people shake their heads, affecting disbelief at my cynicism. A cynicism they all share but are too reasonable (i.e. sober) to articulate. Fuck this, I think. In for a penny . . . 'Cher,' I continue, 'at seventy? Playing keepy-uppy with her fucking jugs? Cunt like a wizard's sleeve? Face like a melted bucket of concrete? Fuck that.'

There's a gasp. Literally a gasp. The manager woman looks like she's about to cry. 'What . . . what,' she says banging the handle of her fork on the table, sending shreds of pastry flying, 'what about women who're still producing important, artistically valid work? Nanci Griffith? Emmylou Harris? Chrissie Hynde?'

'Come on,' I say good-naturedly, 'who really wants to want to fuck any of those cows?'

There's a bunch of shouting – I think she actually tries to hit me – and then Parker-Hall is helping me up and we're out on the street, the cool night air of Soho washing my face as he shouts for a cab.

Americans, I reflect as some Paki drives me back to the hotel, they're so fucking *serious*.

*

Morning manages to find a crack in the heavy drapes and comes crawling across the bed, waking me up. The TV is still on. The adult channel, obviously. I groan and engage the memory banks, fast-forwarding through the previous evening: drinking in the room, cab, gig, drinking, cab, chang, another bar, drinking . . . the restaurant, after that, nothing. Wait a minute, the restaurant. Go back. My leg gives an involuntary twitch, a physical spasm of pain as I freeze-frame on an image from last night: the manager chick's face, twisted in disgust. Bad, something pretty bad happened.

I'm just finishing up a spectacular bout of vomiting (and noticing that I seem to have managed an even more outstanding – and exotically placed – example during the night: the shower stall looks like someone has dumped a tub of dog food in it) when there's a knock at the door. Blanket-wrapped and trembling, a ball of wet Kleenex in my fist I press a watery eye to the spyhole. There's some old Latino chick there, housekeeping or something. 'Come back later,' I shout.

I collapse back onto the bed, scrabbling with the Advil bottle. She keeps on knocking. These fucking people.

Angrily I pull the door open – the abuse already fully formed in my lungs, barrelling up towards my mouth – and it all happens very fast. A short, stocky woman sweeps into the room (hung-over as I am, I get a strong reek of booze from her), throws her raincoat off, and sits down on the edge of my bed, crossing her white-stocking-clad legs. 'You call for a date, honee?' Eh?

'What?' I say. 'What fucking date? Look, I think you've got the wrong room.'

'Room 335?'

'Umm . . .' I look at the TV screen, now showing an ad for 'Co-Ed Foxes', allegedly 'Manhattan's finest escort service'. 'We visit you,' the voice on the ad says, 'day or night.'

'You are Steeeven, yes?' She leers drunkenly, revealing a battered row of teeth so viciously bucked that, for a second, I think she's slipped a chunk of comedy orange peel into her mouth for a laugh. As an ice-breaker.

Looking past her I see the credit cards and the scrawled scraps of paper by the phone. Understanding, memory breaks in on me as I remember making the call a few hours ago before I passed out.

'Right,' I say, taking her in properly now: a buck-toothed dwarf in her late forties, her stomach a crenellated apocalypse of porridgy stretch marks. Graveyard shift. 'Sorry, I've changed my mind. Can you just . . . how much for you to just leave?'

'Full charge, three hunner dollar.'

'Fuck off. I'll give you fifty.'

She leaps up. 'You pay me! You pay now or I go downstairs and get my driver. I go get Ramirez!' Fucking Americans, so serious.

'OK, fucking hell!' I sigh fishing my wallet out and handing over the bills.

'Thanks, honee,' she says, rubbing up against me, friendly enough now she's got the fucking dollar, 'you sure you no want me to stay? I know we can have a good time,' she says huskily into my face. I don't know what she had for breakfast. Pilchards in garlic semen chased down with a mug of gasoline maybe? Her hand flashes through the sheet

I'm wrapped in and starts massaging my bare prick. A good time? To recap: she's an ancient Latino beast, pissed out of her mind, with a mouthful of Stanley knives and breath like a summer fish factory . . .

. . . who turns out to have an incredibly skilful way with a handjob. (I abandoned the blow job after an exploratory sixty seconds of fretful, white-knuckle gobbling. You'd be more relaxed with your cock in the maw of a ravenous Alsatian.) It only takes her about two minutes – all the time she's shouting 'CUM! CUM FOR MY BIG TITTIES!' while, with her free hand, vigorously working a small dildo into my rectum – before I start to shudder and buck. She pulls down her grimy bra and her burst jugs spill down to her stomach. 'CUM! CUM ON MY BEEG TITTIES!' she screams. I swallow hard against the spiralling nausea and unload a wad of spunk all over her.

I collapse onto the bed, foetal with shame, while she gets busy with the Kleenex. 'You feel better now, baybee?' she says, giving me a playful smack on the arse as she staggers towards the bathroom.

I bury my head under the pillow, groaning, and only hear the knocking dimly at first. By the time I leap up the crazy bitch is already tugging the door open.

Parker-Hall stands there looking clean, sober and rested in a crisp white shirt and jeans. Slowly he takes it all in: me, halfway across the room, naked and sweating, trying to cover my half-erect cock with a T-shirt, and the beast, forty-odd years and two hundred pounds of stinking Colombian whore with blobs of spunk still glistening here and there on the ruins of her tits and her stretch-marked stomach. A few feet away from Parker-Hall, directly in his line of vision, the shit-streaked dildo stands proudly on top the minibar. I notice for the first time that a yellow stud of sweetcorn I don't recall eating is stuck to its tip. The room must smell bad.

She grins at him. 'You his fren? You wanna join us eet's extra.'

'I'll see you at the airport,' Parker-Hall says and then he's gone.

We meet again in the BA executive lounge at Kennedy a few hours later. I'm sitting reading *Billboard* and sipping a quadruple Bloody Mary when Parker-Hall strides in. He gets himself an orange juice and sits down next to me.

'Look, Tony, I —' It's as far as I get.

'Listen,' he says, 'this has gone far enough. I don't give a fuck what you do on your own time, but last night you made an utter cunt out of us in front of the American label and it has to stop.' He looks at me coldly. I am dying here. 'I think you might need help,' he adds.

'Help?'

'With the drinking and the coke.'

'Oh come on,' I say, 'I was just taking the piss. She was a pompous old —'

'She's Ashley Werner's fucking *wife*.'

Shit. 'Look,' I say, 'we haven't been working together long —'

'Listen, mate,' he says sharply, cutting me off, 'we might as well get this straight. We aren't "working together". You work *for* me. And as long as you fucking are working for me you'd better shape up. Right? You sign a few fucking hits and then you can get off your nut at dinner and take the piss out of whoever you want because, I'm telling you, you're on thin ice, Steven. Thin fucking ice.'

With that he drains his glass and strides off across the lounge, out through the opaque glass doors, and disappears into the busy terminal.

He's right. This has definitely gone far enough.

I get back to London early the following morning – Parker-Hall and I sat well away from each other on the flight, we avoided each other through the plastic tunnels of Heathrow and took separate cabs in the wet dawn – and get into bed. I don't get out of it for a week.

I call Rebecca. 'A fever,' I tell her and she offers to come over. 'No,' I say.

She cancels meetings and I crumple back down beneath the duvet where I sleep feverishly for short stretches, often waking screaming from terrible dreams: there are dreams where Trellick and I are working in a concentration camp, butchering babies, dreams where I am being raped by a handicapped man, dreams where I am standing on the top of Centre Point watching a shower of nuclear missiles – thousands of them – falling over London, dreams filled with sly, grinning dogs with hypodermics for teeth, dreams where I am married to Rebecca and our babies are crawling all over me and the babies have no eyes, dreams where I cradle Waters' body while I reach into the hole in his skull, almost up to my elbow, scraping around in there for a long time before finally pulling my bloody arm out and seeing that I am holding a fistful of tiny silver statuettes: little Brit Awards, each one the size of a jelly baby.

I wake up screaming – the only light in the room coming

from the TV screen; either a fizz of static or a hardcore shot, as I almost always have a pornographic film on. I watch the video of Annabel Chong fucking three hundred guys five or six times a day. Over and over she pumps and sucks and grinds. Over and over semen is sprayed across her face, belly, breasts and bum. I watch a scene where she upends a used condom over her mouth and greedily slurps down the contents perhaps a hundred times, my thumb shuttling numbly between the play and the rewind. I watch the Rape Tape repeatedly: a compilation Ross had some guy at an edit suite knock up for him; basically all the classic rape scenes from modern cinema – *The Accused*, *Straw Dogs* (is it or isn't it up the Ronson?), *Salvador* (nuns – awesome), *Leaving Las Vegas*, *Clockwork Orange*, *I Spit On Your Grave*, *Thelma and Louise* (well, the bloke nearly gets in there before the dyke shoots him) – spliced onto one video. We wondered about the possibility of selling it commercially. I reckon there's a market but Trellick said you'd have too many clearance and distribution problems.

Every few hours I ring for food and a guy – some gook, some dago – will come to the door with Chinese, Thai or pizza.

Between meals I dry-swallow Valium.

I cry a lot.

A few days into this – having smoked nearly the entire two cartons of cigarettes I brought back from America and needing to freshen my crackling stack of overused hardcore – I try to go the corner shop and find that I cannot leave the house.

So I stay in bed, my hair greasy, my fingernails encrusted with filth, rancid semen-cracked tissues balled up all over the bedroom, overflowing ashtrays teetering on piles of unwashed clothes, waxy pizza boxes and fungal takeaway cartons littered across the floor.

I have been reduced to the bare fundamentals of human existence: eating, smoking and wanking.

Somewhere around the end of the week I am crumpled in a corner of the living room, naked, when I begin to have, well, epiphany is a very strong word, but I'm thinking about all the wrong, all the evil I've done. I'm haunted by an image of Waters' mother at his funeral – trembling her way along the aisle, emitting that crazed, inhuman *woooohooo* sound. Maybe it could be undone. Some kind of atonement? I'm looking at the Karma Bank and it's bad. It's fucking bad. It's like looking at one of my own bank statements; the tumbling, unreal zeros, DR stamped everywhere. Debit, debit, debit. Maybe if . . . if I stop. Change. Do good. Charity. Join the VSO and go and work abroad, nursing swollen-bellied babies, helping African villagers rebuild, I don't know, a dam or something? I could volunteer for spoon-feeding lukewarm soup to skeletal pensioners, or going around the underpasses and subways of central London on January nights, handing out sandwiches and blankets, tucking in freezing derelicts, my only reward being allowed to bask for a moment in the warmth of their grateful smiles. I could move to the country and raise children, try to live happily on the other side of the Prodigy sleeve, the side with the green fields and the smiling people.

The phone rings. Or rather, I become aware of its ringing. It might have been ringing for two days. I crawl across the floor towards it and watch it with dread: six, seven rings and then the machine clicks on.

'Hi . . . Steven? Uh, it's Barry from club promotions. Listen, I need to speak to you. I don't know if you . . .'

I pour a litre of Evian over my head, breathe in deeply a few times, pick the phone up and croak, 'Barry?'

'Oh, you're there. Christ, you sound like fucking shit, mate!'

'Yeah. Flu or something.'

'I've been trying to get hold of you, your mobile's off. Anyway, what are you doing Saturday night?'

'What? Why?'

'You won't believe this . . .'

And Barry tells me first good news I've heard in a long, long time.


'Oh my fucking God,' Trellick says from the back seat, 'will you look at this . . .' We turn a corner and come onto what I guess is the high street. It's eleven thirty on a Saturday night and the tolers – hundreds of them – are doing what they do up North: an overweight girl wearing a thong, a boob tube and high heels is vomiting over a Keep Left sign. A bunch of lads are pissing against a shopfront in full view. Another girl lies unconscious on her back in the gutter, her skirt hauled up and her tights shredded, a bottle of some demented alcopop, some estate juice, still clutched in her hand. 'Are those . . . *chips*?' Ross asks. The four of us squint. As far as you can see, for a few hundred yards in front of us, the air is filled with flying chips, bags of them being hurled upwards as dozens of fights break out. A kid staggers in front of the Saab, blood pouring from a cut in his forehead. He's pulled off the road and disappears under a flurry of fists and kicks as three blokes pile back in, kicking

275

the shit out of him. A handful of chips spatters off the car and I put the foot down.

'Welcome to Rotherham,' Barry says laughing.

'Should have left the car at the fucking hotel,' I say.

The club is a giant metal hangar on the outskirts of town. From the outside it could be a bowling alley, an ice rink, a swimming pool. The giveaways are the dull whump of bass coming from inside and the angry mob fighting to get in. A clutch of bouncers, all in black bomber jackets, all with little earpieces in, stand at the top of the stairs, chewing gum. Their faces are blank, mongoloid. We hang back and Barry talks to one while the tolers of Rotherham look at us strangely – in our dark jeans and black and navy cashmere V-necks. We're the only guys not wearing untucked knock-off Ralph Lauren shirts in head-splitting iridescent shades of lemon, violet and turquoise. It is almost freezing and we're the only people wearing coats.

Finally, with some grunting into headsets and gruff 'excuse mes', a two-bouncer escort is moving us through the throng, the velvet rope is lifted and we're being escorted along a stickily carpeted hallway towards the music by some guy called Steve, the promoter I guess. He seems very pleased to have some London industry types in his shithole. 'You'll 'ave a fooking good crack tonight, lads. The birds in here? Un-fooking-believable, like. We had that FFRR mob up here a while back. Pete Tong's lot, you know 'em?' Barry fields the loser's questions as the music grows louder and louder.

'Here we go, best cloob in't North,' Steve says as he throws a set of double doors open and we bowl right into Hades: two thousand bikini-clad girls and Teflon-shirted

Northern arguments for mass sterilisation are going fucking bananas to some awful cheesy house record. The DJ is suspended high above the crowd in what looks like a metal egg. He is wearing a baseball cap with a giant foam cock-and-balls on top of it. I'm not fucking kidding. Steve the promoter grins proudly.

'Wow,' Trellick says.

'I say we take off and nuke the entire site from orbit,' Ross whispers.

We get given a table in their 'VIP' section: actually a tiny bar roped off to one side of the club with a few fag-burned, booze-stained sofas dotted around. It's rammed with what can only be local VIPS – hairdressers and third division footballers. A few of the boilers are doable in an utterly disgraceful filth kind of way.

'It's grim up North,' Ross says laughing as he opens the bottle of Moët Steve has proudly placed on our table.

We make the best of a terrible situation, talking crap, chatting up girls, draining bottle after bottle of complimentary pooey and ducking down to sneak surreptitious card-edges of chang.

It's nearly 2 a.m. – everyone in the place is *incandescent* with booze: boiled on Stella, Breezers, vodka Red Bulls and speed and Es and all the other terrible crap the penniless spastics in places like this shovel into themselves – when I hear a familiar drum loop and a breathy female vocal. 'Come on,' Barry says, pulling me after him as we head out into the club proper. Packs of girls are charging towards the dance floor, pushing us aside. Guys follow them. Whoops and cheers are going up. Trellick and I look at each other. Then the track kicks in properly.

The whole place goes fucking *ballistic*. We watch open-mouthed. Every girl in the place knows all the words. Dozens of them are doing this funny little dance. It is, without doubt, the biggest reaction to a record I have witnessed in a super-toler nightclub since we all heard 'Saturday Night' by Whigfield for the first time, in some cattle market outside Marbella a few years back. Barry appears, sweating and drunk through the crowd. 'What did I tell you?' he shouts over the Dex and Del Mar remix of 'Fully Grown' by Songbirds.

Ross charges up. 'They've got a dance!' he screams. 'They've got their own fucking dance!'

'Maybe it's just this club . . .' I say.

'Bollocks,' Barry shouts, 'I was in Leeds last weekend. Glasgow too. *It's like this everywhere!*'

Trellick slips an arm around my shoulder, 'This, matey boy,' he says gesturing towards the music, the tolers, all of it, 'is going to be *a fucking smash*,' and then the four of us are dancing a jig, holding our champagne flutes on top of heads and laughing so hard that tears are running down our faces.

Immediately – and without consulting Parker-Hall or Derek – I authorise Barry to *treble* the club mailout. To get the record to every cock-and-balls-on-the-head DJ in the country, to every Ritzy-Cinderella-Rockafeller piece-of-shit, stab-you-in-face-with-a-broken-Beck's-bottle nightclub from Land's End to John O'-fucking-Groats.

Because I got blindsided, didn't I? Sidetracked by detail and nonsense I lost sight of the big picture. Only one thing matters in this racket: Big. Hit. Records. And plenty of them. Sort that out and you can do what you fucking like.

Back at the hotel I turn it all over in my head –

Woodham, Waters, Rebecca, Parker-Hall – and the same question keeps coming back. How far? How far can you go? I root through my bag, take out the dog-eared copy of Hauptman's *Unleash Your Monster* and flip back and forth until I find the passage. *'In every difficult, worthwhile endeavour there will come a point when the easiest course of action is to abandon forward motion, to allow inertia to take over and to return to the status quo. It is the brave and great man who, upon recognising this point, resists inertia and smashes on through to the far side. No matter the cost. I call this juncture the* critical moment of will.'

I underline the last four words several times.

Payback time.

I take Rebecca out to dinner at an obscure Sudanese restaurant to discuss our 'wedding'. Rebecca does most of the talking and I do a lot of nodding. 'We can announce it,' I say grandly, 'at the company Christmas party.'

*'Yeah!'* she coos, excitedly – doubtless imagining all her tunnel-cunted, doomed-to-childlessness, thirty-something secretary friends shimmering with envy as she waltzes around showing off the ring – and continues blathering about arrangements for her wedding that will never happen.

'. . . in gold, or ivory, and then there's place settings, and napkin rings and the like to think about . . . possibly Claridge's – or Babington – but I suppose we'd need to book the whole place out, and then there's the question of how late you can go on . . . DJs or band? Oh! Maybe we could get . . .'

It occurs to me that this is why boilers like Rebecca want

to get married so much – it is the ultimate organisational hard-on.

Earlier today I called Woodham. Without preamble I said, 'Do you want the good news or the bad news?'

'Bad news first,' he says.

'Well, the deal isn't huge and it's with a pretty small publisher.'

'What deal?'

'Your publishing deal.'

A pause while he takes this in. 'Seriously?' he says finally.

'Congratulations,' I say.

'You got me a publishing deal?'

'Yup.'

This was almost true. Having been laughed out of town by every real publisher in the business I rang Benny Gold.

Benny's an old-school has-been who copped the publishing on a couple of big novelty records in the seventies. He's made a little money on property since then but, like a lot of old-school fools, he likes to reckon himself still 'in the business'. He runs a tiny publishing company called Cloudberry Music: going to MIDEM every year and scratching around for deals no one else wants. He's a nice loser, the kind of guy you end up getting pissed with in the Barracuda – hundred-franc notes and whores all over the shop.

The deal I make with Benny is straightforward enough. I will personally sink twenty grand into Cloudberry to become a sleeping partner. I'll then punt acts his way, give him tips on hot bands and stuff. In return Benny agreed to make Alan Woodham our first joint signing (Benny's nearly sixty, he thinks Joe Jackson is a hot new artist, he had no idea if the demo was good, bad, or whatever) and to pay him an advance of ten grand out of my twenty K seed money. The only other condition I imposed was that Woodham never knows I'm involved in the company. He must think the whole thing was Benny's idea. Under the deal we have to pay Woodham five grand of the advance on signature and I max out my overdraft writing the cheque for this. I am up to the hilt on the cards. I am teetering right on the fucking brink, no question.

Woodham is beyond excited. 'How much?' he stammers.

'The advance is only ten grand, but –' I begin.

'Really?' he says, excited, and I have to remind myself that this is probably half his annual salary.

'Yeah. Sorry, but –'

'Oh fuck the money,' he babbles, cutting me off, 'all I ever wanted was a chance.'

Woodham is thinking about fame and success. I am thinking – will this be enough?

'Alan,' I said, my knuckles whitening around the phone, 'about this neighbour of mine who saw me coming home early the morning Roger was murdered.'

A pause while he adjusts to the twist in the conversation. 'When you went out early to get a newspaper?'

'Yeah, but, well, am I in trouble here?'

'Why would you be in trouble for that?'

'I just thought, when we spoke about it on the phone the other week, you sounded a bit . . . pissed off.'

'No.'

'So everything's OK? We're good? I mean, you don't think . . .'

'We're fine, Steven.'

And I want to believe him. I really do.

'Oh no!' Rebecca says suddenly, looking up at me, her fork suspended halfway to her mouth. 'That won't work, will it?'

'What won't?'

'Announcing it at the Christmas party.'

'Why not?'

'Darling, your memory! I won't be here, remember? I told you, I'm going to see my parents. I leave on the first and I'm not back until the new year. Bugger!'

She had told me. Rebecca – like me – is an only child. Her parents live in Melbourne. It's their anniversary soon and she's taking a month off, to fly out unannounced and surprise them. I think quickly. 'Tell you what . . . tell you what. You know I'm going to Thailand with the lads on the 15th?'

She nods eagerly.

'Why don't I cut it short with them and come to Australia for Christmas? I can meet your parents and we can tell them together? I mean, thinking about it, we should keep it under wraps until then, shouldn't we? Your parents should really be the first to know.'

She looks at me in gaping, wide-eyed adoration. 'Sweetie, that's a *marvellous* idea! I'll look into flights in the morning for you. Bangkok to Melbourne. Oh, you'll love my dad!'

She starts talking about her dad, about how funny he is, how laid-back he is, and it's good because now I don't have to listen any more. I can think. I'm thinking – this could actually work out really well. But there are questions. At the flat? Or a hotel suite? And just how hardcore is Woodham? How much does he want it? I think about all this as I push rice around my plate and Rebecca talks on in the background. She's saying, '. . . and you don't want a stretch limo, *so* tacky, but maybe a Lincoln Town Car, we can use Addison Lee for the guests and if we . . .'

As she talks I look up into her face, which is lit a soft orange from a candle which is floating and glittering in a bowl of water in the middle of our table. Rebecca's eyes are bright green. They are glittering too – the zinging glitter of utter madness.

# November

*Michael Hutchence tops himself in some demented wanking frenzy. The Teletubbies are no. 1. Chris Evans buys Virgin Radio. Martin Heath is fired from Arista. A&R guy Jono Cox is given a label deal by Deconstruction/BMG on the strength of this band he's signed called Superstar. He says, 'This is very much a long-term relationship.'*

*'Whatever it takes . . .'*

Casablanca Records motto

Woodham signs his publishing deal. He takes the day off and I take him to the Groucho for lunch.

We're barely into the second bottle of Perrier Jouet when he starts coming out with all the crazy shit they all come out with – '. . . things are gonna happen now . . . I've been trying so hard for so long . . . all I needed was a break . . .' At one point he even starts talking about the 'craft' of songwriting. You what? I think. You're a twenty-eight-year-old *copper*.

As I upend the second empty champagne bottle into the ice bucket and signal the waitress (the cute one I always overtip) for a third, I ask him about his kids. He goes misty-eyed and starts blathering on like they all do, thinking that you give a shit about the howling brats they've conjured up out of some sloppy fuck. He talks on while I think about house prices and money and remixes and chart positions and stuff. I catch the odd phrase – '. . . such a clever little boy . . . takes after her mother . . . the thing about being a parent . . .' Fucking spare me.

'Do you plan on having kids, Steven?' he asks me finally.

'Oh, definitely,' I say. Then, quickly, I add, 'Do you want some fucking chang?'

He doesn't understand so I explain, employing a more widely used noun. There's a pause.

'Here?' he says, glancing around the half-empty bar.

Downstairs into the little bathroom with the little stack of books in it and soon I'm watching the detective constable snort up an icy line of very decent cocaine.

Of course the downside to this is that I soon have to listen to the cunt talking an *incredible* amount of balls: how much he owes me; how, in ten years, I was the first A&R guy to give his music a chance; how he gets laughed at by the other coppers for persisting with his dream in his spare time; how they call him 'Noel'; how his – now dead – father never understood his drive to make music. 'He told me it was a waste of time,' Woodham says sadly, and suddenly I feel a great surge of affection for his dad, for old man Woodham, sagely telling his worthless son what they should all be told really – '*Get a fucking job, you stupid cunt.*'

We're literally a breath away from the same story about how he fell off his bike when he was nine when I interrupt him. 'Listen, Alan,' I say, swallowing and slapping on my gravest expression, 'now we're getting to be . . . well, friends, I suppose . . .'

He nods eagerly and with utter conviction, the coked-up, brain-dead fool.

'There's something I've been wanting to talk to you about but . . . it's difficult. I . . .' I trail off.

'What?'

'Christ, I . . .'

'Come on, mate,' he says, his jaw is set at a mad gak-angle and I am pretty sure he will believe anything I am about to tell him.

'It's just, when you were talking about how much you loved your kids earlier . . . it got me thinking. Oh God . . .'

'Steven,' Woodham says, setting his drink down, putting a hand on my shoulder, 'what is it?'

I wait for a long time, looking like I'm really weighing it up, before I say, 'There's this guy at work . . .'

I tell him.

He sits there for a long time. He looks very angry. Finally he says, 'Are you sure about this, Steven?'

'Pretty sure. Things he's said, when he's drunk.'

'Right. What's his name?'

I spell it for him.

'I'm going to make a phone call. Right now.' he says, pulling his mobile out.

'No phones in the club, Alan.'

'Oh, right.' He sways off towards reception, dialling as he goes.


Afternoon drinking blurs into evening drinking and I take Woodham on a whirlwind blitz of the West End; from the Groucho to Soho House to Black's to the Two Brydges club before cabbing it up to Hyde Park Corner, to the Met Bar.

It's Friday night and the place is *rammed*. Scary Spice has a big corner table with a gang of minders and shrieking drunken mates. Jay Kay from Jamiroquai is on the dance floor, wheeling about like a fruit. For some reason all the male members of the cast of *Friends* are hunkered around one of the central banquettes. We elbow our way in at the bar and Woodham stands there, bathed in the light from the backlit spirits bottle – the golden glow of the Scotches, the emerald of the gins, the platinum white of the vodkas – taking it all in, astonished. 'Shit,' he whispers out the corner of his mouth, nudging me, 'that's James Dean Bradfield, from the Manic Street Preachers.' I look down the bar to see that Bradfield is indeed buying a round a few feet along from us.

'Oh yeah, you a fan then?' I say, cracking a credit card down.

'God, not half.'

Jesus wept. Bradfield comes through the crush beside us, heading for his table. 'Hey James,' I say, extending my hand. He shakes it and it takes him a couple of seconds.

'All right . . . Steve? How you doing, mate?'

'Good, thanks. Out on the town?'

'Ah, me and the Hedgemeister just came out for a couple.' He indicates Mike Hedges across the room, the man-mountain who produced the last Manics album. 'Too middley,' Waters had said. Waters' tongue, the tongue he had used to say those senseless words – and millions more – lying on the floor next to the Nick Hornby novel. While Bradfield and I exchange pleasantries Woodham is twitching and shuffling spastically, begging to be introduced.

'James, this is Alan.'

'All right mate?' Bradfield says, extending his hand to Woodham. Woodham shakes it reverently and then he slurs the following. Oh yes he does.

'It's an honour to meet you, Mr Bradfield. I have to say, I think you're an amazing guitarist.'

I close my eyes but Bradfield just laughs it off. 'Ah bollocks,' he says. 'Have a good night, lads.' And he's off.

A sour-faced bumboy materialises behind the bar.

'What can I get you?'

Woodham dives in. 'I'll get this.'

'No, my treat tonight Alan.'

'No, you've been buying all the drinks. My turn.'

'OK. Double vodka and tonic.'

'Same for me please.'

The guy goes off to fix the drinks. Woodham leans into me and says, 'I suppose that wasn't very cool, was it? With James just then.'

'Ah, don't worry about it. I'm sure he gets it a lot.'

'I had to tell him.'

'Sure.'

'How do you know him?'

How did I know him? I didn't really. 'Oh, just from around, you know.'

Woodham nods and says, 'It's another world.'

The virus carrier returns with the drinks, which come in huge, heavy ice-packed tumblers. Woodham holds a tenner out and the barman looks at him like he's lost his fucking mind. Woodham reaches into his wallet and upgrades to a twenty, which still isn't going to cut it. 'I'll be back in a minute,' I say and head for the toilet for a bump, leaving the barman talking Woodham through the bill.

When I come back ten minutes later Woodham is still blinking at the receipt.

It's midnight when we get back to my place and Woodham is *hammered*.

We're sat on high stools at the granite kitchen counter which separates my kitchen area from the living room. On the worktop between us is a CD case (*Give 'Em Enough Rope*, which we are listening to, Woodham's choice) with a mound of gak on it, my Amex, a rolled fifty, a bottle of Stoli, a bottle of tonic, a half-full ice bucket, some sliced limes and two heavy crystal tumblers. Woodham is getting a bit giggly now, possibly feeling the effect of the half E I ground into his first drink almost an hour ago. (I thought it best to slip him small and gradual doses.) 'I *love* this song,' says Woodham, leaping off his stool and stumbling over towards the massive speakers. He turns it up.

My mobile rings and I look at the screen. Rebecca. Bang on time. 'Hi there,' I drawl.

'Hello, sexy,' she giggles, 'are you home yet?'

It's Rebecca's last night in London before she goes to Australia, to surprise her parents on their anniversary. She wanted us to spend it together but I told her I had a couple of gigs and a meeting. Why didn't she go out with the girls and we could meet up later at my place? Have a late supper? She could stay the night and I'd drive her to Heathrow in the morning. She thought this was very sweet of me.

'I'm a bit tipsy and feeling very naughty . . .' she giggles. She sounds smashed beyond human belief. Sen-say-shunal.

'Really?' I say. 'Get your arse in a cab then.'

'Do you need anything? What's that racket?'

'Ah, I've got a mate here. He'll be leaving soon. Oh, you could get some champagne. That place on the Harrow Road will still be open. I'll pay you back when you get here.'

'Mmmm, lovely. OK, sweetie, see you in twenty. Big kiss, Mwwah.'

I hang up and watch Woodham, who is swaying in the

middle of the room, eyes closed, as he plays air guitar along to the Clash. What a fucking loser.

Later, in the bedroom, I look up at Woodham and he looks back at me. The look on his face is an incredible cocktail of expressions: joy, terror, pleasure, embarrassment, confusion, shame, panic, hilarity, disbelief . . . they're all fighting for position. I look down, at Rebecca's naked rump, at my cock appearing then disappearing into her, at the back of her head, her dirty-blonde hair bobbing as it moves rapidly up and down over Woodham's crotch. Rebecca is on all fours on my bed with Woodham and I positioned at either end of her in classic double-ender stylee.

Don't get me wrong, it wasn't easy to pull this off. It took *two fucking hours.*

Rebecca had been a little surprised when she toppled in the door – pulling her little trolley-suitcase behind her, and carrying two bottles of champagne (fucking Moët) – to see Woodham there. But only a little. I'd mentioned a few times that I'd been seeing a bit of him, and she knew I'd demoed his songs. Woodham, pilled up, drunk, chang'd and randy, had been *delighted* to see Rebecca.

The three of us did more coke. We had drinks and danced around to disco records. After an hour or so of this I convinced both of them that we should all do an E *('it's Friday night for fuck's sake!')*. I took an aspirin while Rebecca necked her first pill and Woodham chucked a whole one back on top of the one and a half I'd already slipped him.

More drinking, dancing and coke until, an hour later, the

three of us are stretched out on the big sofa, Rebecca in the middle.

'It's . . . another fucking world,' Woodham says, gazing around at the flat, his pupils like manholes as he takes in the gorgeous girl, the drugs and empty champagne bottles, the evening meeting pop stars. The kind of life he thought he might have when he was a guitar-strumming nineteen-year-old? Woodham told me he lives in Forest Gate with the hag and kids. I nodded, but I do not know where Forest Gate is.

'Listen,' Rebecca says, taking Woodham's hand, her jaw juddering, 'if Steven believes in your music then it's got to be good. He's got the most *amazing* taste.'

I smile, allowing the compliment.

'I know,' Woodham says, looking like he might cry. 'C'mere, mate . . .' He lurches towards me. Oh Christ. Woodham hugs me passionately. 'I fucking love you,' he says into my neck.

'Hey,' says Rebecca, as she squeezes in and the three of us hug. Woodham – almost delirious now – buries his face in her cleavage and makes moaning noises. Rebecca shrieks delightedly. I leave them rolling around on the sofa and tool over to the breakfast bar, to the mirror where I've prepared three big, chunky lines. The three lines are near identical, except for the fact that one of them is simply cocaine while the other two are a brain-rupturing blend of 70 per cent pure ketamine and 30 per cent cocaine. I snuffle up the coke-only line. 'Here,' I say turning back to the sofa, holding out the mirror.

A few moments later Rebecca is lying back in my lap, her eyeballs vibrating gently. I've freed one of her breasts from her dress and am slowly massaging the dark brown nipple while Woodham watches stupefied. I mean, he's foaming at the fucking mouth.

'Shall we adjourn?' I say thickly and I lead the two of them into the bedroom, carefully stepping over the broken champagne bottle which lies on the floor at the foot of the bed.

So, here we are. The three of us are buckled and sweating and exhausted in a heap on my bed, the detective constable having just sprayed a goodly load all over my 'fiancée's' breasts and chin. 'Oh God,' Rebecca says, giggling and dabbing at herself with a Kleenex, 'how did this happen?'

'Holy shit,' says Woodham.

'Go get us some more drinks, Alan,' I say.

'Uh, sure. Vodka and tonic?' I nod and he stumbles off, leaving us alone.

'I love you,' Rebecca says.

'I love you too,' I say, before adding, casually, 'could you pass me up that glass of water?'

She crawls to the edge of the bed, hangs over the side and reaches down. Somewhere down the hallway I can hear Woodham clattering around in the kitchen. Music – fucking Radiohead now – hums from the living room. '*Rain down . . .*'

I jump on top of Rebecca, pushing her down into the mattress, grabbing her hair and pulling her head back. 'Ooof! Gerrof!' she giggles, thinking I'm fucking around.

Critical moment of will.

With my free hand, I bring the thick, jagged stump of the Dom Pérignon bottle up hard and plunge it into the base of her throat, ripping it upwards towards her chin, feeling the flesh tear, feeling her larynx come apart. There's a terrible, flapping, sucking sound as she gasps and breathes in, the breath going into her body now through the fist-sized slash in her throat. It sounds like when the waste disposal gets blocked. Then she breathes out and a wash of syrupy blood sprays everywhere, all over the bed, the seagrass carpeting and the twelve-hundred-quid cherrywood cabinets from Heal's.

I throw her forward – naked – into the pool of her own blood and she writhes onto her back, kicking and thrashing, her hands scrabbling at her throat, trying to get hold of the stump of the bottle, which is jutting out of her neck like a mad, half-arsed tracheotomy. Apart from a frothy gurgle she makes very little noise, I guess because I've just slashed her voice box to pieces.

*Hello, you.*

Very quickly – the whole thing has taken less than a minute – her kicks start to subside, becoming little random jerks as her staring, incredulous eyes begin to glaze over, and I take off – running full pelt and blood-spattered down the corridor and screaming, *'Oh Christ! Alan! Alan! Help!'*

# December

*Big A&R buzz on Campag Velocet. The Spice Girls LP is certified as the biggest selling American release of the year. Nick Mander, an A&R guy at Epic, signs a band called Headswim. He says, 'We have been developing a strong reputation for breaking exciting new acts. Headswim can be the next one.'*

*'I'm all in favour of the Conservative values of personal responsibility, hard work and enjoying the fruits of your success.'*

Geri Haliwell

London gets really cold and I develop a major thing for Natalie Imbruglia, this Aussie soap star whose debut single 'Torn' is all over the radio. Can she be fucked? I wonder. She's A&R'd by Mark Fox over at BMG who I don't really know. Cowell knows him though. Is it worth calling Cowell and testing the water? Nigel Godrich has worked with her. Is it worth giving him a bell? I think about the ins and outs of it a lot.

'Fully Grown' by Songbirds has been no. 1 on the club chart for two weeks now. Demand filtering in from the shops is starting to look huge and I've put the release date back to the week before Christmas. It's a gamble, but if it comes through . . .

I pull into the car park early, around half ten. There are two police cars parked close to the front door of our building. Two uniformed coppers come out of the entrance; the first one is carrying a computer monitor, the second has the keyboard balanced on top of the hard drive. As I lock the

Saab I watch them carefully loading the stuff into the boot of one of the squad cars, overseen by some older plain-clothes guy.

I stroll into marketing on the first floor. It's a morgue, no music playing, people sitting about in shock. 'Morning, all,' I say brightly, as I cross the open-plan space. I've been a bit of a god in marketing lately, a few of the girls have even put bets on Songbirds being the Christmas no. 1. But, this morning, I get no reaction beyond a couple of muted 'hellos'.

I stick my head around Ross's office door. He's on the phone, talking quietly. 'Listen, hang on,' he says as soon as he sees me, 'I'll have to call you back.'

'What's up with the coppers?' I say, strolling in.

He looks at me for a moment before asking, 'Have you been upstairs yet?'

'No, I just . . .'

'Shut the door and sit down.'

I do it.

'Strap yourself in,' Ross says standing up.

'For fuck's sake . . .'

'The police arrived about an hour ago, no one's been allowed to go up to A&R since then. We only know because Jeannie came down and told us. It's . . .' He stops, shaking his head in disbelief.

'For fuck's sake mate, *what is it?*'

'Parker-Hall's been arrested. They've found obscene images of children on his computer. I mean, proper hardcore stuff. Babies and shit like that.'

I let my jaw drop. 'You. Are. Fucking. Joking.'

'I swear to God, Steven. The cunt's a paedo.

\*

So Woodham came crashing and stumbling down the hallway behind me. I stood aside and let him see. Rebecca, naked, dead and twisted in a mad heap, her green eyes staring and the green stump of the champagne bottle still jutting out of her throat, blood still pumping weakly over her brown freckled skin and trickling down her breasts and belly.

'Oh my God. Oh fucking Christ.'

'We were messing about, play-fighting. She . . . she fell off the end of the bed. The bottle . . .'

He inched towards her and extended two trembling fingers to the side of her neck. I picked up the phone and started to dial.

'What are you doing, Steven?'

'Calling an ambulance.'

'She's dead.'

'We need to –'

'Don't be fucking stupid.'

He took the phone from me and sat down. 'Fuck!' Woodham said. 'Fuck it!'

'We have to –'

'Think. I'm a policeman. We're off our heads. There's drugs all over the fucking place, she's full of them. We've both . . . do you know how this will look?'

'Oh Jesus. Oh Jesus, Alan.'

'Shhh. Let me think.'

I sat down on the bed and buried my face in my hands and pretended to cry while Woodham thought.

'Right,' he said, 'give me a hand. Wrap her up in this sheet and we'll, yeah, strip the bed. Here . . .'

Later I sat in my bathrobe, cradling a half-pint of Glenfiddich, chain-smoking and watching MTV with the sound turned way up, the ceaseless din of the videos – Jamiroquai with the floor moving under him (I wonder if we could get Jonathan Glazer to do the Songbirds video?), Pulp, Kula Shaker, Mansun – partially obliterating the sounds of sawing, splintering and hacking coming from the bathroom. Well, I reflected, the four hundred quid on that set of Japanese butcher's knives hadn't been completely wasted after all.

It took almost two hours for Woodham to cut Rebecca up into manageable sections (torso, hips, limbs and head) that would fit into my two biggest suitcases. We sat in silence for a while after he'd finished. Finally he looks at Rebecca's suitcase and turns to me, remembering something we must have been talking about earlier. 'She said she was going to Australia today?'

'Yeah.'

'To visit her parents, but it was a surprise? They don't know she's coming?'

'No.' I'm acting kind of numb.

'She must have her passport on her.'

'Yeah.' It was in her coat. I'd checked.

'How long was she going for?'

'Till the new year.'

'Right. Good.'

Then he got up, got showered and dressed and, just before the sun came up, we hauled the suitcases out to my car. I handed Woodham the keys. He said he had a place in mind and that it was probably best if I didn't know any more.

I watched Woodham drive off, the silver Saab disappearing towards the Harrow Road as the feeble sun came up. Then I walked back through to the bedroom. I picked the digital video camera up – its black eye had been peering through a crack in a pile of sweaters – and turned the little switch from 'record' to 'rewind' to 'play'. I had a decent shot of the naked, bloody Woodham saying, 'Think. I'm a policeman . . .' I put the camera in a drawer and went off to sleep in the spare room.

Remind me not to get sent to prison.

Trellick and I are sitting in the visiting room of Wormwood Scrubs waiting for Parker-Hall to appear and sipping plastic coffee from styrofoam cups. The room seems to be unchanged from the 1960s: brick walls glosspainted in filthy white and brown, chipped Formica tables, those orange plastic seats with the holes cut out of the back.

And then there's the people – these lifetime losers and their broods. The dads sunk down into their striped pyjama-style prison shirts with their matted hair and stubble, wearily listening to the hags they married banging on about money and gossip, wondering which of their mates or neighbours is lumping it into her in their absence. The wives are, of course, something else entirely. At the top end of the scale there's a couple of council-estate readers' wives (a type I'm not *completely* averse to) *Razzle* rejects, bottle-blonde jobs in tight jeans and crop tops who look like they'd take you into a side room right now and break your cock off for forty quid. Down the bottom end of the market it's the twenty-stone thirty-year-olds who look sixty-five, women who look like they've had their cunts kicked in from dawn till dusk every single day of their lives since birth and who expected nothing else. The kind of women who, when their man looked up and told them 'before we get married you should know, darling – I'm a convicted rapist with a history of GBH who's wanted for armed robbery', replied 'let's do this fucking thing', and started cheerily humming 'Here Comes the Bride'.

Their kids sit sullenly, fidgeting, kicking their cheap supermarket trainers at the worn lino, headphones on, tinny drum'n'bass audible, all lost in their own little ragga worlds, already hatching their embryonic schemes for greatness: cashpoint muggings, ram raids, crack deals and lifting your Nokia at knifepoint. Everyone – even the kids, the babies in their tattered strollers – seems to be smoking roll-ups. I mean, roll-ups for fuck's sake. Where's your self-respect? You'd just quit, wouldn't you? (Then again, self-respect can't be too high on the agenda if you're in here for arse-fucking a struggling nine-year-old, for taking a chisel to a granny for eight and a half quid.) People are shouting at each other and banging the tables. Women are crying. The air is flinty with tension and barely suppressed rage. It reminds me of something. Business Affairs meetings. It reminds me of Business Affairs meetings.

I say we take off and nuke the entire site from orbit.

'Fuck,' Trellick whispers as Parker-Hall appears, shepherded over to us by a warden. He manages a cracked shaky grin as he sits down. Jesus Christ. He's only been here for three days and he looks *appalling*. There is a glassy terror in his eyes, like he's numb with horror, like he can't believe it's happening, and yet he's twitchy, nervy, like he knows it could all get much worse at any moment – the sharpened teaspoon in the dining hall, the ebony hand, black as a grand piano, on his shoulder in the showers.

'You know,' he asks us, head bowed, 'I didn't do anything. Don't you?'

'Course we do,' I say.

'No one believes it,' Trellick lies.

I slide across some magazines I've brought him – *Q*, *Uncut*, *Mojo*, *NME*. 'There's a good live review of the Lazies in there,' I say but he just stares at the magazines dumbly, perhaps feeling too keenly the distance between his old life and his current one.

'Why is this happening to me?' he says to no one.

'Listen,' Trellick says, using his best let's-get-a-grip-shall-we? Etonian voice as he counts off the positives on his fingers, 'a) you'll get bail next week, b) the company will pay it, whatever it is, and c) that was an old computer in your office. Christ knows who's used it over the years.' Trellick talks law for a bit, burden of proof, beyond reasonable doubt stuff.

'But what are people going to say?' Parker-Hall looks very small and very young now. He looks like he might cry.

'Listen, Tony, everyone at the label is behind you,' I say, 'and Derek's totally put a lid on discussing it outside the company. Don't worry, it's not going to get into any of the papers.'

Well, this wasn't strictly true. The first call I made when I left the meeting where Derek put a complete ban on discussing the Parker-Hall situation was to Leamington. His next call, as I knew it would be, was to one of his mates at *Music Week*. Front page next week. With a little luck, if they pick up on the man-who-discovered-Ellie-Crush angle, it will be all over the tabloids in time to coincide with Parker-Hall's release on bail.

'Thanks, guys,' he says to us, wiping his eyes.

'Don't be daft,' I say. 'You're a mate.'

Monica is telling Joey and Chandler off about something. She has her hands on her hips and her hair tied back. The tits are good and high in a tight black vest thing. I'd like to fuck Courtney Cox and idly wonder how the planets would have to align in order for this to be possible. (A huge hit record in the States? I'm on tour with the act, they're in LA playing the Hollywood Bowl, she comes backstage, David isn't there, she gets a little drunk, I'm being charming and 'English' . . .)

It's a Christmas episode; the girls' apartment has a huge tree in the corner and outside, through that big many-paned window, snow is – of course – gently falling on the sound-stage Manhattan. It's almost Christmas here in London too, but no snow. Rachel comes in looking really hot – tiny black skirt with black tights and knee-high leather boots. Yeah, forget Monica, Rachel – now there's a proper fuck-jar. The sound on the TV is off, I'm listening to rough mixes of tracks from the Songbirds LP, lying on the enormous sofa in my new house in Notting Hill, drinking Scotch and eating guacamole. The songs are mostly utter donkey. It doesn't matter. We're about to have a huge hit with 'Fully Grown' and we've got two more killer singles. I've even got one of Woodham's less offensive numbers on the LP, which should recoup the idiot's publishing advance and pay me back.

You should see the video for the single. It's incredible.

Annette, Kelly, Jo and Debbie – dressed as schoolgirls, as pubescent spunk-worshippers, as teenage cock addicts – throw themselves around a gymnasium in tight hardcore porno-choreography. Tanned and toned, rehearsed to death and sumptuously lit, they are a living, grinding-sucking-pumping monument to what can be achieved with crazed ambition and near unlimited funds and bear no resemblance whatsoever to the council-estate prostitutes who fidgeted in my office six months ago.

The girls have been reacting to their sudden success in the usual manner. There have been strops, walkouts and catfights. There have been tears and tantrums. Bulimia and bitching. Less believably they've taken to referring to themselves as 'artists' and voicing opinions about the kind of material they're being offered to sing. There are rumblings from Debbie about her songwriting ambitions. (If they really start selling some albums next year I'll probably have to start listening to some of this fucking nonsense. Jesus wept.) For the moment, however, it's fine. It's all manageable. They've worked hard; let them preen and strut and enjoy the short window they'll be afforded before they're spat out the other end. (Spat reeking into rehab and from there onto the daytime TV confessionals, the presenting jobs, the ghostwritten autobiographies – '*I always knew I was different from the other kids*' – and taking a good fucking kicking from their footballer husbands before drifting into middle-aged mega-obscurity.)

It's some rush, the process of having a hit record. A proper hit record, I mean. Not some stinking indie piece of shit that pops up on the midweeks at no. 12, drops to 17 by the Friday, and charts at 21 on Sunday. No. I mean *a proper fucking hit*: a record that slashes and burns its way in at no. 1 and then plants itself in the top five for weeks. A record that every lowlife toler, spod, pikey, uber, granny and foetus in the country is going to be singing for months to come. You turn on the radio, any station, and you hear it. You flip channels and you see the video. You go into a nightclub and every sour-cunted working-class sow in there is throwing herself around her fake designer handbag, smouldering Kensington in one hand, tumbler of vodka and sugar in the other, all doing some mad quasi-synchronised dance they've invented.

It's at moments like this that you genuinely feel like you've contributed to the culture in some way.

'Fully Grown' is now the most played record on Independent Local Radio. It's the third most played record on Radio 1, who, having blanked the single first time around, have sensed how huge a hit it's going to be and have come on board with a vengeance on the Dex and Del Mar remix.

Daily now Dunn sidles into my office. He joshes. He punches me on the arm and talks about football and fucking as he gives me updates about TV appearances and airplay. He even, over two beers after work, goes so far as to tell me how he knew right away that 'Fully Grown' would be a hit, it just needed a little time. A sleeper. He says he always had his doubts about Parker-Hall. His banter, his forced jocularity, has the desperate tang of a man trying to joke his way out the gas chambers, showing a card trick to the guards even as they're forcing him to strip and are sizing up his gold fillings.

He is a dead man and he knows it.

Through the glass wall at the end of my office the new temp Jo (twenty-five, great rack) taps away at her computer, sucking thoughtfully on a strand of her blonde hair. She treats me appropriately, which is to say she treats me like a god with a hangover. She doesn't know it yet, but in the new year, when Rebecca mysteriously fails to return from Down Under, she will be offered the job on a permanent basis.

Last week Derek invited me to a drinks thing over at his house, his virus pit. I declined, but still. He knows he backed the wrong horse. He knows that the industry perception is that he's the raving iron who hired a rampant paedo. To my surprise a lot of people haven't really needed all that much prompting to put together the desired equation. It's roughly something like this: queer + Internet access x cocaine = potential paedophile. We're having lunch together next Tuesday – right after the Songbirds midweek arrives – to discuss my new job.

He is going to pay.

A few hundred yards away on the Portobello Road people are already buying Christmas tree lights and wrapping paper. They're buying hot sausages with fried onions. My one present was bought some time back: tickets for my mother and her friend to go to the Caribbean for Christmas and New Year. It's a present that works both ways, as it means I won't even have to see her over the holidays, which is fortunate – I won't be here anyway.

Ross – that dickhead – strolls in and joins in the argument, taking the girls' side I think, and Joey and Chandler stomp off to their place, Chandler turning round and getting a good crack in before he goes. I wonder, not for the first time, about the viability of a series of pornographic *Friends* videos; filmed on a replica set, with quality lookalike actors and decent production values, although super-hardcore of course. *The One with All the Fisting . . . The One with Phoebe's Double Penetration . . . The One with the GHB and the Ben-Wa Balls . . .* You could even do a sideline for the faggots and the diesels – Joey and Chandler finally go for it, looking tenderly into each other's eyes, a thick rope of milky jizz connecting Chandler's mouth to Joey's twitching prick. Monica and Rachel in a long, rapturous 69. *The One with the Ten-Inch Strap-On.* Massive legal problems of course, you'd have to keep the whole operation untraceable, but I'm sure there's a huge market.

As someone who makes their living from anticipating, from shaping, the tastes of millions of tasteless morons, you have to tell yourself that the things you feel are universal, that the things you think and feel are thought and felt by millions of other people.

I turn the stereo off with the remote and lie back, looking up at the cream ceiling fifteen feet above me. Six months later than billed, and nearly a hundred grand over budget, Murdoch and the Albanians are finally gone. The room I'm in, the ground-floor living room, is really two rooms knocked into one. It is forty-four feet long and eighteen feet wide, narrowing to fourteen feet towards the back of the house. The huge windows overlook the corner of Basing Street and Lancaster Road. The only furniture in the room is the sofa, a massive hardwood coffee table, and a matt-black wall of TV, VCR and stereo equipment. I won't be here long. Shortly after I get back from holiday in mid-January I'm letting the place to a banker, some Sherman.

The monthly rental is absolutely horse-choking. Foxtons are handling everything.

Next year Trellick and I are looking to buy a bigger place together. Paint the whole gaff cream, seagrass matting throughout, chuck a couple of nice fireplaces in and sell it sharpish.

I top my glass up and wander over to the window. A couple of streets away, along Basing Street, left on Westbourne Park Road, right onto Ledbury Road, is Parker-Hall's place. It's on the market and stupidly overpriced. It would be pleasant to stand here – in this huge, warm, soon-to-be profitable room, with Glenmorangie fumes tickling my nose and tearing up my eyes – and picture him: shivering in the dark, turning over in his bunk to face the cold, brick wall, pulling the grimy pillow over his head to drown out the sound of his cell mate aggressively masturbating, but, sadly, the CPS wound up dropping the charges a few weeks later. Trellick was right; insufficient evidence. Still, there was comfort to be had.

The day after he made bail, the headline on page four of the *Sun* raged, 'PAEDOPHILE POP GURU!' Below two starkly contrasting photographs – one of Parker-Hall with his arm around Ellie Crush at the *Q* Awards and one of him being led into court by two coppers – the story continued, '. . . *the talent scout responsible for discovering multimillion-selling Brit winner Ellie Crush was arrested after police seized computers from his west London office. Detectives later found files containing HUNDREDS of depraved images of child pornography. Managing Director Derek Sommers, 45, confirmed today that Parker-Hall's recently signed employment contract was "under review"* . . .'

Parker-Hall's contract remained 'under review' until the *Star* ran with the story on the front cover the following day. Then it was terminated. Last week, after the charges were dropped, Parker-Hall took a flight to Canada. Apparently he's got relatives out there.

Another funny incident last week too . . .

Saturday night and we – me, Trellick, Ross, Darren, Desoto and a few waifs and strays – wound up, unusually, south of the river, in Club UK. Three a.m. and we were all separated, wandering around, pilled up, moving from room to room, checking out boilers. I was standing by the dance floor, swaying, pleasantly off my tits when I become aware of a black guy smiling at me. There was something familiar about him – beyond the usual they-all-look-the-same business I mean. He continued grinning and began nodding downwards, urging me to look too, his expression saying 'take a peek at this'. I followed his gaze down – half expecting to see a cock or something – and saw another black guy, his head at about waist height. In the dark and noise of the club it took me a few seconds to realise who it was. One side of his face was all screwed up – from the beating? from the brain haemorrhage that followed? – and one side was sort of loose and flabby. It looked like he was sucking a lemon with one half of his mouth and trying to blow bubbles with the other. Something chrome sparkled all around him in the dark. I looked up at the guy pushing him, recognising him now as the guy who kissed his teeth at me at the gig that night. 'It's Steven, ain't it?' he said.

'Yeah.'

'He wanted to say hello,' he nodded at the deformity in the wheelchair.

'Hello, Rage,' I said. Rage tried to say something but only managed to produce a frothy bubble of saliva.

''E don't tawk no good since his accident.'

I nodded. Rage beckoned me closer with a twisted, flopping hand. 'T . . .' he said.

I continued nodding, smiling indulgently, like you do at children and mongoloids. It dawned on me that Rage wasn't just a metaphorical mongoloid any more – he's the real fucking deal.

'T . . . tu . . .' he went on, producing a lot of spit, but starting to get somewhere, and now I noticed that the wheelchair wasn't some vamped-up custom job, with power steering and alloys. It was a bog-standard NHS number. Leather-look vinyl and wheel yourself. Times, I concluded, must be hard.

He finally got it out: 'T . . . T . . . TUNE!' he spluttered, gesturing at the air around us, at the record pounding out of the speakers. Some drum'n'bass nonsense.

'Yeah!' I said, giving him a thumbs up. 'Fucking tune!'

The minder, or helper, or whatever, leaned down to Rage and did two things: first he wiped the (considerable) drool from Rage's mouth and chin, then he held a thumbnail of cocaine up to Rage's quivering nostril. But Rage couldn't inhale it – maybe something to do with the loss of motor functions or something – so the guy just rubbed it into his gums, over the chrome and gold teeth, the teeth themselves now a relic, a reminder of something Rage once was.

The minder glanced quickly around the packed dance floor and held a grubby thumb towards me. 'Bump?'

'Nah. I'm all right thanks.'

He did it himself and we stood there nodding along to the music for a moment, me wondering how quickly I could get the fuck out of there, when we both became aware of a terrible stench. We looked down together. Rage was twisting and puffing and jerking his head about. 'Facking hell. Sorry, mate. Happens sometimes.'

I gave the only possible response. I nodded slowly.

'Do you know where the bogs are?' I didn't, but I pointed off into the middle distance anyway, pointing anywhere away from me.

They trundled off and I stood watching them go, wondering if the minder's just a mate or if he's on the payroll. If so, how much? What's the going rate for scraping the crap out of a former 'drum'n'bass superstar's' caked pants? Well, at least it keeps him off the streets.

Rage, of course, is literally *off* the streets. The cunt's in a fucking wheelchair.

I found Trellick in one of the smaller rooms – his shirt off and going bananas to some techno tune. I leaned in and screamed in his ear, 'Have we actually dropped Rage yet?' I had to repeat it a few times. He shook his head. '*Don't*,' I said.

'*Don't what?*'

'*Do. Not. Drop. Rage. Yet. Got an idea.*'

The theme music from *Friends* comes on very softly in the background. '*I'll be there for you* . . .' I walk to the coffee table and drop fresh ice into my glass and then listen to it splinter under the amber wash of Glenmorangie. I walk back to the window and sip my drink, resting my left palm on the windowpane.

It's cold out there.

Generally speaking I don't like Christmas. It reminds me of childhood and me and my mother, just the two of us, exchanging gifts; me handing her the usual box of bath salts or whatever and her reciprocating with the envelope of cash.

This year is a little different. This year I don't mind the half-hearted decorations in the office, or the extra crush and traffic around Regent Street, or the struggle to get a decent table anywhere.

Yeah, Christmas looks a whole lot brighter when you have the Christmas no. 1.

Derek and I go to lunch at the River Cafe. I have duck, he has the penne. We both drink champagne. On the mid-weeks that morning 'Fully Grown' by Songbirds is outselling its nearest rival by nearly two to one. Un-fucking-touchable. Derek does the contrition thing, phrases like 'tremendous asset' and 'great ears' are freely bandied about. At one point the deluded bender – high on the festive spirit and a couple of Bellinis – even goes as far as to tell me he knew we'd 'always had a great respect for each other'. I generously tolerate this nonsense for a while before graciously accepting his offer of the position of Head of A&R.

He stammers and splutters a little as I spell out the insanely avaricious terms of my acceptance – bonkers salary increase, signing-on bonus, profit-share, car upgrade, etc.

– but he pretty much agrees to everything. My lawyer can work it all out with Trellick in the new year.

In the new year I intend to have a platinum album with Songbirds.

In the new year Derek's own contract comes up for renewal. I am going to make life very difficult for Derek.

In the new year I am going to have Dunn fired.

I am going to have Nicky fired.

I am going to fire Rob Hastings.

Everyone is going to pay.

Derek signals for the bill. Outside the plate-glass windows of the River Cafe people, poor people, walk by, their chins jammed hard down into their collars and scarves and their hands in the pockets of thick coats. I'm leaning back from the table in shirtsleeves. Although I can't feel it I know there is a freezing, salty wind blasting up off the Thames and rolling over the pavements and people of Hammersmith. The Thames is not quite frozen yet, here where it bends and heads out towards Oxfordshire. Guys in canoes slide along it. The trees along the riverbank flatten back in the chill wind. A *Big Issue* seller – who looks far too fat to be genuine – has his tattered copy blown from his frozen hand.

The cold doesn't worry me too much. When Derek's paid the bill we'll stroll the three yards across the pavement to the waiting car, a toasty chauffeured Merc from Addison Lee, and trundle the half-mile back to the office, where the temperature is the same every day of the year. Later, when my busy day is done – there are final travel arrangements to be made for Thailand, the interior of my new Range Rover to confirm, the clearing out of my new office (Parker-Hall's old office, Schneider's old office) to supervise, a rough cut of the new Songbirds video to approve – I'll walk the eighteen feet from reception to my new parking space next to Derek's. (Parker-Hall's old space. Schneider's old space.)

No, I'm not worried about the cold at all.

Derek's mobile twitters its deranged ringtone. He pops it open. There are a lot of dusty old houses on these side streets, in the strange hinterland along the river, between Hammersmith and Fulham. Ash-streaked net curtains, non-opening, fifty times painted-over window casements, dead gardens. Probably all full of old boilers who've been living there since the Blitz. Probably all undervalued to fuck. Find yourself a simpatico estate agent – bish, bash, bosh. I must talk to Trellick about this.

'No! Oh God *no*!' Derek says, his hand going to his mouth in that queenly way. My first thought is that something unthinkable, something truly terrible, has happened: somehow one of the records behind the Songbirds single has had a dramatic sales surge and has overtaken us.

'What is it?' I say, but he turns away from me, finger in the ear, still listening. This can't be happening. We were outselling the nearest record by . . .

He hangs up and turns to me, his mouth hanging open.

'Tony Parker-Hall's committed suicide.'

The sensation of relief I experience is tidal, almost orgasmic.

Finished. Game Over. See you later, Sooty.

'Thank fuck for that' almost comes out of my mouth but I manage to say, 'Oh my God,' because I suppose that's the kind of thing you're meant to say.

\*

Bangkok Airport on New Year's Eve.

Ross, Leamington and I are knocking back the local brew, which is called – brilliantly – Chang. It's barely lunchtime and already half a dozen fat, brown empties are lined up on the Formica tabletop. We're Chang'd up to the max and waiting for Trellick, whose flight out from Heathrow has been delayed. It's a billion degrees outside but we've managed to wedge ourselves right under the air conditioner, so we're laughing.

I feel great, tanned and fit. We've been here over a week, taking it easy down at Koh Samet. Beer and beach. Books and Discmans. Backgammon, tom yam gai and floating in the body-temperature ocean. No ostros. No class As. No quadruple Rockschools. This is, of course, all set to change with Trellick's arrival. Later today we fly down to Phuket for a fuck-off party; tonight is when the real shit begins. It's a boiler-fest down there – clean-tasting Scandinavian backpackers a go go. We're also planning to pop into the human toilet of Pattaya and catch a few shows: bare-knuckle midget boxing and teenage ostros firing ping-pong balls, goldfish and frogs out of their cunts; pulling razor blades, butcher knives, landmines and Christ knows what out of their arses.

We're larging it.

'Any more for any more?' Leamington asks. We both give him a thumbs up and he pootles off towards the bar, weaving a little.

I'm leafing through a week-old copy of the *Guardian*. Tony Blair is larging it too. He's in the Seychelles, staying at some massive fuck-off gaff where (apparently) they filmed the soft-porn flick *Emmanuelle*. They reckon Tony will have spunked seven and a half million quid on travel and entertainment in his first year in power. Meanwhile, back home, he wants to slash benefits to single mothers. Top lad, Blair.

There's a little piece about the upcoming Brit Awards. I want to be back in London for 12 January, for the nominations at the Café de Paris, where Songbirds are going to be nominated for Best Single. I gave an expansive interview to *Music Week* about the girls just before I left London. I said, 'I've dealt with a lot of bands, but these girls are the best songwriters I've ever worked with.' And I said, 'They're real music fans. Trust me. They can give you the bar codes on their record collections.' Then, refuting a slight accusation that they were just another manufactured pop act, I said, 'You wouldn't believe the IQs of these girls. No one tells them what to do.' Then, finally, I looked the journalist in the eye and, with an absolutely straight face, I told him: 'Songbirds will be around for a long, long time.' Oh yes I did.

We're putting the second single out end of February, album beginning of March. There's two more potential singles to come after that. Bish, bash, bosh.

I've got another big album shaping up for next year too. You won't believe it, but the press have gone mental for the Rage story we leaked out: the whole 'a crippled man dislocated from his environment communicating through electronica' bullshit I drummed up with the press office went down a storm. He's being perceived as some kind of drum'n'bass Stephen Hawking. Front covers with *NME*, *Muzik* and *Mixmag*. They don't know he finished the record months before he got quadra-spazzed. And what does it matter that the record's an unlistenable pile of shite? He's riding his steel wheelchair across a massive wave of PC goodwill. Are you going to be the journalist who sits down and tells this poor, drooling mess that his record sucks? No one listens to this sort of album anyway, do they? You buy them and stick them down on your Habitat coffee table so that the cretins at your dinner party think you are on it. I'm not even releasing a single. We're spending fuck all on marketing. It's all being done via press and word of mouth. I reckon we'll just about ship gold, which is little short of a miracle considering what we had to work with. Rage. The last turkey in the fucking shop sprouts some wings.

Ross drains his beer. 'Ahhh,' he yawns contentedly, 'it's a hard knock life.' I light a duty-free Marlboro as Leamington reappears, three fresh Changs tinkling together on a plastic tray.

'Hey, look at this,' he says, slapping down a copy of the *Sun* he's found. It's dated 28 December, three days ago. Leamington flips as fast he can through the tired, soggy pages until he comes to the half-page story. There's a photograph of Ellie Crush in a black dress and sunglasses. She's a little out of focus, it's clearly been taken with a long lens. Above the photograph, the headline: 'ELLIE GRIEVES FOR SUSPECTED POP PAEDO'.

We all hunker round and read the story. It's the usual guff – '*ace record industry talent spotter . . . Brit winner Crush . . . police seized computer . . . sacked . . . six-figure salary . . . charges later dropped . . .*'

Towards the end there's a quote from Parker-Hall's

father, also Anthony, a solicitor, 57, from Hampstead, north London: '*Anthony was innocent and we know we will clear his name. Now we hope we can be left alone to mourn our son.*' There's no photo of him and I wonder what Anthony Senior looks like.

'Shocker,' says Ross, setting his beer down, 'absolute shocker.'

We're all quiet for a moment. 'Do you think he was guilty?' Leamington says. 'I mean, topping your fucking self? If you were innocent surely –'

'I can't see it,' Ross says, 'I mean, they dropped the charges, didn't they? Now, if it had been Derek . . .' He trails off, leaving us to join the dots ourselves, to make our own solid connections between irons and paedos and demi-paedos. (*Queer + cocaine x Internet access . . .*)

'What do you reckon?' Leamington asks, turning to me.

*Gak, chang, nose-up, bag, beak, charlie, krell, powder, chisel, bump, posh, bugle, sniff, skiwear . . .*

What do I reckon? I pour more Chang into my plastic cup and the foam volcanoes up, lathering down the sides and running over the *Sun,* darkening the paper, bleeding into the blurry photograph of sad-looking Ellie. He was buried at Kensal Rise cemetery, at the corner of Harrow Road and Ladbroke Grove, near the William the Fourth. Good chips in there. Nice Bloody Mary. Crush's face disappears beneath the expanding circle of golden bubbles. I wonder if Parker-Hall ever fucked her? Surely to Christ he must have? I wonder if he fucked Marcy from the Lazies? Because this is something that's definitely on my 'to do' list for next year. It'll be tough as she hates my fucking guts. But that may all change now, given that I'm her boss. We're meeting soon.

To discuss producers and recording budgets and the like. I'm thinking Steve Albini.

Woodham called the office just once after that night, to see if there had been any interest in his songs. I didn't speak to him. Jo gave me the message. I didn't bother calling him back. I think we've definitely reached an understanding there.

We stayed in Bangkok last night, at the Ramada. This morning I got up bright and early and strolled to an Internet café near the hotel. I tapped into Rebecca's Hotmail account (her password, obtained during a little good-natured pillow talk, is – fairly unbelievably – 'Steven') and sent the following email:

From: Rebecca_spears21@hotmail.com
To: stevens@******records.co.uk
Subject: I'm sorry . . .

Steven – I'm so sorry, but I won't be coming back to work after the holidays. I think you'll understand. What with Roger and losing the baby and everything, I'm just really messed up right now. I need to be on my own for a while. Sorry to leave you in the lurch, especially when you've been so understanding this year.

Love R x

Back home, after the holidays, I'll be forced to tell people that Rebecca was pregnant with Waters' child. She didn't know what to do, whether to have it or not. She confided in me. Then she had a miscarriage. She was depressed . . .

Other than in these very practical terms I don't think about Rebecca much. And I'm definitely not planning on fucking Jo in a hurry. I mean, there's a level of fallout, of grief, you'll take from doing a secretary – the frosty silences, the substandard work, her sporadic dashes to the bathroom with the red eyes and the balled Kleenex – and a level of grief you won't take. (Like, for instance, a ketamine-addled copper dismembering a fucking corpse in your en suite.)

'I don't know,' I say finally, shaking my head, 'you just don't know about people, do you? Anyway,' I yawn, turning the page, 'fuck him. One less guy we have to compete with.'

'Christ, Steven,' Leamington says, 'you *are* hardcore.'

I *am* hardcore. I am the fucking King.

'OI! OI!' Ross shouts and I turn round.

About seventy yards away, I see Trellick appearing out of the handful of International Arrivals. He comes towards us pushing a trolley. He hasn't seen us yet and he has that air about him that people do when you see them before they see you; alert, scanning, vulnerable, self-conscious.

'OI! *LOSER!*' I shout and a few Thai heads turn.

He sees us now and his face lights up reluctantly. He's grinning as he trundles towards us through all the people, using his elbows to keep the trolley on line as he gives us a really stupid thumbs up. People, mostly Thais in their shitty sub-Western dress – tracksuit trousers and 'The Pope Smokes Dope' T-shirts, like Scousers from 1988 – get out of his way, darting and dodging around his trolley, all smiling their heads off and it strikes me that the airport is pretty busy considering it's New Year's Eve, but then I remember that the holidays don't mean much out here because they're all Buddhists. I mean, they don't give a shit about anything, do they?

Based on the
bestselling novel by
**John Niven**

LIES. BETRAYAL. MURDER.
JUST ANOTHER DAY AT THE OFFICE.

Nicholas **Hoult**

# KILL YOUR FRIENDS

## IN CINEMAS NOVEMBER 6

Discover more  *KillYourFriends*  *KillFriendsFilm* #*KillYourFriends*

# ALSO BY JOHN NIVEN

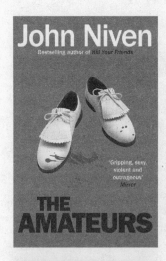